FIRST

WHAT WOULD YOU GIVE UP TO KEEP YOURS?

Yolanda Callegari Brooks

BOW Press

LONG BEACH, CALIFORNIA

A LEGACY OF UPLIFTING LITERATURE

The author's scriptural references are taken from the Holy Bible, King James Version.

BOW Press
3553 Atlantic Avenue, Suite 301
Long Beach, CA 90807
www.bowpressonline.com
bowpress@attbroadband.com

Printed in the United States of America
First Printing: February 2002

Cover photographs by Anthony Burries
Front cover design and photo retouching by Parry Havelaar
Book cover layout and interior design by Bookcovers.com

First Edition

Library of Congress Cataloging-in-Publication Data
Callegari Brooks, Yolanda
First Love - What Would You Give Up To Keep Yours?: a novel /
Yolanda Callegari Brooks. - 1st ed.

p. cm.
LCCN 2001098222
ISBN 0-9716274-7-9

1. African Americans—Fiction. 2. Women—Fiction. 3. Young Adult—Fiction. 4. Interpersonal relations—Fiction 5. Spirituality—Fiction. 6. Christian Fiction, American. 7. Los Angeles (Calif.)—Fiction. I. Title

**To my Lord and Saviour, Jesus Christ
Thank you for "picking me up" in more ways than one**

"For the Lord thy God bringeth thee into a good land,
a land of brooks of water, of fountains and depths
that spring out of valley and hills; A land of wheat, and barley,
and vines, and fig trees, and pomegranates;
a land of oil olive, and honey;
A land wherein thou shalt eat bread without scarceness,
thou shalt not lack any thing in it;
a land whose stones are iron, and
out of whose hills thou mayest dig brass.
When thou hast eaten and
art full, then thou shalt bless the Lord thy God
for the good land which he hath given thee."

Deuteronomy 8:7-10

"For it is written, As I live, saith the Lord,
every knee shall bow to me,
and every tongue confess to God.
So then every one of us shall
give account of himself to God."

Romans 14:11-12

Dedication

I dedicate this book to the memories of

Missionary Eula Mae Alfred,

Bishop Bennie Lee Archie,

Rev. Thomas Jefferson Brooks,

Deacon Milbert Callegari,

and

Bro. Jimmy Hall, Sr. & Sis. Eula Mae Hall

They were on the battlefield fighting for the Lord
May those of us they left behind fight as valiantly

Acknowledgments

It is with an attitude of utmost gratitude that I thank the following:

For Spiritual Assistance:

My Heavenly Father: I thank You for taking every disappointment and every hurt I've ever experienced and using each one to mold me into the woman You created me to be. I praise You for faithfully completing the work You've begun in me and for choosing me to write for You even though I am still "under construction."

The anointed men and women of God who have spoken into my life—through various means: A few have given me direct words of prophecy while others have preached the uncompromising Word of God from the pulpit. From many, I've learned through your television, book, and music ministries. I am especially grateful for my pastor, Dr. Gary Greenwald, of Eagle's Nest Ministries, who read my manuscript "by the spirit" during dinner one evening. His inspiring words were confirmation for me to go forth.

For Editorial/Writing Assistance:

James Clayton, thank you for thoroughly critiquing the skeleton of a novel that I brought to you and for loving "my baby" immediately. The "name" has since changed, but its essence has remained. I began my journey into the land of revision using your critical analysis of my manuscript as a roadmap. Dr. Joyce Johnson, thank you for directing me to him.

Victoria Christopher Murray, I "happened" upon your self-published version of *Temptation* in ordained time. I appreciate your taking time out of your busy schedule to meet with me and for giving my manuscript its first story edit. You helped me to grow as a writer through both lavish constructive criticism and lofty praise. Thank you for your unwavering belief in my talent. You are a courageous woman of God and I admire you very much.

Maxine Thompson, I thank you for sharing your literary gifts with me by first critiquing my manuscript and later editing it after I had done my best to implement many of your suggestions. Without a doubt, you are making a positive contribution to the literary world. I also appreciate the insightful book review you wrote of *First Love* once we were satisfied "it was finished."

Tia Shabazz, of Pentouch Literary, I hereby crown you "Grammar Queen." Your copy editing expertise helped to increase the pace and improve the flow of my novel. In addition, your straight-to-the-point comments and inquiries, byproducts of your acute attention to detail, helped to further enhance my manuscript. Thank you. As you continue to share your literary talents with authors, the bar for self-published fiction, in particular, will continue to be raised. I am pleased that our paths crossed.

Adrienne Starkey, of Pentouch Literary, I thank you for your meticulous and prompt proofreading of my manuscript. I'm glad that you enjoyed reading it. I appreciate you!

Dr. Rosie Milligan, of Milligan Books: Thank you for hosting the six-week writing class that Victoria Christopher Murray taught as only she can. It was there that I met Maxine Thompson. I appreciate your zeal for assisting self-published authors and your one-of-a-kind mother's wit. Dr. Milligan, you have greatly contributed to the world of African-American literature. I wish you continued success!

For Photo Shoot Assistance:

My male model and his wife: Mark Dorsey, thank you for being so willing to help this sista realize her dream that you gave up your two days off to take pictures for *free*. If that weren't enough, you barely flinched when the photographer said the "mustache had to go." Mark, I have deep gratitude for your champion attitude. The pictures came out great. You're a natural! Paula D., thank you for loaning us your husband and for supporting him during the photo shoots, every step of the way. Also, thumbs up for bringing me that picture of Jasmine. Mark and Paula, I'll never forget your generosity.

My female models and their mothers: Ashley Chambers, thank you for working the camera like you did, girl! Your pictures are gorgeous and your confidence and talent are obvious. Look out, Hollywood! Toni Lankford, thank you for chauffeuring Ashley and for staying for the entire shoot. Jasmine Wingfield, thank you for rearranging your work schedule (twice) so that you could take the pictures. Your pictures are lovely and your sweetness and beauty shine through on every photo! Valerie Davis, thank you for allowing me to have pictures taken of Jasmine.

Anthony Burries, photographer extraordinaire: Anthony, in divine time, you stepped in with your easy smile, positive energy, and awesome talent. What a joy to watch a pro in action! Thank you for doing an outstanding job with the pictures you took of the models and with those you took later of me. Annette, of Drama, in Carson: Thanks for styling my hair for my photos and showing me how to maintain it. I appreciate you!

Michelle Edmond, owner of TLC (Tender Loving Care) in Inglewood: Michelle, thank you for doing a superb job of styling Jasmine's hair for both photo shoots. Your hands are blessed, girl! Mary Smith, the make-up artist: Mary, thank you for coming over with your huge make-up kit and for doing a professional job on the models' faces. You have anointed hands!

Pastor Reginald and First Lady Althea Sims of Gospel Temple, C.O.G.I.C.: Thank you for graciously allowing us to use your beautiful facility for the church photos.

For Graphic Design/Web Site Assistance:

Kim D'Angelo of Book Covers Design: Kim, you pressed through to help me realize my vision for *First Love*. Thank you for giving your all to match my concept for the interior and book cover layouts. I appreciate your patience with me.

Parry Havelaar: Parry, thank you for creating our BOW Press logo and for designing the perfect cover for *First Love*. You did a stunning job of retouching the photos. You've been an invaluable resource throughout my journey to publication. Parry, I am in awe of your talent and your spirit of generosity.

Bruce Cadiz: Thank you for developing Website application templates for the auto-responder. You were a big help to Bernard and to the project.

For Confirming My Reality:

My family, friends, and co-workers: Thank you for taking the time to read *First Love* when it was a work-in-progress or a "finished" manuscript, or for simply believing that I could write a book and being excited for me. Heartfelt thanks to Bobbie and Audra Anderson, Mary Andrew, Charlotte Ashford, Gwendolyn Battle, Darlene Berry, Yvette Bluitt, Yi Booker, Ethel Borders, Penny Brooks, Audrey Brown, Lynda Carraway, Anita Clark, Mi'quael Cottrell, Marsha Cuyjet, Paula Dorsey, Candace Edwards, Rosalind Emel, Kathleen Etter, Angel and Juanita French, Lisa Fulbright, Delores Hall, Darrin Hardgraves, Brian Harvey, Mark Hemphill, Michael Henry, Catherine James, Deborah Jones, Shaun and Jessica Jordan, Arlene Junior, Jefferson Laurence, Renetta Lipscomb, Eleanor Mack, Tanesha May, Sandra Melson, Danette Molina, Ruthelle Moss, Elynor Olivadoti, Roy O'Neill, Laura Povsner, Richard and Kimberly Redd, Rebecca Roeck, Dorothy Simmons, Ryan Sims, Leona and Lenora Smith, Doris Snoddy, Felisha and Katie Thomas, Brenda Wade, Alyce Walker, Carole Wiezorek, Tullie Williamson, Traci Willis, Essie Wilson, Rose Womack-Hall, and Susie Zachario.

To *every* staff member at Annalee Avenue Elementary School: It has been a plum pleasure working with you. I'm going to miss you!

Special thanks to the Black Writers Alliance (BWA) and every member who has ever shared an interesting article, a writing tip, or an inspiring word that was right on time. In particular, I thank the following: Diane Campbell, thanks for the patois translations! Brian Egeston, I appreciate you! Jamellah Ellis, you are a jewel! Kimberly Hines, thanks for that great line! Journey, hey virtuous sista! Brandon Massey, I am grateful for all of your assistance! Cynthia Moore, I'm waiting to buy my copy of your poetry book! BWA Christian Lit List: I thank Mary Griffith, our mighty moderator, and all of the soldiers on the battlefield "writing" for the Lord. Continue to "write" the good fight of faith! Gina Johnson Smith, I appreciate all you've done to help me. Anthony Louis, I thank you for the great resources you've shared with me.

I am eternally grateful for Samuel Wesley of Praise One Entertainment: Samuel, thank you for sponsoring the *First Love* Release Celebration in conjunction with your Winter Praise Concert. I appreciate your support and all that you've done to spread the word about *First Love*.

Last, But Certainly Not Least, For Family Support:
My parents, Jimmy and Delores Hall: Jimmy, I appreciate you for always being there for us. Mama, you are the epitome of class, generosity, and selflessness—a true virtuous woman. I love you both and thank you for believing in me.

To my sisters, Denise, Sonya, and Yvette, and my brothers, Vincent, Nigel, and my brother-in-law, Elliott: We don't keep in touch as often as we could, but I want you to know that I love you. Special thanks to Yvette for the hours of babysitting you did so that Bernard and I could supervise the *First Love* photo shoots without three little people underfoot. Also, I thank you for being a listening ear during those times when I couldn't see the light at the end of the tunnel. Yvette, I'm blessed that you're my sister, my friend, and my prayer partner.

Special thanks to all of my aunts and uncles who have advised me, cared for me, or encouraged me in some form or another over the last several years. I love you and am glad we're in the same family. Special thanks to my aunts, Linda, Brenda, Sharon, Debra, and my aunt-in-law, Mattie, and to my uncles, Michael and Gregory. I'm especially grateful to my great-aunt, Ada Archie: You are a wise and faithful woman of God. Thank you for showing me that living for Jesus is not a swift sprint, but a steady walk. To my aunt, Arlene Junior: You have always been in my corner. I'm blessed that you're my sister-in-Christ and my friend.

To all of my nieces, nephews, and cousins: If you trust in the Lord and keep God first, all things will be possible to you. I hope that my going after my dreams will encourage you to make yours a reality, too. I love you all.

To my in-laws: Rachel Brooks, Penny Brooks, Erma (Brooks) Williams, Edward Brooks, and the rest of the Brooks clan: Thank you for accepting me as a member of the family. Love to all of you!

My children: Imani Nailah, Joshua Omari-Bernard, and Isaiah Jelani-Bernard, I thank you for daily showing me that God made us to live creatively and for helping me to rediscover the joy in little things. I pray that you will never detour from God's truth and therefore never settle for being less than who He created you to be. Mommy loves you!

Finally, my helpmate, Bernard Brooks: I could write a book about all we have been *through* together. We are now united in spirit and purpose, moving into the center of God's perfect will for us. Baby, this book is as much yours as it is mine. Thank you for holding down the fort and freeing me to write. I am astounded by how thoroughly you love our children and me. In your trademark spirit of excellence, you have built a unique website and put together an impressive press kit. I am so proud of you! Thank you for being everything and more than I could ever want in a life partner. I love you so much!

If I missed anyone, please "charge it to my head, and not my heart."

SEASONS

To everything there is a season, and a time to every purpose under the heaven.

Ecclesiastes 3:1

PROLOGUE

SPRING of '70

BUNKIE, LOUISIANA

"What's wrong with that fool?"

Claudine repeated her question while she traced circles with her bare toe.

Silent moments passed. Olivia stood as frozen as an ice sculpture and, for a moment, it even seemed like the billowing clouds lurching across the sky stopped. Everything, including the breezy gusts of wind lifting her strands, stilled.

Olivia bit her lip and looked away. She was so hurt she couldn't speak. Out of the corner of her eye, though, she noticed Claudine had stopped making toe art and was furtively peeking at her. Without uttering a word, she turned back to face Claudine.

Olivia wondered whether truth or fallacy was in the air. After all, Claudine had been known to confuse the two before. But Olivia didn't think she'd go this far. Why would she? They were more like sisters than cousins.

Olivia's cloudy eyes rested on her cousin's bright ones. Each set of eyes seemed to search the other. She could see that Claudine was extremely uncomfortable with having to be the messenger of Marcus' mess.

But was Claudine telling the truth?

This question lingered longer than Olivia would have liked for two reasons. First, her heart pleaded Marcus' innocence. Secondly, it had already tried and convicted Claudine.

It was no secret how her cousin viewed "the Almighty's Diary," the nickname her grandparents gave the Bible. To Claudine, it was simply a book of "thou shalls" and "thou shall nots."

Twisting from side to side with the flair of a Mississippi blues singer, Claudine would hold her left arm akimbo and snap her right fingers. "Baby Sister, I'm gonna smoke, curse, and dance, wear as much make-up as I want and as little clothing as I choose to. And I'll drink when I feel like it and do it with whoever I fancy."

She constantly mocked Olivia's puritan ways. "I ain't studyin' Papa, Big Mama, or *you* with y'all holy selves. Go 'head and wait to live with Jesus in some golden city. I'm gon' live my life here." She'd roll her eyes skyward. "So heavenly minded, y'all ain't no earthly good."

"Olivia, did you hear what I said?"

Claudine's words snapped her back and Olivia blinked her cousin into focus. She pursed her lips and continued to "hold her peace" as Big Mama had instructed her to do when she wasn't sure about a matter. Rather than respond to her cousin, her eyes followed the flight path of a passing butterfly. Claudine tapped her foot. Olivia knew her silence irritated her cousin because Claudine *hated* to be ignored.

Claudine tilted her head, and placed her balled fists on her hips. "Anyhow, I said, 'What's wrong with that fool, tryna get next to this?'" She brushed her hands over her bosom and down her thighs.

Eyes glazed, Olivia peered into an airless space, a whirlwind of emotions warring inside of her. Disbelief marched through first. Did he or didn't he? Olivia's first reaction was to pinch herself—hard. No, this couldn't be true. She was

3

having a nightmare during the middle of the day. How could her tightly held dreams of happily-ever-after be wrenched from her hands?

Olivia spun around and studied Claudine. Her wide eyes narrowed to slits. She had to quell a sudden urge to slap the smirk she hoped she was imagining from her cousin's face.

Claudine, leaning against the tree's trunk, quickly pushed away from it and pointed to what had been hidden behind her back.

"Baby Sister, remember the summer Marcus used Reverend Shephard's knife to do this? Ha! Too bad that punk didn't mean it." Claudine turned up her nose. "If he did, he sho' wouldn't be tryna get with your cousin." She stopped examining her nails and glanced at Olivia. "I sho' hate ta have to tell ya somethin' like this, Baby Sister." Claudine averted her eyes. "But we blood."

The lines of fury faded in Olivia's forehead as her anger was overtaken by bewilderment. She simply stared at *their* tree. *M.S. & O.D. 4-ever* was carved in the midst of a crooked heart. Sapling figs vied for attention amongst the leaves and branches overhead, but they went unnoticed as she tried to digest her cousin's casual confession. Olivia didn't even realize she was crying until Claudine patted her shoulder.

"Baby Sister, don't waste no tears over that fool. He ain't nothing. It would serve him right if you went out with me tonight. I can ask Juniorman to bring his brother. You know Lil' Earl been likin' you since . . . Shoot! When hasn't Lil' Earl liked you?"

Olivia wiped her face with the back of her hands. "I need to finish my history report. I don't feel like going nowhere anyway." She sniffled. "I can't believe Marcus been lying to me all this time. All his 'Sweet lady, we're going to do things right. Just like God wants us to. When we get married, it'll be the first time for both of us.' Liar!" she scoffed. The words wielded by her cousin pierced her heart and left her with the question only Marcus could answer. Why? Olivia's wet face glowed in the golden rays of the spring sun.

Even distraught, the youngest granddaughter of Wilson and Eula Mae Dupree was a feast for greedy eyes. There wasn't a male, young or old, in Bunkie or the nearby town of Evergreen who hadn't fantasized about claiming Olivia Ava Dupree as his own. Her natural beauty attracted the finest suitors, Marcus Alexander Shephard III being the most suitable of them all.

Olivia's amber complexion perfectly complemented a mane of brown waves that flowed past her shoulders and had no use for heat or lye. The wind and her fingers were her usual combs. A rounded nose, bow-shaped lips, and a pair of doe-like eyes radiated warmth and sincerity from her oval face. Olivia's sexual innocence served to fuel a fellow's fascination.

A look of disgust washed over Claudine's face. She sucked her teeth. "Guess that lyin' dog thought he could practice with me and get some tips from an older woman. Y'all won't be eighteen until August and September. I'll be twenty in another week, remember?"

Olivia barely nodded, then turned from the tree and watched Claudine tug at the thin red fabric masquerading as a dress. The scarlet color accentuated her cousin's smooth ebony skin. Her face, set in a serious mold, stared back at Olivia from under a cap of carefully pressed short curls. Her voluptuous breasts resembled over-ripened cantaloupes and her ample hips possessed the power to tempt even the holiest of men. As it turned out, Marcus was no exception.

Olivia gazed down at the white oxford shirt she was wearing along with a pleated navy skirt and a pair of tennis shoes. *Plain.* She really couldn't blame Marcus for being attracted to her more sophisticated cousin, but what she couldn't understand was *why* he had asked Claudine for sex, especially since he was more adamant about their holding out than she was.

She fingered the cross around her neck.

Confusion and pain spilled from her eyes, flooding the depths of her soul. *How could you do this to me, Marcus?* Disillusioned, she glanced at Claudine as a chilling truth splashed over her. What was the point of being saved? Maybe Claudine had the right idea.

"We can hang out tonight." She waved her hand as if batting away a mosquito. "Forget that stupid report."

Claudine's eyes widened. "What did you say?"

"I said, 'I'll go out with y'all.'"

Olivia took her hands off the cross. She wasn't sure about anything anymore. The one thing she had been certain of— Marcus' love and *loyalty*—was gone. Besides, look what trusting a man had gotten her: a future that would never be. So, she refused to entertain the doubts knocking at the door of her conscience and barged ahead in her mind. "You can help me get ready. Make me look older."

"Now you're talking."

"I don't want nothing drastic. A lil' change is all."

"Baby Sister, for a skinny girl, you got yo'self a knockout body. Just too *sanct-a-fied.* You keep it all covered up. It's awright to show some skin."

Claudine grabbed Olivia's arm and dragged her toward the brick house they shared with their grandparents. Olivia had lived with them since she started George Washington Carver High School and Claudine almost since birth. Claudine's mother had decided she didn't want a husband and baby after all, so she went to visit some relatives up north and forgot to come home. Her father carried the infant to his in-laws as if he had changed his mind about a purchase and deserved a refund. Three-month-old Claudine became a permanent addition to the Dupree household and never let anyone forget it wasn't by choice.

Claudine winked. "I have the perfect outfit for you to wear. I even have a pair of jazzy heels and the handbag to—"

"First I need to call Marcus." She stopped walking. "Wait 'til I talk to that two-faced—"

"Let that holy hypocrite sweat!" Claudine let go of her arm. "You know he's gonna stop by when he leaves work. Like he does every evening." She rolled her eyes. "Won't he be surprised to find his sweet thang done gone out with Cous'n Claudine?"

Olivia's shimmering waves bounced as she shook her head. "I . . . I at least need to talk to him before we go."

"Let that worm squirm tonight. Tomorrow we'll get everything out in the open. Trust me, Baby Sister." She turned, hips swiveling in a circle, and sashayed toward the house.

Olivia surveyed Claudine's sensual saunter as she silently lamented. *Lord, I know the Bible says vengeance is yours and you will repay. This is just a lil' payback from me. I want Marcus to hurt like I'm hurting.* Olivia walked in the dirt trail left by her cousin. Her heavy heart weighed her down as she laboriously climbed the steps to the porch. She brushed aside the second thoughts clinging to what was left of her first mind. "Time to grow up," she murmured, firmly closing the door behind her.

FALL

A time to be born, and a time to die; a time to plant, and a time to pluck up that which is planted; A time to kill, and a time to heal; a time to break down, and a time to build up.

Ecclesiastes 3:2-3

ONE

Present Day

Los Angeles, California

She was born the seventh daughter to a seventh daughter and, though it sounded charming, she sometimes wished she could switch her birth order.

Her mother was at it again. "Baby Girl, don't you remember saying you weren't ever going to straighten your hair?"

Amani didn't answer her right away. She was too miffed. How dare her mother hold her to some promise she had made when she was too young to know any better? "Maybe I changed my mind, *Mother*," she almost snapped.

Although she was the baby of their boisterous bunch, she was anything but. Her older sisters used to tease she'd be a wife, mother, and *grand*mother, but still their mother's little brown baby, wrinkles and all. When they realized how much their kidding upset her, they finally stopped. However, during moments like these, Amani believed their pathetic joke was probably prophetic.

In reply, she rolled her eyes and tried to keep her neck stiff as her mother wrapped an oversized towel around small sections of her hair and squeezed. The heavy, damp strands moistening her face, neck, and shoulders added to Amani's irritation.

A sudden smile lifted her out of her funk as she relished a more savory subject. *It's time for me to be somebody else's chocolate baby.* She lowered her head. *Hmm, his fine, caramel-looking self can be my babies' daddy, too.*

"Ouch!" A firm tug on a handful of her hair prevented her from planning the wedding and forced her to sit up.

Olivia Shephard, seated atop the toilet with the cover down, briskly towel-dried her daughter's hair. "I can't believe this mess you made, Amani Nicole."

Amani remained silent as she sat on the floor between her mother's legs, filing her nails and keeping the peace.

Olivia had just finished washing her daughter's hair for a final time. Amani used an entire bottle of *It's Magic! Hair Oil* in her attempts to straighten her kinky-wavy, sometimes curly, past-the-shoulder mane. It took three washings to get out all the oil. Despite its claim to melt away each of Amani's boring curls, it had only left a greasy mess.

As her mother towel-dried her tresses, Amani stared at her mother's French-pedicured feet and recalled how happy Mama had been when she pledged to always wear her hair natural, too.

Whenever Amani gave her word about something, she took it seriously. Still, she felt that using oil in the place of a pressing comb or chemicals kept her within the bounds of her vow.

This was her senior year at Harriet Tubman Preparatory High School and she was more determined than ever to exercise her independence. Her mother would have to learn to trust her. She loved her Mama, reverenced God, and didn't plan on doing anything drastic. *My goodness,* she thought, *I just want a new hairstyle.* Whenever she blow-dried it straight for a sleek look, it barely lasted a day before reverting back to its natural state.

She thought back to the joke her best friend, Destiny, made earlier that day. "Maybe your mother thinks you'll remain in your virgin state as long as your hair does. As soon as you start pressing it or perming it, look out below! Mani's panties are coming down." Destiny laughed until she started coughing while Amani cringed and slapped—patted her friend on the back.

Olivia's voice interrupted her mental cruise. "Amani Shephard, do you hear me talking to you?"

Before Amani could reply, her mother continued fussing. "I don't know why you would even think about messing with your hair. Besides, you promised."

"Mama, I was only *ten* when I made that promise. You can't possibly expect me to—"

"Well, why not? A woman's hair is her glory. You have hair that most women would—"

"It's just that . . ." Amani blew on a tendril of hair covering her mouth, "I need a change," she mumbled.

"Your hair is beautiful like it is." Her voice rose. "Anybody that tells you differently is either petty or jealous!"

Amani jumped at the force of her mother words.

Olivia expelled an exasperated sigh. "Change ain't always good, Baby Girl." She gently squeezed her daughter's locks from root to end with the towel. "Don't let *nobody* stop you from being who God made you to be. Your Daddy and I . . . You two were so close. We named you Amani for a reason. It's Swahili and—"

"Mama, I *know*—"

"It means faith. With faith in God and faith in yourself, anything is possible . . ."

Her mother's voice trailed off. Amani didn't know what her name had to do with her hair, but she knew her mother's head was somewhere else. Most likely thinking about the only man she had been connected to in heart, mind, and body. Her spiritmate, Marcus Alexander Shephard III.

Mama never tired of telling her daughters "When God made y'alls daddy, He didn't even use a mold." She would smile with a look that hinted at the hidden treasures of the heart shared by two who had become one.

"Mama," Amani spoke softly, "please don't try to stop me from being who I am either. I love you and I don't know any woman I admire more than you, but I'm *not* you."

Amani took a breath before continuing. "I'm going to have my hair straightened for graduation, but I haven't decided whether to have it permed or pressed." She paused. "Mama, I'm sorry if this makes you unhappy, but it's my hair and my choice. At least you have almost nine months to get used to the idea." She chewed her bottom lip and waited.

Olivia placed the towel in her lap, then she arranged Amani's mound of hair on the towel and began massaging her scalp, beginning at her temples. Her circular touches were sure and steady. She knew exactly where to apply a moderate amount of pressure and when to lighten up. Though Olivia used her hands without words, Amani knew. Her mother's nimble fingers did a good job of reminding her.

The love being transmitted through Amani's pores was encapsulating. It surrounded her on every side and had proven to be secure and unconditional. She wanted to forget all about her need for something different. She wanted to remain Mama's little girl for as long as she needed her to. She wanted to promise her mother she would never disappoint her. But she couldn't.

Although there was more on her mind than unruly hair and mother-daughter issues, Amani refrained from speaking. What was she supposed to say? *Mama, I can't stop thinking about the gorgeous guy I met last weekend. We only spoke briefly, but he's tall and strong and . . . I think I'm in love.* No way. Instead, she reached for her mother's hand, kissed it softly, then placed her mother's palm against her cheek.

The ringing of the telephone interrupted their love-fest.

Amani dropped her mother's hand and jumped up. "Mama, I'll just get my hair pressed. Okay?"

She kissed her mother on the forehead. "I love you, Mama O." She overlooked the downcast eyes and tight mouth that signaled her mother's feelings were hurt and rushed into her bedroom. Amani recited what had recently become her favorite prayer: "Please, God, let this be Marley."

Olivia released her pinched lips and exhaled slowly. *It's my hair and my choice.* She wanted to respond, but hadn't trusted herself to maintain her composure. Instead, she had taken a detour. The safest route was to keep her hands moving and her mouth closed.

She'd come home from Centerview Memorial Hospital that afternoon, took one look at her Amani's hair, and almost returned to a place she never wanted to revisit. Her brown mane resembled Amani's in everything except color. She had allowed it to be straightened once in forty-nine years. How could she make Amani understand that her decision to change her hair was more than a simple matter of style? It was the start of her own mother's demise and the beginning of the same destructive pattern each of Amani's six sisters had followed.

First, they changed their hair, then their clothes, and their music. Lastly, their commitment to God was overshadowed by a preoccupation with boys and, although they had voices that could make an atheist shout amen, they didn't even sing in the church choir anymore. The saints at New Horizons Christian Center would "get happy" as the Spirit moved throughout the congregation when the Shephard girls sang.

Only Amani still sang in the choir.

Olivia chose to ignore her youngest child's comments, hoping the longer she delayed her response, the longer things would remain the same.

———————

The butterflies in Amani's stomach were flapping overtime. Of all the girls he could have called, Marley called her. Finally.

Amani felt like she had won the lottery, been crowned Miss America, and heard the voice of God all at the same time. Marley Jamison was in the house. Well, not exactly in the house, but close enough. He was on the line.

However, even in her excitement, she could not shake her best friend's voice. "When I met him, his motto was, 'The truly strong abstain.' But, girl, whatchu gonna do if he changes his mind?"

Those were practically the first words out of Destiny's mouth when Amani told her Marley asked for her number.

She shook her head to clear it so she could concentrate on what he was saying.

". . . go with me to gospel party night at Skate World? You know what they say, 'Ain't no party like a Holy Ghost party 'cause a Holy Ghost party don't stop!'"

"True dat." She laughed. "I need to ask my—What time does it start?"

"At seven for the little ones and that lasts about an hour. Then, from eight to eleven, it's all about the young peeps. I'll pick you up at seven so we can hang out before we get our praise on."

Amani couldn't believe it. She was going on a date with Marley Jamison. She was excited; however, she decided to play it cool. "Hold up! I forgot to check my calendar—"

"Listen, Amani." His voice caressed her. "You're someone I'd like to know better. Having you by my side tonight will make Kirk and Fred and 'nem sound even better."

She could practically feel the rays of his grin through the phone. Amani wired him an involuntary smile in return.

"Now, that's a compliment." *I better save the drama for Jerry Springer.* "I'd love to hang out with you tonight." She blushed and dropped her voice. "And I'm looking forward to it."

"Back at ya. Just remember to wear your wings. I don't want you gettin' hurt when you fall." He rubbed his chin. "I know angels can't skate. That would be too much."

Amani was cheesing her way into the Smilers' Hall of Fame. "You know what the Word says, 'To whom much is given, much is required.' Tonight, it's my duty to skate circles around you."

"I can see you have a whole lotta faith, but I'm not too sure about your ability." He chuckled. "Don't worry. I'll give you free lessons." He kicked off one of his celebrity-endorsed running shoes. "On the court or at the rink, school's in session. You, too, can learn from the Master."

Marley thinks highly of Marley, she couldn't help thinking. Before she could hold this observation up to Shephard scrutiny, she closed her eyes. "All right, Miracle Master Marley, here's my address." Amani gave him directions along with the nearest cross-streets. She didn't want him getting lost. "Repeat the directions for me so I can make sure I gave you the right ones."

"Believe me, Miss Shephard, I will stop at every gas station, every AM PM, every 7-Eleven on the corner if I have to. Somebody would have to help me find the girl in my dreams."

Amani was floating so high above cloud number nine that she had to open her eyes to get her bearings before she crashed to earth—or fell off the bed. She swung both legs on the floor. "See you at seven, Marley. Bye." She gently replaced the receiver on the telephone. The smile plastered across her face made her look like a chocolate-flavored Mrs. Kool-Aid.

Amani reached under her bed and pulled out the storage box that contained her blow dryer. She took it out, plugged it in, and flopped down on the bed.

Staring at her reflection in the mirror, Amani studied her

heart-shaped face, professionally arched eyebrows, her almond-shaped eyes, rounded nose, high cheekbones, and full lips from every angle. Her complexion was the color of burnt sugar. She would never forget when self-doubts about her looks first surfaced.

Five-year-old Amani was using the bathroom when she saw two pairs of feet on the other side of the stall. The voices were talking about boys. She thought her two oldest sisters had changed their minds and were going to wait for her inside instead of out in the church's foyer. She was about to yell out to them when the voice that sounded like Perri changed the subject.

"Those Shephard girls make me sick with they stuck-up selves. Think they so cute. I get tired of listening to them sing *every* Sunday."

The voice that didn't belong to Vanessa chuckled. "They ain't nothing but a whole lotta hair. If they had short hair, nobody would pay 'em any mind. They'd be homely, especially the baby because she's the darkest."

Amani's heart began to beat like it had the time she got lost in the supermarket. She waited for the bathroom door to close before she left the stall, but she didn't let her cry slip out. Then she'd have to tell her sisters what happened. What if what the girls said was true? *Homely.* She wasn't sure what it meant, but she knew it wasn't anything nice.

She decided not to worry too much about her color because Daddy loved it. "Come here, gorgeous chocolate girl." He'd kiss her all over her face and smack his lips. "Mmmm, mmmm. I have my own delicious Hershey Bar doll."

She used to wonder if her father was thankful his daughters all had long hair like their mother. If not, he'd have to pretend he thought they were beautiful.

From that time on, Amani paid careful attention when her mother or one of her three oldest sisters washed and braided her hair. Getting her ends trimmed almost called for her to be restrained until she realized, as she got older, that trims helped her mane to remain healthy. She tolerated trims, but no serious cutting.

Better satisfied than sorry. As long as she could help it, she'd never be dark *and* homely.

Amani stopped staring at herself long enough to attach the comb to the end of the blow dryer. *Get a grip, girl. You must look pretty good for Marley to take notice. Or maybe . . . it's just the hair.*

She shook all skepticism from her shoulders and began the tedious process of blow-drying her tresses though she knew her straight look would not last.

Now, brother Marley. Bald head, locced head, faded head. No matter how you groom it, that's straight-up beautiful. She grinned into the mirror, singing to herself. *"There's something about the name Marley."* Already it was a sweet sound in her double-pierced ears.

Destiny told her several times he didn't believe in sex before marriage. "Just consider him a younger version of A.C. Green. Who knows? Maybe the L.A. Lakers will sign him one day, too," she had teased.

Amani found it amazing her girl didn't want him for herself. Destiny insisted on introducing her to Marley last Saturday when the two of them went on an informal campus tour of the University of California at Los Angeles. They were on their way to the Student Union when Marley strolled out of Powell Library.

Even the sun seemed to brighten at his appearance. When he stopped to adjust the strap of the waist-length knapsack slung over his left shoulder, the sun paid homage. It became a solar spotlight, making his caramel skin glisten. He looked up, waved, and smiled in their direction. The sun reflected a smile so mesmerizing the light of its brilliance blinded Amani.

Destiny elbowed her. "Girl, that's Marley "Miracle Man" Jamison!"

"Who?"

"He's played point guard for UCLA's varsity basketball team since his freshman year *and* he's saved."

"All right now!" Amani would have been content to continue staring along with the rest of the oglers, but Destiny grabbed her arm and steered her toward what had suddenly become Amani's only reason for being on UCLA's campus that day.

Destiny's older brother, Skye, was an assistant coach for the University of Southern California. Destiny met Marley two years ago when Skye tried to recruit him for the Trojans basketball team.

Whatever the reason she'd passed him on to her, Amani was both enthralled and grateful. Miracle . . . Master . . . Marley, whatever he called himself, seemed like he would be a lot of fun. Even more important than his being gorgeous was the fact that he was a Christian.

Six times her mother was unsuccessful in raising a daughter who saved herself for marriage. For Amani, it was not debatable; the Bible was the final authority. It clearly stated, *"Marriage is honorable and the bed undefiled."* Who was she to argue with that?

Amani had made a promise to herself, to her mother, to God. Mama would not fail a seventh time. She would see to it.

———————

Several minutes passed before Olivia lifted herself from where she sat with Amani. She couldn't help but remember the times her girls confidently submitted their hair, hearts, and lives into her hands. Back then, she craved time and space for herself, not appreciating that all too soon they grew up.

"God grant me the serenity to accept the things I cannot change, courage to change those things I can and wisdom to know the difference," Olivia recited the Serenity Prayer passionately, but quietly.

With a sigh, she stood and began straightening the bathroom. She rinsed the comb and brush in warm soapy water and hung the towels she used to dry Amani's hair over the shower door. Once they had dried thoroughly, she would transfer them to the silver wicker laundry hamper.

Looking around, she was pleased with what she saw. She and Marcus had been unable to hire an interior decorator on a single income, so they bought *A Place to Call Home* magazine for valuable do-it-yourself tips.

They finally agreed to paint the walls lilac and to trim the moldings in white. Luscious green plants in silver pots adorned the counters, and an assortment of pastel abstract paintings lined the walls, giving the bathroom a tranquil feel. The Jacuzzi-style bathtub was separate from the see-through shower and the toilet was enclosed in its own little room.

The double sink counter offered space for all of her hygienic and beauty essentials as well as her favorite mementos. There was a silver sculpture of a man carrying a child on his shoulders, two silver candles in a sterling silver holder, and her favorite photo encased in an elegant silver frame.

That photo had been taken on their wedding day. They were young and in love. She cherished that picture because the photographer was able to capture the confidence they felt in doing what was honorable in the sight of man and holy in the sight of God.

As the minister made his final declaration, "I present to you Mr. and Mrs. Marcus Alexander Shephard III," the young lovers gazed into the camera's eye as if the strength of their love alone would carry them into a future filled with much promise and little heartache.

Since Marcus' death, this bathroom had become her sanctuary.

Olivia bolted to the door and locked it. As was her ritual, she turned and leaned against it while bitter tears fell from her eyes. Blindly, she stumbled to the shower and twisted both knobs as far as her might would allow. With one hand stifling her cries, she trudged back to the counter, fell into the vanity chair, and listened to the flow of purging water.

Her eyes were drawn to the mirror.

Olivia was a more mature-looking version of Amani and her sisters. People continued to be amazed at how closely they resembled each other. The physical differences between the eight Shephard women were mainly variations in shades of brown, hairstyles, body sizes, and taste in clothing.

Though Olivia's golden complexion was radiant, the eyes that returned her stare bore witness to deep sorrow. Even still, her beauty was undeniable. At forty-nine, she regularly rejected the advances of potential suitors. In her heart, she remained married to Marcus . . . and to her past.

Olivia returned her attention to the wedding photo. She lifted the picture and stared unwaveringly into the eyes of the young man who joyfully returned her gaze. "I'm so sorry, Marc," Olivia moaned. "Please forgive me." Rocking the newlyweds in her bosom, she sank to her knees.

Her chest heaved from the force of her soul-wrenching sobs. Finally, after a temporary cleansing of her conscience, she lay almost motionless on the floor, still clutching the photograph.

TWO

Amani was completely captivated as she watched Marley glide through the skating rink as if he owned it. He was carrying two bottles of spring water in one hand and a hot dog smothered in relish in the other. He stopped beside her, nodded his head, then placed the food in front of her. Like a large cloth napkin, his jacket hung over his arm.

With a wave of her hand, Amani smiled. "Very well. You are dismissed."

He grabbed her hand and pressed his soft warm lips against it. "You can't get rid of me that easy, girl."

Amani eased her hand away and picked up her hot dog. "Thank you, sir." With a shy grin, her eyes acknowledged his. "You actually believed me when I said extra extra relish." She took a bigger bite than she normally would have because his playful kiss had a serious effect on her.

"Well, in my business, I aim to please." He pretended to shoot a free throw. "Swoosh. Nothing but net."

Swoosh. I'm drowning. Amani took a long swallow of her water. It seemed as if Marley drank all of his in one gulp before pulling his electric blue skates with yellow wheels from his bag. Amani watched as he kicked off his shoes, and smiled. *Officer, please arrest this thief before he steals my heart and breaks it.*

Amani finished her hot dog and water, balled up the paper tray, and then picked up their empty bottles. She dropped the paper in the trash can and the bottles in the recycle bin before slowly scoping out the rink. The place was packed. On the floor, parents held the hands of children whose legs struggled to support them.

Amani's eyes focused on a little girl, about four or five, whose neon green overalls covered a bright orange t-shirt. Her white skates displayed identical pictures of a black Barbie. Her long hair was braided in a single French braid that hung down her back.

Each time she fell, a man Amani assumed to be her father picked her up, steadied her, and sent her on her way. She would skate about ten feet and down she would go. Whenever she began to cry, he would encourage her. She rewarded his attention with a sweet smile.

The scene reminded Amani of St. John, Chapter 14, Verse 18, a Bible verse her godmother made her memorize when her father died. It was a promise Jesus made. *I will not leave you comfortless: I will come to you.*

Amani often dreamt that her father was still alive. What she wouldn't give to trade places with the little girl she watched enviously.

"Stomp," one of her favorite Kirk Franklin cuts, roared in the background without her automatically adding her voice to the choir. Amani didn't feel like stomping because she doubted she'd ever get the victory over the longing she still felt for her father's presence. She yearned to hear his soothing voice and feel his comforting hug.

As she continued to observe the little girl and her father, Amani could almost sense her own father beside her, cheering her with one of his silly raps. "It's okay to pout when you feel mad, okay to cry when you're oh so sad, but don't forget to rejoice when you're feeling glad."

A sliver of a smile broke through her mist. Her father had been a real-life superhero in her eyes. Instead of using gadgets to overcome evil, he used the Word of God. A few more minutes passed before she realized the first group of skaters was clearing the floor to make way for the teenagers and young adults hurrying onto it. It was obvious that the young folks were in a rush to show off a little and get their praise on a lot.

Amani watched the enthusiastic crowd for a moment, enjoying the show. Whoever thought being a Christian was reserved for geeks and wallflowers needed to check out this party. Fashionably dressed males and females were boldly lifting up Jesus, L.A. style.

She hoped deejay Reginald "Salt Shaker" Cooke brought business cards with him—in case she decided to have a graduation party. The music was slamming and the Salt Shaker was bopping his head so hard it looked like he was going to give himself whiplash.

He bellowed over the steady beats of the music. "In Matthew 5:13, Jesus told his disciples they were called to be the salt of the earth. However, he warned them if salt loses the power to do what it was created to do, it's worthless. Well, tonight, we want to commit to staying salty. Here we go." He smiled into the crowd. "When I say, 'Salt,' you say, 'Shakers.'"

"Salt."

"Shakers!"

"Salt."

"Shakers!"

He ended their call and response with a hearty "Hallelujah!" The crowd's energy intensified when DJ Salt Shaker then mixed in the latest cut by Brent Jones and the TP Mobb.

Amani stopped people-watching and gave in to the music.

Swaying to the rhythms, she looked around for her skating coach. She was ready to see him in action.

Amani spotted Marley and was surprised—no, shocked—to see Destiny talking to him. *What's she doing here?*

Her friend hadn't mentioned anything earlier about coming to the skating rink. Amani had called Destiny as soon as she finished drying her hair. *Oh, well.* Amani had known her friend long enough to know Destiny basically answered to no one.

"Where do you think Destiny's Child gets all of their ideas, including the name of their group? I'm the original independent woman," she used to quip.

For this reason alone, Mama never fully appreciated her status as Amani's best friend. On a regular basis, she admonished Amani to stay prayerful because birds of a feather usually flew into the same rough winds.

Amani started walking toward the table on which Marley was casually sitting. Whatever Destiny was saying to him must have been deep. Marley had broken off eye contact and was now watching Amani, but Destiny continued talking, her eyes never leaving his face.

When Amani stood beside her, Destiny finally followed his gaze and reached out to hug her friend. Amani could smell they were both wearing Purely Pear Body Mist. *Time to start rotating my perfumes more frequently,* Amani immediately decided. *At least we look nothing alike.* "What's up, Destiny?" she asked dryly.

Unperturbed, Destiny bumped hips with her girl. "Hey, diva. After we got off the phone, I decided skating sounded a lot more interesting than UPN's Friday night line-up. Hope you don't mind, this being your first date and all. I promise to stay out of your way."

Lose the 'tude, Gertrude! Destiny introduced y'all. Amani felt she needed to make amends. "Girl, get serious," Amani assured her friend before she sat down next to Marley. "This is cool. I get to enjoy the company of my best friend—" She grabbed Destiny's hand "—and my new friend." She hesitated before patting Marley's hand.

Destiny looked over at Marley. "I don't want to intrude. Are you sure you don't mind? Just because I played Cupid doesn't mean you have to keep me around. Give me the word and I'm outta here."

Marley shrugged. "Actually, my best friend, Taylor, and his girlfriend were planning to meet us, but Regina's not feeling well. My boy's sprung, so he'll be a no-show, too." Marley lifted himself from the table and reached for the roller skates he rented for her.

Amani noticed this was the first time his smile did not reach his eyes. However, she wasn't sure if it was due to his friend's absence or her girl's presence.

Marley pulled her down next to him and began removing her shoes while she did her best to remain calm. Amani was glad that she had moisturized her feet with the peppermint foot lotion she usually reserved for the times she gave Mama and herself pedicures.

Since wearing socks tended to make her feet sweat, she took an extra precaution and powdered them, too. *Thank you, Mommy.* Olivia Shephard raised her daughters with the belief that the true mark of a lady was she took as much care of the parts of her body she did not normally show to the world as she did with those parts constantly on display.

The Shephard girls had learned the routine by heart. Olivia would start out lecturing them about the importance of being well-groomed and end up preaching on the necessary qualities of a godly wife and mother. Mama would quote verses from Proverbs 31, one of her favorite passages of scripture. Her sister, Mia, dubbed it Mama's VWT, her Virtuous Woman Thang.

Amani, however, loved it. One of her favorite verses was "Who can find a virtuous woman? For her price is far above rubies." The other was "Favour is deceitful, and beauty vain: but a woman that feareth the LORD, she shall be praised."

She wasn't in the place where she gave little thought to her outward appearance, but her primary desire was to please the Lord. Right now, her burning desire was to get to know one of His children a whole lot better.

She looked down at Marley busily tying the laces on her right roller skate, then glanced at Destiny who was also watching Marley. Amani tried to catch her friend's eyes.

Failing, she turned her attention back to Marley who had moved on to the laces of her left skate. *Yeah, I fear the Lord,* Amani thought, *but I also fear the effect this brother is having on me.*

Marley got up, pulled Amani to her feet, and wrapped his arm lightly around her waist. She was dreaming with her eyes wide open.

As if from a distance, she heard Marley bragging, "Don't forget. I promised to teach you a thing or two tonight." He began leading her toward the floor.

Suddenly, a dazed Amani remembered her friend. "Go rent some skates so you can come party with us."

Destiny shook her head. "I already have a pair that I bought a couple of years ago. They're in the car. I'm just going to watch for a while." She started popping her fingers and moving rhythmically to the song's beat. Fred Hammond and Radical for Christ's song, "The Spirit of the Lord," was blaring through the speakers.

"Oh." Amani was confused. "I didn't know you even knew how to skate." Dancing was the only hobby Amani knew her friend to be interested in. Since they were little girls, they had taken classes together. This skating business was news to her. "Why didn't you ever invite me?" Her curiosity was piqued.

"Girl, please! You were too busy studying so you could stay at the top of the honor roll or practicing your vocal exercises trying to be the next Yolanda Adams. Getting you out of the house on the weekend would have been like getting Pastor Chamberlain or Sister Rachel to preach an uninspiring sermon."

Amani laughed. She remembered her fastidiousness, as her sister, Krystal, called it, when she first entered high school. She was a senior now, however, and wanted to get out more. It was a good thing, too, because if she hadn't agreed to go with Destiny last weekend, she wouldn't have met Marley.

Being a Christian didn't mean she had to be a hermit. She thought of "This Little Light of Mine," a song she used to sing in Sunday school. With her mind on Marley and Marley on her mind, she rewrote the lyrics. "This great big light of mine, I'll let it shine. Every moment I'm with Marley, I'll let it shine. This humongous light of mine, I'll let it shine. Let it shine, all the time. I will let it shine." That's exactly what Amani was doing and her light was shining brighter than it had in a good while.

Destiny watched Amani and Marley, totally oblivious to everyone else around her. Several times she saw him give high-fives to a couple of guys thrilled to be skating along with UCLA's Miracle Man. He was somewhat of a celebrity to them because of his well-known commitment to God and his miraculous skill on the court.

Although her brother had been unable to nab him for the Trojans, he was still reverential when he spoke of him. Skye's far-from-profound editorial when it came to Marley Jamison was simply "Baby got game."

And my best friend, too. Destiny shook her head sadly.

She hated to admit it, but Amani and Marley looked good together. Real good. They both wore jeans. Amani wore hip huggers and Marley, Levis. She had topped hers with a red scooped-neck blouse that was short-sleeved, form-fitting, and shimmery. Brother Marley was doing a dead-on impression of Soul Train's former host Shemar Moore. He had covered his sculpted chest and bulging biceps with a white short-sleeved shirt.

They both had dark brown eyes and Amani's smooth Hershey-brown complexion and long jet-black hair perfectly complemented Marley's caramel-brown skin tone and the sandy brown hair he wore in a short faded cut. At six feet seven inches, Marley did not overpower her friend's five foot ten and one-half inch frame.

Anyone watching them would think they'd known each other forever. Destiny had had a feeling the two of them would get along great. *Yeah, like peanut butter and chocolate in a Reese's Cup.* That was why she had decided to introduce them. Yet, the more she watched them, the more she regretted her impulsive decision. She would become too through when the peanut butter would get too thick too fast and, it never failed, the chocolate always melted just as quickly. She always hated Reese's Cups. Now, she knew why.

DJ Salt Shaker announced he was slowing it down with an oldie but goodie and she quickly recognized BeBe and CeCe Winans' "I'm Lost Without You." Destiny cringed when Marley began to sing the song, not to God as the brother and sister duo intended, but to Amani. "Oh, Lord. I need to get out of here," she whispered.

Rushing toward the exit, she felt herself sinking on her own private Titanic as a wave of salty tears streamed down her face.

Destiny turned to look one last time before she left the rink unnoticed, exactly as she'd arrived. She turned just in time to see Amani trip over something on the floor and begin to lose her balance. Marley was so preoccupied with singing to her that he reacted a moment too late to prevent the inevitable.

Amani Nicole Shephard, her best friend since kindergarten, fell flat on her butt in the middle of the skating rink and Destiny Lafawn Ross smiled her first real smile of the evening.

THREE

Creeping up the darkened stairway as she held onto the banister with her right hand and gripped her nightly companion with the left, Olivia Shephard stepped cautiously. Vapors of steam led the way. When she reached her bedroom, she carefully made her way to her king-sized mahogany canopy bed and eased onto it. Wearily, she set the cup and saucer down on the nightstand, turned on the lamp, and tightened the belt on her white terry cloth robe.

She brushed away the night's final tear then settled down on her husband's side of the bed. This time she cried so long she had to settle for taking a cold shower. Usually she made it into the shower while the water was at least lukewarm.

Something different was happening in her spirit.

She couldn't shake the feeling she needed to talk to someone about these crying spells. Olivia took a deep breath and picked up the phone to dial the one number she was sure she could dial blindfolded if she had to—the number to the Armstrong residence. Why not? *I've been dialing this same number for almost thirty years.* After just one ring, she hung up the telephone. *I can't do it. What would Oneita think of me?*

Her hands shook slightly as she raised the teacup to her mouth and pursed her lips. She blew the raspberry tea for several seconds before taking a long sip. As the honey-sweetened, lemon-tinged liquid made its way down her throat, soothing warmth enveloped her.

Olivia replaced the cup on the saucer. Determined, she lifted the receiver again and called the Armstrong residence. She bravely allowed the phone to ring twice before hanging up. "Guess it's just you and me, Lord," she concluded.

Dejected, Olivia retrieved her teacup and sipped. As she welcomed the tea's comfort, she was relieved her friend Oneita stubbornly refused to utilize any of the telephone service options she said prevented one person from having a decent conversation with another.

Oneita would go on about how, for the sake of convenience, there was the-more-the-merrier calling, and I-gotta-go-because-someone-better-is-on-my-other-line calling, and you-can't-fool-me-I-see-who-you-are calling, and if-you-call-and-hang-up-I'll-find-out-who-you-are calling—all for a nominal fee.

Olivia never tired of hearing her friend's entertaining commentary on modern telephone service. If she were to pinpoint one of Oneita's greatest contributions to their friendship, it would have to be the gift of laughter. Indeed. Through the years, her friend's ability to minister an uplifting prayer along with her good-natured humor helped to turn many of Olivia's tears of past sorrow into tears of joy remembered.

'I can do all things through Christ who strengthens me' was a scripture Oneita often used to encourage Olivia. When Marcus was killed, a year shy of their twentieth wedding anniversary, that verse became a lifeline to her.

The prayers of her church family and Oneita's constant, gentle reminders that their Heavenly Father was the giver, not the taker, of life sustained her and kept her able-to-maintain sane during the first couple of weeks following her husband's fatal car accident.

Long after distant relatives and friends left Olivia to grieve on her own, Oneita stayed.

Olivia would never forget Oneita's dedication during the time she personally "walked through the valley of the shadow of death." That was the only part of the twenty-third Psalm Olivia meditated on back then. She didn't want to believe God was with her, couldn't believe his goodness and mercy followed her still.

Fortunately, Oneita stepped in and attempted to gather the pieces of Olivia's resolve that had crumbled completely after Marcus' memorial service.

She practically moved in, taking seriously her pledge to be a substitute parent. Since she was godmother to all seven of the Shephard girls, she had to wear several different hats.

Oneita alternated between being the resident chauffeur, cook, homework checker, housekeeper, and tear-drier. When grief drove the girls to lash out at each other, she acted as referee. Oneita even established curfews for Perri and Vanessa, the two oldest girls, who sought a release from the pain through one social event after another until home was nothing more than a place to sleep, shower, and change clothes.

Although Olivia knew her emotional absence was hard on the girls, she befriended depression and toyed with self-anni-hilation, the latter only in her mind. She was afraid to fend for herself but more afraid of hell's torment. Yet she believed the God of Abraham, Isaac, and Jacob had, undoubtedly, for-saken her.

The last traces of summer crept into fall. On the trees out-side of her window, Olivia imagined leaves dressed in their God-designed orange and yellow apparel dancing in the light autumn breeze. She refused to look.

Olivia kept her curtains drawn. The most she could bear was to leave her window open so she could listen to the sounds of the world turning without them. Marcus was gone and life moved on. She was expected to do the same.

Day would break and fade to black and Olivia remained in bed. The day-to-day household activity orbited around her. She would strain to hear his voice and long to embrace his laugh. At night she yearned for the touch that could be tender one moment and tantalizing the next. Her heart, mind, and body ached for her husband and her spirit was restless.

She kept her eyes closed, but seldom slept. Instead she replayed the tape of the afternoon that had become their final farewell. A careless comment changed nine lives forever.

As a result, a drunken fool barreling through a red light sideswiped Marcus' cab. The voices in her head were not being unmerciful. On that balmy August evening, she killed her lover, helpmate and friend.

Absently, Olivia tapped her fingers in a staccato rhythm on the nightstand's edge. She lifted the teacup, sipped, then allowed herself to become part of still another memory.

It was nearing Thanksgiving when Olivia felt gentle hands caressing her cheeks. The contact was comforting. Finally, her visitor spoke. "It's time to stop crying."

Familiar hands traced the dry trail of tumultuous tears that lined her face and her guest addressed her more firmly.

"Mommy, Daddy's in heaven." Amani pulled at one of her ponytails. "But you still have me and my sisters and Godmommy and Goddaddy and *Jesus*."

Olivia opened her eyes, sat up and pulled her closer. She allowed her daughter's warmth to melt away the icicles that had formed over her heart. Fresh, hot tears slid across her cheeks and nose and into Amani's hair. She sniffled. "I sure do, baby. Thank you for reminding me."

Olivia released her daughter, tweaked her nose then kicked off the covers. After planting both feet firmly on the ground, she smoothed down Marcus' rumpled v-neck t-shirt and kissed God's sweet messenger on the forehead. Before she could change her mind, she hurried to the open bay window and drew back the curtains.

Amani walked over to the window and stood in front of her mother. She nestled her face into her mother's soft womb. Olivia brushed the French braid that hung down her baby's back with her palms and squinted toward the sun. The dismal reality of a world without Marcus hurt her eyes.

She struggled to pray. It had been months since she had, but she finally croaked out the words. "I will lift up my eyes unto the hills from whence cometh my help. My help cometh from the Lord who made heaven and earth." She stopped to clear the grainy voice that sounded unfamiliar.

She was about to say the third verse of Psalm 121 when the door opened. Amani squirmed and peeked around her mother. Olivia continued to peer out of the window. Moments later, she felt another set of well-known arms embrace her. Strengthened, she was determined to open her eyes fully and look directly into the light.

After a few moments of sacred silence, Oneita spoke. "Unless you're trying to get your name in the Guinness Book of World Records, I'll run you a bubble bath or you can take a shower and wash your hair."

Olivia raised an eyebrow and cocked her head to one side. "Are you trying to tell me something, Sister Armstrong?" she asked, trying her best to sound like herself.

"Just looking out for my best friend." Oneita's eyes searched Olivia's. "I've been worried about her."

"I'm going to be all right." Olivia squeezed her hand. "Thank you for everything."

"You'd do the same for me."

Olivia nodded.

Amani yawned and moved away from the window. They watched her climb onto the bed, curl up on her Daddy's side then stick her thumb in her mouth. She fell asleep immediately.

The two women turned back to the tree. Its roots ran deep, allowing it to stand as a testament. Olivia's eyes lingered on the loosening leaves. The breath of fall blew leaves from their branches and the lace curtains away from the window. The breeze brought refreshment to her spirit that was as dry as a lackluster leaf separated from its life source.

Tonight, in the lamp's light, Olivia swallowed liquid now as lukewarm as her faith had grown then.

She often thought of that long ago afternoon as her resurrection day. Olivia knew she would have never made it through without God and Oneita. In His infinite grace and boundless mercy, He had purposely placed her in their lives. Shaking the past from her shoulders, she chanted one of her daughters' silly childhood sayings, "You're my friend. 'Til the end? 'Til I die? You're a lie." No lying. Olivia Shephard and Oneita Armstrong believed God Almighty had ordained their friendship. They believed the fact that they had similar first names was a sign they were destined to be sister-friends.

For the last twenty-nine years, they'd shared in one another's hopes, disappointments, triumphs, and sorrows, but there was something Olivia hadn't ever shared with her friend. She doubted she ever would.

Her biggest regret had been buried with Marcus.

The shrill ringing of the telephone interrupted the silence and startled Olivia out of her thoughts. Herbal tea spilled over the sides of the teacup, pooling onto the saucer beneath the lemon wedge. She carefully set them on the nightstand before answering. She instantly recognized the voice and smiled.

"Hey, Neita, I was just about to call you."

FOUR

In spite of all her earlier boasting, Amani hadn't skated since she was a little girl. Marley held Amani snugly around the waist as they skated in unison to the mellow sounds of "God's Grace" by Trin-i-tee 5:7. He hadn't let her go since he gently lifted her from the floor moments earlier.

She tried to convince him that only her ego was bruised. "Marley, I'm okay. I'm more embarrassed than anything else."

"You think I'm gonna let you fall again? Naw, not on my watch."

"Don't forget I'm a Christian. We fall down, but we get up." She gave him an impish grin.

"Donnie McClurkin has the right idea." His eyes gleamed. "Even still, I got you."

Amani decided not to force the issue because she could think of few things better than being in his arms. Not even her favorite roller coasters, Ghost Rider at Knott's Berry Farm or Magic Mountain's Colossus, could make her stomach dance the way Marley's arm around her waist was doing. She was experiencing a collage of intense feelings. At times, Marley's nearness made it hard for her to stay focused on skating, but, whenever he relaxed his hold to high-five an admirer, she had to resist the urge to pull him back.

Marley Jamison was her first real date outside of a high school dance. She loved the fact that he possessed the three "C's". He was cute, cool, *and* Christian. Of course, the last "C" was the most important on her list. He knew every song the DJ played and didn't mind singing—loudly—though he was definitely a save-it-for-the-shower singer. She called herself sneaking a peek at him, but he was peeking right back. *My, my, my, my.*

Amani's racing heart, light head, and tumbling tummy were an intoxicating combination. She needed to take a break and check in with Destiny. As she and Marley glided around the floor, Amani's eyes anxiously searched the concession and arcade areas for Destiny, but she didn't see her friend anywhere.

Marley brought his face next to hers. "You need to hook up with your girl?" His breath warmed her cheek. She smelled peppermint and a hint of mustard. "Just say the word. I'm here to protect and to serve."

I need protection all right . . . from you. His eyes held her captive as his full mouth curved into a smile worthy of its own billboard. The '80's song, "Your Smile," that they regularly played on KJLH, her favorite radio station, popped into her head. Amani really enjoyed listening to some of the old school songs, especially the slow ones. They painted pictures without being crass like many of the contemporary love songs. Maybe her and Marley's song would be "Always and Forever" by Heat Wave or "Inseparable" by Natalie Cole or . . . She shook her head at her presumptuousness. This was their first date and she was already picking out *their* song.

Believing she was answering his question, Marley's energy level soared. Amani could gossip with her friend later. For now, he could continue skating with the sun-kissed beauty on his side who made him feel God was definitely smiling on him.

He had the perfect place to take her when they left the skating rink because he was already convinced she was going to be his girl. When it came to the inevitable subject of sex, he would have to "stay prayed up" for those times when his spirit and flesh engaged in a tug-of-war.

His Christian upbringing played the major role in his decision to remain celibate, but there was another reason.

He was afraid.

Marley Isaiah Jamison always did things to the extreme.

If the coach told them to do fifty push-ups, he had to do at least seventy-five. Take it easy on the fried foods a day or two before the game. Not a problem. Only fruits and vegetables would pass his lips for at least a week. They needed to maintain a two point five grade point average to be eligible to play. Nothin' to it but to do it. He earned a three point five average during his freshman year and planned to top that this year.

Marley was reluctant to have sex because he knew once he did, it would be all over. He'd take it to the max. That was just the way he lived his life. On the court and off. But he wasn't *loco*.

The Miracle Man had a plan and jeopardizing his shot at the NBA was not part of it. Besides, he was committed to Christ. For him, sex was in the same category as alcohol and drugs. Off limits.

He didn't want to end up infected from sleeping with all of the groupies willing and ready to give him play or be the sperm donor for some of the same groupies looking to enhance their financial portfolios through procreation with a future member of the National Basketball Association.

He wasn't even going out like that.

Once an NBA team drafted him, he would think about settling down like his big brother, Kingston. If he wanted to, he could even hook up with a cheerleader like Kingston had.

Tamara Thompson had certainly been making her intentions clear to him since his freshman year. She was fine, but lacked the classy touch he preferred. A couple of his teammates had warned him about her. The running joke was that the cheerleader had been bounced more than a warped basketball.

Amani, on the other hand, had a pleasant personality, a sweet aura, and enough grace to loan to a few of these homegirls who didn't know the difference between scandalous and sexy. Her mama must have raised her right. She was a lady and he was definitely digging that.

Marley removed a strand of hair from in front of her eye and placed it behind her ear.

"Thank you."

"My pleasure."

"I don't doubt it."

She smiled up at him and his world seemed to spin. *Chill, Miracle Man. It's just lips and teeth.* She was turning him on with her confidence. Not the loud, boisterous all-eyes-on-me type, but the unpretentious kind that came from knowing who she was. She didn't even seem fazed by all the attention being directed at him, female or otherwise.

For the first time in his life, Carmen Jamison's baby boy was concerned about measuring up to the standards of a female other than his mother.

He and Amani together would be a serious dream team. On the court, he played to win. With Amani, he'd have to play to avoid the cut because something about her told him he'd better come correct or not at all.

There was one other thing that concerned him. What was in this for Destiny? It didn't make sense to him that she'd purposely set him up with her best friend? Maybe she had a change of heart and had changed her sneaky ways. He hoped so and silently thanked Destiny for bringing Amani into his life. He had a feeling Amani could be the one and that their destinies included each other.

———————

Destiny hastily threw herself across the passenger seat of her brother's first car—an old beat-up four-door sedan. Another minute and they might have noticed her parked almost directly behind Marley's black Cadillac Escalade.

She held her breath as she listened to their laughter and the slamming of one door then the other. The hum of the engine sounded as Marley backed out of his parking space. Destiny exhaled, sat up and watched them drive off.

When she'd rushed from the rink, she had had the misfortune of bumping into Chazz Monty, a forward for USC's basketball team. Last semester, out of sheer boredom coupled with her brother's approval, Destiny had gone out with the sophomore several times. He was a decent brother.

Despite his being gorgeous with a golden complexion, hazel eyes, and light brown hair that he wore in sexy ear-length twists, he could not hold her interest for long. She did, however, enjoy the attention she received from being seen with one of the Trojans' star ballers. If Chazz were two inches taller, he'd be a full foot taller than her five feet eight inch frame. If she were to cut her shoulder-length bob and wear twists, they could pass for sister and brother.

Destiny wiped her eyes with the back of her hand and exchanged pleasantries with Chazz as she attempted to make her getaway as swift as possible. He must have missed going out with her because he milked dry their chance meeting. When he stopped talking long enough to notice her tears, she lied that she had allergies and that something must be in the air.

Alone inside the darkened car, Destiny rested her head on the steering wheel as her tears freely flowed. When she was twelve years old, her favorite book was Judy Blume's *Are You There God? It's Me, Margaret.* She could still relate to the young girl in the story who felt uncertain of God's availability to her. Most times, Destiny seriously doubted God even liked her as well as He did other people.

Destiny rolled down the window and stuck out her head, turning her face toward the heavens. The sky sparkled as thousands of stars danced across it while the cold night air stung her face and dried her tears. Destiny continued gazing upward then raised her hand and lifted her voice.

Shaking her fist in the air, her voice choked. "Why not me?" she repeated until her anger subsided, replaced by a weary resolve.

Destiny pulled her head inside and rolled up the window before turning the key in the ignition. "I met him first." She let out an exasperated sigh. "Why can't he be *my* man?"

For two years, Destiny had envisioned her and Marley engaged in a steamy game of one-on-one. It was a dream from which she still had trouble waking.

———————

Amani felt as cozy as a well-fed baby who had just been given a warm bath. The twinkling of the stars against the black expanse of the sky and the feel of Marley's arm around her waist lulled her into a comfortable state of being that she never wanted to leave. They sat on the hood of his car, gazing at the starlit sky.

Amani jazzed up "Twinkle, Twinkle, Little Star" and "Star Light, Star Bright" as she repeatedly sang one and then the other. Outside of the Shephard residence and her church home, she was sometimes modest about sharing the gift of song with which she'd been blessed. Tonight she felt compelled to sing.

Maybe it was the wonderful time she was enjoying on their first date. Or the inspiration of the glistening stars against the background of the pitch-black sky. Or simply the feel of Marley's embrace. Whatever the reason, she knew she would never forget her first time viewing the stars from the Long Beach Harbor Lookout Point.

Her rich alto rose to the heavens then down to earth again. She was so caught up in the moment that it took several minutes before she noticed Marley staring at her, his eyes shining and his mouth wide open. A few seconds passed before he spoke.

"You been holding out on me." He shook his head slowly. "I sing about as well as you skate."

She smiled and poked him in the arm.

He moved his shoulder away from her. "But at least I tried. I wanted you to know how happy I was. You sing like . . .like Mariah, Toni, Brandy, Monica, Whitney *and Yolanda Adams* all rolled into one. But you didn't sing a note while we were skating. You ain't nothin' nice, Miss Shephard. I'm hurt."

She locked her arm in his. "I'm sorry."

"No, you're not either." He untangled their arms and lightly held her hand.

"Yes, I *am*."

"For what?"

She smiled softly and lowered her voice. "For holding out on you."

"I think I know a way you can make it up to me." He hooked their arms together again.

"Huh?"

"What's your middle name?"

Her left brow rose. "Nicole."

He lifted his free hand. "Raise your hand and repeat after me. 'I, Amani Nicole Shephard, promise to sing to Marley Isaiah Jamison . . .'"

She lifted her left hand and played along. She pretended to be smacking on gum as she spoke.

". . . everytimeIgetachance."

She said the words as quickly as he had, this time with a southern accent.

All of a sudden, he slowed down the pace of his impromptu pledge. "For the rest of my life."

She tilted her head and hoped he could read her *"Now you're going too far"* look.

"For the rest of my life," he repeated, his eyes locked on hers.

The words wouldn't move pass the lump in her throat. *What's wrong with you?*

He tickled her palm. "I'm waiting," he half sang.

Girl, he's not serious. Y'all just met. She leaned her head against his shoulder. *Say it, silly! He's just playing.* "For the rest of my life," she said quietly.

Marley leaned over and rested his head on hers. "I promise to give you many reasons to sing." His voice suddenly became husky. "Look at me, Amani. I want to see myself in those stars you call eyes."

She didn't know whether to laugh, cry, or run as far away from him as she could. But there was one thing of which she was sure. Their game was becoming more real by the minute. Her heartbeat did a crazy stampede as she lifted her head from his shoulder.

He gently placed his hands on her face. "Your skin looks like chocolate silk." Time stood still as he memorized every detail. Then, in what seemed like slow motion, he lowered his mouth to meet hers.

She had imagined this moment all evening and now that it was here, she was afraid. She put both of her hands on his chest and pushed him back. "Wait!" Amani whispered as his lips touched hers.

Marley opened his eyes and saw the alarm in hers. "What's wrong, Amani?"

Her words rushed out. "You need to know upfront I'm a *sold-out* Christian, and I plan on staying that way." Amani didn't want to use the word virgin, but that's what she meant. Sometimes it seemed that being "untouched" was some sort of aphrodisiac. Whenever she mentioned that she was a virgin, a hot-blooded male would get as charged up as a bull going after a red flag. She needed Marley to be different.

He tapped his chest. "This is Marley, baby. I'm tryin' to live right, too." He began to massage her shoulders.

Trying. She brushed his hands off. "I'm not going through some phase. If you can't get with that, there's no point in *this* going any further." She bit her bottom lip.

Marley placed an arm around her shoulder. "Amani." Softly he gave her a peck on the forehead. "I'm." He playfully nibbled her right ear. "With." Tenderly, he kissed her cheek. "That." With the stars above to witness their first kiss, his mouth caressed hers.

As their excitement mounted, she was relieved he felt the same way she did. They finally came up for air and resumed their earlier stances, communing silently with the majesty of the star-filled sky and each other.

This time, Amani did a quick remake of a Parliament classic: *Faith, don't fail me now.* She knew dating Marley would be her first real test, and not even she was sure if she'd pass or fail.

———

Marley expertly maneuvered the freeway, keeping one hand on the steering wheel while the other held Amani's. Was it just her imagination or was he driving much slower now that their time together was ending?

She kept sneaking sidelong glances at his strong profile. He was extremely handsome, but he was also a gentleman. Not once had he allowed his hands to roam where they shouldn't have. Amani was glad she didn't have to check a brother. She let out a satisfied sigh.

Amani never knew stargazing could be so fascinating. Okay, who was she kidding? Marley patiently and repeatedly pointed out the Big and Little Dippers along with a couple of other constellations. Composing different variations of "Twinkle, Twinkle, Little Star" and "Star Light, Star Bright" and occasionally viewing a full moon rounded out her total interest in astronomy.

She finally told him. "Science isn't my thing."

He looked surprised. "Most ladies would have at least pretended."

"I better warn you now. I'm *not* most ladies." She sent a half-smile his way.

Marley's stomach did a flip-flop. "Most definitely."

She did tune in at one point during the astronomy lesson. They were standing side by side and his arm rested lightly around her waist. She sensed a shift in the flow of the conversation/lecture and glanced up at him. He looked as if he was in deep contemplation.

"You know something, I never understood how some people can deny the existence of a Creator. Look at those stars. They didn't just happen. God designed them for a specific purpose."

Amani was tingling from the top of her head to the soles of her feet. *Marley took me to a gospel skate party, didn't force anything past a kiss, and now he's talking 'bout my Heavenly Daddy. Thank you, Jesus.* She began to button up her waist-length jean jacket. "I think people believe whatever's easier for them to believe. For some of us, it's easier to believe what the Bible says about creation. In the beginning, God created the heaven and the earth. Simple. End of story." She stifled a yawn. "But for other folks, it's easier to believe some big explosion formed the world or that human beings derived from apes which doesn't make *any* sense to me because—"

"Who created the apes?" they asked in unison.

They looked at each other and smiled.

Marley took his arm from around her waist and stood in front of her. "You know something I find hard to believe?"

"What?"

"That you don't have a man."

"Well, believe it."

"I'd like to change that if I can."

Her eyes twinkled. "If you can . . ." She waited a beat. "You'll be the first to know."

Amani turned on the sincere smile Marley was beginning to crave and he saw the light. It was good. It was very good.

———————

Every few seconds, Olivia checked the grandfather clock as she sat on the sofa in the living room. It was a quarter to midnight and she was waiting up for Amani.

Listening to the repetitive tick-tock of the clock, she watched the methodical movement of its hands ushering in the beginning of a new day. The clock stood proudly against the back wall covered with more priceless memories of her life with Marcus.

She and Marcus had known each other for years, having been raised in the same church where they sang in the youth choir and served as junior ushers on fourth Sundays. Nine-year-old Olivia knew she wanted to marry Marcus the day he punched Vincent in the stomach for calling her a big snaggle-toothed baby.

Marcus got a whipping from Sister Clarice, the head usher, but it didn't appear to faze him. After the service, Olivia had gone all out of her way to say good-bye. He and some of the other boys, including Vincent, were coming from the candy store when she found him.

The candy store was really just a stand that one of the neighborhood ladies set up across the street from the church each Sunday. It was for those kids who did not have enough of the fear of God in them to put in *all* their coins when the offering plates were passed.

As Marcus and his friends walked toward her, she smiled,

being very careful not to show any teeth, and waved. He looked right at her, took another bite of his licorice and winked. After that, as her daughter, Krystal, would say, "It was on like hot buttered popcorn."

They were married within a week of their high school graduation in May of 1970 at Holy Trinity Baptist Church. They were seventeen years old. Marcus' father, Reverend Marcus Shephard, Jr., officiated the ceremony. His mother, Evangelist Nadine, played the organ. It could have almost been considered a shotgun wedding except for one thing. Young Marcus "held the gun" on himself.

She smiled as she thought of her father's father, Wilson Isaac Dupree. Papa was fond of saying, "Back in the day, when a girl was in the family way, a young buck got married or buried." He and Eula Mae, known throughout Bunkie, Louisiana, as Big Mama, were married for sixty-nine years before they passed on to glory within six months of each other. Olivia thought she and Marcus would be married almost forever, too.

The hum of a motor brought Olivia's attention back to the present. She checked the regal-looking clock. 11:58 P.M.

She peeked through the curtains and watched a sports utility vehicle pull into the driveway and out of her line of vision. Seconds later, she heard voices approaching the porch. She remained at the window until she could make out Amani's. Only then did she go to the kitchen and place her empty cup and saucer in the sink. Olivia yawned as she retraced her steps to the bedroom where she had taken refuge all evening.

The wooden floor creaked as she knelt beside her bed next to her nightstand. Fervently, she prayed that her baby girl would not fall into temptation. She glanced at her digital alarm clock. At 12:16 A.M., she heard Amani's footsteps on the stairs. Olivia Shephard rose from the floor and got into bed. Bone tired, she closed her eyes.

Marley couldn't stop grinning as he made his way home. Usually he couldn't stop muttering about the traffic on the 405 freeway. Tonight he barely paid attention to the other motorists or their lack of driving skill. He was traveling by rote because his concentration was elsewhere. Marley did an instant replay of their goodnight kiss.

As they sat on her porch swing, he leaned down to sample her sweet taste for the second time.

Amani placed her hands on his chest and pushed him back a little. "I need to warn you about something else."

"What's that?"

"Chocolate can be addicting."

"So I hear."

Their lips reintroduced themselves and they joined hands as they kissed tenderly. Soulful sensations surged inside of him. It was as if he had never been kissed before tonight.

The blast of a car horn interrupted the detour his mind had taken. Marley looked left then right before passing through the intersection. Amani's warning came too late. He was already hooked. Marley cranked up the radio as Usher's "U Got It Bad" confirmed the course he was on and carried him toward an unchartered destination.

FIVE

Sunlight filtered through the oat-colored Venetian blinds. Amani lifted the pillow from her head, checked the time on the digital clock, and rolled onto her back. Yawning, she stretched her arms, arched her back as languorously as a cat, then pointed her toes. She sighed deeply and rested her head on the pillow this time, folding her arms underneath. She could hear the blue jay that often sang near her window twittering with his mate. A gentle smile touched her lips as she replayed last night's kisses. Those were actually her first real kisses. She doubted they were Marley's.

Suddenly she bounded from the bed and ran to the dresser where she stared at her reflection for a few seconds. The two long braids hanging over her shoulders made her look like a dark brown Pocahontas. She turned her back to the mirror, wrapped her arms around herself, then looked back over her shoulder. She tried to imagine how she must have felt in Marley's arms.

She unwrapped her arms, picked up her Bible, and began searching frantically for the scripture that now held new meaning for her. Song of Solomon, Chapter 1, Verse 2. Her grin broadened as she read the scripture aloud. "Let him kiss me with the kisses of his mouth: for his love is better than wine."

Her pastor regularly remarked, "The Bible is just plain real." Amani was inclined to agree with him. She closed her eyes and held close the memory of Marley's intoxicating kisses until she was rudely interrupted by a voice from downstairs.

"Come on down, Sleeping Black Beauty."

Amani frowned at the sound of Rosalind's hollering. She had forgotten. It was the third Saturday of the month. That meant all six of her sisters were downstairs, ready to get their grub on and get all in each other's business.

Mama established their breakfast tradition a few months after Daddy died. Because of the various extracurricular activities they were involved in, a set dinnertime was impossible to maintain, so Mama had been creative.

Once a month, they came together to share in one another's lives. How they shared depended on the circumstances. Sometimes they encouraged. Other times they cried. On rare occasions they vented, but most times, they laughed and teased.

Despite their differences, Amani believed this breakfast kept their family ties strong. It had come to mean as much to them as it did to Mama.

Before running into the bathroom, she opened her closet, pulled out a pair of jeans and an orange halter top, and threw them on the bed.

Fifteen minutes later, a freshly showered Amani walked into the kitchen and hugged Mama from behind. "I'm sorry for missing my curfew last night," she whispered. "It won't happen again."

Olivia nodded in acknowledgment. She was busy arranging orange slices around the edges of the champagne glasses they normally used when celebrating special occasions with sparkling apple cider, or getting the 4-1-1 on each other at least one Saturday each month.

She turned and handed Amani the crystal pitcher containing fresh-squeezed orange juice. "Go set the table." Her mother looked regal in a geometric-patterned caftan and matching leather choker set in pale blue and yellow. From her head a crown of brown waves flowed behind her.

Amani took the orange juice, leaned against the island counter, and surveyed the scene before her. As she looked around, a wave of nostalgia hit her. This scene reminded her of when all her sisters still lived at their two-level stucco home nestled on top of one of the winding streets in Baldwin Hills. On a clear, smog-free day, from the glassed-in family room, they had a panoramic view of Los Angeles and the Santa Monica mountains looming on the horizon. This was the place they all called home, even now when everyone except Amani had vacated the nest.

Twenty-nine-year-old Perri, the oldest Shephard sister, was buttering the biscuits she always baked using their godmother's recipe. In place of her usual French roll, her wrap hairstyle, parted off-center, swung across the middle of her back. She was sporting a pair of jean overalls instead of the tailored suit she customarily wore to Alfred & Alfred Law Offices where she worked as an attorney.

Vanessa was dicing tomatoes, mushrooms, and bell peppers to go into the scrambled eggs. The layers of her thick bob grazed her cheeks and neck. As a fashion designer, she was wearing one of her own designs, a canary yellow tube dress that hugged every one of her size nine curves. One year younger than Perri, she was also single. However, for the past year, she'd been dating Khalil Love, the president and chief executive officer of Lovin' Us Creations, a company specializing in both casual and chic clothing.

Krystal, her face framed by a set of tiny individual braids that hung past her shoulders, was frying salmon croquettes. The Capri jeans she wore with a Girl Power t-shirt made her look much younger than her twenty-six years. Because of her exuberant spirit, she had an easy time connecting with her fifth graders at Sojourner Truth Magnet Elementary School.

Twenty-four-year-old Nola was the middle sister, and at size sixteen, she was the most voluptuous Shephard female. Nola Shephard Mills referred to herself as a domestic engineer and encouraged the rest of the family to do the same. She and Ahmad Jamal Mills, the thirty-five-year-old assistant pastor at New Horizons Christian Center, were the worn-out, but proud parents of three-year-old twins, Malachi and Micah, whose mission in life was to leave no stone, chair, knick-knack, bug, or anything else unturned.

Twenty-two-year-old Rosalind, who worked as a computer systems analyst, stirred the pancake batter and worked the griddle. Four months earlier, she had married twenty-seven-year-old Simeon Nelson Banks within a week of receiving her degree.

Then there was Mia, Mama's baby for three years before Amani was born. She was carefully peeling and slicing two halves of a cantaloupe. Hair master Mia was styling a long wrap style parted on the side with the layered ends curled under. Her black jeans were topped with a white t-shirt displaying the name All That Hair Salon & Spa in red letters on the front. A black-and-white photo of Roland Jones, the salon's owner, was on the other side. Amani wished Mia would get a clue and dump that monkey on her back.

Mia caught her sister staring. "Where were *you* last night? Mama called to see if you had stopped by to show off your new *boyfriend*."

Amani blushed and tugged at one of her thick braids. "I went to Skate World. On Friday nights, they play gospel music. I hadn't skated since we used to go with Daddy, but by the end of the night I was holding my own." Swaying to the music inside her head, Amani snapped her fingers. "We had a good time."

"We who?" Perri interrogated. Her cross-examining skills were tens times sharper than the butter knife she held in her hand.

"We—Marley and me." Amani blushed.

Still in honeymoon mode, Rosalind gushed, "Ooh! Your first real date. Start at the beginning and don't leave anything out." All eyes were riveted on Amani.

"I . . . I have to set the table." She scurried through the doorway that led to the dining room. Carefully placing the pitcher in the center of the table, she absentmindedly walked over to the china cabinet and counted out eight of Mama's fanciest plates. There were only two things on her mind: one, when would she see Marley again and, two, when would she kiss Marley again?

———

Marley picked up the phone on his nightstand and quickly put it down. *Gotta stay focused.* The risk of meeting some-one who could get next to him like Jade had gotten next to his brother, Kingston, was the very reason Marley didn't seri-ously date. Never-been-sexed Kingston left for UCLA with a full four-year basketball scholarship and a shot at the NBA. By the time he graduated, he had gotten his girlfriend preg-nant, married her, become the father of a set of twins and a certified public accountant at Cookin' Up A Storm, the Ja-maican soul food restaurant their parents owned and man-aged.

Even though Marley dated a few times during his freshman year and had even experimented with dating outside his race, nothing clicked until Amani. He looked forward to seeing her again. Holding her again. Kissing her again. Right now, he'd settle for simply hearing her voice.

He wanted to call and tell her how much he enjoyed last night but he couldn't. He never had to in the past. The designated date from the previous evening would call him the next morning and invite him to breakfast, lunch, dinner, and a midnight snack. Depending on her ethnicity, it would take from a few days to several weeks—sometimes months— before she'd finally get the hint and lose his number.

Things were different this time.

He pretended to try to remember if he had given Amani his number when they met. He knew he had, but feigned memory loss since he knew he would have to initiate contact. Next, he lifted the receiver to check the dial tone. It was working. Lastly, he checked his mirror to make sure he was still who he thought he was. The Miracle Man stared back at him. Then why wasn't his phone ringing? *Stay focused.* He shrugged. *You need to devote one hundred and ten percent to your game.*

He was on his way to being a major contributor to the NBA and Amani was already proving to be a distraction. He needed to break this off before it went any farther. He lifted the receiver for a second time. He was going to put the brakes on before any damage was done.

A vision of her loveliness flickered in his mind and he immediately reconsidered. Amani was as invigorating as a bottle of Gatorade after an intense workout. She was the most charming young lady he had ever met. He would fail a polygraph test if he attempted to lie. He was equally impressed with Amani's face and figure. The fact that she appeared oblivious to her beauty and was comfortable in her skin impressed him even more.

He lifted the receiver for the third time and dialed her number from memory. The phone rang. *No harm in saying hello.* And rang. *Wanna find out if her mother tripped 'bout her gettin' in late.* Finally, he heard her. The smile in Amani's voice made him smile, too.

"Hi! You've reached Amani. Thought for the day: dreams can come true. Leave your number. I'll get back at you."

"Miss Mani, it's Marley. You have my number so give me a call. Peace."

He hung up the phone and rubbed his chin. *This girl's gonna make me work.* Right then he made a swift decision about the future of their relationship. Amani Nicole Shephard was definitely the one.

Olivia sat at the head of the dining table, her back to the china cabinet. Perri sat at the other end. Amani sat between Rosalind and Mia on the side of the table closest to the kitchen. On the living room side of the table, Vanessa sat across from Amani between Krystal and Nola.

The eight women joined hands as Mama led prayer. "Heavenly Father, we thank you for blessing us to see another day. This is the day you have made. We will rejoice and be glad in it. Thank you, Lord, for choosing me to give life to the seven beautiful, talented, and virtuous women of God seated at this table. I praise you for keeping your hands on them and for this time of fellowship. We thank you for this breakfast and for your faithfulness. In Jesus' name, I pray. Amen."

"Amen." Seven Shephard sisters cosigned.

Perri cut her pancakes into bite-sized pieces then looked up. "About three weeks ago, we hired a new paralegal. He's got to be the boldest brother I've ever met. Thursday he asked me when *I* was taking *him* to dinner. I'd hate to see that brother with a law degree."

Nola giggled. "'Cause he's already *way* too satisfied with himself. Guess what?" She waited to gain everyone's attention. "I'm thinking about entering Big Beautiful Woman Magazine's Supermodel Search."

"Do yo' thang!" Mia enthused.

"I'll be a big beautiful woman myself," Rosalind eyed her ring, "if I have all the kids Simeon *thinks* he wants. Two boys and two girls."

Olivia smiled at Nola. "That's great, baby. We need more African-American models to show the world that beauty comes in all sizes."

"Dawn, last year's winner, is definitely representin' for us voluptuous women, but she could use some help." Nola's smile waned. "The only thing is I'll need to have some pictures taken and y'all know how Ahmad feels about this *fantasy* of mine."

"Although you're committed to taking care of him and the boys, it's good for you to have outside interests," Rosalind responded.

Perri took a sip of orange juice and faced Rosalind. "Spoken like a clueless newlywed. Simeon *lets* you work now, but he might change his mind when y'all add on to your family. Especially since real estate has been *bery, bery good to him*. He doesn't need your income."

Even Rosalind's blonde streaks seemed to frown. "I didn't go to college for four years so I could stay home, clean up behind Simeon Junior and Ava Simone all day, and—"

"Ava Simone? I already love my future granddaughter. Ava Simone Banks. Has a nice ring, doesn't it?" Olivia Ava Dupree Shephard beamed.

Rosalind was pleased with her mother's reaction. "It's a small tribute to you, Mama O."

"Small nothing. It means a lot." She squeezed Rosalind's hand. "Thank you, baby."

"You're welcome."

"I'm hip to the game, Roz. Mama couldn't possibly say no to babysitting her namesake." Krystal took a bite of cantaloupe. "I ain't mad atcha."

"You're starting to sound like those fifth graders you teach." Rosalind cut her eyes at her sister. "What I was saying was I didn't get a degree so I could stay home and watch Sesame Street and the rest of those educational kiddy shows on PBS." She set down her glass. "Guess the highlight of my day would be story time at the local library."

Nola, the round-the-clock manager of Mills Family, Inc., the pet name she'd given her household, swiveled her head, but before she could respond, her mother interjected.

"Your father and I decided early on that I would stay home until Amani went to kindergarten." Olivia put a large piece of croquette in her mouth and chewed slowly.

She had actually waited until Amani started first grade before enrolling in UCLA's School of Nursing. She applied for and received so many grants and scholarships that her tuition was taken care of. She attributed the fact that she had always worked the morning shift, and then only during the week, to God's favor.

Unfortunately for her, God's grace did not extend to turning back the hands of time. Olivia wished she could have taken back words she never meant. A vacant look shadowed her eyes.

Perri silently studied her mother's face. She started to say something but changed her mind.

Rosalind touched her mother's hand, and looked over at Nola. "I'm not devaluing the noble and demanding job of raising children full-time. Both you and Nola are to be commended. It's just not something I plan on doing. We will pay for the best childcare our money can afford, or we'll hire a nanny."

"When your last name is Banks, you can buy whatever you want," Mia joked.

Nola was the only one who didn't laugh. "Not even a nanny can substitute for a child's mother or father being there." She traced the rim of her glass with her finger. "It's just that I wish Ahmad could at least acknowledge my desire to model. When our M&M's start school, I would like to do something besides wait for my Mills men to return home each day."

Olivia reassured her. "Don't force the issue. If God is in your desire, it'll work out."

Krystal twirled a thin braid around her finger. "A lot of

women would love to have a husband who can afford to take care of them and the children and who *wants* to. All I keep meeting are brothers talking about 'I need somebody who can bring something to the table.' You don't realize how blessed you are," she added quietly.

Olivia looked at Krystal. "God is no respecter of persons, baby. Stop getting in His way and allow Him to choose a mate for you, too."

Mia laughed. "Perri won't date anyone and Krystal dates everyone."

"Apparently your boyfriend and I have the same problem," Krystal shot back.

"Don't get it twisted. Roland owns a salon. It's his business to be friendly with all of the clientele," Mia returned. "The *only* reason he didn't offer me a position when I got my cosmetology license was because he didn't want to mix business with the pleasure of being *my* man. He wouldn't have been able to concentrate and his business would have suffered."

"Great alibi, Roland." Krystal smirked. "I guess love is blind *and* dumb.

"I hear you, Lord." Mia clasped her hands and looked heavenward. "Bless them that persecute you. Bless and curse not."

Krystal chuckled. "You really are amazing. You readily quote some verses while completely ignoring others."

"Better get that tree trunk out your own eye before you start worryin' 'bout the branch in mine." Mia put down her fork. "Anyway, my future *husband* and I plan on becoming partners in a few years. The Many Expressions of You Hair Salon & Spa will be a Roland and Mia Jones enterprise."

Before Krystal could respond, Mama turned to Vanessa. "So how is Brother Khalil coming along? He has everything most women say they want. Looks, money, a relationship with the Lord, and—"

"A wife and two children." Vanessa took a bite of her cantaloupe.

"What?" Amani brow furrowed. It was time to stop daydreaming and join the discussion. "I thought his wife died two years ago."

"She did, but we've been dating for six months and he still wears his wedding ring." Vanessa sighed. "His wife was a designer's dream. A combination of beauty, grace, and sensuality. That's how I met Khalil. The supermodel Milan Love agreed to model one of my designs at an Ebony Fashion Fair Showcase. She said she wanted to help a Christian sister out. A few months later, she was dead of ovarian cancer."

"Don't be too hard on him, Nessa. When you lose someone you love and have built a life with, it takes time before you're ready to move on." Olivia shook her head. "Sometimes it seems you'll never get there. But he has those girls, and they need a mother. How old are they?"

Vanessa smiled. "Karrington Marie is nine and Kennedy Anne is four." She tugged at her ear. "Khalil claims he loves me and I'm falling hard, but I'm not sure I can compete with an international supermodel's ghost or handle being part of a microwave family."

Mama stared at her hand. "Your plot in life is never more than the Lord strengthens you to plow." She turned back to Vanessa. "Pray for Khalil and give him time, baby. Those girls have grown so fond of you. It would be a shame for them to lose you, too."

Vanessa nodded, her eyes brimming with tears. Nola patted her hand and Krystal hugged her around the shoulders.

Olivia poured more syrup on her pancakes. "All right, Baby Girl, we're listening. Tell us all about this miraculous—"

"*Miracle* Marley, Mama." Just saying his name made Amani glow. "Well, what do you want to know? He's—"

"Can he kiss?" interrupted Rosalind. "That's all I want to know 'cause if he can't you need to throw that fish back in the water with a quickness. Simeon is a great kisser! That's one of the reasons I mar—"

"That explains it, Roz." Vanessa jumped in, her emotional moment over. "I wondered why you dated so many bums before Simeon. You kissed first, then found out later the only transportation dude had was an expired bus pass."

Rosalind stuck out her palm to Vanessa. "Girl, you know you need to quit. Before Khalil, all you dated were wannabe models with cash flow problems. You done hooked up with a millionaire and now you're trying to forget where you've been."

Vanessa shivered and hugged herself. "Does anyone else feel a draft in here?"

"Look, Nessa, don't start none won't be none," Rosalind retorted.

Krystal shook her head and sighed. "You two are so pugnacious."

Rosalind and Vanessa looked at Krystal, each other, then back at Krystal. Somehow it was decided Rosalind would be the spokesperson. "Excuse us, Dr. Marva Collins, but—"

"Nubian queens, please. It is imperative that we momentarily elevate our minds," Nola interrupted with a smile.

"Try breaking that down for those of us who never dated a prison scholar before," cracked Mia.

Nola rolled her eyes. "Straighten out your facts, little girl. Lyon's brother went to jail. Lyon went to juvenile hall."

"Baby Girl, give us the real scoop." Perri leaned forward. "Is he *foine*?" she asked, doing her best homegirl impersonation. They all stopped, stared at her, then burst out laughing.

Rosalind waved her hand. "From the office to the 'hood. Miss Corporate America's black poster girl is ghetto fabulous."

Olivia laughed with her daughters before asking, "Is he saved, Baby Girl?"

"Yes." Amani nodded, still smiling.

Mama shook her head. "Now I'm not talking about a person who believes in God. I'm talking about a born-again, spirit-filled, tongue-praying, holy-living, Bible-reading, sin-confessing, quick-repenting Christian."

"Let the church say 'Amen!'" Mia raised her hand like the saints in church did if they agreed with the Pastor Chamberlain or Sister Rachel's point and that point didn't hit too close to home.

"Marley loves the Lord, Mama," Amani solemnly replied.

Olivia pointed with her index finger. "That's the only scoop that matters." She wiped her mouth with her napkin then stood and walked over to the piano against the wall. She sat down on the bench and opened her well-worn hymn book, then turned around and peered into Amani eyes. "I want you to remember something. You are priceless so you don't give discounts or play yourself cheap."

Gracefully Olivia began to play the piano that was an anniversary gift from her in-laws. As her fingers moved deftly over the keys, Amani recognized the chorus to one of her favorite gospel hymns.

Before joining in, she closed her eyes and listened to the soulful voices of her sisters. Somehow she sensed she would never again effortlessly sing "All to Jesus, I Surrender." In her heart, she felt certain she would soon be forced to choose to whom she would ultimately submit everything.

The Shephard quartet times two had retired to the family room to continue playing catch up with each other's lives. Olivia relaxed in her leather recliner, amused and dismayed at some of the things coming out of her girls' mouths. Amani sat at one of the two bar stools at the counter that separated the family room from the kitchen. Krystal sat next to her. Mia and Perri were sitting on the floor. Nola, Rosalind, and Vanessa were seated on the sofa.

Mia jumped up in mid-thought and hurried to her small leather backpack and then over to the CD player. "I want y'all to hear this jazz CD by a friend of a friend of Roland's. His name's Jarel Posey, but his stage name is Jarez. He's bad." When the first song came on, she started swaying to the sultry sounds of a saxophone.

Rosalind looked up from admiring her ring. "I like this. What's the name of the CD?"

Mia did a little bop-de-bop and plopped down. *"No Pressure."*

Rosalind smiled. "I'm going to have to pick one up for my baby. Simeon loves jazz almost as much as he loves his wifey."

Perri shook her head in disgust.

"I think it's cute." Krystal frowned at her eldest sister. "Everybody can't be as glacial as you, Perri. If I didn't know any better, I'd think you hated men or something."

"Or something." Perri rolled her eyes. "I make a hundred twenty-five thousand dollars a year, work in one of the largest law firms in L.A., drive a brand new Lexus coupe, and own my own home. What can a man do for me?"

Mia laughed. "Girl, if you don't know, you're worse off than I thought."

"What's that supposed to mean?"

Nola took her turn at bat. "It means we hardly recognize you sometimes. You used to be warm, caring, and sensitive. You know, *human.*"

"I don't need a man telling me I can't fulfill my dreams. That the only thing I'm good for is wiping runny noses and providing him with a hot meal and a warm body."

Olivia sat up. "Perri, your mouth is runnin' over your brain!"

Nola's voice rose. "I love Ahmad and our boys! And I'm willing to put my dreams on hold as long as I need to."

Perri snorted. "I'll believe that when you do."

Olivia glared at her oldest daughter.

Perri refused to back down. "Why don't you ever tell us the *whole* story, Mama, about your decision to stay home?"

Olivia averted her gaze. "I don't know what you're talking about."

Perri nodded slightly. "All right, Mama O."

"Your daddy knew I planned to pursue my dream of being a nurse when Amani started school and he supported my decision. You were seventeen when we lost him." Olivia's voice faltered. "Perri, you know your father was a good man."

"But Daddy wasn't perfect, Mama," Perri said softly. "Why not allow us to remember the beauty and the flaws that made Daddy who he was? We won't think any less of you or him."

"I'll keep that in mind." Olivia clasped her hands in her lap. Her lips were drawn in a tight line.

"Perri, Mama's not on trial. There's no judge or jury here, so save the interrogation for the courtroom." Amani was going for a homerun. *Nobody* messed with her mother. "It's not Mama's fault or Nola's that you don't have a man. "Ice, ice baby. Too cold, too cold." Amani chanted teasingly. She stuck out her tongue at her eldest sibling. "That's your problem."

"I bet you believe that mess you see in the movies." Perri's words were laced with sarcasm. "Boy meets girl, they fall in love, get married, and live happily ever after." Her eyes narrowed to slits. "I hate to burst your joy bubble, Baby Girl. Marley *will* disappoint you. If not sooner, then later."

Amani sucked in her breath, then simultaneously chewed on her sister's words and her bottom lip.

Krystal placed her hand on top of Amani's, then fixed her eyes on Perri. "Why you got to go there with her? I swear. You are so cantankerous."

Mia attempted to lighten the mood. "Krys, I bet your students have the best vocabularies at Sojourner Truth."

"Ain't no point in shielding her." Vanessa pulled at the top of her yellow tube dress. "I have to agree with the ice queen on this one."

"Whatever." Perri rolled her eyes for the umpteenth time that afternoon.

Vanessa shifted her body on the sofa and turned to Amani. "From what you've told us, Marley sounds like the bachelor of the new millennium. He's handsome, spirit-filled, and on top of that, he has the potential to make millions. Women go crazy for brothers with power—athletes, entertainers, politicians, pastors—"

"Assistant pastors." Nola was quite familiar with this issue.

"Salon owners." Mia was practically related to the topic.

"Real estate developers." Rosalind voiced her acquaintance with the subject.

"High school principals," Olivia blurted out.

"God-fearing, handsome, charismatic educators like daddy." Vanessa smiled at her mother and then continued. "CEO's of major corporations, entrepreneurs, and designers with their own lines of clothing." She pulled at her earlobe. "If you continue dating Marley, Baby Girl, you need to be certain of one thing." Her expression clouded. "Make sure you're down for the drama—his and theirs."

———

Marley was still hung over from the time he spent with Amani last night. Her presence was refreshingly intoxicating and he looked forward to quenching his thirst in the depths of her eyes. *Focus.* This morning he was on another type of outing.

Marley smiled down at the little dude who enjoyed nothing more than hanging out with his "big brother" and trying to be just like him. Marley was cool with that. As the saying went, "Imitation was the sincerest form of flattery."

They made it to the mall within seconds of it opening. Marley held out his hand and it was eagerly accepted.

"What should we do first? Eat or shop?"

Tyreek's smile was wider than Marley's. "Shop. I already know the shoes I want. They're made for brothers with moves like mine!"

"Is that right?"

"Yep. First we'll go to Footlocker. Next, Hot Dog on a Stick, and then we'll get some ice cream. Let's go to the movies after that." His eyes shined with happiness.

Although the mall had a few early bird shoppers milling about, it was a good time to shop. Marley knew he wouldn't have to stand in a long line.

"Hold up. Your mother said you have piano lessons in a couple of hours. We'll have to catch a movie next month."

Tyreek snatched his hand away and stuffed both in his front pockets.

"That's how you treat your big brother? Cool. I'll tell pastor I need to trade in my little brother for a new one. Maybe Brother Curtis and I can switch. I'll take William and he can have you."

"Uh-uh." Tyreek shook his head vigorously. "Brother Curtis can't help me with my game. He's too old."

"Forty's not that old. I bet you think I'm old."

"Nope. You're still a teenager. My mama was nineteen when she had me." He thought for a moment. "How come you don't have kids?"

"It's not my time yet. I still have to graduate from college and get married."

Tyreek looked confused. "You don't have to be married to have a baby. My mama's not married and she has me."

"That's true, but some people think it's better to get married before they have kids."

"Is that a God thing?"

Marley palmed the top of Tyreek's head and guided him inside the store. "Most definitely."

Tyreek wiggled his head from Marley's grasp and placed

his small hand inside of the much larger one. "I'ma wait 'til I get married, too. Then I'll be like God and the Miracle Man."

A warm feeling spread throughout Marley's chest. "You do that."

Marley watched as an attractive saleslady approached them. She smiled at Marley. "I've seen you play before." Her steady gaze never left Marley's. "You're exciting on the court. They call you 'the Miracle Man,' right?"

"That would be me."

"What can I do for you?"

"My little brother needs some tennis shoes that will support his magnificent feats on the court."

One blond eyebrow raised over a blue eye.

"That would be me," Tyreek piped up.

She looked down, noticing him for the first time. "Oh, I didn't even see . . . hi. Aren't you handsome?" she gushed.

Tyreek grinned. He was accustomed to receiving all kinds of attention when he was with Marley.

Marley nudged him on the back of his head. "What do you say?"

"Yep, I'm very handsome. Just like my big brother."

"Boy, you better—"

"It's okay, especially since it's true." She glanced down. "What's your name and how old are you?"

"My name is Tyreek Wallace, Jr. and I'm eight years old."

She threw a handful of blond tresses over her shoulders and turned to Marley. "Isn't your last name Jamison?" She looked flustered. "I thought you said he was your little brother."

"He is. I'm part of the Big Brother program at my church."

Her eyes widened. "Your church?"

Tyreek spoke up. "We've been brothers for two years."

"Right, right." Marley made a fist and Tyreek quickly followed suit. The two males expressed brotherly love as they tapped fists. "I'm going to sit right here and make a phone call while you show—"

"Jenna." She pointed to the nametag fastened over one of her bosom buddies.

Marley turned back to Tyreek. "Show Miss Jenna the shoes you want. Remember your mother only gave me sixty dollars, but I got twenty-five that I'm giving you for your birthday."

"Thanks, Marley."

"You're welcome, lil' bro." He took out his cell phone. "You can get a pair of kicks that cost a total of eighty-five dollars *including* tax, or you can get a sixty dollar pair and keep the cash. It's your call."

Jenna smoothed down the black miniskirt she wore with her tight black and white striped shirt, then lifted a well-shaped leg to adjust the strap on her platform shoe. She looked at Marley, but addressed his little brother. "Come on, Tyreek. I'm sure you already know which shoes you want." Her smile was not bashful. "I usually know what I want, too." She stared a few seconds longer before strutting away.

I bet you do. As Marley watched the advertising Jenna was doing for his benefit, he knew all he had to do was say the word and he was guaranteed to get more than a pair of tennis shoes. He peeled his eyes away before she could catch him looking and dialed Amani's number. He pressed the seventh digit just as Usher's "U Got It Bad" began playing over the store's speakers.

He bobbed his head to the music. No point in lying, deny-ing, or justifying. He wanted Amani to be his lady so at the sound of the tone, he took it like a man and left another message.

———

Their family meeting was adjourned, but Olivia felt one more thing was necessary before they parted ways. She had never forgotten the hurt of being rejected by her own mother and sisters, so she did what she could to keep her clan connected. From the time they were little, especially after times of "intense fellowship," they would take turns hugging each other. She would start off by embracing each daughter, beginning with Perri and working her way down the line to Amani, giving words of encouragement to each one.

Olivia wrapped her arms around Perri and whispered in her ear, "You're not angry or cold, baby, just scared. 'God didn't give you a spirit of fear, but of power, love, and a sound mind.' You're fearless when it comes to legal matters. Don't fear matters of the heart either. Ree-Ree, you deserve to love and be loved. Stop being afraid. I *love* you and I'm praying for you."

Olivia pulled Vanessa close. "'The trying of your faith worketh patience. So let patience have her perfect work that you may be perfect and entire lacking nothing.' Do you rush your creativity when you're designing? Trust the Lord with Khalil and be patient, sweetie. Those girls need your beautiful spirit and so does he. I love you, Nessa, and I'm praying for you." Vanessa stepped over to Perri.

Olivia pulled Krystal into her arms. "'Delight thyself in the Lord and He'll give you the desires of your heart.' You want a husband? Stop playing house with the imposters the devil sends your way. Spend some time alone and discover how valuable you are. Your students are *so* blessed to have the astute Miss Shephard for a teacher. I love you, Krys, and I'm praying for you." Krystal went to her sisters.

"'Your husband and children rise up and call you blessed.'" She put her arms around Nola. "Ahmad praises your homemaking abilities to anyone who'll listen because your house is filled with love and peace. Ahmad knows the wife sets the tone in the home and he also knows beauty doesn't stop at a size ten. LaLa, don't give up on your dreams. Give them to God. I love you and I'm praying for you." Nola moved to join her sisters.

Olivia squeezed Rosalind's body against hers. "'He that finds a wife finds a good thing.' You are a good thing Simeon has found. You are intelligent, witty, and generous. Decide whether or not you'll stay home *before* you get pregnant with Simeon Jr. or lil' Ava. Don't do it because you think you should, Roz. Do it because your heart tells you to. I love you and I'm praying for you." Rosalind walked over to her sisters.

"'Trust in the Lord with all your heart and lean not to your own understanding. In *all* your ways acknowledge Him and He shall direct your paths.'" She enfolded Mia into her arms. "You have been blessed with artistic hands, incredible business sense, and too much personality for one body. Mimi, you don't *need* Roland to make the Many Expressions of You Hair Salon & Spa a reality. God will help you if you let Him. I love you, Mimi, and I'm praying for you." Mia joined her sisters.

Olivia hugged Amani tightly in her arms. "'Who can find a virtuous woman? For her price is far above rubies.' I hope Miraculous Marley realizes he got himself a genuine jewel with a heart for the things of God." She held Amani at arm's length. "You're going to be tested in the coming months, Baby Girl, but if you stand on the word of God, you won't fall or fail. I love you and I'll be praying overtime for you." Her mother released her and started toward the Shephard huddle.

Instead of receiving words of edification from her mother, she was given a warning. She felt slighted and unappreciated. Amani swallowed her disappointment as she slowly made her way to her sisters.

When they were through with their individual gestures of love, they stood in a circle and placed hand atop hand. Olivia did the countdown. "Five, four, three, two, one."

"Sisters for life!" they exclaimed in unison. Then they laughed and exchanged a group hug with their mother in the center.

Olivia was pleased with the positive energy that now flowed in the family room. She wished she could have shared the honest relationship with her own sisters that her daughters enjoyed. She was happy for them, but also a little jealous. At times, she felt the same way when she was around her best friend, Oneita, and her husband, Bennie. And she even felt sometimes that God was punishing her for past deeds. Olivia wondered when her debt would be paid in full.

Amani shut her bedroom door firmly behind her and threw herself across the bed. She usually loved spending time with her sisters but they had worked her nerves for real. *Make sure you're down for the drama.* She was just getting to know Marley, and they already had her doubting him and any future relationship. *He will disappoint you, sooner or later.* And her mother's prayer didn't help matters. *I'm praying overtime for you 'cause you're going to be tested.*

Her mother acted like she and Daddy were the only couple in the history of western civilization to ever save themselves for marriage. *Excuse me. I think you missed something, Mama. He's saved, too.*

Amani knew her mother was concerned, sometimes overly, and had high hopes for her. Although none of her sisters had done so, her mother hoped Amani would remain a virgin until marriage. There was the hope that she'd leave her hair alone even though her sisters had fried, dyed, and tried all sorts of styles with theirs.

Then there was the hope she'd carry on the Shephard tradition by attending UCLA in Westwood. Though Mia had graduated from a school of cosmetology in L.A., she was only taking business courses part-time at UCLA. Nola married Ahmad at the end of her sophomore year and gave birth to the twins at the end of her junior year. She still had three quarters to complete before getting her degree and now she was talking about plus size modeling.

It wasn't fair! Her sisters lived their lives as they saw fit while she felt pressured to live hers according to her mother's hopes. And there was also her desire to please the Lord with the choices she made. Of course, this also made her mother happy. Why did staying in her mother's good graces matter so much to her?

Sometimes Amani resented her mother and all her hoping. Whoever thought being the baby of a large family guaranteed a person a charmed life needed to spend some time in the skin she was in.

Amani reached for the telephone and called her message center. She entered her password and mailbox number and waited, doing some hoping of her own. She had three messages. Her frown faded fast. Two of them were from Marley. All of a sudden, there were no warnings, expectations or stresses to contend with. After hearing Marley's voice, nothing else mattered and everything was already alright.

———

An hour and a half later, Marley pulled up in front of Tyreek's apartment building in the section of L.A. called "The Jungle." Tyreek jumped out of the car and turned to Marley with a big grin on his face. "You know why I want to be a baller baller, shot caller?"

"'Cause you love the game as much as you love your Mama?"

"Naw!"

"'Cause you dream of playing basketball when you go to sleep at night?"

"Nope."

"Because basketball players get paid, have shoes named after them, and have their own commercials?"

"Uh-uh."

"Help a brother out."

"'Cause ballers get *love*."

"What you talkin' 'bout, Tyreek?"

"Miss Jenna wanted to take us to lunch, that pretty Chinese lady wanted to give us free hot dogs and lemonades, and the Mexican lady at Baskin Robbins was smiling so hard *my* face was startin' to hurt."

"You got jokes."

Tyreek took advantage of every opportunity to be like his big brother. "Most definitely." He grinned as he pressed the intercom. A sweet voice flowed out of the box. "Hello."

"Mama, buzz us in."

"*Excuse me!*"

"Mama, will you buzz us in please?"

"Sure, baby."

Wanita met them at the door. Her short cut was layered to perfection and her flawless nutmeg complexion was in stark contrast to her son's vanilla hues. She was tiny, standing about five foot one, and weighing no more than a hundred pounds.

"Hey, you two." She kissed Tyreek on the cheek. "I hope he wasn't any trouble."

"Mama, wait until you see my new shoes. I'm—"

"Tyreek, do you see me talking?"

"Yes, ma'am."

"Say good-bye to your big brother then go inside and watch TV. You can show me your shoes in a few minutes."

Marley reached out and hugged Tyreek. "Check you next month, bro. I'll let you know which Saturday I'm free, then you can find out where the movie you want to see is playing."

"Okay. Can I come to a couple of games this season, too?"

"Most definitely."

"Cool." Tyreek started inside.

Wanita blocked him with a quick hand against his chest. "Didn't you forget something?"

Tyreek turned to face Marley. "Thank you for taking me to the mall today, Brother Marley, and thanks for the birthday money." He flashed two crisp bills at his mother.

"My pleasure, bro."

"Figure out ten percent for your tithes," Wanita reminded Tyreek.

"Two dollars and fifty cents."

"What's your mission?" Marley called to his young friend.

Tyreek spun around. "To stay focused and give one hundred and ten percent to everything I do." He grinned at Marley and his mother.

Wanita gave him a thumbs-up sign.

"Bye, Marley."

"Bye, Lil' Tee."

Tyreek grinned at the nickname. "I don't want you to trade me, but if you ever did, you could give me to your best friend, Taylor. Now, Big Tee's got game." Tyreek dribbled an imaginary ball as he gripped his new shoes and made his way to his bedroom.

Wanita's brow furrowed and her eyes questioned Marley.

Marley winked. "It's a man thing. You wouldn't understand."

"O-kay," she said slowly. "Marley, I want to thank you for the time you take with him. It makes a difference. I'm glad Pastor started the mentoring program." She pulled at her overalls. "How old are you now?"

"Nineteen."

"That's how old I was when I had Tyreek." A look of regret crossed her face, but an optimistic expression cut the visit short. "I've done some wrong things in my life, but keeping my son was the *best* thing I ever did. It's hard being a single mother but worth it."

"Wanita, you're doing an excellent job with him. He's a great kid."

"Thank you. Having people like you in our lives helps a lot. I know this is being nosey, but Tyreek never mentions it." She stopped. "Oh, never mind."

"Now you know you got me curious. What's up?"

"Do you have a girlfriend?"

Man, I need some cologne named after me. He didn't want to hurt her feelings. "Wanita, I'm flattered, but..."

Wanita reared her head back on her neck, fanned a dismissive hand at him and gave him a "Get serious" look. "Boy, I'm asking for my cousin. She's a freshman at Cal State Dominguez Hills and she's also a Christian."

"Whoa! For a moment, I thought the Miracle Man magnetism had gotten to you, too."

As she smiled, Wanita's braces made her look much younger than her twenty-seven years. "You are *too young* and *too big* for me, but I think you'd be perfect for my cousin."

"Thanks for trying to help a brother out." He tugged at his blue and yellow jersey. "Not that I need any help."

She playfully pushed him. "Check the ego, Mister Potato Head."

"Seriously, though, I met someone recently and I want to give us a chance."

"What's her name?"

"Amani Nicole Shephard."

"Ooh, she's got you blushing! I like her already." She glanced in the direction of her son's room. "I wish more brothers could be loyal to one sister at a time."

"Somebody's gotta represent for the brothers."

"I hope she appreciates what a good brother you are."

Marley winked. "How could she not?"

Wanita shook her head. "We'll see you in church tomorrow. Are you bringing *Amani Nicole Shephard* with you?"

"If I introduce her to my parents and church family, she'll think I'm serious."

"Well, aren't you?"

"Wanita, I got it bad."

"Good, but don't forget you're God's man first."

He rubbed his chin. "Most definitely."

———————

Between classes, assignments and their corresponding due dates, basketball, and choir practice, Amani and Marley had to purposely make time for each other. They willingly sacrificed in order to bask in each other's presence. Tonight they had gone to dinner followed by a movie at the Magic Johnson Theatres in Baldwin Hills. Amani reluctantly agreed that Jet Li's *The One* was pretty good while Marley was shocked to discover that pouring a box of Raisinettes into a bucket of popcorn actually tasted delicious.

Their date was ending and Amani was home again. Marley turned the radio up when India Arie's "Brown Skin" swam through the airwaves of KJLH. He shifted the gear to park, then turned the key in the ignition, stopping the engine but not the flow of music. They were encased in darkness as they sat in front of her house savoring their final moments together. Marley sang along to another of his favorite songs. He held Amani's hand in both of his as he crooned off-key. Her blush caused her cheeks to burn. She was certain her brown skin was turning bright red.

Marley's praise of her skin tone reminded her of something that happened with her father the day he left for New York never to return. The memory was bittersweet and she didn't know if she could get through it without crying, but she wanted to share it with Marley. She bit down on her bottom lip and stared through the front window shield.

Marley had learned early on what her unconscious habit signaled. "What's wrong, baby?" The music stopped when he turned the car off completely. "Is my singing that bad?"

She shook her head. "Daddy was always complimenting me . . . all of us. Your singing . . ." She blew out a stream of air.

"Talk to me, Amani."

76

She looked out the passenger window and sighed again. She didn't want to cry. She was so happy. Before Marley, the only men she had ever cared about had been her father and her godfather, Bennie. But her father had been the love of her young life.

Marley squeezed her hand and waited.

She glanced at Marley, then peered straight ahead. "The last time I saw my Daddy, I was five years old. It was August and he was going to New York . . ."

Amani became a part of the sights, the sounds, and the sensations of that day.

"Marcus!" Olivia yelled upstairs. "We need to go, baby. Hurry up!"

Marcus bounded down the stairs. He was wearing a pair of khakis with a cream oxford shirt. His dark brown skin gleamed, and his goatee made him look younger than his thirty-six years.

Olivia was wearing an orange short set. Her brown waves were pulled back in a ponytail. A few strands had escaped captivity and hung loosely here and there framing her face. Six of her daughters stood with her at the bottom of the stairs.

She gazed up at her husband. "You're the featured speaker at the Soaring High School Principals Conference. Would be nice if you were there. You act like you don't want to go."

He smiled at his wife, then his daughters. "What sane man would want to leave all this loveliness?" He glanced at his daughters. Suddenly he frowned. "Where's Nikki?"

Mia put her hands on her bony hips. "She's watching cartoons. I told her to come tell you bye, Daddy."

He lifted one of Mia's thick ponytails from her shoulder. "And what did she say, MiMi?"

"Nothing. She's in there crying."

Olivia started toward the back of the house, but Marcus put his hand on her arm, kissing her softly on the lips. "Y'all wait for us outside." She didn't budge. "Go on now, woman."

She turned around and he playfully swatted her behind.

"Ugh, Daddy!" the younger girls groaned. The older ones rolled their eyes. "Gross!" All six sisters had the same thought. *Daddy's nasty.* Olivia had two different thoughts that amounted to the same thing. *My bed will be so empty.* She shuffled her daughters out the door. *It's going to be a long week.*

Marcus poked his head into the den, then he strolled over to the sofa, sat next to Amani, and scooped her into his arms.

He kissed her temple. "Daddy's going to a big meeting to speak to thousands of principals. Remember when I went to San Diego to do the same thing?"

Amani sniffled. "Yep."

"Didn't I come back home?"

She turned her wet face to him. "Uh-huh."

"I'll be back this time, too."

She gave him a funny look. "I know that, Daddy."

"Then, Baby Girl, why are you crying?"

"I don't see any dolls on TV that look like me." She paused. "Mia said they don't show Black dolls on TV 'cause they think Black girls are ugly." Her sorrowful eyes questioned her father's. "Am I, Daddy?"

Marcus' eyes widened. "What? You mean nobody told you? I thought Mommy told you. Well, I'll tell you if you promise never to forget what I'm about to say. You promise?"

Amani's moistened eyes focused on her father's face. She nodded. "I promise."

"Television sets all over America would disappear."

Amani giggled. "Daddy! You're telling a story."

Marcus shook his head. "No I'm not either. Poof! No more TV's. Baby Girl, these television sets can't handle your kind of beauty. Your skin is as smooth as chocolate." He nibbled her arm. "Mmmm, delicious." He patted the corners of his mouth with an imaginary napkin. "Excuse me, where was I? Oh, yeah. God's spirit living in you makes you shine as bright and as hot as the sun. No television set can handle the energy a true beauty sends out." He wiped her face with her pajama top. "If they tried to show a doll that looked like you on a commercial, TV's all over the world would vanish without a trace. Poof! There goes another one. You wouldn't want that to happen, would you?"

Amani shook her head soberly. "Nope. Then I wouldn't be able to watch cartoons on Saturday." She looked over at the television, then back at her father. "Daddy, you made that up, huh?"

"That's right, but let me tell you something that's real. You are a beautiful black princess. You're smart, brave, and a child of God. The Lord has given you power on the inside. Use it to make your dreams come true." Marcus kissed her nose. "You remember who you are and it won't matter if other people forget." He stood and offered her his strong hand. "Ready to walk me to the car?"

She stared up at him through glistening eyes. "I love you, Daddy."

"I love you more, Princess Amani."

She granted him a smile and took his hand.

Reluctantly, Amani returned to the here and now. "That was the last time . . .I saw my daddy."

Marley lifted her hand and kissed it. "I have some big shoes to fill."

Amani tried to blink back the beginning of tears as her eyes met Marley's.

He cleared his throat. "I know I can never take the place of your father. Even though I never met him, we have something in common."

Amani arched an elegant eyebrow.

"I already think of you as my chocolate sunshine." He licked his lips. "Will you be my girl, too, Amani?"

She nodded as hot tears raced down her cheeks and slipped off her face. The pain of her loss was a deep puncture wound that had healed superficially. Her last memory of her father had reopened an old wound and released a floodgate of fresh tears.

He extended his arms and his heart to her. "Come here."

Amani leaned into his embrace. "I still miss him, Marley." Her breaths came in short gulps. "I . . . miss . . . my daddy."

Marley surrounded her pain with his gentleness. "Let it out, Sunshine. It's all right. I got you." He rubbed her hair and back. "I got you."

Inspiration struck as a divine hand ushered in the newness of another day. Amani was at her desk, putting the finishing touches on a poem inspired by her last evening with Marley. She could not get over his reaction to her sharing her last memory of her father. Amani smiled as she thought of how sweet he'd been not to laugh or back away when she cried. She stood and went over to the phone on her nightstand and dialed Destiny's number.

Her friend answered on the third ring. "To what do I owe this honor?" Destiny asked, using her best sarcastic tone.

Amani knew Destiny didn't answer the phone without first consulting her Caller ID. "Don't trip! I want you to be the first person to hear a poem I wrote. Remember what I told you about the other night?"

"You boo-hooed and the Miracle Man got a chance to show off his sensitive side. He didn't even try to push up on you like some brothers would have. Isn't he precious?"

"*Anyway*. The title is 'I Remind Myself.' You ready?"

"I was born ready."

"Destiny using a cliché? I don't believe it."

"Stop the hate and spread the love. Wasn't there a purpose behind the interruption of my beauty sleep?"

"She's wide awake now." Amani gripped a sheet of notebook paper that only she could decipher, then began reciting in a voice full of conviction.

I Remind Myself

Daddy used to call me princess
and make me believe I was beautiful,
that there was nothing I couldn't do,
no goal I could not reach.

So I trusted him and grew strong and admired the person
that met me when I looked into my mirror.

But, one day, Daddy left and never came back.

In his absence, my spirit withered
and my mind became cluttered with
doubts and thoughts of insecurity.
Handfuls of self-esteem slipped through
my fingertips.

The me that I was ceased to exist and
I no longer recognized the person that met
me when I looked into the mirror.

As time passed, I went on a sojourn for truth.
Took a trip to find myself.

And I discovered God's spirit within me,
empowering me to be courageous.

I discovered God's spirit inside me,
infusing me with faith to believe again.

Discovered that God's spirit abides in me,
indwelling me with the knowledge that
the time has come.

I must do what I relied on another to do before.
I must love me, encourage me, praise me,
and honor me.

It was difficult at first, but it's easier now.
When circumstances make me
forget—or question—who I am,

I simply remind myself.

"Well, what do you think?" Amani held her breath.

"Sister Maya could learn a thing or two from my girl." Destiny laughed. "Amani, girl, you have a gift."

"Thank you."

"Maybe one day you can write a poem about our friendship. Talk about how I was always getting into fights because you were so busy turning the other cheek."

"Get outta here! I constantly had to take up for you. Then again, it's still early so you're probably suffering from selective amnesia. You remember the time Byron Evanston said Destiny was a stupid name because it was a word? Who was about to kick his butt for you?"

"*Mia.*" Destiny chuckled. "You didn't start getting loud until she came to the second grade play area."

"Stop! I didn't see her. My back was turned."

"Who needs to see Mia? You can always hear her first."

"Oooh! I'm telling."

"You better not."

Amani opened her heart. "Dee, I'm scared of messing up. I'm falling for Marley, but I don't want to disappoint Mama,

God, or myself. What if he does change his mind?"

"Keep your legs closed and stay on your knees."

"That's easy to say. Celibacy hasn't been a challenge because I didn't have a boyfriend."

Destiny spoke softly. "Mani, I have a feeling you'll do fine. You know what? I bet we're the last two virgins at Tubman."

"Probably." Amani paused. "Well, Dee, an extraordinary sista's got to do—"

"What no ordinary one *ever* could," they said in unison.

They reminisced and kidded one another for a few more minutes, then hurried off the phone to get dressed for school. Amani was a senior and felt it her duty to give her schoolmates a look at the latest "Lovin' Us" designs for fall. She really wanted Vanessa to work it out with Khalil, Karrington, and Kennedy Love. *At least until I get my new college wardrobe.* She felt a tug in her spirit. *Hey, I've kicked a lot of business his way. It's a mutually beneficial relationship.* She went to her closet and pulled out a burgundy suede miniskirt, a long-sleeved, white silk blouse, and a pair of wedge-heeled, shiny burgundy boots. She grinned. *Hang in there, Nessa.*

S I X

Olivia had a date and was in a hurry. Goblins, ghouls, witches on brooms, laughing jack-o'-lanterns, and black cats greeted her as she walked the corridors of Centerview Memorial Hospital. This time each year, she prayed for a spirit of peace to reign amidst the hospital's annual Halloween festivities.

A few of the doctors, and many of the nurses had come dressed to scare or delight their patients. Olivia was wearing her usual costume, a long white dress with white rubber-soled shoes. Her face had been lightly dusted with a powder that sparkled, her brown mane rested under a sequined halo, and her lips shined under a frosty pink gloss.

Holding a book she had been reading every day for the last several weeks to one of her favorite patients, she pushed open the door of room 111 and ushered in the fragrance of pine cones and forest lilies.

Gestures of goodwill, in the form of balloons, flowers, and cards, filled the small room. Montana lay back on the bed with his eyes closed.

She sat on the edge of the bed and watched his lips form into a smile. He had detected her scent. Olivia placed the book in her lap and gently reached for his hand.

"How are you feeling?"

"Like the last enchilada at a Cinco de Mayo celebration."

Olivia smiled. "You always have a joke."

"If I'm laughing, I won't cry, and neither will my papi."

"Are you sure you're just six?"

He opened his eyes. "Uh huh, but I'll be seven next September."

"That's almost a whole year away. I hope you won't forget to invite me to your fiesta."

"No way." Glowing eyes and an invincible spirit contradicted his gaunt appearance.

"Bueno." She picked up the book. "Are you ready?"

"Wait a minute. Let me see your costume first."

She set the book on the bed and stood with outstretched arms.

He looked her up and down.

"Well?"

His dark eyes lit up his face as he smiled. "Una hermosa angel negra."

"Gracias." The beautiful black angel sat down and opened the book.

The social hall of New Horizons Christian Center had been transformed into a magnificent array of fall colors. The banner displayed across the stage read *Welcome to N.H.C.C.'s 20th Annual Harvest Festival.* Streamers in brown, yellow, and orange decorated the chandeliers; golden helium-filled balloons floated across the ceiling; and stacks of hay lined the side walls.

Booths were set up on the back walls. Face painting, caricature drawing, and carnival games were offered at some booths. Caramel apples, hot dogs, potato chips, cotton candy, and sodas were exchanged for tickets. The middle of the floor was clear for dancing to the live band.

Amani loved her church home because her Pastor and First Lady were enthusiastic and supportive of their younger members. It seemed every year the festival was better than the year before. Amani knew this year would definitely be her best.

She smiled as Marley sauntered over, carrying a caramel apple in one hand and the fake club in the other.

"Hey, you," he said, sitting down on the haystack beside her. He stretched his long, muscular legs in front of him.

"Hey, yourself. Where's mine?" she asked, eyeing the caramel apple.

"Right here." He grinned and held out the apple.

Yabba dabba doo! Amani's eyes slowly traveled from his face to his sandals then back to his face. Her smile widened when Marley blushed and shook his head, his hand still extended.

He was dressed as Bam Bam and she was Pebbles. They had rented their outfits from the Costume Connection on Centinela and LaCienega. It was where she and Destiny bought all of their costumes and dance gear.

"Thank you," she said, finally taking the apple from him. "I thought you wanted one, too."

"I do, but I decided we could share yours."

Resisting a smile, she held her lips in a straight line. "Oh, really." She arched an eyebrow.

"You don't want to share with me?" he asked, turning his puppy-dog face sideways.

She laughed. "I hope you're housebroken." Amani pressed her lips together to set her lipstick, then took a bite of the apple and handed it back to him. Purposely, she raked her fingers through her hair and shook it just like the actresses did on television.

Mesmerized, Marley watched her before turning the apple to the exact spot where she had taken the first bite.

"Baby, if Eve looked even *half* as good as you do, my boy, Adam, didn't stand a chance." He shook his head, took a bite of the apple, and passed it back.

"Are you saying another person could keep you from obeying God?" Amani drilled him. She twirled the caramel apple by the stick and tried to conceal how serious she had become.

"Yeah . . . no . . . time out!" Marley made the signal with his hands. "I'm just saying after I watched you bite that apple, I wanted a bite, too. Maybe Adam figured eternal life without Eve wasn't really living, so he did what he had to do. Isn't that what y'all call commitment?"

"But what about his commitment to God?" Amani countered.

A familiar voice butted in. "Hey, cool it. This is supposed to be a party. Save the theological debates for Sunday School." Destiny grinned. She and Chazz stood in front of them, each holding a can of soda.

Amani sniffed and wrinkled her nose. *They stank.* Apparently, they had doused themselves with cologne, but the unique odor of a cooked hemp plant remained. *I don't believe this girl.* Amani's expression hardened as she checked out her best friend the same way she had done Marley earlier. From head to toe and back again. She could still come up with only conclusion. *My eyes better be lying to me.*

Chazz leaned down and shook his basketball rival's hand. "What's up, shot caller? Looks like great ballers think alike." He raised his club against his shoulder and pulled a smiling Destiny to him. "Come here, Pebbles."

"Girlfriend, you're gonna have to seriously forgive a sista. I couldn't remember who you said y'all were gonna be." Destiny bent down and put her can on the floor. "Sorry."

The band started playing "Ladies Night" by Kool and the Gang. Destiny took Chazz's can of soda out of his hand and placed it on the floor next to hers. Then she stood and adjusted the straps on her costume, smoothed it down over her hips, and fluffed her hair. Destiny pulled Chazz by the hand. "I'm ready to get my Bedrock boogie on." She called over her shoulder, "Later, clones."

Marley grabbed the apple from Amani's hand, took the last bite, and then shot it in a nearby trash bin. "Good thing for your homegirl we decided to leave Dino at home," he joked, trying to head off the tornado he saw brewing in Amani's eyes.

"Nope. Good thing friends are the family you choose for yourself 'cause I'm about to disown her." She shook her head disapprovingly. "I *know* you could smell them, too. That girl is straight-up trippin'! She was with me when I rented our costumes." Amani pulled at her dress. "Said she didn't know who she wanted to be yet. That weed is already jacking up her head."

"At least you don't have to worry about them drinking and driving," Marley volunteered. He rubbed the back of his neck with the oversized bat and followed his girl's attention to the dance floor.

Amani's eyes narrowed as she watched Destiny grab Chazz's hands and put them around her waist. The last she had heard Chazz wasn't the one. Amani wondered what was going on and felt like going over there and laying hands on Destiny for real.

"Miracle Man to Miss Mani, do you read me?" Marley asked, his hand cupped around his mouth.

"What?" she snapped. Why couldn't he see the seriousness of the situation? Her best friend was getting high and had purposely humiliated her.

Not usually one to engage in tit for tat, Amani refused to shake off this slight. One of her godmother's southern sayings seemed appropriate. *Fair exchange ain't no robbery.*

"Come on, Marley," Amani whispered in his ear. "I want to dance with the only Bam Bam for this Pebbles."

Marley attempted to steer her clear of the imposters as they weaved their way through the crowd. Amani shook his hold, walked briskly ahead, and squeezed in right next to Destiny and Chazz.

Destiny smiled and waved when she saw them. Amani raised her hand and wiggled her fingers. Her face tightened, but Destiny continued smiling. Amani was copying her every move. When it came to hip-hop dancing, Amani had been crowned the undisputed queen while Destiny's forte was ballet and modern dance. Every movement she now improvised, Amani did it smoother with hyped glamour, confidence, and style.

When Chazz became more interested in watching Amani than in dancing with her, Destiny realized she had been outdone. She slowed her movements until she came to a complete halt, then looked over at Amani who coyly returned her stare.

"I'm thirsty," Destiny announced, rolling her eyes at Chazz. She stopped dancing and stomped off the floor, fanning herself.

Chazz's cluelessness was clear. He shrugged his shoulders at Amani.

Amani shrugged in return and lifted her palms, but Marley shook his head at her. "You're wrong."

Wanting to savor the victory, Amani followed Destiny's retreat with her eyes. Yet, her troubled heart would not gloat. She had always believed in the solidity of their dynamic diva duo and had never purposely competed with her best friend. *Was there any storm a twelve-year friendship could not weather?*

Thoughts of Destiny evaporated when Marley took her into the circle of his arms and sang "Here and Now" along with the Luther Vandross stand-in.

Amani breathed in his musky scent and closed her eyes, choosing to believe the recent tension between Destiny and her would blow over as quickly as it had blown in.

On the sidelines, Destiny fumed. Of course she would not get an opportunity to showcase her gift tonight, but wait until the church's talent show in June. She would have them falling out in the aisles. When she danced, the Holy Ghost choreographed her entire performance.

With burning eyes of coal, she watched Amani blissfully wrapped in Marley's arms while he lyrically pledged to love her faithfully. Destiny imagined his breath being sweet warmth in Amani's ear. The sigh she released came from deep within.

She deserved a man like Marley, a man who honored the Lord, walked in integrity, and would cherish her as a gift from God. The fact that he was going to make millions playing pro ball was an added, though unnecessary, bonus.

It was never too early to lay claims on her future husband. She would not make the mistake of marrying a man who even slightly resembled her father.

Solomon Ross. What a joke! King Solomon had asked for infinite wisdom while it appeared Solomon Ross requested a bottomless supply of liquor.

Harmoni Ross was the wife for whom he eternally pledged to forsake all others. Too bad he couldn't turn his back on a drink.

Praise the Lord, everybody! Sister Ross would shout at the start of Wednesday night Bible study, giving her testimony of how the good Lord done blessed her to be in her right mind with a reasonable portion of health and strength.

Either God had shortchanged her or she was lying. A strong woman with good sense would have long ago left an alcoholic who disrespected himself and her.

And if God was truly good, why couldn't He stop her father from getting drunk or at least from yelling at her mother when he was wasted?

Destiny struggled to wholeheartedly trust a God who allowed her mother to suffer. But despite her lack of consistency in fighting the good fight of faith, she still prayed for a man who walked with God. She didn't want a man like her father or her brother, Skye, who had given up on going to church altogether.

Futile were their mother's attempts to explain that only by genuinely loving God and transferring that love to their father would he come to know the Lord in a way that mattered. To this, Skye's refrain was standard: *He's gonna bust hell wide open with a one-way ticket.* Destiny only hoped he didn't try and take their mother with him.

Destiny blinked when Chazz passed his hand in front of her face. She turned her gaze away from the dance floor and headed for the door. Chazz eagerly followed her.

Once inside his car, he pulled open the ashtray and took out his favorite method of stress release. He lit it, hit it, and passed it to Destiny. She hesitated, then extended her hand.

She had tried it a few times before the party and almost coughed up her lungs. This time she inhaled smoothly, exhaled nonchalantly, and handed it back, almost guilt-free.

There was a half-smile of contentment on her face. She closed her eyes, but not even the melancholy feeling she was experiencing could make her believe Chazz was the *other* Bam Bam.

———

Their first time attending church together was almost perfect. Since Marley met her Pastor and First Lady at last night's Harvest Festival, Amani agreed to attend church with him this morning. She was wearing a gray silk wrap dress courtesy of Lovin' Us Creations with a pair of black ankle-strapped heels. Her kinky waves were parted down the center and brushed off her face, her lips were covered with a berry matte lipstick, and her neck and ears were adorned with a black double-strand choker and matching stud earrings.

Abundant Faith Christian Center was a converted warehouse. At first Amani found the set-up disheartening, but she soon lost herself in the familiar atmosphere of humble worship and high praise. Yet, once the teaching began, she found that once again her comfort zone had been dismantled. Of all the subjects Marley's pastor could have covered, he said he was led by the Holy Spirit to teach on the blessings of covenant relationships between spouses, church and family members, and *friends*.

It was hard to sit and listen to him because he made so many good points about the sacredness of marriage, spiritual and natural kinship, and friendship. She focused mainly on the significance of the latter, since she was too through with her best friend and enjoying the budding relationship she was establishing with the brother on her right.

She was having difficulty listening to Marley's pastor for another reason. Marley was wearing a charcoal gray suit with a royal blue shirt left open at the collar. Marley's warm hand covered hers, and the light-scented cologne he wore was making its own point.

His pastor's voice boomed from the pulpit. "Turn to your neighbor and say, 'God made us to be in covenant with each other.'"

Amani's cheeks were glowing as she faced Marley. A wide smile covered his gorgeous copper face. "God made us to be in covenant with each other," they declared in unison. Unaware they were being spied on from both sides, they reveled in mutual gazes of adoration.

Marley's parents observed them looking like two chipmunks that had found a barrel of assorted nuts. Ira Jamison's lips curved downward while Carmen Jamison smiled softly, a catch in her throat.

His sister-in-law gave the couple a knowing glance. Jade poked Kingston in his ribs and whispered, "Your baby brother's falling in love."

Kingston suppressed a laugh. "Wait 'til Zoie and Zachary find out about this. Let's pick them up from your mom's house before we go to dinner."

Jade shook her head. "I don't think so. They'll have to meet their uncle's girlfriend another time. I want to enjoy my meal without someone sitting in my lap for a change."

Kingston nodded. It would be nice to eat without having to deal with the twins' whining and teasing. (Daddy, Zachary hit me. Mommy, Zoie stuck her tongue out at me). He turned to see that Marley and Amani were still gawking at each other.

Their pastor chuckled deep in his throat. "Brother Marley's got the right idea. You should certainly acknowledge the person with whom you would like to be in *spiritual* covenant." Amani lowered her head to study the church bulletin in her hand. Another rush of heat flooded her cheeks. Marley turned shining eyes toward his pastor and nodded. "Most definitely." The members who were aware of the visual exchange between the two sweethearts roared in laughter.

———

At the end of the service, a little boy in a dark blue suit ran over to Marley dragging a petite woman wearing a navy skirt set trimmed in white with him. He wrapped his arms around Marley. "Hey, big brother Marley.

Marley grinned. "What's up, man?" Marley squeezed Amani's hand. "This is my buddy I was telling you about."

Amani stuck out her hand. "Hi, Tyreek."

He firmly shook her hand, a quizzical look on his face. "You know my name, but I don't who you are."

Before she could answer, the woman reached out and hugged her then stepped back. "I'm Wanita Richards, Tyreek's mother." Her small stature and braces made her look like an older sister rather than his mother. "It's good to meet you, *Amani Nicole Shephard*," she said, a twinkle emanating from her eyes.

Amani didn't think it was her imagination. Marley was actually blushing. "A pleasure to meet you, Wanita, and you, too, Tyreek." She continued to address Tyreek. "Marley told me all about your church's program and how glad he is to have you for his little brother."

"Really?" Tyreek turned away.

"Excuse me, young man." Wanita placed a firm hand on her son's shoulder and looked up at Amani. "He knows better than to be rude. I don't know what his problem is." She cast a worried glance toward Marley.

Marley nudged his little brother. "I didn't tell you I had a girlfriend because I figured third graders weren't interested in that kind of stuff."

"She's your *girlfriend*?" Tyreek scrunched up his face. "Yuck! Girls make me sick."

Wanita's voice was sharp. "Tyreek Wallace, Jr., you better check yo—"

"He's just surprised." Amani wanted to pinch him until she remembered how difficult it was for Vanessa to gain Kennedy and Karrington's trust when she first started dating Khalil. She also recalled her godmother's words. "Properly entreated, you can get anything from anybody." Amani finally understood what that meant.

She stooped to his eye level. "Maybe you'll let me hang out with you and Marley one Saturday. Bet I could learn a lot about guy stuff from you. I have six sisters and no brothers."

His face lit up. "My mama has six brothers and no sisters! She knows all about being a guy and—"

"Gee, thanks!" Wanita laughed. "I'm just one of the guys,

huh? Do I need to grow out of this short cut and trade in all my jean overalls for more skirts and dresses?"

"Why, Mama? I like your overalls and your hair." He stared at his mother as if she had grown a third eye.

Wanita patted his cheek. "Never mind, baby."

"Just some girl stuff," Amani added.

Tyreek mulled over Amani's earlier request. "Guess you can hang out with us guys. . . every now and then."

Amani loosened her hand from Marley's grip and extended it to Tyreek for the second time. "I'm looking forward to learning a lot from you." She smiled. "Every now and then."

Marley's chocolate sunshine and little brother shook on it and then turned to the one person with whom they both enjoyed spending time. Marley offered a hand to each of them and winked at Wanita. She discreetly gave him a thumbs-up sign.

SEVEN

A t the ringing of the final bell, students jetted out of their classes into the halls of Harriet Tubman Preparatory High School. Animated conversations saturated the air as the games began.

The high profilers leaned nonchalantly against their lockers, waiting to be admired, or stood in groups of three or four, cruising with their eyes. Those in the less popular crowds disappeared into the sidelines.

Amani could see Destiny retouching her lipstick and maintaining her flawless bob in the mirror she kept in her locker. Securing a position as a top-ranking member of the player's club was a full-time job.

Amani trudged over to her friend. The knot in her stomach went along for the ride. She hadn't seen Destiny since her hasty exit from the party on Saturday night. Normally, she would have seen her girl at Sunday service.

If Marley had elbowed her one more time during his pastor's teaching on covenant relationships, she would have shouted for real. She wasn't serious about dissolving her friendship with Destiny. They had been best friends too long. She was only venting. After hearing the pastor's sermon, she felt even worse about challenging Destiny to a rhythmic showdown she had no chance of winning.

Standing behind Destiny, their eyes met in the mirror. Not wanting to be on the receiving end of Destiny's infamous stare that could freeze a volcanic eruption, Amani decided against their old greeting: *"Mirror, mirror on the wall, where are the divas who surpass them all?"* With much attitude, Destiny would respond, *"Here we be!"* They would end with a high five and a "Hel-lo."

Instead, Amani raised the flag she had taped together using a pencil and notebook paper during Mrs. Taffey's lecture on Langston Hughes.

Destiny saw the flag, smiled in the mirror, then slammed her locker shut and turned to Amani. The two friends hugged as if they hadn't seen each other in years.

Amani let go first. "You're still my bestest bud?"

"You know it!"

"I'm sorry about Saturday night."

"Me, too."

"Love ya, Dee."

"Back at ya, Mani."

Earlier, when Amani constructed her peace offering for Destiny, she had paid close attention to her English teacher because her deepening feelings for Marley made her acutely aware of the power in poetry. One day, she planned to pen a poem in honor of their relationship. For now, Amani turned her attention back to the present.

Amidst the whistles and flirtatious comments from the brothers, they strutted, arm in arm, toward the student parking lot. They jumped in Destiny's 2002 Toyota RAV4, a birthday present from her folks, and slammed their doors. Destiny's parents paid her car note and her brother, Skye, paid the insurance.

Amani envied her friend. Even when she turned eighteen,

she already knew her mother could not afford to buy her a new car. Maybe she could drop a few hints to Perri. For now, she'd have to settle for borrowing her mother's old Land Cruiser.

As a result of having repeated kindergarten, Destiny reached eighteen shortly after the start of their senior year. During her first go-around in kindergarten, she became ill with meningitis and stayed out most of the school year. Her mother ended up taking a leave of absence from work to nurse her back to health.

The two girls met during that following school year at New Horizons Christian School, where they quickly become loyal friends.

Amani asked Destiny if she remembered their childhood nicknames.

"Are you kidding? Chocolate Mani and Vanilla Dee. We were as inseparable as two scoops in a waffle cone. Girl, I could hardly keep a straight face when my parents took Skye and me to get ice cream. If someone ordered a scoop of chocolate and a scoop of vanilla, forget it."

They laughed and reminisced about old times as they rode to Amani's house. Suddenly, Amani quieted and stared out of the window. Destiny sensed the shift in her mood. "What's the matter?"

Amani shook her head. "Nothing."

"Girl, please."

"What! You read minds now?"

Nervously, Destiny insisted. "Just say whatever it is!"

"Since when did you start getting high?"

Destiny was relieved. "I just tried it that night with Chazz. It's no big deal."

"I don't believe you! You are way too smart to start messing with that junk."

"Maybe I'm not as smart as you think," Destiny answered, keeping her eyes on the traffic.

"You made the High Achievers Honor Roll last year. I know you know better than to start smoking weed."

"Maybe I got book sense, but no common sense."

Amani cut her eyes at her friend. "Meaning?"

Destiny took her time before answering. "A person with good sense probably wouldn't have introduced her best friend to the Miracle Man."

"Marley's not trying to convince me to have sex if that's what you're worried about."

"Stop being naïve. Even young, hot-blooded Christians can only take celibacy so far. Marley's gonna flip the script. When he does, I bet all your 'I'm-staying-a-virgin-until-I-get-married' talk will end up on the editing floor!"

"Why? Because yours would? Along with your panties?"

"Only a fool's wouldn't!"

Amani spoke evenly. "If you feel that way, Destiny, why did you introduce us? Are you hoping I'll slip up?"

"No," she said softly. Destiny stopped at a red light, but kept her eyes straight ahead. "Personally, I'm getting tired of just saying no. Ain't *nobody's* business if I change my mind!"

Amani looked out her window. "I hope you think long and hard before you do something crazy. Like Pastor Chamberlain says, 'We can choose our actions but we can't choose their consequences.'"

"Consequences aren't always bad, you know."

Destiny's response was too quick and too smooth to be unrehearsed. Amani figured she had been practicing that line, attempting to justify what she seemed set on doing.

If Amani were honest with her friend, she would have to admit she did think about making love with Marley, but when those thoughts came, she did her best to chase them away. *Give no place to the devil and he will flee.* Lately, Amani had to work extra hard to keep the devil on the run.

They pulled into the Shephard's driveway. Amani faced her friend. "I'll talk to you later." She grabbed her backpack and got out of the car, silently praying her friend would come to her senses before she chose a route that led straight into the path of an eighteen wheeler with faulty brakes.

As she watched Destiny back out onto the street, Amani thought of another of their pastor's spiritual nuggets, and mumbled, "There's no such thing as an illegal U-turn with God."

EIGHT

Miracle Marley was in high form, giving his admirers yet another stellar performance on the court. It was their first home game at Pauley Pavilion since returning from a road trip.

"Defense! Defense!" The crowd roared and stomped their feet as Marley stole the ball, dribbled down the court, and sank a three-pointer at the buzzer, giving the Bruins the victory.

Amani's heart was pounding, and her eyes were riveted on her man. He flashed a smile and pointed upward as he accepted the congratulatory pats on the behind from his teammates. The spotlight was shining solely on Marley. He was the star of the show and he was hers.

People rushed onto the court as many in the crowd stood in the bleachers cheering, "Miracle! Miracle! Miracle!" He flashed a triumphant smile at the crowd, holding two fingers in a V sign. Then he strode over to shake hands with the Arizona players.

Amani stood, willing him to look at her. She wanted to share in his victory.

A couple of cheerleaders stopped him as he left the opposing team's side. She could tell that this after-game chat was customary. He looked very comfortable as he laughed with them. They were equally at ease. One of them kept touching his arm, his hand, his chest. Marley finally walked over to his team's bench. Suddenly, he turned and scanned the faces of the stragglers in the bleachers.

Their eyes connected and Amani's heart beat again.

Marley effortlessly trotted up the steps and took possession of her hands. In sacred silence, they feasted on one another with joyous eyes. Neither wanted to be first to break the honesty of the moment.

Engulfed by the intensity of her feelings for Marley, she bit her lip to prevent tears of delight from flowing. Amani knew she had to speak now or float away in the name of love.

"You represented me well out there. Especially with that last shot."

"I gotta make sure my lady can keep her head up when she enrolls here next fall."

"Marley, you know I haven't decided yet. I've just narrowed my choices to two. Cornell *or* UCLA."

"What's to decide? Your parents and all your sisters came through here one way or another. How can you even *think* about going to Cornell after what happened to the World Trade Center and the Pentagon a couple of months ago?"

"Just like terrorists attacked the east coast, they can do the same thing here. We have to trust God, the only *true* super power. Like my daddy used to say, 'My times are in His hands.' And my pastor has been encouraging us to regularly pray Psalms 91 and 121. You need to do the same thing." She pondered the fact that attending UCLA had become some sort of Shephard tradition. "I'm not sure I even want to attend college in California. It might be good for me to get away."

"From what? Me?" he asked huffily.

Amani moved closer to hold him, sweat and all. At first he stood stiffly. Then he returned her embrace with a passion that made her reconsider. Perhaps she should stay exactly where she was. Home.

Marley went to the locker room while Amani waited for him in the gym. She sat on the team's bench and daydreamed about being married to a professional basketball player.

Despite the money that could buy her everything she wanted and allow her to be a blessing as Pastor Chamberlain taught, she imagined that more time with Marley would be her great-est desire. She smiled as she remembered their first kiss.

A laugh startled her out of her thoughts. "The only people who want to be like Mike are the ones who've never seen the Miracle Man in action."

Amani turned to see her friend standing beside her and wearing a huge grin.

"Hey! I didn't know you were here."

"The Miracle Man's got game and he's on his way to fame!"

"O-kay." Amani chuckled, then frowned. "Why didn't you come sit with me?"

Destiny sat down and spoke quickly. "I apologize for what I said the other day. Will you forgive me?"

"I've known you long enough to realize you have a bad habit of speaking first and thinking later."

"Ouch!" Destiny frowned. "But do you believe I meant what I said?"

Amani thought back to the gist of Destiny's comments. *Only a fool wouldn't give in to Marley if he wanted sex.* She stared directly into her friend's eyes. "What I believe is you're as committed to celibacy as I am, despite all your talk." Amani reconsidered. "Hold up. The Word does say 'Out of the abun-dance of the heart, the mouth speaketh.' Destiny Ross, I hope you're not serious about—"

"You always got a word for somebody!" Destiny stood

abruptly. "I hope your precious words don't fail you when that wannabe Kobe Bryant is ready to do the do, and I'm not talking 'bout no soda either." Destiny spun around on her heels.

Amani jumped up and watched her make her way to the nearest exit. She jumped when Marley put his arms around her from behind.

"What's up with your girl?" he muttered.

"I wish I knew. She acts like she's jealous of our . . ." Amani quickly turned and faced him. "Did you and Destiny use to date?" Amani knew his eyes would answer her.

Marley put his gym bag on the bench and sat next to it.

"I don't believe this! Why didn't you tell me?" She eyed the *God Rules the Heavens but the Miracle Man Rules the Court* sweatshirt she designed for him in her visual arts class. "I thought I could trust you."

"Amani, you *can* trust me. It's not what you think. We went skating a couple of times with her brother and a girl he was seeing at the time." His dim eyes met hers. "You know Skye tried to get me to play for USC. I hadn't mentioned it because I wasn't sure if Destiny told you and I didn't want you thinking I was interested in her."

"Hmmm. Anything else you need to tell me?"

"Yeah." He pulled her onto his lap and stared directly into her eyes. "It's all about you, Sunshine," he continued, tugging at his shirt, "and I'm only wearing this corny sweatshirt to prove it to you."

Marley's lips met hers and Amani hoped her kiss relayed her response. She was already convinced. As their kiss deepened, she wondered if she'd ever have to prove herself to him.

WINTER

A time to weep, and a time to laugh; a time to mourn, and
a time to dance; A time to cast away stones, and a time to
gather stones together; a time to embrace and a time to
refrain from embracing.

Ecclesiastes 3:4-5

NINE

They held hands and strolled through the twinkling lights of Westwood—UCLA's college town. The stores, streets, and trees were decorated in anticipation of the upcoming Christmas holiday. Amani was giddy and felt so blessed. She already had all she wanted for Christmas: Marley Isaiah Jamison. UCLA's Miracle Man and her gift from God.

Males and females of all ethnicities high-fived him or patted his back as the two lovebirds strolled through the crowds. She could sense he thoroughly enjoyed the attention though he tried to appear unaffected. Amani was excited for him and only became a little perturbed when several of the young ladies made it clear they wouldn't mind walking a while in her shoes. The more flirtatious they were, the more tightly he held her hand.

He quickened their pace as they approached the restaurant. They were going to be adventurous and dine on Thai cuisine for the first time. The pungent aroma of garlic, onions, and soy wafted down the street to greet them as they approached Thai Time. A whiff of welcoming smells met them at the door as Marley held it open. He kissed the back of Amani's neck as they entered the brightly lit, contemporary-styled eatery. Amani noticed the walls were decorated with color photos of UCLA athletes. She also noticed that many of the diners in the full restaurant stared openly at them.

Amani listened as Marley charmed the hostess. Miss Mini-Miniskirt kept her eyes glued to his face. Suddenly their twenty-minute wait had become 'Right this way, please' and she led them to a table for two near the window. Marley pressed his palms together and bowed his head, Japanese style. Their hostess grinned broadly. When Marley pulled out Amani's chair, Miss Mini-Miniskirt acknowledged her with a long, cool stare.

"Good evening." Amani smiled in return.

Miss Mini-Miniskirt grunted, then placed a menu in front of each of them. "Your server will be right with you," she informed Marley.

"Thank you."

As she walked away, Marley leaned across the table and kissed Amani, then picked up her menu and handed it to her before picking up his own. As Amani watched him studying his menu, she could clearly understand her best friend's dilemma.

She was sure Destiny wanted to be happy for her, but it was difficult because she wasn't accustomed to having to share Amani. She probably also had a crush on Marley back in the day. The uncertainty Amani faced was whether to feel flattered or threatened at this discovery.

Although it was her thirteenth Christmas without Marcus, this holiday season was still one of the hardest times of the year for Olivia. It ranked right up there in difficulty with the anniversaries of their wedding and his death as well as Father's

Day. The magnitude of the pain had lessened, of course, but her longing for his presence had not.

She looked around before she returned to her seat at the head of the dining table. Krystal sat at the kitchen counter between Karrington and Kennedy. Being an educator came natural to her because her interest in children was genuine. The Mills family sat across from each other, forcing Rosalind and Simeon to sit at opposite ends of the kitchen table. Olivia was certain having to look at each other without being able to put their hands on each other would be a stretch for the newlyweds. She smiled and sat at her designated end of the dining room table while Bennie sat at the other end. To Olivia's right sat Amani, Marley, Vanessa, and Khalil. To her left were Perri, Roland, Mia, and Oneita.

Each year since Marcus' death, Bennie faithfully carved the turkey in his spiritual brother's place. For this Olivia was as thankful as she was envious. She sometimes imagined it was her husband who asked if she'd like white or dark meat. Her meat selection depended on her mood. She chose dark meat if she was feeling jovial and wanted to talk more than she chewed and vice versa.

Tonight, she chose white meat.

Usually she put forth a fine effort of masquerading as a joyful hostess. However, seeing Amani and Marley together reminded her so much of young Marcus and Olivia that an excruciating sadness was slowly, but surely, saturating her.

A masculine voice returned her to the present. "Mrs. Shephard, my mother was afraid I'd miss the Jamaican dishes she adds to our traditional Christmas fare, but your cooking made me forget all about curried goat," Marley volunteered. "Of course, I wouldn't dare tell her that."

"I taught her everything she knows," Mia kidded.

Roland gave her a sidelong glance. "So you can make a Christmas feast, but not my breakfast."

All eyes turned to him. Olivia's lingered the longest.

Mia kicked him under the table.

"Ouch!" Roland's smile was apologetic. "I bit my tongue."

Olivia turned to Marley. "I'm glad you enjoyed it, Marley. Which part of Jamaica are your parents from?"

"They're both from Kingston. Bob Marley country. My dad was a great admirer of his. That's how I ended up with the name Marley. My brother's name is Kingston."

"What are your middle names? No, let me guess." Mia paused thoughtfully. "Rasta and Farian."

Olivia gave Mia the same look Mia had just extended to her beau. This time, Roland took another bite of dressing and chewed slowly while Amani glared at her sister.

But Marley grinned. "A few months before my brother was born, my mother became a born-again Christian. My father chose our first names and she picked our middle names from the Bible. I'm Marley Isaiah and my brother is Kingston Elijah. About a year after I was born, my father accepted the Lord. It took several years, but she never stopped praying in faith for him."

"There's awesome power in prayer." Oneita agreed.

Khalil put down his fork. "I met my wife on a photo shoot in Jamaica." He fingered his ring. "It's a beautiful island."

Perri tried to catch her sister's eye, but Vanessa kept her head down as she tugged her ear and took a sip of punch.

Bennie chuckled and clapped his hands together once. "I'd have to say the names Marley Isaiah and Kingston Elijah beat the name Bennie Lee any day."

Oneita quickly spoke up. "Granted those are very beautiful names, but if we had had a son, he would have been Bennie Lee Armstrong, Jr., or Bennie Lee Armstrong II, whichever you preferred."

Bennie patted his wife's hand as she smiled at him and ate a spoonful of Olivia's cornbread dressing. Speaking to no one in particular, he said, "Oneita and I were unable to have children, but we thank God for the school we have run together for the past twenty-five years at New Horizons. There we've been blessed with hundreds of children. With seven beautiful goddaughters to love, we've tasted the ups and downs of parenthood."

Vanessa leaned over Khalil and grabbed her godfather's hand. Bennie smiled and continued. "The Lord always has a ram in the bush."

Marley turned to Olivia. "Seven daughters is an exceptional feat, Mrs. Shephard. But did you and Mr. Shephard ever want a boy?" His steady gaze never left her face. Olivia knocked over her glass.

Perri jumped up to get some paper towels. "They almost put Mama out of the hospital, she was so excited Nola had a set of twin boys." She tossed her hair over her shoulder and started toward the kitchen.

"Sit down, honey," Olivia spoke firmly. "I'll go. I need to work off some of this food before it settles around my middle."

As soon as she entered the kitchen, Olivia's grandson who was her pride, and his twin brother who brought her joy, jumped out of their chairs and ran to hug her waist.

"G-mom, we ate all our food, even our greens and string beans!" Micah's golden face beamed under his curly fade cut.

"Now we can have a big piece of your chocolate Hershey cake?" Malachi spread his arms as wide as he could. "G-mom, yours is way better than Mommy's."

Everybody but Nola laughed at that. Ahmad grinned, but his wife's glare promptly ended his faux pas.

Olivia kissed them both on top of their heads. "I made the cake for you guys so you get to have the first two slices." She was glad for the distraction. She needed to avoid Marley's question and the answer she was unwilling to give.

———

After they joined in the family's traditional reflection of the birth of Jesus through the reading of scripture and the singing of their most cherished Christmas carols, her godparents said goodnight. Next to leave were Rosalind and Simeon who almost knocked the tree over in their rush to return to the privacy of their townhouse in Culver City.

Shortly afterward, Vanessa and her crew departed for Anaheim Hills to spend time with Khalil's parents. Then Roland left alone to "holla at his peeps" while Nola and her gang left Baldwin Hills to make their rounds in South Central L.A.

Three Shephard sisters were in the family room watching the original version of *A Miracle on 34th Street*. Only one was alone by choice. Perri had no one she wanted to be bothered with, Krystal's top selection had chosen someone else, and Mia's boyfriend conned her with a whispered promise. An exhausted matriarch had gone upstairs to soak in the bathtub.

Amani and Marley, both dressed in purple, sat at the bottom of the stairs watching the twinkling colors of the Christmas tree that gave off the only light in the living room.

Marley sang "This Christmas," a classic holiday song in her ear. Amani couldn't stop smiling as he sang about hanging mistletoe and getting to know her better. However, she recognized if he shot hoops the way he sang, he'd ride the bench more than he played.

Still, Amani loved it. She sat beside him and swayed to his song. When she could no longer restrain herself, she joined in with her own soulful stylings, concurring that this Christmas was a very special Christmas indeed.

Marley immediately stopped singing. "Baby, you can sang to me any time."

Krystal yelled from the den. "Go on, girl, serenade your man!"

For her encore, Amani put her hand on the side of his face and kissed him.

He stared into her eyes. "Merry Christmas, Amani."

"Merry Christmas, Marley."

"I have a little somethin' somethin' for you. Will you bring me my jacket, please?"

Amani went to the foyer closet. On her way back, she picked up a small rectangular box from under the tree. She handed the handsomely wrapped gift to Marley along with his leather jacket. "Open mine first," she requested.

He carefully unwrapped the present before lifting the golden lid. Smiling broadly, he picked up the 14-karat gold I.D. bracelet. It had been engraved *S.O.S. 8:7.*

"Thank you, Amani. This is *really* nice." He studied the inscription. "S.O.S. stands for Song of Solomon, right? But what does Chapter 8, Verse 7 say?"

"I'm not telling. You're going to have to look it up," she teased. She grabbed his wrist. "Let me put it on for you." Marley rested his arm on her knee. A warm glow passed over her and she took her time fastening the bracelet. He kissed her on the forehead when she finished. Then he held out his wrist and admired the gold against his caramel skin.

"Thank you, Sunshine. It's beautiful, and so are you. I'll never take it off." He reached for her hand and lightly caressed it. "It won't turn green if I shower in it?"

She punched him playfully on the shoulder. "No, silly."

"Just checking." Marley took an envelope from the inside pocket of his jacket and handed it to her.

Amani kept her face stiff to hide her disappointment. As much thought as she'd put into his present, all she got in return was a gift certificate. She prepared to fake her enthusiasm as she tore open the envelope.

But a moment later, her eyes widened and her mouth fell open as she studied its contents. "Oh, my goodness, Marley! Are you serious?" She hugged him, hopped down from the stairs and ran into the den. "I'm going to Jamaica for Spring Break!" she shouted to her sisters, jumping up and down with them for a few minutes before she hurried back to Marley.

In her excitement, Amani hadn't heard the doorbell ring, so she was slightly surprised to find her best friend and Chazz Monty standing on the porch when she returned. Destiny was under the mistletoe Amani had attached to the outside edge of the door frame in anticipation of Marley's yuletide visit.

Marley widened the door and stood against it to let them in. Chazz waved Destiny ahead of him. She stepped into the doorway, then leaned forward and kissed Marley softly on the cheek. She smiled and winked. "Merry Christmas." Destiny laughed at his expression and pointed to the mistletoe.

He quickly regrouped. "Yeah. Thanks. Merry Christmas."

Amani rushed over and stood beside Marley. Destiny kissed her best friend, eyeing the envelope in her hand.

Destiny was wearing a black cashmere sweater and black mini-skirt with a pair of black knee-high leather boots. Her bob was parted down the center and she had blended in the bangs she normally wore for a more elegant effect. She wore a coral lipstick that shimmered and made her complexion radiate.

Chazz followed Destiny, and Amani could see he had called ahead for a wardrobe check. He wore a black corduroy shirt with matching pants and a pair of loafers with a silver band. He was holding a bottle of Martinelli's Sparkling Apple Cider with a red ribbon around its neck.

Chazz leaned down and kissed Amani on the cheek.

"Merry Christmas, Amani." He handed her the bottle.

"Merry Christmas, Chazz." She lifted the bottle. "I love sparkling cider. Thanks so much."

"You're welcome." Chazz gave Marley the true soul brother one-arm hug and handshake. "Merry Christmas, Miracle Man. Your game's been on point."

"This your world, Mighty Monty. I'm trying to keep up with you."

"I hear you, man."

Marley closed the door, then followed Amani to the dining table where she had placed four dessert plates, forks, cloth napkins, glasses, and a pitcher of water after she helped her sisters clear the table and clean the kitchen. Marley pulled out Amani's chair and helped her move it closer to the lace-draped table before sitting down beside her. Amani placed the envelope next to her plate. On the other side of the table, Chazz helped Destiny into her seat.

Destiny smiled at him and shook her hair. She didn't have the length Amani did, but when it came to having a head full of thick, luxurious hair, not even Oprah's rivaled hers. Much energy and many hours went into Destiny's cover girl look.

Longingly, she eyed the four sweet potato pies, chocolate cake, and 7-Up cake that lined the table. One bite and she'd have a zit or two to contend with by morning. For a moment, a mini-war raged inside her head. Right now, her acne-prone complexion shone clear. She grabbed the crystal Mikasa pitcher, poured some water, and took a long swallow. The last thing she wanted was to bring in the New Year with unwanted visitors lounging on her face.

Destiny turned away from the enticing desserts and allowed her eyes to rest on the envelope. "I see you got gift certificates for Christmas, too. These brothers must think all we do is shop." She snapped her fingers. "Baldwin Hills Plaza, here we come."

Amani smiled and pushed the envelope across the table. "Not even close, girlfriend."

Destiny pulled out the stapled tickets and placed them on the table. She stared, wide-eyed, at a round trip ticket to Kingston, Jamaica. She looked at Amani. At Marley. Then back at Amani. "Dang. Merry Christmas, baby. Too bad Mama Olivia won't let you go."

Amani's happy expression soured. She had neglected to factor in her mama's most likely response to the gift.

Chazz remembered something Destiny's brother had told

him. "Your family goes down every year, right? Maybe her moms will be cool with that."

"Please!" Destiny took another sip of water. "You don't know Mrs. Shephard."

"My mother wasn't crazy about the idea either, but she came around. I started hinting around Thanksgiving that all I wanted for Christmas was a ticket for my girl." He placed a hand on top of hers.

Amani spun toward him. "I didn't realize your mother didn't like me. Guess I'm not foreign enough for her, huh?" She glanced at Destiny for backup, but the smirk on her friend's face caught her off guard. Amani's brow furrowed. "Maybe if I were West Indian or even African, she wouldn't mind me going with y'all. No. You tell me." She tilted her head. "What's the problem?"

His mother's heavily accented words echoed in his ears. She purposely slipped into patois when making a point. *Lard, have mercie! Wa mek yu no tek some time fi know yuself first? How yu gowin' court wen fimi milk still de pan yu breath?*

He held back a grin. "Girl, stop trippin'! My mother likes you. She's still getting used to sharing me with another woman. Jade has Kingston. She's not ready to lose her baby, too."

"I hear you." Chazz laughed. "Moms still rings my dorm room every morning to tell me to be careful. She's a single mother and I'm her only child. 'Nuff said." He bit into the slice of chocolate cake Destiny cut for him. Before handing him the saucer, she had pinched off a tiny piece.

"I hope your parents can get their money back, Marley. Destiny's right. Mama's not going to let me go all the way to Jamaica." She sighed. "It's all right since your mother doesn't want me to go anyway."

"Squash that. If my mother didn't want you to go, you wouldn't have this ticket. She and my Pops bought it." His eyebrow rose as he searched for a solution. A slow grin snaked across his face. "Bet. I'll have my mother call yours tomorrow.

You're *going* to Jamaica with us in April."

Destiny reached for the pitcher. "I know your nickname is Miracle and that's exactly what it's gonna take for Mama O to let her baby girl out the country. Marley, you know your mother would have preferred your brother marry a Jamaican girl or at least one that was West Indian." She took a quick sip of water. "It's not too late for you. That's why she don't want you taking no Yankee to Jamaica. Especially when you can have your pick of one of those spicy island gals." She raised her arms above her head and wiggled her hips. "Shoot! You could probably change up every day. Be around there singing "No Woman, No Cry" for the ones you didn't choose."

Marley shot a hard look at Destiny. He was suddenly reminded of the reason they had never hit it off. That mouth. He watched her refuel with a long gulp of water.

Chazz nodded at his cross-town rival, an apologetic grin on his face. "Definitely out of bounds." Then he passed Destiny a look that promised private lessons if she was game.

She finally sensed that all eyes were on her. She sat the glass down and scanned their faces. Destiny's eyes locked with Amani's, pleading for her friend to clue her in. "What?"

"I can always count on you to keep it real, Dee."

Destiny smiled. "No problem, mon."

After Destiny, Chazz, and, later, a reluctant Marley left, Amani trudged to her bedroom with her ticket in her hand instead of joining her sisters in the family room. Without turning on the light, she unzipped her black leather boots, slid open the closet door, and placed them back in the box on the top shelf. Then she walked around her bed to the bay window and sat on the built-in bench. She pressed her back against one wall and stretched her legs to rest her stockinged feet against the opposite wall.

Amani looked down at the ticket in her hand, then rubbed her temples as she thought about what Destiny said. Because she and Marley were both close to their mothers, it seemed as if they were caught in a love rectangle. She and Marley were the two shorter sides attempting to exert their independence against the longer sides of their mothers' influence. Make that a pentagon. Their love for God was the unifying thread that joined them.

In the distance, she heard the wail of an ambulance. She prayed the prayer she usually did whenever she heard the cry of any emergency vehicle. "Heavenly Father, divinely intervene on behalf of the recipients." Amani needed Him to do the same for her if she was going to Jamaica in the spring.

Moments later, Amani watched the Shephard trio leave. She could see them laugh and joke like the good friends they were before heading to their separate destinations.

She shut the blinds, stood, and stretched before walking over to the white dresser. She pulled a short silk robe from the top drawer then placed the ticket at the bottom and closed it. Why should her mother deny her the opportunity to go to Jamaica? Not once in seventeen years had she given her any reason to distrust her and, before Marley, she had never seriously dated anyone. Hanging out with Destiny at the mall had been the zenith of her social life.

Still thinking about her years in high school, she turned around and threw the robe on the bed. She unzipped the royal purple mini-skirt she had worn with a matching, v-necked sweater set. Next, she slipped out of her black, sheer stockings.

It wasn't that she had trouble attracting admirers. She just wasn't interested. Before Marley, her spare time was invested in her schoolwork and browsing through college brochures.

Amani had been thinking of breaking the Shephard tradition and venturing outside the Los Angeles area for college. However, Cornell, UCLA, USC, or UC Berkeley had become three thousand miles away from Marley, a dorm room away from Marley, a freeway away from Marley, or a road trip away from Marley.

She took off the sweater, then pulled the vest over her head. Amani folded her outfit and placed it on top of the dresser. Still in the dark, she put on the robe, then returned to the dresser and picked up her black brush. Amani briskly brushed her hair, and then picked up her comb.

An alarm clock/radio sat on the white pine-trimmed nightstand. Amani turned it on and opened her bedroom door. She quickly walked down the cold maple hallway. With the exception of Mia occasionally spending the night, she had the bathroom to herself. At last.

Her bare feet welcomed the feel of the plush burgundy carpet. Amani closed the bathroom door and stood in front of the mirror. She parted her hair down the middle and plaited it in two braids that she tied with rubber bands at the ends.

Her one-track mind was on autopilot.

Amani grabbed her shower cap from the hook then reached for the bar of Neutrogena. Nowadays, her most conscious moments involved being with Marley or imagining she was with Marley.

Using circular motions, she massaged her skin with her fingertips. She peered closely into the mirror, searching her almond-shaped soul's windows for the answer to the question she asked herself nightly. *What would I give up to keep Marley?* Her final answer eluded her still as she rinsed with warm water.

She slipped out of her robe, put the wooden toilet seat down, and draped her thigh-high silk robe across it. Her eyes briefly rested on the burgundy, gold, and green painting of flowers angled directly above the toilet. Then she pulled open the shower curtain that displayed flowers in the same rich tones. Sitting on the edge of the tub, she studied her selection of bath gels before deciding on one.

Tonight, she would smell like apples as she dreamt of him.

———————

Several miles and a heartbeat away, Marley lay on his back in his king-sized bed. He was having his nightly talk with God, thanking Him for his athletic talent and the opportunities it gave him, praising Him for a family that loved and supported him, and worshipping Him for having brought Amani into his life.

He smiled as he thought of her expression when she saw the ticket. When he got back to his apartment, the first thing he did was call and ask his mother to give Mrs. Shephard a call in the morning. She hesitated slightly before agreeing. Remembering Amani's gift to him, he turned on the lamp on his nightstand and opened his Bible.

Marley flipped through its pages and stopped at Song of Solomon Chapter 8, Verse 7. He read the scripture aloud, "Many waters cannot quench love; neither can the floods drown it." Marley took it as a sign. No way would their game of love be cancelled because of Destiny's gloomy report. He yawned, shut his Bible, and turned off the light.

Their first Christmas together had been cool, but the heat they'd generate during Spring Break would be off the charts. Marley imagined he and his girl romping in the crystal-clear waters of Jamaica's island paradise. Whoever said Jamaica was for lovers had the two of them in mind. He pictured his girl in swimwear: a one-piece, a tankini, a bikini.

A wide grin inched across his face as he closed his eyes and tried to sleep.

TEN

Destiny looked at her visitor through the peephole before slowly opening the door. The last person she expected to see standing on her porch actually seemed sincere in wishing her a Happy New Year. It had been exactly one week since she'd seen her best friend.

When Chazz drove her home Christmas night, he told her she should have considered keeping a couple of her comments to herself. It never failed. She spoke first and thought later.

Amani noticed Destiny's hesitance. "I can tell you're thrilled to see me. May I come in?" Destiny widened the door enough to let her pass. Amani started down the hall to the bedroom and Destiny touched her hair that was wrapped around her skull with half a dozen silver clips holding it in place. She hated for anyone to see her when she wasn't looking her best. *Too bad. I wasn't expecting company.*

Destiny shrugged, then followed Amani whose hair was perfectly smoothed into a high ponytail. She was wearing a Casual Wear for Kings and Queens outfit—a pair of jeans with a vest worn over an orange long-sleeved t-shirt.

Amani sat on the bed, lifted the flap of the cardboard box, and picked up a slice of pepperoni pizza.

Destiny stood in the doorway, leaned against the frame, and planted one bare foot on top of the other.

"You want something to drink? We have milk, water, cola, cranberry juice, and orange juice." She tugged at the burgundy and gold USC t-shirt that barely covered the top of her thighs. "Want me to warm up some pizza for you?" she asked politely, but stiffly.

Amani licked her fingers and shook her head. Her ponytail swayed from side to side. "No, thank you. This is fine, but I would like some water."

A few minutes later, Destiny returned and sat on the edge of the bed. She handed Amani a white ceramic mug with their black and gold high school emblem and the phrase "Harriet Tubman High Achievers" surrounding it.

"Thanks." Amani took a sip. "I can see your mom didn't cook chitlins today. Girl, you should smell our house." She scrunched up her face.

Destiny grinned. "When Skye told me what they were, I couldn't eat them anymore. Ugh! Hel-lo, black people. We're not still on the plantation."

"Okaaay!"

"And you know my mother always goes to the Prayer Bowl at church on New Year's Day," Destiny continued. "She usually cooks them the night before, but she didn't cook at all this time. Destiny picked up a slice of pizza. "She and my father will probably go to dinner afterward."

"Your father went to the Prayer Bowl with your mother? Praise the Lord!" exclaimed Amani. "With all of those different pastors preaching back to back, he'll probably get saved and start speaking in tongues at the same time."

"I guess God does answer prayers," Destiny added quietly.

Amani traced the flower pattern on the comforter. "Destiny, we've always tried to be truthful with each other. That's probably why we've been friends so long. Marley told me you all went skating a couple of times with Skye and one of his many women. I guess it's a little hard for you to think of us as a couple sometimes. Believe me. I understand. I never told you this before, but . . ." She bit her lip. "I'm sort of jealous of one of your relationships, too."

Destiny's spirits immediately lifted and the tension in her face eased. "Yeah? Which one?"

"I know you hate it when your father drinks, but you are a daddy's girl for real when he's sober," Amani replied. "My sisters and I each believe *to this day* that we were our father's favorite. He had a way of making you feel that you were the most important person in his world. . ." She paused. "Regardless of your father's problem, you still have him." Her tears came easily. "Don't take that lightly."

Destiny handed her a napkin and nodded. "You're right." The two friends fell silent. Destiny finally interrupted the room's thundering quiet.

"I'm sorry I didn't tell you about the skating thing." She paused. "He's an awesome brother. I hope y'all make it."

"Thank you." Amani smiled wistfully before looking away.

"Come on, Amani. Please don't hold anything back," Destiny urged her friend.

"When you and Marley dated. . ." She took a deep breath. "Did he ask you for sex?"

Destiny stared at the ceiling for a long time before looking at her best friend. Water began to fill her eyes. "I wouldn't call it dating, and no, he didn't ask me for sex. Would I have liked him to? She nodded. "I think I wanted him to be my first. I'm sorry, Amani, but I'm being honest."

Destiny folded her legs Indian style on the bed. "One day, when we were in the tenth grade, I ditched and caught the bus to his house. When you called me later, I told you I left because I wasn't feeling well. I knew Marley was getting out of school early that day. He opened the door and just stood there when he saw me. I didn't think he was going to let me in. We watched television for about twenty minutes. Any other guy would have at least kissed me, but he didn't touch me at all."

"When a commercial came on, I asked to use the bathroom. I went in and gargled with the mouthwash I had in my backpack. I blotted my lipstick and put on some more perfume, then I snuck into his bedroom. I stripped down to my bra and panties and got in his bed. We had never gone out without Skye and one of his girlfriends. I thought if he saw me in a different way, he would know this sixteen-year-old wasn't a little girl."

Pain-rain fell across Destiny's cheeks. "About fifteen minutes passed and I could hear Marley calling my name. He knocked on the bathroom door a couple of times before he opened it. A few minutes later, he started turning the doorknob to his room. I almost peed on myself."

She brushed away her tears. "Marley found me and I'll never forget his expression. It was a mixture of shock and disappointment. He picked up my clothes from the floor and threw them on the bed, then he turned and walked out. I was so embarrassed. Before he took me home, he asked me to forgive him if he had misled me in any way. Of course we never went skating again."

"Amani, even with all the mistakes I still make, I want to serve the Lord. "Sometimes it seems so hard." For the first time that afternoon, she looked directly at her friend. "You ever feel that way?"

A very relieved Amani put a napkin into Destiny's hand and gave it a squeeze. "When I think about being five years old and having to understand my daddy is never coming home, I wonder why I should even trust a God who would allow that to happen, but then I force myself to remember, Destiny. A whole lot of stuff happens outside of God's will. It's God's perfect will for my father to still be with us and for yours—"

"To stop drinking," Destiny finished quietly. She crawled over to where Amani sat on the bed and put her head on her shoulder. Unashamed, the two friends wept together. They cried tears of relief and reconciliation.

———

Something inside of her wanted to get back at Marley for not telling her about the incident with Destiny. She had purposely stayed at Destiny's longer than she planned to because she knew he'd be looking for her. It didn't matter that they didn't know each other when Destiny's little scheme backfired or that he was probably trying to spare her friend from further embarrassment. It was the heart of the matter. They weren't supposed to have any more secrets between them.

She shut her bedroom door behind her and reached for the telephone. The anticipation of hearing Marley's voice was usually enough to set her butterflies in motion. Tonight their fluttering was subdued.

"Hello," he answered on the first ring.

"Hi."

"I was beginning to think my sunshine was gone."

"Why's that?"

"You obviously haven't checked your messages. I called you *several* times. Where were you?"

"Out."

"With who?"

"Happy New Year to you, too."

"We brought in 2002 together, remember?"

"Abundant Faith's Watch Night Service is almost as big a party as New Horizon's."

He wouldn't let her change the subject. "Who were you out with?"

"A friend."

"What's up with you?"

"Nothing."

"This is one of those PMS things, right?"

"No, it's one of those 'I-thought-we-weren't-going-to-keep-any-more-secrets things.'"

She heard silence on his end.

"Marley?"

"Just be straight with me. What are you talking about?"

"Guess."

"No, you tell me."

"Destiny . . . Just forget it, okay."

She disconnected the call, left the phone off the hook and went into the bathroom to take a long, hot shower. She couldn't believe she hung up on him but, in the midst of the call, she realized she wasn't angry. The warm soothing spray of water helped her to think.

This was the second time some situation with Destiny had come up. If Marley didn't think she deserved to know her best friend had tried to sleep with him, what else would he keep from her? Had he turned Destiny down out of respect for his Christian beliefs or out of fear Skye could cause trouble for him down the road if things didn't work out between his sister and the Miracle Man? Maybe he was suppressing his true feelings for Destiny. Maybe she was the real reason he had chosen UCLA over USC. He didn't want any conflict of interests. Maybe she was too dark and *homely* for him. Or maybe Marley really wasn't the person she thought he was.

If he was keeping secrets this early in their relationship, could she truly trust him with her heart?

She turned off the water and wrapped her towel around her. In a haze of hurt, she brushed her teeth and then crossed the hall to her bedroom where she took her time moisturizing her body. When she was done, she put on a pair of emerald green lounging pajamas and a Sade CD. Though Marley hadn't actually done what she was accusing him of, she sang every line of "Somebody Already Broke My Heart" as if she had written the song herself. As soon as the song ended, she pressed repeat. *Play it again, Sade. I feel you.* "Somebody Already Broke My Heart," she bellowed.

Olivia banged on Amani's door and then opened it. "Did you hear me calling you?"

Amani turned the volume down, then faced her mother. She was in such a funk that she almost answered, "Did you hear me answer you?" However, she was melancholy, not insane.

"Marley's downstairs."

"Oh." None of the excitement that normally followed this proclamation was present.

Olivia started to comment on her daughter's lack of enthusiasm, but changed her mind. "I'm going to bed. Make sure you lock the door when he leaves." She kissed her daughter on the cheek. "Good night."

"Good night." Amani didn't even check the mirror before she left her bedroom.

Marley met her at the bottom of the stairs. He was wearing a pair of tan khakis with a matching long-sleeved button-down shirt. His golden cross and ID bracelet accessorized his freshly starched attire.

He kissed her cheek. "Hi."

She crossed her arms in front of her. "Hello."

"You had me scratching my head all the way over here. The only thing I can think of is the day your girl dropped by my house unannounced."

"You didn't think you should tell me about *that*?"

"We didn't even know each other then, Amani."

"So."

"*So* why are you trippin'? I already told you I'm not interested in her. Never have been, never will be." He sat on the stairs and pulled her next to him. "I have who I want."

She leaned away from him. "We promised not to have any

more secrets between us. That's why I'm *trippin'*."

"I never told anybody about that. You expect me to tell you everything that happens to me, every thought I have, how many females that look at me during the course of a day?"

She tilted her head. "Yeah."

"What about you?"

She picked at a piece of lint on her sleeve in response.

"You gonna do the same?"

"Tell you about all the females checking me out?"

He raised his eyebrow and gave her a sidelong glance.

"I just don't want there to be any secrets between us, Marley." She pressed her back against the banister and placed her bare feet across his lap. "We need to be honest with each other."

"You're right." He massaged her heels. "You have nice feet. Where are your toe rings?"

"Thank you." She studied her feet with new eyes. "I haven't got around to buying any yet."

"All right then. You first."

"Huh?"

"Tell me something about you that nobody else knows."

"Mmmm, let me see." She swept her hair from behind her back so that it lay across her shoulder. As she thought, she combed her fingers through it. Finally, she spoke. "A couple of years after my dad died, I saw the Wizard of Oz. Not the original. The one with Diana Ross and Michael—"

"Jackson. He was the scarecrow and she was Dorothy. It was called 'The Wiz.'"

"'*Scuse me.*" She nudged his palm with the heel of her foot. "I'm telling this."

"Sorry."

"My favorite part was when Lena Horne, who played Glenda the Good Witch, told Dorothy she already possessed the power to get back home. It was within her reach the whole time. All she needed to do was click the heels of her red shoes together and say, 'There's no place like home.' I think she had to do that three times." She tapped her heels together. "That was deep."

"And?"

She stared at her French-pedicured feet. "For weeks after I saw 'The Wiz,' whenever I was dressed for church in my black patent leather shoes, I would click them together three times, like Diana Ross did, and whisper, 'Daddy, come home.'" She gave Marley a wistful smile. "But he never did."

He shifted her feet to the steps below them and moved next to her until their shoulders were firmly touching, then he placed her head on his shoulder. "I'm sorry, Sunshine."

She reached for his hand. "Your turn."

———

Olivia hadn't planned on eavesdropping. She was in the kitchen turning off the kettle when the doorbell rang earlier. When she came upstairs to get Amani, she forgot about her nightly cup of tea. It helped her to sleep. Now, she wished she had simply suffered a restless night. Her hands were clasped under her chin as she rested her trembling body against the wall beside the stairwell. She wondered what Marley would say if he knew Amani's mother was the cause of her father never returning home. Richard Pryor's Wiz gave the tin man a heart, the scarecrow wisdom, the lion courage, and helped Dorothy and Toto back home. Olivia wished she had the ability to revise the ending to her and Marcus' story.

She loved God, but sometimes . . . sometimes it was a struggle to keep her heart open to Him. In the days and weeks following Marcus' death, she could have screamed every time some saint attempted to wrap up her husband's life with a pat summary. *The Lord gives and the Lord takes away. Blessed be the name of the Lord.* She was supposed to bless the name of a God who would take a man from his wife and seven daughters, ranging in age from five to seventeen, each needing him to continue to affirm, nurture, and love her like only a father can.

There was another summation that still made her cringe. *The Lord moves in mysterious ways, His wonders to perform.* Could someone please explain what was wondrous about the death of a healthy man? One who loved the Lord with his whole heart and whose life mission revolved around making a positive impact on the spiritual, emotional, and educational lives of African-American and Hispanic teenagers?

She didn't know how long her life would last, but she would have joyfully chosen life with her husband for even a few more years over living to be a ripe old age. Thirty-six was too young to die.

More than blaming God, she blamed herself. It was her fault Marcus was dead. Olivia pushed herself away from the wall and quietly returned to her room. Sleep would be even more unsettling tonight though she received a certain comfort from the conversation she had overheard. Amani was learning earlier than she had that every story didn't have a happy ending and there was no such thing as magic.

Amani poked Marley in the side. "Come on. I'm waiting."

He massaged his neck with his free hand. "You already know everything I was keeping to myself."

"No." She lifted her head from his shoulder. "It's got to be something that nobody else knows about, not even Destiny."

He tugged one of her braids. "When I was growing up, my father used to take Kingston and me to air shows." He smiled at her. "The end."

She elbowed him.

"All right." He pushed her with his shoulder. "I was amazed at the stunts those pilots could do and I would dream about getting a pilot's license and showing my father and Kingston what I could do."

Her look was questioning. "Well, why didn't you?"

"'Cause . . .I'mafraidofflying."

"What did you say?"

"You heard me." He stared at her front door. "One day I saw two planes collide and then explode at an air show. Since then, I haven't been too keen about flying the unfriendly skies. And, now, with what happened on September eleventh. . ."

She shuddered. "That was *horrible*. I prayed so much for the families of all the victims. It still gets to me."

"Yeah, me, too."

"Well, what about when your family goes to Jamaica?"

"I usually go as long as I can without sleeping the day before we leave so I'll sleep most of the way there." He chuckled. "I have them convinced I'm trying to be well-rested so I won't miss a thing when we get there."

"That's deep."

He rubbed his hands together, averting her gaze.

She caressed his back with her hand. "Baby, you're going to be a professional basketball player. That's a lot of flying. What are you going to do?"

A wry smile crossed his face as he faced her. "I'll have to trust God and believe what you told me your father used to say. My times are in *His* hands. Amen, sister?"

"*Amen*, brother!"

Ain't nobody's business if I change my mind. That phrase played like a scratched record in Amani's head as she attempted to complete her homework assignments at the kitchen table. Since Destiny's confession about wanting to get busy with Marley, the statement had embedded itself in Amani's psyche.

On one level, she couldn't understand what had gotten into her friend. Every year since the age of eleven, they had made a confession of chastity.

As they grew older and witnessed firsthand some of the downsides of premarital sex, they had even coined a motto for their unofficial Club V. Amani professed under her breath, "An extraordinary sista's got to do what no ordinary one *ever* could."

Almost daily, they overheard conversations where young ladies gave each other the 4-1-1 on who they did it with, where they did it, and exactly how it was. From the sounds of it, the sold-out/semi-sold-out duo was missing out on something good. *Real* good. Amani wondered if all the talk was getting to Destiny the way it must have gotten to her when she pulled that stunt with Marley two years ago. She tapped her pencil against her trigonometry book. *I wonder if Chazz will end up being the one? Now, he would definitely take her up on her offer. Or will she come to her senses before doing something stupid?* Amani hoped so.

On another level, there was no puzzlement, no confusion, no bewilderment of any kind. Amani understood completely where Destiny was coming from.

The sound of Marley's voice instantly brought a smile to her face. The touch of his hand scattered every one of her brainwaves. And when he kissed her, it was a fight to keep her hormones, her hands, the heat from taking over. The Good Book told her to resist the devil and he would flee. However, in her book, having to resist Marley Jamison was something altogether different.

ELEVEN

Ever since she and Marley brought in the year 2002 during Abundant Faith Christian Center's New Year's Eve Celebration, she had been counting down the weeks until this day. Together, they had celebrated the birth of Christ, the start of a new year, and, tonight, they would celebrate their love.

Today had to be the longest Friday in history. TGIF. *Thank God I'm Free*. Amani smiled to herself as she carefully spread the can of Comstock cherry filling over the no-bake cheesecake she made for Marley. It was their first Valentine's Day.

She ate the last spoonful of cherries and frowned. The taste was more tart than sweet. *My baby's kisses, on the other hand, are sweeter than the honey in the honeycomb.* She smiled again. "Girl, you have a terrible love jones." She shook her head. "Nope. I have a serious love Jamison."

They had been dating for four months and she was amazed at what a significant part of her life he had become. Closing her eyes, she imagined Marley's arms around her. In a few more hours, they would be. His embrace was like being wrapped in a warm blanket on a cold, windy night.

Amani was sure there were those who would argue she was too young, naïve, or inexperienced to know a thing about romance, but her infatuated heart would plead her case.

Whenever she was near him, she experienced a surge of delight from the crown of her head to the soles of her feet. She dreamt of him from the rising of the sun to the going down of the same. She loved him.

She opened her eyes and looked over at the bouquet sitting on the counter next to the sink. The dozen red roses had been delivered almost as soon as she had gotten home from school. They were beautiful. However, she was disappointed with the card's bland message: *Wear something red. Marley.*

Amani had eagerly opened the small card accompanying the bouquet, hoping it would contain the three words she planned to tell him before night's end. Although she felt slightly let down at his trio of words, she was prepared to do as he requested.

Last weekend, she went to the Baldwin Hills Plaza with Destiny to buy an outfit for Valentine's Day. Destiny chose a red sleeveless mini-dress with a matching jacket that showed off her dancer's legs. She bought a spaghetti-strapped, ankle-length, clingy red dress that was simple yet elegant.

After Amani showered, her mother would comb her hair in a chic upswept style. The silver necklace and earring set she purchased along with the dress' matching wrap would complete her ensemble. Her favorite silver shoes and handbag accompanied her to most formal occasions and would do so tonight.

Olivia breezed into the kitchen and stopped when she saw the cheesecake. "Where in the world did you find a heart-shaped pan?" she asked with an amused look on her face.

"I borrowed it from my visual arts teacher yesterday. Like the American Express Card, being an exemplary student has its advantages." Amani grinned, pleased with herself.

"We call it being a teacher's pet where I come from."

"I like to think of it as networking."

"Mmmm." Her mother smacked her lips. "That cheesecake sure looks good. Is it for me?"

Amani eyes widened.

"Sike!" Olivia grinned and kissed her daughter on the forehead. "I'm going up to take a bath. I need to soak away this hospital smell." She noticed the roses and turned around. "Your flower arrangement is lovely. What time is Marley picking you up?"

"Six-thirty. The buffet is from seven until eight-thirty and dancing starts at nine. You know Pastor Hilton. I'm sure the last song will end at 11:59 P.M. on the dot."

"I still expect you home no later than midnight. You all have done a great job of keeping your curfew." She thought for a moment. "Except for that first time."

Olivia easily read her daughter's expression. "You don't have to bite your lip, Baby Girl. I'm sure forty-nine seems ancient to you, but I do remember being seventeen and in love." She tweaked Amani's nose. "Just don't forget *whose* you are." She walked out of the kitchen humming softly.

Amani placed the cheesecake in the white box decorated with tiny hearts. She didn't think it was a good idea to tell her mother that if she did forget, it would be on purpose.

———

Valentine's Day was one of Olivia's least favorite holidays. However, she smiled when she saw the white porcelain teakettle that bore Amani's original artwork on her dresser. Her full name Olivia Ava Dupree Shephard was written in calligraphy and four pink hearts separately surrounded each of her names on one side of the kettle. A *Virtuous Woman* was written just as fanciful, only larger on the other side.

From Vanessa, she received a red lace pajama set; Rosalind had a luscious green plant decorated with a red bow delivered to the hospital that morning; and last night, Perri dropped off a crisp hundred dollar bill enclosed in an uncharacteristically sentimental card. Mia took her to lunch and presented her with a gift certificate for an All That Hair Salon & Spa full-day special while Nola had given her a lovely bouquet of flowers along with a picture frame Malachi and Micah had made themselves. Always the teacher, Krystal gave her a book of poems for mothers of adult children.

Their tangible gifts of love caused Olivia to reflect on her favorite line from the virtuous woman passage. *Her children shall rise up and call her blessed.* Despite the challenges they faced as a single-parent family, Olivia had done her best to raise confident, creative, Godly young women. Unfortunately, their fear of the Lord had not prevented any of them from becoming sexually active outside of marriage.

Except for Amani.

Amani had always worked extra hard to please her and until Marley's entrance into her daughter's life, Olivia worried very little about her youngest child. Recently, she prayed without ceasing that her baby girl's faith would remain firm.

———

Under normal circumstances, Amani would have savored each morsel of her favorite foods. Instead, she picked at her meal of Cornish hen, steamed vegetables, and rice pilaf. Not even the exquisite red, white, and silver décor of the social hall could quench her desire for semi-solitude. She wanted to be alone with Marley. Destiny's constant chatter, which she usually found humorous, was grating on her nerves. She felt like screaming, "Will you please *shut up*? I'm trying to concentrate on my baby."

Marley was wearing a black collarless dress shirt with a red vest and black slacks. They had taken pictures shortly after arriving. The photographer was set up in the corner of the room for those couples who wanted to memorialize the evening they spent at N.H.C.C.'s 11th Annual Sweetheart Dinner & Dance. She and Destiny also posed for a set of pictures they planned to split.

Photos finished. Dinner done. As far as she was concerned, they could leave. Amani leaned over, breathed in his aroma, and whispered in his ear, "I'm ready to go, Marley."

"Sunshine, you're feeling my vibes. I'd like to cut out early, too, but not before we have a chance to dance. We can take a drive along the coast and listen to the ocean. It's too dark to see anything, but the sparkle in your eyes is all the light I need."

Lord, I love this man. "I think you missed your calling. You should have been a poet. When you go pro, you can write little poems when you sign your autograph for the ladies."

"I'm only interested in writing words of amour that open your heart's door."

"You're trying a little too hard now, baby."

"Can't help it." He winked. "You do that to me."

A warm glow radiated from the center of her being as Marley led her to the dance floor. The deejay was playing Kirk Franklin's "Revolution." The young lovers sang a duet as they danced to the song's euphoric beats.

Although this was a Christian dance, she wished they would play extremely slow jams all night long because her main objective was to be closer than close to Marley.

If she believed in reincarnation, she would have settled for being his shirt. Even better, the airy cologne he was wearing.

Kirk Franklin was one of her favorite artists, but the deejay could have been playing "Mary had a Little Lamb." Any other time, she'd be focused on getting her groove on, but tonight Marley held her complete attention. He danced almost as well as he played ball, but it wasn't that. His high cheekbones, slightly broad nose, and penetrating gaze were distracting. His hand on her waist was not helping matters.

Marley was the pepper to her mint. The cookies to her cream. The frosted to her flakes. He was quickly becoming her everything and it frightened her a little, yet excited her a lot. She smiled as she remembered the oldie but goodie they played the other day on KJLH. "You Are Everything and Everything Is You" adequately explained her feelings for Marley.

Amani was sure proper dating etiquette required the girl to get the guy to say "I love you" first. Whatever. She didn't have time for tricks. Those were for kids.

DJ Salt Shaker passed the baton to the band that the entertainment committee regularly hired for their dances. Sweet chords from the keyboard floated over the crowd as the female vocalist began to sing "I Just Wanna Be Your Girl" by Chapter 8.

God must have been eavesdropping on her earlier thoughts. A ballad she could have easily dedicated to Marley was the first song they slow danced to. The incomparable Anita Baker was Chapter 8's original songstress, but the lady singing it tonight was holding her own.

Amani's stomach did a somersault as Marley pulled her close, but not too close. She had already warned him that Pastor Hilton had no qualms about embarrassing a couple if he believed they were getting out of hand.

Amani turned her thoughts from her pastor to her man, her miracle. Tonight, she would sing to him before she told him how she felt.

The lyrics erupted from her soul. Amani's rich, expressive alto broke it down for Marley. She wanted to be his girl. There was nobody else for her, and each of her future plans included him.

Her song was for his ears only.

They were moving in sync to the music heard by all and the silent rhythms binding them.

Marley reminded himself that they were not alone and were probably under surveillance. His moistened hand snugly held hers as she serenaded him sweetly. His heart was thump-thump-thumpin' away. He inhaled a whiff of her fruity fragrance. His girl's lovely face was a kiss away, but he knew not to even think about it. Every time they were together it seemed like the first time. And the more time they spent together, the more time he wanted to spend together.

With Amani, he could let his guard down. It didn't matter that he was UCLA's star player or the NBA's next moneymaker. She had no secret agendas or ulterior motives. He marveled at the depth of her sincerity and trusted her to be straight with him. A lump formed in his throat and he swallowed hard. Amani Nicole Shephard had gotten to him like no young lady ever had. She was his sunshine and he had come to depend on her light.

He needed to get a grip. He was Marley "Miracle Man" Jamison and he was used to running things. A ball in his hand was good for at least two on any scoreboard. He was Big Brother Marley to a little dude named Tyreek who bragged they could take on Shaq and Kobe *if* they wanted to. He was a nineteen-year-old college sophomore who felt like some elementary kid having his first crush.

The song ended and the statement he tried to rein in burst forth.

"I love you, Nikki," he breathed into her hair. He could feel waves of heat flooding her body.

Amani arched her neck, her eyes sparkling. "I love you, too, Marley." She tapped his chest with her open palm. "And guess what?"

"What, Sunshine?"

"Daddy used to call me Nikki."

"You don't say." He swiftly blocked an instance of jealousy. "Would it bother you if I call you Nikki sometimes?"

She shook her head, smiling up at him as if he were the embodiment of all that was good, and true, and strong.

Marley's gaze moved from her eyes and rested on her mouth.

"Let's get out of here. I have another present for you."

She wondered what else he had for her since he had already given her roses. She thanked him with a kiss when her mother left them alone in the living room in search of her camera.

"I have something for you, too, but I can't give it to you until you take me home."

The two fugitives quickly gathered their belongings, said their good-byes to Destiny and Chazz, and started to make their getaway.

A few tables away, Pastor Hilton caught her eye and held up his index finger. He was stopped several times on his way over. They remained standing in front of the doorway as they waited for him. Amani wished he'd hurry up.

Pastor Hilton looked more like a CEO of a major corporation in his black tuxedo than a minister of the gospel. His thin salt and pepper hair accentuated his golden-brown complexion and sculpted good looks. Before establishing one of the most well-known churches in Los Angeles, he had been "an alcoholic in need of a Saviour." His love affair with the Lord was real and it had transformed his life and his marriage. Fifty-four-year-old Chamberlain and fifty-year-old Rachel Hilton had hearts for helping hurting people.

"Good evening, Sister Amani." Pastor Hilton kissed her cheek then extended his hand to Marley. "Nice to see you again, son. Your team is having a great season. Keep balling like you've been and you'll be able to name your price. Excuse me." Pastor Hilton shook hands with a couple of passersby before turning his attention back to the young couple. "You have a lot of natural ability, Marley. Just don't buy into the media hype. God is the only miraculous one."

"Thank you, Pastor Hilton. I'll try not to."

"So, you two calling it a night so soon?" he questioned.

Marley looked sheepish. "Yes, sir."

"Pastor Chamberlain, you and Sister Rachel are looking pretty prosperous tonight." Amani knew firsthand that divine prosperity was one of his favorite subjects. "I want to be just like y'all when I grow up."

"Keep God first and nothing will be impossible. He desires that we prosper in every area of our lives. Spirit, soul, and body."

"Amen." Her pastor was prepared to preach. Amani spoke quickly. "Well, I'll see you Sunday. Goodnight." She rushed through the doorway.

Pastor Hilton clapped Marley on the shoulder and retrieved his right hand. "Many years ago, there was a popular saying. 'Real men don't eat quiche', I believe it was. Although it was said in jest, it was absolutely absurd. I can polish off a whole pan of my wife's broccoli quiche in one sitting. But you know what I've found to be true time and time again. A real man can deny himself. I didn't become a man until I learned to align my life with the Word of God." He dropped Marley's hand.

"I've held you up long enough. Goodnight, son, and be careful." He peered into Marley's eyes. "It can be treacherous out there. That's why we have to trust in someone whose ways are higher than ours. Some folks call it a supreme being. We call Him Jesus."

Marley had about two and a half hours before his mahogany Cinderella had to be home. They were playing dress-up and had already escaped from where they were supposed to be. Marley glanced at Amani. Either they could sail their 'love boat' through the streets of Los Angeles, or dock at the nearest pier and stroll on the beach. Maybe, if they were on a 'fantasy island,' but it was an unusually chilly night in L.A. Syrupy-sweet late-night reruns kept him good company when he found it hard to sleep, but he knew not to mistake television for real life.

Amani effortlessly brought out his romantic side. She even had him listening to classic love songs on 102.3 FM in place of his regular hip-hop station. Both he and Natalie Cole had love on their minds. Might as well keep it real. He had something more than that on his, and it was trying to control him. Marley couldn't stop thinking about their last dance. He shook his head to clear another image vying for his indulgence.

Amani placed her hand on top of his. "Let's go to your apartment."

Everything in him rejoiced at her command. This would be their first time going there. *We're just going to talk,* he chided himself. Marley turned the key in the ignition. *Folks who only want to talk go to Denny's.* He ignored the apprehension he felt in the pit of his stomach along with that other voice. *A real man can deny himself.*

He wanted to tell Amani he didn't think it was a good idea, but he couldn't. His spirit was willing to do right, but his flesh was beginning to weaken when presented with the right set of circumstances. Or was it the wrong set of circumstances?

Unfortunately for him, the Creator crafted his first taste of temptation on the day He felt like showing off. Her beauty went past the surface and her name was the most spoken one on his tongue. Although he wanted to rush back inside of their sanctuary, Marley drove out of the church's parking lot and headed to Westwood.

———

Marley turned on the lights. Amani was in awe. She had no idea he was such an art connoisseur. His walls were covered with Black art. She recognized many of the paintings from street vendors she'd seen.

Marley switched on the radio with the remote and magically the room became enveloped with the cool sounds of jazz. Amani sat on the edge of the sofa against the wall opposite the television. Stacks of books teetered precariously on a nearby crate. Leaning against the wall next to the crate was a large rectangular box.

"What's that?"

"It's a bookshelf I bought a few weeks ago from IKEA. I haven't had a chance to put it together yet."

"Next time I come over I'll help you."

"We'll see."

"What does that mean?"

"I don't want to get used to your being here."

Amani walked over to him and grabbed his hand. He was still standing by the CD player. "Let's dance," she breathed in his ear. Walking backwards, she guided him to the center of the small living room.

Marley hesitated before allowing her to lead him to the black and white zebra-patterned rug covering the maple wood floor where a coffee table could have stood.

"This song is perfect." She sensed his reluctance. "Don't tell me you don't want to dance with me either." She pouted, looking like a spoiled but adorable little girl.

His heart was growing fuller by the minute. "Yeah, right." Marley put his hands around her waist and crooned along with the radio. His own lady in red was dancing with him and he was not dreaming. His dream girl stood before him, live and in living color, and he didn't trust himself to close his eyes.

He was in dire need of a distraction.

When the music ended, he quickly took off his vest and threw it on the sofa. Amani's eyes were fastened on his. He started to unbutton his shirt exposing the t-shirt underneath.

Startled, Amani stepped back. "What. . .what are you doing?"

"I told you I had another gift for you." He threw his shirt on top of his vest then slowly rolled up the sleeve of his t-shirt and whispered, "Many waters cannot quench our love. Neither can the floods drown it."

Several seconds passed before she stopped looking at his left bicep and stared into his eyes. "Oh, Marley," she gasped.

He put her hand on his muscled arm. "This tattooed heart is because of you." Then he placed her hand over his chest. "And this real one is yours for as long as you want it." The pounding of his heart beneath her palm confirmed his words.

Tears sprang to her eyes. Amani removed her hand and walked over to the black sofa. She felt overwhelmed. Marley told her he loved her first and now this. Tonight, he was showing her that she was the star of his dreams and his Nikki, too.

Marley followed her to the sofa and knelt before her. She stared at the faint outline of a heart. In its center, *SOS 8:7* was inked inside of a small wave. Everything had been etched in royal blue. Amani gently traced the heart with her index finger. She needed to lighten the moment before she started bawling like some fuzzy-headed baby.

"That's deep! You branded yourself for me? I guess that means we belong together. Like Farmer John and Bessie, the Cow."

"Something like that." Marley's tone was serious. He couldn't have planned it better himself. "Fortunate" by Maxwell pumped through the sound system, a song he could have personally penned for Amani. He guided her to her feet and into his embrace. They flowed as one. She pressed her face against the strength in his chest as she listened to the song wobbling in his voice.

When the song ended, he let her go and turned off the radio. Then he took her hand in his and led her to the sofa, pulling her down next to him. Marley stared at her as if his next breath depended on his being able to see the intensity he felt reflected in her eyes. "I have to disagree with my boy. I'm not fortunate. I'm *blessed* to have you in my world. You feel what I'm sayin'?"

"Yeah." She began to feel off-centered though she was sitting.

To regain some semblance of balance, she did what she did best. She took her turn at singing what was in her heart.

A few soul-filled lines of Natalie Cole's "Inseparable" joined with the electricity in the air. "That can be another one of our songs."

"Baby, you can sing for me anytime, anyplace." Marley grazed her nose with his lips. "So we're inseparable, huh? That means no one or no thing can come between us."

"Not ever," she added.

"I can get with that." He brought their clasped hands to his chest. "I already know I want to marry you, but we'll wait until you get your degree. I'll definitely be playing pro ball by then." He took a breath to steady himself then dived in. "I want to take care of you, Nikki . . . until death do we part. At the wedding or maybe the reception, we'll play "Fortunate" for my dedication to you, but you can sing "Inseparable" to me. What do you think?"

"That the next four years will seem like a lifetime."

Like magnets, they were being drawn closer. Soul to soul. Yearning to yearning.

She tested the waters. "Marley, will we be able to stay celibate that long?"

"I think so." His eyes searched hers. "How about you?"

"I don't know . . . if I want to."

"What do you mean?"

"Marley, I..." Her heart was pounding every ounce of her self-will into a fine powder she could simply blow away with a soft breath. She tried again to express the conflicting emotions erupting within her. "Baby, I love you *so much.*" She trembled slightly. "Maybe . . . maybe we could make love to celebrate our feelings for each other . . . just this once."

"What are you saying, Amani?"

Her voice was barely audible. "I want you."

Breaking free of his gaze, she placed a velvety kiss on the

miniature heart etched not far from the one beating their rhythm of love.

Her up-do was slowly coming undone. Marley lifted her face with the tip of his forefinger and brushed a curl of hair away from her eyes. "Baby, are you sure?"

She leaned into the circle of his embrace. He smelled delicious. "What's the name of your cologne?"

"Fahrenheit."

Amani inhaled deeply. *Hmmm.* That explained the floods of heat radiating throughout her. "It's working." Amani wondered what had gotten into her as she helped him pull the t-shirt over his head. Timidly, she slid her hands up and down the smoothness of his strong back.

Amani wanted to dream this dream forever as Marley summoned her with butterfly kisses along her neck and shoulders.

As she continued to make contact with his bare skin, her touch became bolder. She moved her hands to his chest area and started to explore. Her fingers met with some resistance.

Amani opened her eyes. "What's this?" She gingerly touched the raised j-shaped mark on his well-defined chest.

"An angel's kiss."

Amani leaned down to kiss it then brought her lips to his face. "Now it's official." She nibbled his ear as she continued to finger the curls on his chest and lose herself in his smell, in the strength of his muscles, in the feel of his familiar touch. The passion radiating throughout her body lured her on and she couldn't . . . didn't want to . . . stop herself. It wasn't lust. They loved each other and she wanted to be with him. Tonight. She turned her back to him.

"Unzip me."

Marley's hand turned to stone as he held the zipper between his fingers. Haltingly, he followed its trail to the small of her back until the zipper could go no further. He memorized every freckle on her back as he struggled to shut out his father's voice.

Present your body...
Amani rose above him.
As a living sacrifice.
She kicked off one shoe.
Holy and acceptable unto God.
Off came the second one.
This is your reasonable service.
The first shoulder strap was pulled down.
Be not conformed to this world.
The second strap fell across her shoulder.
But be transformed . . .
Her dress tumbled to the floor.
By the renewing of your mind.
In her lace slip, she eased back in his arms and they kissed slowly, gently. Their kiss deepened and he felt her fingers touch his belt, then move to his buckle.

A real man can deny himself. He almost cursed as those words repeatedly rebuked him. He fought to silence the pastor's voice. Marley concentrated on the rise and fall of their breathing roaring in his ears. Sound effects he preferred. He had been starring in this dream since their first date, but the director always yelled "Cut!" before they got to the good part.

Amani's hands fumbled with his uncooperative belt buckle. He moved his hands from her shoulders and slid them on top of hers. He was as ready as her to turn his living room into a loving room. It was obvious his girl needed help, but he regretted he felt compelled to assist her as a parade of questions raced through his mind.

Why couldn't her pastor have kept his big mouth shut? How could his father require him to uphold some outdated standard? And what possessed him to make a confession of celibacy when he was eleven?

Marley grabbed her hands and Amani blinked. He gazed into her deep brown eyes and shook his head. Amani nodded, tossed her mane like a wild stallion, then brought her face to his. Her voice was a hoarse whisper. "Make love to me, Marley."

Her sweet, searing breath almost melted away his convictions.

A flash of his parents praying over his sixteen-year-old brother and him flickered in his mind. He still remembered the words he and Kingston repeated after their father. "I will keep myself holy until marriage and treat every female as a child of God. Her body is the temple of the Holy Spirit, so I promise to protect, honor, and respect God's property."

Marley slowly shook his head a second time. The only young lady he'd ever loved was ready to slip out of her lingerie and into his receptive arms. His voice projected a calm he did not feel. "Amani, every part of me wants to love every part of you." He picked up her dress and handed it to her. "But we can't."

Instead of taking it, she stroked his cheek and grazed his lips with hers. "Yes. We can, Marley, and I want to. So do you."

He closed his eyes and rubbed the back of his neck with his free hand. Amani was standing half-dressed before him, ready to make a sacrifice at the altar of their love and he was expected to refuse. Again, her pastor's words buffeted him. *A real man can deny himself.*

Marley opened his eyes. "Get dressed, Amani!" He thrust the dress at her. "Now!"

While Amani marched to the bathroom, Marley redressed the top half of his body, leaving the vest on the sofa. He knew he shouldn't have spoken to her so harshly, but he had to stop her before he backed down. His soul and body had long ago given in so his spirit battled alone. Though it fought valiantly, he was ready to surrender. Surrender to the sensations that consumed him as she caressed and kissed him. Surrender to the feel of her soft, warm flesh against his chest. Surrender to sin.

Amani felt like someone had dashed a bucket of ice water on her as she flinched, swallowed back the lump in her throat, then snatched the dress from him. The first tears fell as she darted down the hall to what she hoped was the bathroom and slammed the door.

As she leaned against the bathroom door, slowly inhaling and exhaling, feelings entirely opposite those she had experienced moments earlier enveloped her. How could what had felt so good and so right now feel so wrong? Who was that stranger who had taken over her body? She thought back to their first date when he tried to kiss her. *I'm a sold-out Christian,* she told him. Now, she felt like a fool. Tonight, she had tried to seduce him.

What if he hadn't stopped me? Destiny would still be a virgin and I'd be a . . . How could I be so stupid? What's wrong with me? Fumbling in the dark, she felt for the sink's faucets and turned on the water to drown out her sobs. Several minutes passed before she ran out of tears and slipped back into her dress. She hung her head when she came out the bathroom, unable to look Marley in the eye.

Marley stood as she approached the sofa, then knelt in front of her. She reached for her heels, but he gently took them from her. He wanted to show her she was still his one and only chocolate sunshine.

He wanted her to look into his eyes and see his heart, but she kept her head low and her eyes downcast. He placed the second shoe on her and remained kneeling before her. He cleared his throat. "Look at me, Amani." He gave her a few seconds to respond. Finally, he put his forefinger under her chin and tilted her head upward, but she still averted his gaze. Her long eyelashes shaded her tear-soaked eyes.

When he glanced down at his watch, she shook her chin free. Resigned for now, he stood and extended his hand. She reached for her cape and purse and held them closely against her, still avoiding his eyes. A heaviness settled over him. He had so much to say, but there wasn't enough time. They had to hurry if they were going to make curfew.

Moments later, Marley glanced at Amani who was looking out the window. *I know she's chewing on that lip.* Her isolation cut him deeply, but he had to keep trying. He reached for her hand. This time, she made two fists and folded them inside her arms. His stomach clenched. He turned the radio on then off. Her silence beat listening to a song about making love in the rain. He was thankful there wasn't a cloud in the sky.

He was also thankful he had stayed strong for both of them. He didn't have it in him to be a player and Amani wasn't some hoochie with whom he could just "hit it and quit it." There was something different—special—about her and he didn't want to blow it. That's why he hadn't taken advantage of her moment of vulnerability.

He also couldn't get past the voices of his father and her pastor. Even still he had to talk himself out of crashing through the bathroom door and carrying her to his bedroom. He refused to be responsible for reducing their relationship to regrets and resentment. He had to make her understand.

"Amani, I did what I did for us, for you."

She didn't even acknowledge him with a "Hmmm."

Marley's eyes were on the road, but he was concentrating on Amani. Failing to cross the abyss that separated them, he wondered what she was thinking. Although Amani was seated next to him, he couldn't reach her. *Why won't she talk to me?* He felt inadequate as fear hopped on board and settled in for the ride. He rested his elbow on the windowsill and rubbed his neck.

Kenny Lattimore's "If I Should Ever Lose My Woman" popped into his head. Marley couldn't hold a note any more than a netless rim could hold a basketball but right now, he could do a Grammy–award-winning rendition of the song. Amani was his sunshine and he didn't ever want to lose her. He needed her light. Didn't she know he wanted her as much as she wanted him?

"My feelings for you haven't changed, Nikki. I didn't want us to do something you'd end up regretting." How could he say what he really felt without sounding like some punk? His heart beat faster. "I . . . I didn't want you hating me. I wouldn't be able to stand that, baby."

Amani squirmed in her seat and looked at him out of the corner of her eye. Her heart was beginning to thaw and the haze was beginning to clear.

When they pulled into her driveway, he turned off the ignition and turned to her. Darkness overwhelmed him as he watched her reach for the handle and get out.

He jumped out of the car and rushed to the porch behind her.

Then he remembered. "Amani. You have something for me, right?"

She looked past him, and then nodded. "Wait at the door."

Her words shone a flashlight of hope into his black hole. That was all he had until she returned her heart to him. He watched her go into the house.

Standing in the doorway moments later, she gave him the cheesecake. Marley lifted the lid. Immediately, a smile spread across his face, erasing more of the dark. He leaned down to kiss her, but she turned her head so that his lips brushed her cheek.

"Thank you *so much*, Marley. Goodnight." Amani closed the door softly and the porch light went out.

For a few seconds, Marley stood paralyzed before he was able to raise his other hand. He tapped lightly and the door opened. In the light of the foyer she stood, a sight to be held in his memory until heaven and earth passed away. "Lard, have mercie," he mumbled in patois.

Marley almost forgot why he knocked. He held up the edible heart. "Does your heart still belong to me?"

Amani remained silent, but raised her hand to his branded arm. She delicately traced where she believed the painted heart lay and wondered if this very question was being posed and answered elsewhere in God's grand universe.

She lifted her eyes to meet the sincerity in his.

Opening her mouth, she drank from the spring of love she saw cascading from his eyes. Amani was terrified of being swept away. Still she sipped.

"Yes," she whispered.

TWELVE

When she heard her mother go into the bathroom for her leisurely Saturday morning bath, Amani showered, threw on a pair of jean shorts and a white UCLA t-shirt, then hurried down to the kitchen. The two braids she slept in adorned her casual attire.

Mama wouldn't dare interrupt her when she was looking over her college information. Although Mia was working on a business degree on a part-time basis, Nola still needed to complete her senior year, and Amani was still undecided about the degree she would pursue, Olivia was proud of the fact that all seven of her daughters would have gone to college.

Of course, Mama was quick to say she gave God all the glory, yet Amani knew her mother set aside a corner piece to bask in when one of the single mothers at the church needed encouraging. Or when the reflection in her mirror needed uplifting.

Amani pored over the brochures spread on the counter before her. The soft sounds of KJLH's afternoon love fest played in the background. She usually listened to her gospel CDs more than the radio, but that was before he came along. Marley, Marley, Marley. She sighed deeply as she gripped the arms of the barstool. Sometimes she missed the simplicity of a life without him.

Now, every decision she made became an event of paramount importance. *Do I look prettier with my hair down or up? How do these earrings look? Which fragrance smells the best? What color should I wear today? Should I go to college back east or stay on the west coast?*

Before Marley, she made decisions based on what was right for her. His presence in her life had her second-guessing everything, even her faith.

The words on Cornell's college brochure blurred as she thought about what almost happened. If it hadn't been for Marley, she would have probably gone all the way. In spite of her upbringing, she had been willing to share everything with him last night.

This morning, she felt far, far away from God.

She now understood how so many of her peers became entangled in premarital sex. Her own body's longing to be tangibly connected to Marley's had overridden the gentle guidance of her spirit. The more that she hearkened to the cravings of her flesh, the fainter the soft nudging became until she had listened only to the stirrings in her soul.

Thank goodness Marley had remained loyal to his pledge. But what if he had also had a momentary lapse? Would God have disowned them? Would she have to spend the rest of her life getting Him to love her again? Amani shook her head.

In Sunday school, she learned there was no way anybody could earn God's love. As a gift, He'd chosen to bestow it upon all mankind.

However, Pastor Hilton constantly reminded the church that God's love, grace, and mercy were not to be abused. There were still serious repercussions when the Bible, God's instruction manual for life, was compromised in the pursuit of fleshly or selfish desires.

Amani smiled faintly as she thought of the expression on Marley's face when her pastor stopped them at the door. He reminded her of her nephews, Malachi and Micah. When they were busted being naughty, especially if they were doing something they had been warned about previously, their eyes wore the same guilty gleam.

She found it fascinating that some people seemed to have special Holy Ghost radar. Amani wondered what Pastor Hilton said to Marley after she made her get-away.

She had moved quickly because the last thing she wanted was a word from her pastor. Chamberlain Hilton was a genuine servant of the Most High and God told him things.

Her mother possessed that same x-ray vision, so Amani was armed with her own brand of kryptonite: college brochures, housing information, and financial aid applications in the form of loans, grants, and scholarships.

When Mama peeked into her room earlier that morning, she feigned the sleep that had evaded her since daybreak because then she had been defenseless.

Now, she listened to her mother's padded footsteps descending the stairs. Her tongue became heavy, her palms sweaty, and the brochure trembled in her hand. Amani's mind replayed a solitary thought: *Liars shall not inherit the kingdom of God.* She bowed her head and pretended to read.

Amani felt hands brushing her hair followed by a warm kiss on her forehead. Out of the corner of her eye, she watched her mother fill the teakettle with water from the five-gallon dispenser on the sink counter.

Although she could get hot mountain spring water directly from it, Olivia liked the formality of boiling the water on the stove. Amani averted her eyes when Mama glanced in her direction. "You and Marley sure make a good-looking couple."

In response, she mumbled her thanks. Mama raised an eyebrow, but before she could pursue it the phone rang. Amani greeted the caller and passed the phone to Olivia. Now, her eyes were unable to take leave of the face so like her own.

The whole time her mother spoke on the telephone, Amani felt the sudden terror of a deer caught in the path of a speeding car. Although it sensed the imminent danger, the deer stared helplessly into the oncoming headlights as it remained frozen to the very spot of its demise. Amani too desired to elude the escapable but could not.

Olivia's mouth remained tight-lipped as she repeated "uh-huh" and "I see" throughout most of the conversation. She grasped the phone between her right cheek and shoulder as she filled her teacup and seasoned her tea.

Amani caught a glimpse of a look on her mother's face that was poignant, yet unfamiliar. In the place of the hopeful expression that propelled her mother from one day into the next was a look of defeat. Unwilling to be worn by her face alone, it cloaked her mother's shoulders with the same heavy shroud.

Holding her breath, Amani listened as her mother carried on the telephone conversation. Then, with joviality Amani knew her mother did not feel, Sister Olivia thanked Pastor Chamberlain for calling. Silently, she handed the phone to Amani to hang up, and returned to her stirring.

Olivia Shephard stared into her teacup and braced herself for the answer to the question she regularly prayed there would be no need to ask Amani. She took a long, slow sip of her tea then looked at the girl she was before . . . before . . . She couldn't even face the memory.

Amani tried to look at her mother and play it off as if nothing happened. Instead, after only a few seconds, she looked away. But the habit of telling the truth to her mother was hard to break. "Mama, please, listen—" Amani began, tears already welling up in her eyes.

"Shut up!" Olivia commanded.

Amani flinched, her eyes burning with regret. Right away, she knew her mother could see through her—knew everything that happened or almost happened last night. She felt so ashamed of herself. People in the world were quick to say the church was full of hypocrites—Christians that say one thing and do another. She belonged in that group because she'd disappointed herself, Mama, and God. She broke down and sobbed, her shoulders heaving, her face hid in the crook of her arms.

Olivia's tone softened. "Amani Nicole, I trusted you. Looks like my trust has been misplaced. Where did you and Marley go?"

Amani lifted her face to the one person she tried so hard to please, but turned away. The tears and snot mixing together on her face made her look even younger than her soon-to-be eighteen years. She lowered her head and wiped her nose with the back of her hand.

"Girl, look at me when I'm talking to you. I asked you a question."

Amani lifted her head. "To . . . his . . . apartment." She hiccupped.

Olivia looked like a balloon that had been deflated, but her eyes never left her daughter's. "Are you sexually active?" She drew in a breath.

Amani shook her head. "No . . . I . . . Marley wouldn't. I love him, Mama. How can it be wrong to show that love?"

Olivia exhaled and almost every trace of her disappointment dissipated. She walked around the counter and sat beside her last hope for breaking the curse of her past.

She held her daughter, wishing her distress was the result of a boo-boo whose pain she could simply kiss away. Then she pulled some Kleenex from the pocket of her robe and wiped Amani's face. Being heavy-handed hadn't worked for the others, so she chose a different approach this seventh time. Holding her daughter at arm's length, her voice was loving but stern.

"Baby Girl, you gotta believe for yourself that God's ways

are the best. He loves us and wants us to enjoy a good life, but whenever we go our own way, we mess up." She put her hand under Amani's chin and lifted her head. "Don't forget I was your age when I married your Daddy, so I *do* understand how you feel about Marley."

Amani's sobs quieted.

Olivia wiped a stray tear from her daughter's cheek. "Baby Girl, you need to make up your mind. Either you're going to trust in God's plan for living or man's. If you obey the Lord, no matter what, He'll bless you."

"I'm trying to do the right thing." Amani sniffed. "It's just that all kinds of feelings are tumbling around inside me."

She caressed her daughter's cheek. "I'm sure you get overwhelmed by what you're feeling sometimes." Olivia clasped her daughter's hands in hers. "But I want you to remember something. The confession of chastity you make every year is real and God is holding you to it."

Amani expelled a long, exasperated breath. "I know." She placed a soft kiss on her mother's cheek. "Thank you, Mama."

"You're welcome." Olivia picked up her teacup and looked down at the pile of correspondence in front of Amani. Some of the burden that had just been lifted came back to visit. She stared at the acceptance letters. "Which is it going to be? West coast or east coast? Have you decided?"

"My head says Cornell, but my heart says UCLA. If I become a Bruin, I'll continue the Shephard tradition. However, I think it would be a great experience to go away to college. But if I stay here, I won't have to leave you all . . . or Marley." A light blanket of melancholy fell over her. "I don't know what to do." She turned expectant eyes on her mother.

Olivia placed her hand on her daughter's shoulder. "I still have faith in you, *Faith*," she spoke softly. "I believe you'll make the best decision." Having said her piece, she headed to the living room singing, "'Tis So Sweet to Trust in Jesus."

———————

Marley and Amani sat rocking back and forth on the bench swing on her front porch. Amani peeked at him out of the corner of her eye. She almost did not recognize the haggard young man beside her. He looked as if sweet slumber had refused to beckon him last night. For almost fifteen minutes, they sat shoulder to shoulder in silence.

Marley was unafraid to speak, but reluctant to hear. Last night she claimed she was still his, but he couldn't determine if she was appeasing him or actually sincere. He had the same unsettling feeling he experienced whenever he sat in his dentist's chair. Dr. Brown's pronouncement that he would barely feel a thing was never the case. He was just being set up.

Three times he had called Amani since leaving her last night. Once when he got in and twice that morning. Each time, he received her voice mail greeting.

After the last attempt, he laid his suit of armor on his king-sized bed.

It was time to saddle his horse and go into battle. He hopped into the shower and bowed his head. His war cry was direct. "Lord, you're the God of a second chance. Please give me another chance with Amani. In Jesus' name, I pray. Amen."

Last night, his body had ached to make love to Amani, but as he sat next to her in the light of day, he was thankful he resisted. He cleared his throat.

"You've been avoiding me."

"I'm sorry if it seems that way. I've been reviewing my college material. I'm pretty sure I'll get into all my choices, but I still haven't decided."

Marley grabbed her hand and faced her. He wished he could pretend he didn't care, but Ira Jamison had modeled for his sons his belief that manliness and tenderness were not polar characteristics. "Jamison men love hard" was one of his Pop's signature expressions.

"Amani, please come to UCLA. One of us will always be strong enough to resist temptation."

"Not if we continue to play with fire. I'm grateful you stood last night, but what happens when we're both willing to fall?"

Marley believed God had upheld them last night and would continue to do so. He let out a sigh of relief. "God wouldn't let that happen."

"Get real, Marley. God gives us guidelines, but He doesn't force us to follow them."

"Then we'll force ourselves. Our love is too strong to allow one moment of weakness to separate us. Remember, we're inseparable. No one or no thing can come between us. Not ever." He brought her hands to his mouth and brushed them with his lips.

His soft lips, magnetic eyes, and warm breath set off sparks inside her. She was falling again. "What about your apartment?"

"Off limits if it's just the two of us. And when your roommate is gone, we'll kiss goodnight outside of your dorm. Don't forget I have disciplined Jamaican blood pumping through my veins. We can hold down four full-time jobs while raising a family and earning law and medical degrees."

Amani cracked up. She had recently watched a television sitcom that poked fun at the strong work ethic many West Indian families displayed when arriving in America, their promise land. Jamaican immigrants were favorite targets of that overdone parody.

She punched his arm playfully. "Hey, you don't qualify. You were born here." Her eyes smoldered with the adoration he was accustomed to reveling in.

"Gal, mi still Jamaican to de core," Marley responded in lilting patois.

Her smile spanned the gulf that had divided them and she

moved closer to him. "What will that make our children then?"

Marley gently kissed her parted mouth, teasing himself with its sweetness. He raised his head. "Blessed, mon."

His damsel was no longer in distress, so he put down his sword and surrendered himself to her look of love that now burned unrestrained.

———————

Into the night, Amani continued to be deep in thought as she listened to one of her favorite old songs.

Each lyric she sang seared her soul and intensified her longing. She could have easily written Toni Braxton's "I Love Me Some Him," but Monica's "Angel of Mine" was, without a doubt, her anthem to Marley. The CD was set on repeat, but each time the song played, she heard it anew. So it was with Marley. Sacrilegious she was not, but whenever she was in his presence she felt born again. She glanced at the recently purchased toe rings on her left foot and smiled. Even her toes loved him.

She was attempting to polish them as she sat in the middle of her bed on top of several pieces of newspaper. She swayed gently to the waves of love that washed over her as she held their last meeting in focus. Marley was bending his head to hers. Involuntarily, she lowered her eyelids and inhaled, missing her tiniest toenail and brushing her big toe with Pretty in Pink nail polish. She dabbed a cotton ball with polish remover and wiped away all ten traces of her one-track mind.

The cool L.A. night chased away the remnants of day while sensations of tingling reverberated inside her as she thought of Marley. Amani kicked the newspaper onto the floor, set her pedicure kit on her nightstand, and then lay on her side holding her pillow close. Tenderly, she touched her finger to her puckered mouth and bade him good night.

THIRTEEN

She was becoming an honorary Jamison who looked forward to one day legally claiming that surname. Amani hadn't seen all of Marley's family since she visited their church the Sunday following the Harvest Festival. After service, they had dinner at their family-owned Cookin' Up A Storm restaurant. That was her first time eating curried goat, and rice and peas and today was her first time meeting the twins.

She was sitting between Mrs. Jamison and Jade, watching Marley get his game on against USC and his acquaintance slash rival Chazz Monty. It was cute the way they played mercilessly against each other, yet repeatedly helped each other off the floor.

Four-year-old Zachary sat between Jade and Kingston, and Mr. Jamison was seated next to his wife. Zoie sat on Amani's lap, chattering nonstop. Every few seconds, Jade would lean down to hush her daughter.

Waving their arms around, jumping up and down in their seats, the twins were quite animated as they watched their Uncle Marley play. But while Zoie could not keep her mouth closed, Zachary's eyes were full of awe as he followed the action, only speaking to cheer his uncle on. Amani was impressed that the two women seemed to know as much about basketball as Mr. Jamison and Kingston.

Mrs. Jamison patiently explained the referee's calls to her. Although she had attended every one of Marley's home games, she still didn't know the difference between traveling and double dribbling. Whenever she asked Mrs. Jamison a question, Amani noticed a smug look cross Jade's face, but she refused to let Jade's pettiness disturb her mood.

She was having a great time peeking at Marley's parents while watching him do his thing. Even though his main focus was coaching his youngest son from the stands, Mr. Jamison made it a point to touch his wife often. If he wasn't holding her hand, he was rubbing her back or patting her leg. He even went so far as to massage her shoulders.

When Marley sank both of his free throws, Mr. Jamison hugged his wife around the neck, pulled her to him, and kissed her cheek. "That's our boy!" he shouted.

An emotion she never experienced in relation to Marley swelled within her. At that moment, Amani realized why her spirits were so high. She was imagining that her boyfriend's parents were hers.

Her belief that her father would have been as attentive to her mother as Mr. Jamison was to Mrs. Jamison was her only solace.

The game ended with Marley once again being the leading contributor to the Bruin's success. Her baby had skills, on *and off* the court.

Amani stopped reminiscing about his romantic talents and looked down to see Zachary showing his uncle a few of his moves with his miniature basketball while Marley pretended to be unable to steal the ball from his nephew. Watching his theatrics, the foreign feeling of envy was quickly replaced by a more familiar one—heady love.

Zoie jumped up and initiated a pep rally in honor of her twin. "Go, Zack. Go, Zack. Go, Zack." Her grandparents made an apt audience and she was thrilled. She alternated between shaking her pom-poms high above her head and squatting to her knees. However, Amani was puzzled because Jade's attention was drawn to the court below.

When Amani glanced around Zoie, she noticed the same two cheerleaders who regularly accosted Marley had invited themselves over.

Jade elbowed her. "Girl, you better go down and let those birds know who you are."

A look of surprise crossed Amani's face. Jade had barely spoken to her all evening. She knew Kingston was five years older than Marley and assumed he and his wife were the same age. Amani didn't want to blow their first real conversation by sounding young. "Our relationship is based on trust." She hoped she sounded convincing.

The truth was she did trust Marley, but the desperately-seeking-Marley duo was a-whole-nother story, especially the cocoa-colored one who was making it a point to put her claws on some part of her man's muscled physique.

"Girlfriend, trust me," Jade insisted. "They're not interested in his stats for the season."

Mr. Jamison turned his attention away from his granddaughter and interjected. "You might want to listen to her, Amani. She was a cheerleader when my boy, Kingston, was on the team. In addition to charging slam dunks his junior year, he was changing soiled diapers."

Jade stretched her lips into half a moon and turned her dark-brown eyes to her daughter, but not before Amani observed their gleam instantly evaporate as a definite cold front passed over them.

Zoie exuberantly waved the small pom-poms that were the same color as those held by the self-appointed leaders of the Marley Jamison Fan Club. Amani tried hard to concentrate on the pint-sized pom-pom diva. She was watching Zoie, but her mind had returned to the court. *I bet her long silky hair was manufactured in Korea or Taiwan.* Amani frowned. She hated the stabs of jealousy in her heart.

Pretending to tie her shoe, she reached down and looked around Zoie. Her eyes narrowed as a sudden thought hit her. Some brothers had a thing for shapely legs. Others were all about big breasts, but Marley was obviously a hair man. He seemed mesmerized by all the swinging homegirl was doing with hers. Still, she felt no need to take Jade's advice.

If Marley didn't realize she was a diamond without the rough, he could settle for cubic zirconium.

Zoie started working harder to keep everyone's attention. She chanted in a singsong voice:

"Mommy, cheerleader. Daddy like cheerleaders."

"Mani, cheerleader. Uncle Marley like cheerleaders."

Amani smiled. "No, sweetie. I'm not a cheerleader."

She watched a scowl spread over Zoie's cinnamon-toasted face. "What's the matter, Miss Zee? You want me to be a cheerleader?" Amani was amused. "Okay, will you help me?"

Two thick afro-puffs, worn on either side of the part down the center of her head, resembled a pair of Mickey Mouse ears and bobbed up and down as she nodded. Zoie turned and looked down at the court. Amani's eyes immediately followed. Zoie's uncle was still standing below with her father, brother, and a set of scantily clad cling-ons.

She turned back to Amani. Her dimples beautifully indented the smoothness of her face as she handed her pom-poms to her newfound friend. "Yeah! You're a cheerleader! Now, my Uncle Marley marry you, Mani."

Peals of laughter erupted from Jade and her mother-in-law. Zoie volleyed her head back and forth between her mother and grandmother. Glad to have been the cause of their delight, her round eyes danced in her face. Although she didn't understand what was so funny, she laughed along with her two favorite ladies.

Amani grinned and turned her head toward Marley's father. The mouth that had earlier teased and cajoled was set in a grim line. His eyes stared ahead, hard and unsmiling.

———————

Marley was on a natural high as he strutted into the locker room. After tonight's game, he knew the Most Valuable Player award was his. Being aggressive on the court was a major part of his repertoire and when Amani watched, he took it to another level.

Tonight he played not only to win, but also to make a point.

He'd purposefully continued talking to Tamara and Michelle even after Kingston and Zack returned to the stands. He was banking on Jade's jealous tendencies and knew she was quick to direct Amani's attention below. His sister-in-law knew all about cheerleaders rising to the challenge. The proof was in Kingston's ring on her finger. However, the Miracle Man wasn't about to let tantalizing Tamara get that close. Besides, she was definitely *not* his type.

There was a motive behind Marley's madness.

He wanted Amani to change her mind about life after high school. It was hard for him to believe she was still considering a college three thousand miles away. UC Berkeley would have been a bitter enough pill to swallow, but Cornell was akin to amputation. Without her by his side, he would feel incomplete. He thought of a Kevon Edmonds lyric. *I'm not used to getting no love.* Amani had spoiled him for the single life. Loving her and being loved by her fulfilled him more than he'd ever dreamed possible.

He wondered what his girl thought about his little post-game scenario. Take-it-to-the-max Marley believed in keeping it real. Amani held the deed to his heart, but his eyesight was not for sale.

The two cheerleaders were hotties. Tamara Thompson was mocha brown with long, straight, jet-black hair she wore parted off one side. Her eyes were so dark they shone black and her full mouth was usually covered with glossy wine lipstick. Michelle Grady was fair-skinned with light-brown eyes. Her short auburn hair was usually styled in a layered cut or slicked down and parted on the side. Both young ladies were about five feet nine with slim, but curvaceous figures.

As an incoming freshman, he proudly wore the banner of Christian *and* celibate but Tamara, then a junior, told him if he ever wanted to see what he'd been missing he knew where to find her. She had been giving an encore performance since the beginning of his UCLA basketball career, and her girl, Michelle, usually had a front row seat of the show. When Tamara found out he had a girlfriend, her advances became even bolder. Now, every time they talked she wanted to know if he was still abstaining.

When he told her Amani believed as he did, she quickly chased away the smirk on her face. "How sweet," she said, smiling. Then she stood on her tiptoes and whispered, "If you change your mind and she doesn't, give me a call. I'll take real good care of you for her. She won't even have to thank me. The pleasure will be all mine . . . and yours." Her lips had brushed his ear.

Although his ego soaked up their after-game hype and banter, his heart was no longer in it. He had permanently loaned it to Amani Nicole Shephard. Marley admired Tamara's persistence, but made a mental note to keep a wide space between the soon-to-be graduates of the Class of 2002. One would graduate and receive a high school diploma. The other, her college degree.

Marley was in a rush the first time he showed off his girl to his teammates. The last person he introduced her to was Clifton Hendrix who proved, once again, why "No Class" was one of his aliases. No Class Cliff held onto Amani's hand as he appraised her. "Mmmm, mmmm, mmmm! I need to leave these chickenheads alone and get me a pretty young tender. Tenderoni. Macaroni. Call me Ragu, baby."

Returning his thoughts to the present, Marley stood sock-footed in front of his locker mirror brushing his hair. When every strand had been brushed, he sat down and picked up his sneakers. He wondered which brand he would endorse. His pastor constantly talked about the wealth of the wicked being laid up for the just. If there was going to be a transfer of wealth, he planned to get his share.

"Money cometh to Marley," he grinned, imitating his pastor.

His parents and Sunday school teachers had taught him the importance of tithing before he fully understood what it meant. Since the age of four, he learned to give ten percent of his allowance or any money he had. His parents also made sure he gave offerings over and above the tithe. Abundant Faith Christian Center would be *abundantly* blessed through his tithes alone. His offerings would be directed to the different ministries his church supported.

With the NBA, a major endorsement, and Amani Shephard, his future looked brighter than the Las Vegas strip. There was only problem. His self-control was weakening. He wanted a repeat performance of Valentine's night, closing with a grand finale instead of a premature ending. However, he had been playing it cool since the last thing he wanted was to push her away. They needed to hang out with another couple because he had a strong urge to take her home with him tonight for an encore.

Marley turned and looked over at his best friend, Taylor Wright, UCLA's team captain and starting center. He was sitting on the bench a few feet away looking scholarly, yet casual-cool. Outside of playing ball, witnessing about the Lord, and spending time with his girl, he enjoyed reading. This had earned him the nickname Booker Tee, although all the players dropped the Booker when addressing him to his face. His being six feet nine and two hundred fifty pounds had a lot to do with that.

Taylor was wearing a pair of black Khalil Love jeans with a matching jacket, a white mock turtleneck and a pair of designer hiking boots. Taylor's gold wire-framed glasses and short cut made him look kind of suave. His deep dimples made him a natural for a Casual Wear for Kings and Queens ad.

Those FUBU brothers had used LL Cool J for their ads. Marley "Miracle Man" Jamison and Taylor "The Terminator" Wright could one day endorse Khalil Love's line. Khalil seemed pretty cool when he met him during Christmas dinner at the Shephards'. When the time was right, he'd ask Amani to speak to Vanessa. Maybe she could hook up something.

Marley watched Taylor close his book and stand up. The book's title was *Maximize the Moment*. Amen. He planned on making the most of every moment he spent with his Sunshine. Taylor looked over at him and pointed to the book.

"You need to check this out, dawg. Bishop Jakes makes it plain."

"I saw him on TBN a couple of Sundays ago at my parent's house. They watch him faithfully. Ira and Carmen make sure we get our fill of natural and spiritual food on Sundays. The twins used to run around saying 'Get ready, get ready, get, get, get, get, get ready!'"

Taylor grinned. "The brother's anointed. I try to check him out every Sunday, too." He put the book in his sports bag and closed it. "What are you getting into this evening?"

Clifton was the only other person still in the locker room. He slammed his locker shut and quickly walked over to the bench where Marley was sitting. No Class smelled like he had followed his shower by bathing in cologne. He was wearing his warm-up suit because he bragged it got him mucho play. He put a foot on the bench beside Marley and looked at Taylor.

"I can tell you what church boy is not getting into." He patted his seventies 'fro then turned to Marley. "Amani looks real good to this brotha. If I were you, I'd handle my business, then repent. Man, I don't see how you haven't hit that yet."

Marley's left eyebrow began to twitch. He jumped up and slammed Clifton against the locker behind him. It was time to teach this Jamie Foxx wannabe a lesson.

He pushed Marley off of him. "You better save your energy for later." Clifton stopped. "'Scuse me. I forgot that fast. You don't get none!" He gave Marley a wild-eyed stare, then started laughing as he marched in place, shaking his head from side to side.

After a few seconds of watching him clap his big, ashy hands, Marley's eyes glazed over and the muscles in his neck tightened. He was no longer the Miracle Man. He was that gangly adolescent who was singled out for wanting to please the Lord and for having a last name for his first name.

It was nutrition at Frederick Douglas Middle School. A group of eighth graders were calling him sixth–grade scrub. Resa McClain, a member of his church, was the only girl hanging out with the ratty pack. He had been in love with her since second grade. She whispered something to Smokey, the ringleader, and his eyes bugged out of his head. He grabbed his crotch and looked at Marley. "Check it out, homies. He's not just a scrub. He's a *virgin* scrub."

He and his stooges laughed so loud a yard aide came over to quiet them. Marley turned and walked away. His feelings for Resa died instantly and he avoided speaking to her when he saw her at church or school. The summer before they went to eighth grade, her family moved more than seventy-five miles east to Riverside.

He had never forgotten the incident or her betrayal.

Though his game improved along with a growth spurt, his tolerance for being rejected lessened.

Clifton's laugh jarred him back to the present.

"Church boy has a temper. Better take that to the Lord in prayer."

Breath racing in hot gusts, Marley's nostrils flared as he grabbed Clifton around the collar. *I'm 'bout to bust this fool in the grill.*

Suddenly he felt someone place a calming hand on him. He saw Taylor out of the corner of his eye as his friend squeezed his shoulder. "Let it go, man." After a few moments, Marley's breathing evened. Taylor dropped his hand but remained beside his friend.

Marley slowly released Clifton and sat down. Clifton brushed himself off and stooped to pick up his bag. He straightened and grinned at Marley. "If you don't get with that sweet honey, you must be gay or made of steel." He turned and gave Taylor the chin-up goodbye. "Peace."

Clifton began walking away, then stopped and pointed his finger. "Look up in the sky. It's a bird. It's a plane. No, it's the man of steel!" His raucous laughter trailed behind him.

Taylor, the team's unofficial chaplain, watched Clifton push open the door that led to a bevy of young women willing to do whatever it took to help him feel invincible.

Taylor watched the door close behind Clifton's retreating back. He shook his head disdainfully. "That brother needs Jesus." He turned back to Marley. "You all right?"

"Yeah." The muscle in his jaw was still throbbing. He couldn't believe he'd allowed No Class to drive him to that zone.

"This is Tee you're talking to. What's up?"

"Does it get any easier?"

"Dealing with ignoramuses or letting crap slide?"

"Staying true."

"It's a struggle to the end, homie. You better recognize and decide which side you're fighting on. As far as being true to who I am, I have my moments. But I'm a brother in love with Jesus and my Gina. They both keep me strong." He rubbed his eyes with his index fingers and adjusted his glasses.

"We learned that it's best for us to avoid tempting situations altogether. We've been dating since we were freshmen and haven't gone there yet."

"Why doesn't anybody front you?"

"I haven't always been as saved as I am now," Taylor joked. "I used to be a hothead like you and I gave a senior a beat-down my freshman year. Dudes started giving a brother due respect after that. Clifton was there. He doesn't want me to go déjà vu on his behind." He rubbed his stubble-haired chin. "Not a chance though because this homeboy is growing in self-control.

"If you really think about it, the only one giving you grief is No Class. He's giving the ladies the best that he's got and still ends up with sloppy seconds. You're saving all your love and that makes the ladies want you more.

"Clifton probably wants to have tempting Tamara all up in his face." He smiled. "And if he could have a jewel half as precious as Amani, that cat would think he was the H.N.*O*.C., the Holiest Negro on Campus."

Marley laughed. "Man, you're crazy."

"Seriously. He can't stand you because you make the ladies swoon." He snatched up his shower towel from the bench, put it on his head, and swung his makeshift wig from side to side, letting his wrist go limp. "Ooh, girl! Did you see the Miracle Man? He's so fine he doesn't ever have to score a point. Just keep running back and forth in those shorts and—"

"Chill, Tee." Marley pulled the towel from his friend's head and threw it on the floor. He made eye contact with his confidante. "We had a close call about a month ago. It was our first time in my place. Nature was calling and we were 'bout to answer, but I didn't want any regrets. Plus, we didn't have protection."

"Slow your roll, Double M. You better count the cost 'cause when it goes down, you're gonna pay one way or another." He tapped his chest with his fist. "Stay strong, bro. Any fool can have sex. It takes real heart *not* to do what everybody else is doing."

Marley nodded his head, then stood and took one last look in the mirror. "You and Gina wanna grab something to eat with us?"

"Sounds like a plan, but I'm warning you, she'll end up preaching before the night is through."

"A brother needs all the help he can get." Marley started strolling toward the door.

"Hold up." Taylor reached into his bag. "Here. Listen to the third cut."

Marley looked down at the Men of Standard *Feels Like Rain* CD in his hand. "Thanks." He turned it over. "In Your Will" was song number three. He was trying to stay in God's will but, more importantly; he wanted Amani to stay with him. Tonight, he figured the company would do them good. Cliché or not, it was true. He muttered the words under his breath, "There's safety in numbers."

————

Sleep came quickly, but rest bypassed Tamara. They were coming into her room again. Dwight, her little brother's father, climbed into her bed and put his hand in her panties while placing her hand on his privates. When eleven-year-old Tamara confided in her mother, she didn't believe her. She'd called her a little tramp and told her to stop lying, and then accused her of being spiteful just like her father.

Two years later, Dwight moved on and Big Chris moved in.

Tamara pretended she was dead while his chubby fingers fondled her developing breasts and poked around in her underwear. Late one night, he decided it was time for more. He told her to undress and watched her pull her flannel gown over her head, and then he took off his tank shirt and sweats. Tamara waited for him to climb back into the bed before she let out a spine-tingling scream. He tried to cover her mouth, but she bit his finger then continued yelling and flailing her arms and legs.

Vivee flung open the door and stared at the scene before her. Big Chris was sucking on his throbbing finger and trying to pull up his sweatpants. Tamara cried hysterically, holding the blanket against her nakedness. "I wasn't lying about Dwight, Mommy. See?"

Vivee's eyes narrowed and she let out a string of expletives. "Both of y'all get out of my house. Now!"

"But Mommy, he—"

She turned a venomous eye on her daughter. "Call one of your aunts, Michelle's people, somebody. I better not see your face when I wake up."

Tamara clung to her cover. Her wet face was contorted with tears as she rocked her body back and forth.

Big Chris faced the floor. "Vivee, what about my son?"

The look she gave him should have struck him dead. "You wasn't thankin' nothin' 'bout him when you brought yo' fat sloppy behind in here. You said she been comin' on to you. Don't you come 'round her no mo'." She slammed the door so hard the walls shook from the velocity of her anger.

Big Chris leered at Tamara. "Might as well finish what we started."

She shook her head vigorously. Her heart ached it was pounding so fast. "No, please . . . "

He yanked away the blanket and fell on top of her. His rolls of stomach pressed her into the mattress and his slimy tongue licked her ears and face. Big Chris repeated a lie as he invaded her body. "Daddy loves you so much, sweet Tammie."

Tamara wondered if she should be thankful her own father left before he started to hurt her like this, too. Then she wondered if she should try to hold her breath until the pain stopped. Finally, she wondered if she could dial 9-1-1 without looking.

She grasped for the telephone on her nightstand but it fell out of her hands. Her baby brother's father was killing her, but she wasn't ready to die. There was only one person she knew to call.

Tamara's eyes snapped open. Though she hadn't seen Big Chris in almost ten years, she could still feel his weight crushing her and his body violating hers. The wounded look of a desperate animal flashed in her eyes as she howled for help.

"Mommy!" Her heart was racing and her silk camisole was drenched with sweat. "Mom—my!" She almost knocked the lamp on her nightstand to the floor as she struggled to turn on the light. "Mooooomeeeee!" Tamara bolted up in her bed, clutching her comforter. She wrapped her arms around her knees and rocked back and forth, back and forth, back and forth. Waiting. But this recurrent nightmare imitated real life, so nobody came to save her. Not even her mother.

S P R I N G

A time to get, and a time to lose; A time to keep, and a time to cast away; A time to rend, and a time to sew; a time to keep silence, and a time to speak.

Ecclesiastes 3:6-7

FOURTEEN

The sun peeked from behind thick clouds hanging in an overcast sky. The air was kind of nippy but not cold enough for him to put a jacket over his UCLA jersey. He was parked in a prime location. Marley leaned against his car and idly watched students rapidly exit the main entrance of Tubman. The end of that path led directly to him. It seemed like a lifetime ago that he was in high school.

He was still checking out the scenery when a pleasant-looking young lady wearing a super-sized French roll and pulling a roller backpack practically ran into him.

She extended her hand. "Hi, Marley! I'm Shawna, a good friend of your girlfriend's. Amani and I have a lot of the same AP classes. You know, advanced placement. We're both in the Magnet Program. We've been in most of the same classes since ninth grade." She finally took a breath and let go of his hand.

"Pleased to meet you, Shawna." He didn't want to be rude. Amani had never mentioned her to him, but he just played along. "Do you know where she is?" He smiled. "She doesn't know I'm here."

She turned suspicious eyes on him. "There's no problem or anything because if there is I don't want to get involved. I was watching a movie last night where this woman broke up with her boyfriend, but he wouldn't—"

"No. It's nothing like that. I'm surprising her."

"Whew! For a minute, I thought you were stalking her or something. I was ready to go get security because the last thing—"

"Would you mind taking me to Amani's locker?"

"Well, I'm not sure if—"

"I'd really appreciate this favor, Miss Shawna." He looked directly in her eyes and grinned. "It would mean a lot to me." He reached for her roller bag. "Let me carry this for you." He pushed the handle down and lifted it and started toward the entrance before she could answer.

She caught up with him. "Her locker's on the ground floor, but she's probably hanging out with Destiny on the quad by now."

"What's up, man?" and "Hey, baby" were shouted to him as he and Shawna moved through the crowd. She was telling anyone who would listen that this was Amani's boyfriend, Marley "Miracle Man" Jamison, who played for UCLA. Marley was impressed because she even knew some of his stats from last season. He already knew who would end up representing Tubman's Class of 2002 as valedictorian or salutatorian as well as being voted "Most Likely to Succeed" or "Most Likely to Talk in Her Sleep."

They finally made it out to the quad. She stopped abruptly in front of him and pointed. "There she is."

Amani and Destiny were holding court in the middle of the quad. They were surrounded by a group of African-American and Hispanic guys. His jaw clenched. *Why she got all these cats up in her face?* He turned to Shawna. "You coming?"

She shook her head. "I'm already behind schedule." She reached for her bag and hurried away.

"Thanks, Shawna," he called after her. "Bye."

She lifted her hand in response.

Marley put his hands in his pockets and turned around. Amani had spotted him and was waving him over. He put on his take-no-prisoners game face.

Amani was wearing a purple sweater with a pair of black jeans and black riding boots. Her hair was pulled up in a high ponytail and a pair of gold hoops dangled from her ears. "Hey, baby!" She didn't try to hide her excitement.

"Hey." He gave a general nod to the entourage that consisted of six older dudes dressed in slacks and shirts. Six leather briefcases sat on the stone bench next to Amani and Destiny's backpacks.

"Hi, Marley." Destiny was dressed similar to Amani in an orange sweater, brown slacks, and brown riding boots. Her bob, fluffy and flawless, shimmered in the sun as she swung her head.

"What up?"

Destiny and Amani exchanged glances.

Amani smiled at her honey. "Everybody, this is Marley. He—"

"I know who he is. Remember, I played football for the Bruins back in the day." The short, stocky one with the clean-shaven head extended his fist. "James. You got game, bro."

Marley relaxed as they tapped fists. "Thanks."

The other five made their affiliations known as well.

"Frank. Northwestern."

"Wyatt. Washington State."

"Sly. USC, baby!"

"Calvin. Penn State."

"Aaron. Stanford."

Marley was impressed. "Who y'all playing for now?"

Sly smiled. "Ourselves."

The Miracle Man couldn't conceal his confusion.

Frank interjected. He stood with one fist resting on the other as he explained. "All of us were injured during college so we never made it to the pros."

Too bad and too sad. Marley shook his head. "That must have been rough." He looked down and picked up Amani's backpack, freely assessing the Battered Bunch. *Let me get out of here. I'm not interested in listening to some anti-sports infomercial. They've probably made discouraging black boys and girls from dreaming of being pro athletes their one mission in life. Misery loves . . .*

"We didn't have time to be bitter," Wyatt interrupted Marley's thoughts.

"Sarge taught us too much for that," Calvin added, "so we focused on getting our degrees."

"When one door shuts, get yourself a hammer and build your own." Aaron smiled. "I had no idea what that meant until my football career was taken away."

James pointed to his head. "When your body wears out, what can your mind do?"

"It's not a man's outer strength, but his inner spirit that makes the difference," Frank said.

Wyatt grinned. "And his all-time favorite. If you think you can—"

"You can," they said in unison, tapping fists with each other.

"Sarge had all kinds of sayings. Most original, some borrowed." Sly's thin mouth curved into a smile. "We wanted to honor his memory. After we graduated from college, we pooled our resources and established Each One, Reach One Financial Services. We show families, individuals, students, retirees, nonprofit organizations, small businesses, and large corporations how to manage and invest their money."

Marley's face was one big question mark. "Who is *Sarge?*"

Every one of the men blinked at him in disbelief. Destiny laughed. A look of adoration crossed Amani's face. "My father. A lot of his students called him Sarge because he ran this school like a drill sergeant. Today was our Spring Career Fair and Each One, Reach One gave a presentation."

Marley looked at the men like he was seeing them for the first time. "Are you dudes saying Mr. Shephard had something to do with y'all wanting to 'give back to the community,' as they say?"

Calvin made direct eye contact with Marley. "That's exactly what we're saying."

"What year did y'all graduate?"

"Nineteen eighty-nine in the house!" they shouted, making "T's" with their index fingers. Their pride at being Tubman High graduates was evident.

Marley caught Amani's eye. "That's the last year your father was principal."

Amani validated him with the sincere smile that was her trademark.

Even Destiny was impressed. "He shoots and he scores. Our girl's dad was something else, huh?"

Marley saluted the six soldiers in front of him. "Most definitely."

James grinned. "That reminds me, Amani. How are the two eldest Shephard sisters doing?"

Amani giggled. "I was wondering when you'd get around to asking. They're good. Perri's practicing law and Vanessa's designing clothes that only a celebrity can afford."

"Mmmm, mmmm, mmmm." Sly shook his head. "Are they still so fine they could drive a brother outta his mind?"

Destiny and Amani burst out laughing.

"Oh, yes!" Marley answered.

Amani tilted her head. *Excuse me.*

"Air ball," Destiny announced.

"It ain't this brother's fault." Wyatt gave Marley the soul brother handshake. "Sarge had great genes."

"And Perri and Vanessa wore their jeans well, too," Sly said.

"That sho' 'nuff is a mouthful of truth," Frank agreed.

"All right, *gentlemen.*" James was obviously the captain of the team. "We need to head out."

Sergeant Shephard's six star recruits kissed each young lady on her cheek and hurried to the school's parking lot. Destiny walked with them. Marley practically dragged Amani out to the front of the school. He wanted to see what these dudes were rolling.

A few minutes later, Destiny's SUV swooped in front of his. "Call me later," she yelled to Amani over the blast of the latest Fred Hammond and Radical for Christ CD.

"Okay," Amani yelled back.

Marley was puzzled again. *Didn't they spend all day with each other?* He took his time opening and closing Amani's door, keeping a close eye on the parking lot. A beautiful red Lincoln Navigator pulled out of the parking lot. *That's sweet.* He looked closer. The only difference from the ones he usually saw on the street was the doorplate on the side. Each One, Reach One. Marley rubbed his chin. *I'm down with that.*

In fact, he was a step ahead of the game. He was already investing his time and energy into two worthy individuals: his little brother Tyreek and his sweet lady Amani. Some nights, he dreamt of the various ways he'd like to reach *her*.

————

Amani was as nervous as she'd been the night she sang the solo part and their choir won the annual McDonald's Gospel Fest. It was already her third trip to the bathroom. As she turned on the water to wash her hands, she noticed the same girl coming into the bathroom she had passed on her way out twice before. Either homegirl has a bladder infection or she's anxious because her boyfriend was nominated for a couple of awards, too, Amani thought.

She shut off the faucet. Before she could reach for the paper towel dispenser, the young lady turned the handle, carefully tore off a piece, and handed it to her.

Amani smiled. "Thank you. I guess this is the hot spot tonight."

"Yeah, girl. Whenever I'm nervous, I pee a lot."

"Me, too. My boyfriend will probably get the Most Valuable Player award tonight, so I keep having to use the bathroom."

"A real good friend of mine is up for the same award, and he's definitely got the skills to pay the bills."

Something about her was familiar but Amani couldn't recall having met her before. She extended her hand. "Since we have so much in common, I might as well introduce myself. I'm Amani Shephard."

She wondered what happened because the amiable spirit that embraced them at the onset of their conversation evaporated like morning dew in the summer sun. Amani was about to chide herself for being too sensitive when the girl spoke.

"I'm Tamara Thompson, captain of the cheerleading squad. You're Marley's girlfriend, right?"

"I thought I recognized you, but how do you know me?"

"We all know who you are. The Miracle Man is one of our favorite players. You struck gold. I hope you realize that."

"I like to think he's been blessed, too."

Tamara flipped her hair over her shoulder. "I heard you were one of those hard-core Christians."

"I don't know your definition of hard-core, but I am a Christian."

"Girlfriend, let me be the first to make the announcement. Praying ain't gonna change a thing when Marley's ready to dunk his basketball in your hoop. If you're too holy to handle your business, I'll gladly come from the sidelines and finish your game."

Amani returned the young lady's stare. "I know miracles still happen, but I already got yours." She brushed past Tamara. "Excuse me."

On the way back to her seat, she congratulated herself. Mia and Krystal would have been proud, but Amani wasn't stupid. She knew Tamara was not alone in her attraction to Marley. With his being a shoo-in for the MVP award, even more females would flock to him. Even if she were no longer a threat to his ban on sex before marriage, there would be plenty of temptation awaiting him. What if he did change his mind?

She didn't want to lose her virginity before marriage, but she didn't want to lose Marley either. To lose the former would break the heart of God, but to lose the latter would be to take a sledgehammer to her own.

Anyway, God was almighty. His heart would mend in the twinkling of an eye. She wouldn't be surprised if hers never fully recovered because, as far as she was concerned, Marley had the home court advantage.

Her heart was familiar territory.

———————

As the warm water from the showerhead pelted her skin, Tamara drowned her tears. Weariness and hopelessness claimed her. She was running out of time. She'd be graduating in less than three months and had yet to get a date with Marley, let alone a proposal of marriage from him. And now, Marley had a girlfriend. She hated to admit it, but homegirl was beautiful and sweet looking. *What am I going to do?* All her life she had attempted to prove that she wasn't anything like the woman who gave birth to her.

Any woman who took the words of two lowlifes over her own daughter's didn't deserve to be a mother. Any woman who would turn her back on her own flesh and blood in the midst of a crime being committed was as guilty as the perpetrator. Any woman who could ignore frantic pleas for help coming from her thirteen-year-old child's bedroom wasn't fit to live.

Tamara hated her mother but hated being alone at night even more.

She turned off the water and stepped out of the shower to let the air dry her body. She moved into her bedroom, laid her towel on the bed and sat on it before carefully lotioning her body with a sensual, scented lotion. Then she powdered herself with the same scent and slipped on a white two-piece lingerie short set. She admired her hair in the mirror as she brushed.

She slicked one side behind her ears and let the other fall softly at the side of her face. Her slightly wide eyes, mouth, and nose were beautifully proportioned. She kept her eyebrows professionally arched and applied her make-up like an expert. She took out her make-up bag. Tamara knew she was as pretty as Amani, so she didn't understand why Marley never gave her a chance. *I don't have naturally wavy hair, but he's more real than that. More real than the guys I've been dealing with.*

For her first two years at UCLA, she dated a lot. After a couple of months, the faces became a blur. It was the same routine. Dinner, movie, sex. She would have accepted being held in place of anything more. 'We'll cuddle afterwards', most of them lied. So Tamara took the comfort of not being alone at night with whatever came with it.

During her junior year, the Miracle Man came to UCLA. If she hadn't met him, she wouldn't have believed there were other brothers with integrity like Taylor Wright. She and his girlfriend, Regina Simms, lived in the same dormitory freshman year. Regina was outgoing, loving, and fearless. Tamara wasn't tempted to tangle with her. Taylor was off limits, but Marley was free and clear. The only thing holding him back was his convictions.

He was sweet, saved, sexy, and, from past conversations, she knew he was also a little cocky. Tamara had been trying to get next to the Miracle Man since his freshman year. Her friend, Michelle, had tried to tell her to give it up, but she couldn't.

Marley was the kind of man who would never purposely hurt or abuse any female. With everything in her, she wanted to be his woman. She was on a mission to be his woman. She didn't know how and she didn't know when, but one day she would be his woman. Until then, she was just passing time and hosting sleepovers.

The chime of the doorbell rang through her thoughts. She took one last look at herself and saw her mother's face. Tamara lit the row of scented candles on her dresser and turned off the lights. It was too late for dinner and a movie, but she needed to be held and was afraid of being alone.

FIFTEEN

The future owner of the Many Expressions of You Hair Salon & Spa was busy with one of her favorite nonpaying clients. Mia was experimenting with simple hairstyles for Amani's upcoming trip to Jamaica. Amani sat at the edge of her bed while Mia stood beside her. She turned her head right and left as they checked out the low ponytail Mia had given her. Amani was snapping her fingers to her favorite song.

Mia frowned as she teased her sister. "Dag. Don't you play any other songs on that Monica CD? I'm convinced. Marley J's an angel."

"But, Mama Mia, he really is," Amani said, trying to sound Italian.

"Make sure your angel wears a condom in the land of sun, surf, and sex."

Amani eyed her sister through the mirror. A few seconds passed before she spoke. She turned around and put her hands on her hip.

"You've been misinformed. Point number one, Marley and I are on the same wavelength when it comes to sex. Point number two, it's not that type of party. Marley's parents and his brother's family are going, and we're all going to stay in their summer home outside of Kingston." She stuck out her tongue at Mia's reflection.

Mia rolled her eyes. "And point number three. Six months ago, I let Roland's hands roam a little too freely. The next thing I knew, Dr. Peters was giving me a prescription for birth control. Since I got on the pill, we've been finishing what we started."

She clipped a silver butterfly above each of her sister's ears. "Mama called and he answered the phone one morning. You know she wasn't pleased with my decision, but at least she doesn't have to worry about me bringing home any crumb snatchers. Anyway, we're going to get married as soon as he gets his financial situation together."

"See, your first mistake was getting involved with someone who doesn't share your beliefs. Roland doesn't even go to church. All he cares about is making his salon the most popular one in L.A. That's why every time I see you, you have on that tired t-shirt. Roland's a smart businessman though. He's got his whole harem giving him free adver— Ouch!"

Amani plied her braid out of Mia's hand then continued. "Anyway, the one time Marley and I did get carried away, *he* stopped it."

Mia wound her sister's thick braid into a bun at the nape of her neck. "Don't fool yourself. There will be a next time. RJ and I dated for a year and a half before we made love. I had to do something. Those desperados at the salon were out of control." She inserted a couple of hairpins to hold the bun in place then stopped and stared at Amani.

"Baby Girl, let me make an appointment for you with Dr. Peters . . . just in case."

"Are you listening to yourself?" Amani rolled her eyes. "I

don't have to go all the way to Jamaica to have sex with Marley when he has his own place in Westwood."

Mia pushed her sister in the back. "Point number four. Unless you're dumb enough to think being a teenage mother is fashionable, you need to handle your business."

Amani glared at her sister's mirror image. "The only control we need is self-control."

Mia returned her sister's stare, then shook her head sadly. "Love makes you do what you wouldn't ordinarily do." She walked over to the portable CD player on the top shelf of the small white entertainment center that stood against the wall, released the CD's repeat option, cha-cha'ed out the door, and firmly closed it.

Mia hesitated a moment outside of her sister's fantasy world. Regardless of what Amani thought, Marley was no angel. He may have been fearfully and wonderfully made, and yes—she had to give the Miracle Man his props—he was fine. However, he was still just a man.

SIXTEEN

Glorious mountains outlined the clearest azure sky she had ever encountered. She shielded her eyes as she stood at the top of the portable staircase adjacent to the plane. The view was silver screen perfect. A gentle breeze blew away the vestiges of doubt that held her tensed during the plane's descent. Marley's hand fastened around hers as he guided her down the stairwell to the welcoming ground below.

He was laughing and speaking so rapidly to his parents and Kingston that she couldn't understand what he was saying, especially since they were using their Jamaican dialect. Amani wanted him to herself, if only for a few minutes, so she prepared to flash him the smile she smiled just for him.

She had faithfully practiced it in the mirror ever since they went to get ice cream after a recent movie date. That afternoon, they were listening to 94.7 The Wave as they cruised down Crenshaw Boulevard. After 7's remake of "Sarah, Smile" was playing. Marley joked he'd like to see a smile bad enough to make a grown man beg.

Amani was inspired to create a special I-love-you-Marley smile. It began with a gleam of adoration in her eyes. For a few seconds, she would offer a playful, closed-mouth smile before stretching it into a perfect half-moon that framed the top row of her even white teeth. An air kiss and a left wink concluded the smile designed to knock the chill off Marley's coolness.

She stopped reminiscing as her gift from God said, "Welcome to Jamaica" as soon as they reached the bottom of the stairwell.

Amani couldn't help teasing him. "Your Jamaicanese is perfect."

He kissed her cheek. "So are you."

Amani gazed into his face and presented him with the smile custom-made for him.

The fragrant Jamaican breeze caressed her face and hair.

Marley received the kiss, caught the wink, then blushed as he removed a strand of hair from the corner of her mouth and placed it behind her ear. Mission accomplished. Amani turned to the rest of her travel companions.

Kingston and Jade looked worn out as Zoie and Zachary bounced up and down around them. *The Energizer bunny needs to start working out, or the Z-team will have his job.* Amani smiled and called to them, "Hey, you two! I've never been here before so I need you to be my tour guides."

They ran over to her and each twin took a hand as they dragged her toward the terminal behind their grandparents. Kingston and Jade gave her a grateful smile while Marley looked impressed.

Amani was more fascinated than the two Jamaican jumping beans boiling over with excitement beside her. She already sensed an obvious allure hovering over the tropical island and sensed this trip would be a turning point in their relationship. Marley could have had his pick of beach beauties during his spring break, but wanted her with him.

Amani didn't doubt she made any man look better, but it was exciting to realize Marley was as into her as she was into him.

On the plane, Marley had managed to stay awake practically the entire trip though he wasn't very talkative. Things became quite turbulent toward the end of the flight. As the plane rocked, quavered, and rolled, she watched his shoulders stiffen. He was squeezing her hand so hard, it hurt. She leaned over and whispered in his ear, "Your times are in His hands." His posture instantly relaxed and he loosened his grip on her hand, but the only times he let it go were to use the restroom. Where Marley was subdued, Amani chatted on and off with the woman seated next to her as if flying across the country with the man she loved and his family was no big deal.

In reality, she had to fight for her seat on that flight.

Her mother's immediate reaction was for her to return the ticket because she felt the gift was too extravagant. Even after speaking with Mrs. Jamison the day after Christmas, her mother still hadn't made up her mind. Amani recruited each of her sisters to plead her case. Not even Perri, the legal expert, could make any progress. Her sons-in-law, Ahmad and Simeon, brought in the male points of view to no avail. Khalil even took a turn. When her godparents were unable to change her mother's mind, she almost gave up.

Amani finally started doing her own campaigning then. She reminded her mother that not one of her sisters had lost their virginity in another country. Every one of them had engaged in premarital sex right in sunny California.

Ironically, a week after Valentine's Day, her mother conceded. She came into Amani's bedroom on her way to the hospital one morning. Although she was still a little groggy, her mother's words rang clear. "I won't be in Jamaica, Baby Girl, but God will. No matter where you go or what you do, He's watching."

The twins' excited chatter, as they followed their grandparents through the terminal, could not overshadow the memory of Mama O's surrender or Destiny's recent remarks.

Twice within the same week, predictions for protection were made in her bedroom. First, by Mia, then by Destiny.

She had been lying belly-down across Amani's bed, flipping through the latest edition of *Essence* magazine.

"I don't think you should get on the pill because I know you're not planning to have sex on a regular basis. But maybe you should take a couple of condoms so you'll be ready in the heat of the moment." Destiny lifted her head from the magazine with a ridiculous grin on her face. "Losing your virginity in Jamaica. Now, that would be romantic."

Destiny smiled slyly. "And at least you're not old enough to be his mama." Suddenly, she began kicking her legs up and down, laughing so hard tears formed in her eyes.

Amani giggled. "What?"

"You better hope no Stella looking for her groove sees Marley in Speedos."

Amani returned to the present. Mr. and Mrs. Jamison had reserved a white Ford Excursion for their week's stay. Amani sat on the third seat next to the passenger side window. Marley squeezed his bulk into the middle and Zachary fell asleep with his head resting on his uncle's side. On the center seat, Zoie slept with her head in her mother's lap while Kingston's hand rested on the back of Jade's neck.

Up front, Mr. and Mrs. Jamison's patois whirled out of the open windows, across the narrow tar-capped roads, and rose to the tops of the Blue Mountains they passed. Marley and Kingston's voices matched theirs. The rhythmic cadence of the lingo inside the car somehow authenticated Amani's first trip to Jamaica.

A few days earlier, Mrs. Jamison told her Jamaica was known as the pearl of the Caribbean. She said it with a lot of pride. Amani asked Marley why his parents immigrated to America if they loved their birthplace so much.

"My parents believed the United States had more to offer in terms of opportunities for advancement. I'm thankful they felt that way. If they hadn't, we wouldn't have met." He seemed slightly annoyed as he took a long, hard sip of his chocolate shake. He released the straw, then remarked. "Aren't you glad they came to the land of the freeways and the home of the brave motorists?"

She grinned and pretended to give some thought to her answer. They were holding hands across the table. He was wearing blue sweat pants with a pair of Nikes. His navy tam and windbreaker were emblazoned with the same Nike symbol. Except for the hat, they were matching down to the running shoes they wore on their feet. The question marks in his eyes flashed as he waited for her response.

Amani dipped her final nugget in honey and put it between her teeth. She leaned in toward Marley. He met her and bit off the exposed half of the chicken. Amani chewed and swallowed. "Aw, suki suki now. I definitely must thank your parents for bringing you to me." She smiled. "God bless America, and my Boo, too."

Later that same evening, they sealed their serendipity with a kiss that expressed how grateful they both were for his parents' decision.

Amani allowed that remembrance to fade as she attempted to focus on Jamaica's fertile plains and towering Blue Mountains. The lush beauty of the landscape caused her to reflect on its Creator. She, too, had been created for His purpose, but Amani was beginning to understand the course her life took would be a testament to the choices she made along the way.

She felt powerful. She was the master of her private universe, yet she felt burdened by God's selfless gift of free will. It reminded her of the song, "Open My Heart," by Yolanda Adams. Amani didn't want to do the wrong thing, and she was certainly afraid of disappointing God. She let out a slow breath. The Lord was omnipotent. Why couldn't He just *make* His children do right?

Zachary stirred in his sleep, choosing to rest his head against the window in place of his uncle's steely abdomen. Marley shifted and put his arm around her shoulder as he sang along with Bob Marley, still one of Jamaica's favorite sons. "I don't wanna wait in vain."

Although Amani's intellect knew better, she turned away from the window and glanced sideways at Marley who was checking out the view on the other side. Though off pitch as usual, he passionately sang along with his namesake. She continued to stare until satisfied he was not attempting to convey some covert lyrical message.

———

The Jamison's beach house looked like a small Spanish villa. Surrounded by a courtyard on three sides, it had its own back door with a private view of the ocean. Banana and palm trees encircled the house. Aromatic, enticing smells of Jamaican cuisine whispered on the ocean breeze. The sound of the surf played an ongoing serenade to Amani. She watched with a sense of wonder as pelicans and sea gulls dotted the horizon. Amani stood alone, taking it all in. "Thank you, Jesus," she prayed, feeling both peaceful and blessed.

Later on, as day faded to night, they sat on the steps of the front porch. Her head rested on his shoulder as their hands and hearts connected. The screen door slammed, breaking the stillness. Zachary had come out to join them. He sat quietly on the step below his uncle. A few seconds later, he jumped up and pointed into the dark sky. "Look, Uncle Marley! The moon followed us to Jamaica!"

Marley rubbed Zack's head. "It must love us because when you love somebody, you want to be with them all the time."

Zachary giggled. "You must love Amani a whole bunch then, 'cause you're always with her."

In the light of the moon, he kissed the head that lay on his outlined heart. "True ting, bwoy. Mi luv dis gal hard. Wid nuff luv an' every ting inna mi."

––––––––––

The white sand warmed her feet as they stood holding hands, side by side. Their bodies swayed to the music's distinct reggae beats. Amani was relishing the steady rays of the Caribbean sun, the wind's gentle zephyr, and the shimmer of the aqua blue sea.

Yet, the magnificence of the island's scenic beachfront paled in comparison to the sight of Marley's muscle-layered body in a pair of yellow Speedo shorts and a matching jacket. The golden cross glimmered on his bare chest and the bracelet sparkled on his wrist. His newly grown goatee connected to his mustache, making him the only sight she truly cared to behold. Amani remembered Destiny's comment and quickly looked around. She caught a couple of "Stellas" checking out Marley. Amani held his hand tighter and grinned. She couldn't blame them.

Mr. and Mrs. Jamison traveled to St. Andrew to visit family and friends they hadn't seen since last year's trip. Kingston and Jade gladly left their shadows in their grandparents' care to be shown off, hugged, admired, and cuddled by acquaintances familiar and new. It was the first time since their arrival that the two couples had formed a foursome. The not quite native sons decided they would begin the afternoon at a reggae festival.

They went directly to the hotspot on the beach where the concert had already begun. Jade did a modest imitation of the men and women who were winding their hips to the enticing tempos.

Scanning the crowd, Amani turned up her nose. Some of the couples looked indecent.

Kingston laughed at her expression. "They're dancing rub-a-dub style." He placed his hands around his wife's waist and did his conservative version of the dance along with her.

Jade turned to Amani and grinned. "The first time I was here, I wondered why some of them didn't just go on back to their hotel rooms. Or go reserve one." She looked around. "A lot of these folks are freaky deaky nasty."

Marley shrugged. "Jamaica wouldn't be Jamaica without rub-a-dub. There are different degrees to the dance. The couple determines how far to go."

Amani looked around again and finally noticed she was also being observed. Feeling a bit exposed, she tightened the fringed, yellow scarf Jade had helped her to tie around her orange and yellow two-piece bathing suit. Truthfully, she was extremely proud of her body. Her dancing lessons had given her toned legs, thighs, and buttocks, but she didn't feel comfortable displaying all the goods, especially in front of these drooling lookey-loos.

When Amani finished fixing her scarf, Marley grabbed her hands and looked into her eyes. "You wanna try it?" Sensations of tingling engulfed her.

"Dream on," she spoke bravely, knowing she was afraid to get *that* close again. Amani knew she couldn't give the devil any room if she wanted to return home with nothing more than a suntan and a few souvenirs.

Marley turned her around and rested his chin on her shoulder. She inhaled peppermint as his lips brushed her cheek. "I'm ready to make my dream a reality."

Three down. Four to go. Amani was enjoying her stay, but was somewhat homesick and a little tired. Every waking

moment was spent exploring, eating, shopping, visiting tour-
ist attractions, or Marley's relatives and friends.

Today, she had decided to sleep in.

When she finally got out of bed, she quickly showered and
dressed in a pair of faded blue jeans and a red tube top. Her
hair was in two thick ponytails that grazed her shoulders.
Mrs. Jamison was the only other person left in the quiet house.
She was sitting at the kitchen table snapping green beans.

She smiled when she saw Amani. Her bronze face shone
under chin-length double-strand twists. Amani walked over
to the table.

"Good morning, Mrs. Jamison."

"Good morning, Amani." She picked up a bean. "There's a
plate on the stove for you."

"Thank you." Amani picked up the plate, then sat across
from Mrs. Jamison. She took the paper towel off the dumplings, corn beef, and plantains and hungrily dug in. The sweet,
almost banana-like taste of the plantains was growing on her.
She looked around. "Where is everybody?"

"Kingston, Jade, and Marley went to the market. The twins
went with their Papa to visit some of his old buddies. He's
been witnessing to them for years. The same commitment he
had for the Rastafarian lifestyle, he now has for Christianity."
She beamed. "In fact, he's even more radical for Christ."

Amani smiled, her mouth full of plantains. She ate the rest
of her breakfast in a comfortable silence. When she finished,
she went to the sink, washed, and rinsed her plate and fork.
Amani returned to the table and stood in front of her future
mother-in-law. "Can I help?"

Mrs. Jamison went over to the cabinet under the stove and
pulled out another silver bowl. She patiently showed Amani
what to do. Nevertheless, Amani's movements were clumsy.

Marley's mom smiled. "This is your first time snapping
beans, huh? City girls don't care much for cooking. My boys
love good food, especially Jamaican food. I still enjoy prepar-

ing meals for them, even though all three Jamison men can practically out-cook me."

"Then Marley and I won't have any problems. When we get married, he can do the cooking."

"You better take notes from Jade, honey. She knew how to get Kingston."

Amani's mouth dropped and her eyebrow lifted.

Mrs. Jamison noticed the young girl's distressed look. "Forgive me. Sometimes I don't say all that I mean. Jade practiced Kingston's favorite dishes until she could cook them to West Indian perfection. Rice and peas. Curried goat. Jerk chicken. Plantains. Dumplings. You name it, she can cook it. I'm proud of the way that girl takes care of her family."

"Even though she's not West In—" Amani stopped, feeling embarrassed.

Mrs. Jamison grinned. "A lot of times, an American daughter-in-law makes the best kind. If Jade knew how much I've grown to love her, she might stop trying so hard to impress me." She winked before the smile left her face. "Still, I hope you and Marley don't end up doing what they did."

Amani stopped snapping beans. "You don't think I'd make a good wife for Marley?" She chewed her bottom lip.

Mrs. Jamison chuckled. "I'm doing it again." She stopped and stared at Amani. "You both are so young, sweetie. Don't do nothing now you'll regret later. Take your time. True love is lasting and it can wait."

Mrs. Jamison went over to the sink and began rinsing the beans. "You come from a different spiritual heritage than Jade does. Your faith in God is probably strong enough to keep you if my boy decides to let his hormones rule his head." She turned to face Amani. "You're a beautiful girl and men can be so weak." The older woman's brows furrowed as she watched an invisible movie on the wall behind Amani.

The pace of Amani's heartbeat quickened, and her eyebrows formed a bridge over her nose. No matter to whom she found herself speaking lately, some variation of this conversation took place. She took the few beans she'd been trusted to snap over to Mrs. Jamison.

"You're right about me, Mrs. Jamison. I do want to please the Lord." Her misty eyes glowed. "But I love your son and I don't ever want to lose him." She lowered her head because she didn't want his mother to see the truth shining in her eyes. When it came down to it, she had been the weak one.

Mrs. Jamison turned off the water and wiped her hands on her apron. She gently took the bowl out of Amani's hands, then rested the young girl's head against her ample bosom.

The gesture was as natural to her as the patois that flowed from her full lips. "Gal, yu live in de cement house. No worry de hurricane."

Amani surrendered to the embrace while she restrained rains of uncertainty from pouring forth. Her heart's plea was straightforward. *Lord, help me to stay strong.*

The next three days passed in a whirl of activity. Horseback riding, kissing, scuba diving, caressing, windsurfing, laughing, souvenir shopping, cuddling. They even stood as long as they could under a waterfall, wearing matching red swimwear. His was worn without the tank top. Marley gripped her tightly as waves crashed over them. Amani was grateful for its camouflage because of the joyous tears she shed that day. She was completely in love and could not imagine making any choice that would separate him from her.

Later that afternoon while drying off in the sun, they sat in a secluded spot on the beach and fed each other mango. The fat fruit's juices ran from their hands to their elbows. When Marley took its flesh from her fingers, then slowly licked each one, she was tempted to run back to the cool cascading showers.

It was their last day in Jamaica and they were being chaperoned by strangers. Marley and Amani sat on the beach watching the sun settle behind the mountains. Hues of orange, purple, and pink designed a mosaic across the sky that was theirs alone. The evening concert was beginning. Marley lifted the hand enclosed in his own and kissed it. Amani shivered.

"You're cold?" He let go of her hand and draped his arm around her shoulders.

"No." She stretched her arm around his firm waist.

The night's rhythms were calling him.

He looked at the crowd of people gathering around the stage and sprang to his feet, then helped Amani to hers. She was wearing an ankle-length pink, blue, and white floral dress that flowed delicately when she moved and fit like it was custom-made for her. A set of toe rings she had bought for him adorned of her feet.

If a Jamaican genie were to approach him, Marley already knew his first wish. He wanted to be alone with his girl. Wishes two and three involved removing the dress and taking its place. He shuddered before continuing his visual journey.

Her thick hair was pulled into a bun at the nape of her neck and sparkling silver butterflies were clipped on either side of her head. Her high cheekbones formed delicate mounds under a complexion that had been toasted under the West Indian sun. Arched eyebrows highlighted eyes into which he never tired of gazing. Her rounded nose belonged on that face, and her luscious lips shimmered under a barely-there brown gloss.

Marley was amazed. His lady looked as beautiful with every strand of hair brushed away from her face as she did with her carefree curls framing her head and shoulders.

He brushed specks of sand off his khaki shorts and white short-sleeved cotton shirt that he wore unbuttoned over a blue tank top, and then stooped to pick up their sandals. They held hands as they strolled over to their last Jamaican beach party for the spring.

Claiming their turf on the fringes of the group of frenzied dancers, Marley felt the crowd's heat mixing with his own.

A light vanilla scent perfumed Amani's body, teasing his nostrils with the desire to inhale her from head to toe. Teasing his lips with the desire to follow his nose. In a rush, he dropped their sandals. He faced her and put his hands on her hips, moving them in a circular motion. He purposely left an obvious opening between them. She smiled, though her eyes held a question.

He answered with a query of his own. "You trust me?"

"The spider asked the fly." Amani laughed.

"I'm serious." The combination of deepening moonlight, music, and Miss Mani was mesmerizing. He was hoping for more than a tan to remind him of spring break.

The smile faded and her eyes united with his. "I trust you."

"Then loosen up. It's only a dance. You're the dancer so you know dancing is nothing more than another form of communication. We're talking with our bodies." He was winding his hips as passionately as any native on the beach while guiding her to match his movements. He stepped closer. Still, he did not completely bridge the space between them.

The dance had become a soul-to-soul conversation that was igniting sparks, despite the distance.

"Can you hear me?" Marley's voice was filled with his desire to close the gap.

She didn't answer. Waves of heat flooded her body, causing her to tremble.

"What am I saying, Amani?"

Her eyes stared into his, but she remained silent.

The campfire inside of him was fast becoming a raging inferno. "Talk to me, baby. Do you feel what I'm feeling?" He stopped dancing.

She followed his lead. "Yes . . . but—"

"Shhh." Marley put his finger on her lips. Without removing it, he spoke quickly. "I could get a room. Remember what you said on Valentine's. Just once, as an expression of our love. I brought some condoms with me. Nikki, please." He searched her eyes. "No one would have to know."

The last time he called her Nikki, she'd been ready to show him she belonged to him heart, mind, *and* body. Now, her mother's words reminded her. *I won't be in Jamaica, Amani, but God will.* She removed his hand. "God would know, Marley, and you know I wasn't thinking straight that night."

"I haven't stopped thinking about that night and sometimes I wish . . . Amani, being with you and not being able to be *with* you is getting rough." The pain in his eyes bore witness to his words as he rubbed the back of his neck.

"It's difficult for me sometimes, too, but being a Christian is not some garment we can try on then return to the rack because we don't like the fit." She lowered her voice. "Believe me, Marley. I want to share *everything* with you, but I want to hold off until our wedding night."

Amani placed the palm of his hand against her face and rubbed her right cheek against it. Then she placed her hands on top of his. She guided them from her face to her neck, over her shoulders, slid them down her bare arms, and across the womanly outline of her hips.

She raised his sleeve and kissed the colored tribute on his left arm. Liquid love filled her eyes. "I'm saving myself for you, my future husband." Amani rested her face against his pumping heart to declare what lived inside her own. "We'll have a lifetime to make love." She lifted her head and stared into his eyes. "Please wait for me, Marley."

Reggae rhythms punctuated the night air and the throng about them vanished. For an eternity, he stared above her head into the everlasting waters gently splashing where the ocean intersected the seashore.

Marley's gaze returned to her face and his eyes burned into hers. "Girl," he whispered, gently tilting her chin. "I make love to you every night in my dream." He lowered his mouth to hers.

Their lips met and Marley's appetite was semi-satisfied. Amani picked up her sandals and held on to him to steady herself as she slipped them on. She stepped lively, in search of a haven to protect them from their heat.

His eyes hungrily followed the graceful execution of her hips as she sashayed through the crowd. Marley touched his cross in agony. "Lard, have mercie."

———————

Thousands of miles later, Amani and Marley were spending a lazy Sunday afternoon rocking in her porch swing and observing the ancient sky, each wishing there was such a place as utopia.

In an ideal world, Amani would want what he wanted. In a flawless world, Marley wouldn't even think of asking her to be someone else. In a perfect world, heads would rule hormones so hearts could love freely. Amani was afraid of losing him. In a supremely excellent world, there would be no reason to fear.

She adjusted her head on his shoulder and her hand on his chest.

Marley interrupted the silence. "Have you decided about school?"

He knew she received acceptance letters from four schools. Cornell, UC Berkeley, USC and UCLA. The way he saw it, the right choice was obvious. His asking was merely a formality.

She released the breath she was holding. "I'm still not sure."

Marley's arm dropped from her shoulders. She lifted her head and removed her hand.

Amani snuck several peeks at the side profile that, no matter what, would be forever seared into her heart, her spirit, and her memory. The thought of leaving his side almost took her breath away, but she had set goals before ever setting eyes on him.

Finally, he turned sad eyes to her. "We're supposed to be inseparable. No one or no thing can come between us. Not ever." His mouth curved into a joyless smile. "Those are more than just words to me."

She repositioned her head against his shoulder and searched the cotton candy-filled sky in response.

"You know we're supposed to be together. I'd be a crazy man without you. I love you, Sunshine." He raised her hand to his mouth and kissed the back of it.

The familiar and welcoming feel of his warm mouth started her to thinking. *UCLA would be a good choice.* Her lips curved into a wry smile. *It is a Shephard tradition.* Amani's voice quivered. "I love you, too, Marley, and I want to spend the rest of my life with you." He embraced her tightly and any future regrets were released inside the circle of his arms.

As she watched him drive away, a few minutes later, she hoped she could afford the price she might have to pay later. She rushed back inside to complete the form she started filling out after church, and then took a quick stroll to their neighborhood mailbox. *We're inseparable.* She wanted to send in her response letter before she changed her mind. Her heart beat faster as she approached the large metal container. She prayed she was making the best choice and that Marley truly believed the words he declared. *No one or no thing can come between us.* He had to because her decision would daily test the strength of their commitment to God and to each other. Olivia's baby girl pulled back the blue lid and stuck an unsteady hand inside. *Not ever.* Marley's sunshine let the envelope go.

Marley continued to ponder Amani's college situation as he undressed for bed. The thought of losing her to a university almost three thousand miles away was making him desperate. If he could make love to her soon, he was certain she would make the right choice, the only choice. His girl placed too high a value on sex to give herself to him then fly away. Once they made love, she would belong to him completely—heart, mind, and body.

He was Marley "Miracle Man" Jamison and he did all things well. Pleasing Amani would be another skill he would hone until he excelled. Once she enrolled at UCLA, they could practice until they met with perfection. When he was ready, they would get married. Marley's mission was to do whatever it took to keep Amani in Los Angeles because he was sure of one thing. If Amani moved to New York, their love story would inevitably end.

SEVENTEEN

It was a perfect day for flying lessons. The sky was a powdery blue and there wasn't even a whisper of a cloud in the sky. She wished it could have been as clear to Marley that her not wanting to have sex had nothing to do with her feelings for him. Marley's Caribbean request coming on the heels of that cheerleader's warning scared her. When they returned from Jamaica, she had begun to sense a restlessness in him that wasn't there before the trip. Or, at least, she hadn't noticed it.

Amani had begun to pray about their situation and believed Marley would soon realize their relationship was stronger than those of couples who confused sex with intimacy. She and Marley were friends, they enjoyed each other's company, and they shared an obvious attraction and a mutual faith. She knew the love they shared could equal a relationship as meaningful to Marley as it was to her, then sex could be taken out of the equation altogether.

While she waited for Marley to fully recognize the value of their relationship as it was, she brainstormed for a way to show him how much his happiness meant to her. Finally, she thought about the secret he had shared months ago and an idea had taken flight. James, from Each One, Reach One Financial Services, had called in a favor from a friend and gotten Amani a remote-controlled glider airplane.

She was sitting on a blanket at Cherry Beach Street Park in Long Beach. Tyreek and Marley were having so much fun flying that they were glowing. They were supposed to take turns but most of the time they shared the remote. The glider plane soared, dived, and somersaulted. The look of pure joy on each of their faces was priceless.

Today, she felt serene as she watched the plane sail.

A friendship had blossomed between two lovely flowers since their Jamaica trip. Amani was in the master bathroom of the Jamison residence, sitting on top of the closed toilet. Jade was attempting to bathe Zoie and Zachary, who were splashing, laughing, and soaking everything in sight. Jade's rich brown hair was pulled back in a ponytail. Her slightly slanted eyes gleamed as she watched her children. Brown lipstick covered their faces, shoulders, and arms.

"Mommy, kiss me right here." Zoie dangled her leg over the tub. Jade picked up the leg and gave it a full-lipped smack.

Zack got on his knees and leaned against the tub. "Don't forget my angel kiss, Mommy." Jade placed a brown kiss on the slightly elevated j-shaped mark on his chest.

Amani's eyes widened. "That looks just like the one Marley has."

Jade turned her head. "You didn't notice his or Kingston's birthmarks when we were in Jamaica?"

Amani shook her head. How could she? Her eyes were too full of her miracle.

"Girl, it's so weird. Mr. J, Kingston, Marley, and Zack all

have one in the same spot. Mr. J said his father, grandfather, and great-grandfather had one, too."

Amani smiled. "What's that old saying? Mama's baby, Papa's maybe. If it's a Jamison boy, the truth is on his chest."

"Hel-lo." Jade high-fived Amani, then rolled up her sleeves and knelt beside the tub. She was wearing one of Kingston's old shirts over gray sweats. She smiled at her children. "Time to wash all the kisses off so you'll have room for more after your bedtime story."

Zoie leaned forward and whispered in her mother's ear. Jade looked at Amani and nodded.

Amani's eyebrow raised as Zoie shared the secret message with her brother. He moved his ear away from her mouth and immediately started clapping his hands against the water.

Amani laughed and wiped her face with her t-shirt. "Hey, I took a shower this morning."

They moved down the hall to the twin's bedroom after Jade finished bathing them and brushing their teeth. Amani helped her to dry, lotion, and dress the Z-team. Afterward, she stood and looked around their bedroom admiringly.

A different scene from Noah's Ark covered each wall. Next to the built-in bookcase was a small table, surrounded by chairs in the shape of an elephant, lion, horse, and camel, and their twin beds were covered with matching animal print comforters. A painted wooden giraffe stood proudly as a coat and hat rack while the corner shelf above Zack's bed held a golden birdcage that had been mounted to the ceiling. Inside, a counterfeit dove held a palm leaf in his beak.

Amani looked over at Jade who was helping her children to pick out a story. She chose an orange book and showed it to them. They cheered and nodded enthusiastically.

Amani interrupted them. "Girl, your decorator got down in here!"

Jade looked at her and smiled. "Thank you. I had the most fun doing their room." She placed her hands on their shoulders. "They inspire me."

Amani's mouth dropped. "You did this?"

She laughed at her young friend's expression. "And wall papered, too."

"Wow." She shook her head. "You have a gift."

"Thanks. Kingston is making decent money as an accountant, however, I plan to finish my degree when they're older and open my own business. Jade Jamison Interior Designs. What do you think?"

"I'm feelin' that. You're going to have family discounts, I hope?"

"Girl, with the paper Marley'll be banking, I'll make sure to charge y'all full price." She laughed, then looked down at Zack and Zoie who were each tugging at her damp shirt. "I haven't forgotten." She smiled at Amani. "Will you please read *Chicka Chicka Boom Boom* to my two Nickelodeon rugbrats, I mean, rats?"

"I'd love to." Amani grinned. "Come on Phil and Lil."

A couple of hours later, Amani and Jade were alone on the small patio adjacent to the master bedroom. It contained a couple of potted trees, a round table, two chairs, and a view of their backyard complete with a swing set and fenced pool.

Jade took a sip of her lemonade. "I understand you have a few gifts of your own."

Amani placed her glass on the coaster. "Well, I enjoy singing and writing poetry, but I don't think I want to make a career out of either one. They're just hobbies."

"I used to want to be the next Whitney Houston."

"Oh, yeah. What happened?"

Jade smiled. "My hot water turns lukewarm then ice cold as soon as I even think about singing in the shower."

Amani laughed.

"It's that bad."

There was a shift in Amani's spirit as she realized something. "Isn't it amazing that God decides who gets which gift? I sing and write. You paint and decorate."

"I never thought of it like that before." Jade placed her glass on the table and reclined in her seat. "You know, Amani. I didn't start going to church until I met Kingston at UCLA." She broke off eye contact. "I thought Kingston was the most beautiful man I'd ever met. He was kind, confident, gorgeous *and a virgin*. That just blew my mind." Her lips turned upward. "I knew I wanted to marry him the first time I met him. Crazy, huh?"

"Nope."

"Anyway, we started dating but he was holding firm to celibacy. I had never been in a relationship that didn't basically revolve around sex. Girl, I was having a hard time. All I could think about was being with him."

Her eyes squinted as she remembered. "I gave him ultimatums, cold shoulders, pressured him, and finally seduced him. We had been dating for two years when he broke. The one time we had sex, I got pregnant.

"I don't think he's ever stopped believing that he disappointed God, his parents, and himself. The worst part of all was he and Marley used to be so close, but after I got pregnant, he distanced himself from Marley and their relationship changed."

"You know what?" She smiled faintly. "I admire you."

"Huh?"

"I love my bambinos but if I knew then what I know now, I would done things differently. I would have honored Kingston's commitment."

"That's deep. Well, this time, Kingston's little brother is doing the pressuring."

Jade's eyes held Amani's. "Don't give in."

"I'm trying not to." A wistful smile rose on Amani's face. "Pray for me, girl."

Jade bowed her head.

Amani's smile widened. When she realized her friend was

serious, she quickly followed suit and squeezed her eyes shut.

Jade's sincere words were comforting. "Father God, I thank you that greater are you who lives in Amani than he that is in the world. Help her to stand firm, Lord. Heavenly Father, help her to choose your instructions over the world's opinions. Help her to be an example to all who will travel this road. When her body screams 'yes,' empower her to tune in to your Spirit whispering 'no.' In Jesus' name, I pray. Amen."

"Amen." Amani lifted her head. "Thank you, Jade."

"Stay strong, girl."

For a brief moment, Olivia thought about pulling her comforter over her head and ignoring the solar beckoning of the May morning sun.

What would be the harm in lying in bed all day? It was her holiday, a day to do what pleased her. Right? Today she'd stay where she was. When she heard a light tapping at her door, she sat up reluctantly but said nothing. The tapping became louder. Seconds later, the door was cracked and two eyes peeked at her then disappeared.

Amani walked into the room, carrying a tray. "Happy Mother's Day, Mama." The tray bore a vegetable omelet, a glass of orange juice, a cup of tea, and a bran muffin. In the top right corner sat a small glass vase adorned with a single red rose. She plastered a smile on her face.

"Thank you, Baby Girl. Everything looks good." She took a sip of orange juice. "Mmmm." Olivia quickly bowed her head and closed her eyes to give thanks before taking a bite of the omelet. "Delicious. Your omelets are every bit as good as the ones your daddy used to make." Olivia sighed and looked out the window.

Amani put her hand on top of her mother's. "I still miss him, too, Mama."

Olivia turned to her daughter. "He would have been so proud of you, of all of you."

"Daddy would have been proud of you, too, Mama. You've done a great job raising us. Thank you for the example you've set. I love you, Mama O." She leaned over and kissed her mother's cheek.

"I love you, too, and thanks for the kind words." Olivia smiled through misty eyes. "I needed them."

Amani chewed her lip.

"Uh-oh. What is it?"

She tilted her head. "How did you know Daddy was the one you wanted to spend the rest of your life with?"

Olivia took a moment before answering. "I loved the fact that your Daddy was confident, but humble. Strong but gentle. He was also a God-fearing man who wasn't afraid to stand up for what he believed in. And he adored me and loved me unconditionally. To top it off, he wasn't bad on the eyesight."

"Mama, Daddy was very handsome."

"I didn't want to seem superficial." She laughed. "Your Daddy was a Cheeto in a bag of Lay's."

Amani wrinkled her nose. "Where do you get this stuff?"

"Six-year-old Montana Rios. His name means mountain and we all call him Monte for short. His body may have leukemia, but his spirit is untouched. I prayed I wouldn't see him again when he left the hospital last fall." She sighed heavily. "But he had a recent relapse."

Amani could tell her mother was as personally involved with this patient as she was professionally. She touched her mother's shoulder. "I'll send up a prayer for him, too."

"Thanks, baby." Olivia patted her hand absently.

Amani knew she was being selfish, but she wanted to talk about *her* situation because she was trying hard not to have a relapse of her own. She stared at a picture of Marcus and Olivia on the dresser then turned to her mother. "I love Marley, Mama. I believe he's the one, but I want to do things the right way. Like you and Daddy did."

Olivia took a sip of her tea and nodded her head. "Ask the Lord to give you the strength to do the right thing, especially when doing wrong seems easier." She looked toward the window for a few minutes before speaking again. "We better hurry and get ready for church. There will be so many mothers there today, it's gonna look like the Million Mama March."

Olivia chuckled at her own joke while Amani said a silent prayer for Monte, and then one for herself. She was doing her best to march to the rhythms of her spirit's drum, but her flesh was singing a different tune, a song Amani found herself humming whenever she was with Marley.

———

In place of Pastor Chamberlain Hilton bringing the Word, his helpmate and co-pastor, as petite as she was powerful, was slicing up the bread of life. New Horizons Christian Center was holding its annual Women's Day Program. The morning's message was "This Womb Holds Greatness."

Sister Rachel walked up and down the aisles of the church, making eye contact with those sisters strong enough to hold the intensity of her gaze. The spirit was high and a silent tempo beat steadily. Only those who had come prepared to dine heard it.

Her silver close-cropped mane had an earthy, yet elegant effect. The first lady's golden-hued complexion glistened not from perspiration, but from the anointing that rested upon her. Sister Rachel wore a gray two-piece skirt set with silver buttons. The same pink carnation worn by every female congregant rested over her heart. She was holding a pink lace handkerchief in her French-manicured hands.

"Ladies, when you know who you are and the potential you carry, you force yourself to say no to ungodly relationships. You don't spend dangerous time on your back, underneath any and every man that makes your temperature fluctuate. You are able to plant your feet firmly in the face of raging hormones and stand your ground. You *practice* being strong."

Sister Rachel wiped her face. "Young Mary was tenacious and determined. Imagine for a moment, if you will. She was engaged to marry another man when the Holy Spirit hovered over her and claimed her as a vessel fit for the Master's use. Her womb became a place of honor for it contained the manifested presence of God in the flesh. Je-sus. He who would become the Saviour of the world."

She paused. "Nowadays, we take our bodies, our wombs so lightly. All it takes is for some man to say he loves us, and we allow him to plant seeds in our wombs. For some of us, it don't even take that. A movie and a Big Mac and he's in like Errol Flynn." She shook her head. "Don't have marriage license the first. In those cases where a marriage license does exist, either your name ain't on his or his ain't on yours. "Y'all don't know the man well enough to know what other grounds he's been farming, or even how well he takes care of the crops once the harvest arrives.

"I submit to you this morning that the same Holy Spirit that impregnated Mary has impregnated us." She rubbed her right hand over her stomach in a circular motion. "This womb holds greatness. Your womb holds greatness. I'm not talking about the ability to give birth to a baby. That truly is a blessing from God, but He chose only one woman to give birth to His son. For the rest of us, our awesome task is to give birth to the visions, dreams, and talents our Heavenly Father has placed inside of each and every one of us."

She placed her hands on her hips. "The next time lust whispers in your ear, you tell that foul devil 'You got the wrong one, baby. My womb holds greatness. I don't let just any seeds up in here. My body is a living, breathing, holy temple of God and I'm gonna use it to birth His plan and purpose for my life.' This morning, we submit ourselves to His perfect will and we declare that we shall bring forth all that God has placed within us. Stand to your feet and let's worship Him."

Sister Rachel walked back to the stage and sat at the organ. The earlier rhythms that could only be felt by the spirit were now pulsating throughout the building.

Olivia looked on with bewilderment as all seven of her daughters rose and took their places on the raised platform. The eldest Shephard girl stepped forward and spoke on her sisters' behalf. "Where would we be without praying mothers? The prevailing prayer of a woman moves things. We'd like to dedicate this song to our awesome mothers, Olivia Shephard, our natural mother, and to our godmother, Oneita Armstrong, as well as to all the mothers and precious women of God gathered here today. Happy Mother's Day."

Perri stepped back. From oldest to youngest they formed a semi-circle. They either wore white, gray, pink, or some combination of those colors, and could have headed straight to an *Essence* magazine photo shoot after church. Soprano mixed with alto and tenor to blend into an eternal stream of salvation. Tramaine Hawkins' "A Change Has Come Over Me" invited hand waving, self-reflection, and private repentance among both listeners and singers alike.

They sang of Jesus' ability to change lives, set folks free, and wash away sins, leaving once broken people whole and delivered.

Their voices were a mixture of jazzy chords with down-home gospel flavoring. The Shephards' Voice, a name their father gave them years before, raised their hands and harmonized as the river flowed.

Perri wept for the many mistakes she made before she stopped dating altogether. Vanessa wept for those times she allowed her body to be a dumping ground, and for the uncertain future she faced with Khalil and the girls. Krystal wept because, in her quest to belong to someone, she failed the Lord time and time again.

Nola wept because God had forgiven her and blessed her with three beautiful Mills men. Rosalind wept because the Lord had wiped her slate clean and sent her Simeon. Mia wept because her desire to snag Roland far outweighed her desire to please the Lord. Amani wept for the final decision she would have to make and for the compromises she had made along the way.

Olivia beamed as she wiped her own tears away. Yet, a portion of her heart cried for a burden whose weight had become too heavy to tote alone. She looked across the aisle at her sister-friend. Their eyes locked. She felt as proud as Oneita looked.

Olivia Dupree Shephard stood with the rest of the church. With her head and hands lifted to the Lord, she resolved to wade through the troubled and murky waters of her soul.

It was time to take her life back.

SUMMER

A time to love, and a time to hate; a time of war, and a time of peace.

Ecclesiastes 3:8

EIGHTEEN

They were alone in Marley's apartment for the first time since their February fiasco. Amani was thrilled that Marley had chosen to cook her dinner in honor of her eighteenth birthday. The menu consisted of curried chicken, rice and peas, plantains, a tossed salad, and for dessert, he baked a seven-up cake.

He sang as he brought the cake from the kitchen and made room for it on the small, circular dining table. Amani joined him in singing the Stevie Wonder rendition of "Happy Birthday." She felt content and grateful as she said a silent prayer. *Thank you, Jesus.* She was wearing a pair of flare-legged jeans with a navy tube top that covered her entire midriff area and a pair of wide-heeled silver sandals.

Marley pulled her close and kissed her gently on the nose. "If you can help me sing 'Happy Birthday,' I should be able to help you make a wish." He let her go and reached into the front pocket of the blue and white Hawaiian shirt he was wearing with a pair of faded Levi's. *Mmmm, mmmm, mmmm.* Her baby was wearing those jeans and that beard surrounding his full mouth made him look even sexier.

She grabbed his free hand. "Have I told you lately that I'm feelin' that goatee?"

Marley rubbed his chin. "Yep." He smiled. "Have I told you lately that I love you?"

Amani's heart beat furiously as she nodded. She knew any minute it would burst from her chest and land in the middle of the cake. Marley's cologne, along with his lavish attention, was making her weak. Her present was in his hand. "Close your eyes," he ordered in a low voice.

Kirk Whalum's sweet serenade played softly in the background, adding to the evening's ambiance. She felt him fastening her gift around her neck. His lingering hands and virile nearness made her want to be nice and naughty. Though it was the month of June, she was hotter than July.

Marley's hands moved from her neck to her bare shoulders, down her spine and started back again. He expertly massaged all points of contact as he journeyed.

"Marley—"

"Give me your hand, baby."

Like a blindfolded puppet, she complied as she hesitantly followed his lead.

Marley straightened the necklace then placed his hands on her shoulders. His lips brushed her ear. "Open your eyes."

She was now standing in front of the mirror that hung over the low bookshelf. Amani gasped. The silver cascading pearl necklace complemented her skin and her outfit. "Oh, Marley, it's beautiful." She kissed his cheek then faced the mirror, wrapping his arms around her waist. "Thank you, baby."

"You're welcome."

"You really do love me."

"With all my heart." He kissed her shoulder. "No one or no thing can come between us."

"Boomerang, Miracle Man. We're inseparable."

They stared at each other with flames of love simmering in their gazes.

"Even if I wasn't UCLA's Miracle Man, I'd still want to be me. You got me on a natural high and I've gotten used to wearing this feeling." He rested his head gently on top of hers.

She wanted to prolong this moment. For in her heart, she knew this night would change her forever.

Like statutes carved from flesh and blood, they posed in the looking glass. "Amani, it's not my birthday, but I have a wish—"

"Marley, don't—"

"It's not a new wish. It's what I wish every time I taste your kiss, inhale your perfume, hold you." He turned her around to face him. "I want us to make love, Amani."

He was even more breathtaking face-to-face. And that goatee—it did something to her. He was a man wanting to be with his woman. She was a woman wanting to hold on to her man. She could feel herself falling, just like in her reoccurring dream about falling from a cliff. Amani could never tell if she had jumped or been pushed. No matter. In her dream, she always managed to wake up before it was too late. This time, she was dreaming without a safety net, and she feared it was already too late.

Breaking through the fog, her mother's voice haunted her. *No matter where you go or what you do, God's watching.* She shook her head slowly. "I . . . we can't, Marley. You're not my husband."

"I want to be with you now, Amani, not down the road."

"You made the same commitment to God."

"How can it be wrong for me to express how I feel about you in all the ways a man shows love for his woman?" He placed his forefinger under her chin and tilted her head. His eyes bore into hers. "Are you my lady or still your daddy's little girl?"

She jerked her chin from his hand as her brown eyes turned misty. "Please don't do this." Her words were soaked with tears. "It sounds like you're giving me an ultimatum."

"You can call it what you want." He quickly turned, walked to the sofa, and fell onto it. "I'm sick of this crap." He put his elbows on his knees and dropped his head in his hands. Amani watched him and knew he had become the reason why she sang, smiled, breathed. After a few moments of silence, he looked up at her. As if on cue, a silent tear slid down his face. Amani ached to go to him, but she held back.

Marley looked like a lost little boy. Everything in her wanted to help him find his way back to her. She longed to lead him to the home they had built, one caress at a time. But she knew if she touched him now, they would not stop until they discovered that sacred place within each other.

The last musical note played on the CD player and a quiet tension invaded the room. She wondered what happened to the young man who had prevented them from going too far on Valentine's night. When her passion had overtaken her, he was the sensible one. Tonight was her opportunity to return the favor and tomorrow, he would thank her. No matter what, she would stay strong for both of them.

She walked to the sofa and sat beside him. Coasting on the verge of tears, she reached for him and placed her hand on his bare arm. His face wore a combination of hurt and anger while her emotions were masked under a façade of cool control.

"Marley, we don't have to make love to prove our feelings. That's the world's way. Let's think this through."

"I already have. My heart ain't nothing but a studio for the Amani Shephard Show. I think about you as much as I do basketball. I love you, and I want you to be my first." His mouth curved into a wry smile. "That's supposed to be your line." As suddenly as he'd smiled, his expression hardened. "The prom is in a week. If you're really into me like I'm into you, you'll be ready to take our relationship to the next level."

Until that moment, she had no idea heartbreak was more

than a figure of speech. His words ripped her heart as if it were crepe paper. Her tears washed away all traces of her "collectedness" and her mask slipped off. Amani's hand fiercely grasped his because she was drowning and he had become her lifeline. She felt five years old again—vulnerable, needy, and insecure.

Her wet face leaned into his. "What are you saying, Marley?" Her heart beat faster when he wouldn't even look at her and a feeling of doom pervaded her senses.

He snatched his hand away and got up. After programming a new song on the CD player, he moved to the table and cut himself a slice of cake. She watched him in disbelief. With a lump the size of a watermelon in her throat, she hurried over to the table and sat across from him. He kept his head down as he ate his cake. Suddenly, a rush of heat overwhelmed her. This man was not sitting there eating *her* birthday cake with pieces of the heart he broke all over it. She wanted to slap him for real.

After several minutes, he lifted his head and met her gaze. For a moment, his eyes told the whole truth. Before she could freeze the confused longing she saw in them, a cloud of nonchalance rolled in and he got up and walked into the kitchen.

Amani's teeth sunk into her lower lip as she toyed with her pearls. Searching her bank of memories, she withdrew those supporting her belief that the investments they had made in their eight-month relationship were solid. A myriad of emotions tossed around within her, but there was one thing she knew for sure.

She needed him and he needed her.

However, Boyz II Men sang it differently. In harmony, they informed her that Marley could do just fine without her. She looked over at him washing dishes, more gorgeous than she'd ever seen him, singing in the off-key voice she adored.

Another song was in Amani's heart. Sade's "Love is Stronger than Pride" encouraged her as she got up and walked into the small kitchen separated from the dining area by a doorway. She squeezed herself in between the sink and Marley, put her hands under his shirt and began caressing his back. Without looking at her, he turned off the water and rested his soapy hands on the counter.

She kissed his chin and nuzzled his neck. The scent of him set her soul to stirring. She whispered in his ear. "I love you, Marley, and I want you to be my first *and* only."

He gave her a seductive grin and hastily dried his hands on his jeans, then placed them on her shoulders. "Do you mean that, baby?" Marley knew she would stay in L.A. if they made love.

Amani's hands glided from his back to his chest. "Yes." She kissed him with a fervor that reinforced the truth of her statement. After a few minutes, she stopped. The muscles in her neck were tight and cramped. She massaged it, hoping her kiss had succeeded in reminding him that she was worth the wait.

He effortlessly picked her up and placed her on the counter. Gazing into her eyes, he put his hands on her forearms. "You're so beautiful, Nikki," he breathed into her ear. "I promise I'll never leave you."

His mouth spoke the words her heart wanted to hear.

Marley put his hands in her thick mane and teased her waiting mouth with a game of tongue tag, giving her a succession of short and sweet afterthoughts. His touch moved below her neck and she rested her face on his shoulder, allowing his fingers to do the talking. Her body responded automatically because her willpower was no match for his eloquent hands.

His exploring hands and fingers were naturally skilled and if she didn't stop him soon, their destination would be clear.

Why couldn't she just give in? *No matter where you go or what you do, God's watching.* As she lifted her head, she forcefully removed his hands.

Undaunted, he placed them on her hips. "I bought a box of condoms before we went to Jamaica. I guess I was hoping we could finish what we started on Valentine's night, but that's okay. Your prom will be our special night."

Amani looked down. She could see his excitement was not only in his voice. Their bodies were speaking the same language. How many more times would she be able to say no? She braced herself before looking into his eyes.

"We've gone almost a year without having sex, Marley. We can go until we get married if we stop setting ourselves up like we've been doing. Look at Taylor and Regina. They've been celibate for almost four years. If they can—"

"I'm not trying to hear that!" He removed her hands from around his waist and stepped back. "You're not Gina and I'm not Tee. You have one week to decide if you're ready to make love."

"And if I'm not?"

"It's been real." He continued staring at her. "Wanna know something? You have no idea how many females want to be you." His steady gaze challenged her and his chilling words pierced her heart.

Amani's left hand grabbed the spot where her pledge of allegiance to Marley resided as he brushed past her. Tears of frustration burned her eyes. She jumped down from the sink counter and leaned against the doorway watching him. How could being in love hurt so much?

Marley was standing in front of the portable CD player on top of his bookcase. Searching through the tall, rectangular CD stand, he found what he was searching for. He replaced Boyz II Men with his new spokesperson.

Marley glanced at Amani then strolled down the hallway to his bedroom.

Amani remained glued to the doorway of decision.

They had advanced from kissing only to kissing and caressing. She had hoped it would remain enough to satisfy him, especially since they both belonged to Christ. But he was obviously bored with the appetizers and ready for the main course. It seemed the closer they became, the more they distanced themselves from God.

She had stopped reading her Bible and listening to teaching tapes and gospel music the way she used to. Her regular talks with God had become scarce. Amani didn't have much use for praying because every prayer she had ever prayed was manifested in the gift of Marley's love.

Amani's strength to say no to Marley was connected to her ability to say yes to God. She sadly realized her desire to please the Lord had taken second place to her need for Marley's companionship.

Make love or lose Marley?

Either way, her decision would cost her something meaningful. The sound of the telephone ringing in the kitchen jarred her out of her thoughts.

Through blurry eyes, she stared at the digital clock on the microwave. 11:09.

Marley rushed into the kitchen wearing only a pair of red silk pajama pants. His eyes told her he was surprised to see her still standing where he had left her twenty minutes ago. She stretched out her hand to him, but he stepped out of her reach and grabbed the phone.

Her eyes followed him and rested on the insignia he wore on his bare arm. She wondered why he would do something as permanent as a tattoo if their relationship could be only temporary? Though she'd presented him with her heart of flesh, it wasn't enough. Amani intently listened to the voice that had come to mean more to her than any other.

"Hello. Naw. I'm still up. I was just thinking about you, too, sweetheart."

Marley covered the mouthpiece. "Happy Birthday, Amani. Goodnight." An animated Marley went into his bedroom with another woman and shut the door.

There was no holding back the stream of tears flowing across her face. Amani gathered her sweater, purse, and the keys to her mother's Toyota Land Cruiser. She looked at the cake on the table. It was missing a big chunk just like her heart. She carefully lifted it from the plate and quickly carried it into the kitchen where she dumped it in the dishwater. It sank to the bottom, quickly overtaken by suds.

Though she had won all previous battles, she doubted she could win this war. She loved Marley too much and, although she felt completely humiliated, her love for him remained intense. Amani loved God, too, but this was different.

Marley's presence in her life took her back to days with her father.

Her father's eyes told her she was valuable to him and precious. So did Marley's. Her father's strong arms made her feel safe from all harm. So did Marley's. Her father left and never came back. If she kept her commitment to God, so would Marley.

On her way out the door, Brian McKnight's "One Last Cry" made her sob even harder.

———

Marley placed the telephone on the receiver and jumped off the bed. He walked to the door and cracked it. All he heard was his boy Brian singing his heart out. He walked over to his dresser, picked up her favorite cologne, and gave his bare chest and back a light spritz. Next, he opened the miniature bottle of Listerine he kept in his dresser drawer and took a swig. He'd never met anyone like her and she was driving him loco.

His thoughts and feelings were all twisted up. Instead of buying a necklace for her birthday, he almost charged an engagement ring on his credit card. He hadn't expected to see her standing there when he walked into the kitchen, but his mother couldn't have called at a more opportune moment. He almost laughed at the sorrow-filled expression on Amani's face. She needed to feel the hurt he felt. He hadn't experienced rejection since his middle school days. The memories were usually fleeting, but Amani took him back there every time she turned him down.

In the past, he boldly let many a female know his definition of safe sex was saved sex. Before Amani, his motto was "The truly strong abstain." Before Amani, he used to think Kingston was a wimp. Before Amani, he had never failed a test. but God didn't grade on the curve and he was flunking out. Now, he fully understood the disarming effects of love. Being repeatedly told no, however, was becoming a problem. He wasn't about to get used to receiving rejection from any female, not even one he adored with everything in him.

He respected her desire to live according to the Word and he had the same desire. However, a part of him was beginning to believe there was such a thing as sex in moderation. He and Amani could make love occasionally because they planned to get married. As long as they refused to allow sex to become the center of their relationship, they would be all right and, perhaps, God would understand. There was also another part of him that hated being weak when it came to his commitment to celibacy until marriage. Even still, the primary thing on his mind outside of shooting hoops was making love to his lady.

He put his hand on the doorknob. If Amani was still there, she had already changed her mind, and they would make love tonight. Or else they would in seven days. If she had gone home after hearing him on the phone, allegedly talking to another woman, she was going to stand her ground.

So would he.

Marley turned the knob, feeling like he did when he was fouled and had to go to the free throw line. He always gave it his best shot. Inwardly, he agonized over whether victory or defeat awaited him. He widened the door and walked out under the pretense that it was time to change the tune.

Forcing an air of indifference, he sorted through his collection of CDs. It took only a few seconds for him to realize that, though the aroma of Amani's presence lingered, he was alone. Marley re-programmed "One Last Cry", this time setting it on repeat. Then he went into his bedroom and yanked open a drawer.

He bypassed the unopened box of condoms that sat in the narrow space between two stacks of underwear and dug around for the little black book he had almost thrown out when he met Amani. She had it like that.

Marley did a belly flop onto his bed and began flipping through his customized version of the yellow pages. He reached past the picture on his nightstand and picked up the phone and dialed. The phone rang several times. He was about to hang up when she answered.

"Hello."

Silence.

"Hel-lo."

"Hey."

"Marley?"

"Yeah."

"Stop playing. Who's this?"

"It's me."

"What's up, Miracle Man?"

"Come over."

"Why?"

"I need a friend."

"Where's your *girlfriend*?"

"Don't have one."

"Y'all broke up?"

"Something like that." His ego was in need of repair. "How fast can you get here?"

"Quicker than in a hurry."

"You remember where I live?"

"Is fat meat greasy?"

His smile was faint. "All right then."

Marley hung up the phone and stared at the photo they had taken at the Sweetheart Dance. Every time he looked at it, he thought about what almost happened. He thought he was doing the right thing that night. Tonight, he wanted to kick himself because he couldn't have been more wrong. If they had made love then, they'd probably be making love right this minute. Instead Amani had forced him to celebrate the rest of her birthday with somebody else.

It was obvious his girl didn't love him as much as he loved her. It felt frightening and unfamiliar for him to want some female more than she wanted him. He would make sure it never happened again. Sticking the picture in the bottom drawer of his nightstand, he slammed it shut.

Then he rolled over and went to use the bathroom. When he finished, he washed his hands, then pulled open the bathroom drawer and brushed his hair. Staring at his reflection, he was glad he had grown the goatee. It added character to his boyish face, and Amani let him know more than once how much she loved it. All the females did and they told him through their eyes or with their words. His mother was the only one who didn't like it. *Bwoy, yu lek a likkle bwoy a barrow him papa face.*

The cross his mother gave him when he turned eleven glared at him. It was a gift for his having made the same commitment to celibacy Amani had made regularly for the last several years.

His eyes locked on the tattooed tribute. She left her mark in more ways than one. Right now, he needed someone to help ease the pain he felt. Tamara would have to do. The only other time she'd been to his place was for a get-together he hosted in honor of his nineteenth birthday. That was Friday, September 28. Earlier that evening, his parents presented him with a brand new Cadillac Escalade. Two weeks and a day later, he met the only female who had ever gotten next to him. The only female to make him lose control. The only female ever to reject the Miracle Man.

Marley may have been a fool in love, but he was no dummy. There was one thing he knew for sure. Only Amani Nicole Shephard could erase the big, black 'keep out' he hastily scrawled across his rebounding heart.

———

Bitter drops of rain washed away her sense of time and place. Amani remembered crying like this only once before when she'd had to tell her daddy good-bye. Forever. Hiccupping, Amani wiped her eyes and face with the back of her hand. Then she took a tissue from the Kleenex box in the passenger seat and blew her nose. Seven days to decide whether to disregard the vow of chastity she had lived by for seven years.

She let down the visor and looked at herself in the small, lighted mirror. "Oh, Daddy, what should I do?"

The Holy Spirit gently reminded her of a scripture. *Put on the whole armor of God, that you may be able to stand against the wiles of the devil.* Her pastors had encouraged the members to memorize that verse and where it was found in the Bible. Ephesians Chapter 6, Verse 11. Of course, Marley wasn't the devil, but the devil was behind the spirit of lust egging him on.

If she chose to do things God's way, their love was lost. If she followed Marley's lead, she would lose herself.

Amani turned the key in the ignition and prayed aloud. "Give me the strength to do your Will, Lord." Although she hadn't spoken to God in awhile, she knew He heard her. Before driving off, she glanced into the side mirror then started her journey home.

Half an hour later, Amani pulled into the driveway and reached for the garage door remote. Her hand quickly dropped onto her lap when she noticed her godmother's Jaguar parked on the other side of the driveway. Even in her disheveled state, Amani found it strange that she was visiting so late.

Then she remembered that Father's Day was swiftly approaching and that her mother became slightly depressed this time every year.

Amani didn't want to mess up her first time driving on her own by leaving the Land Cruiser in the driveway, but she didn't feel like exchanging pleasantries, which she would certainly have to do if she went in through the garage that led to the kitchen. Olivia and Oneita were probably sitting at the kitchen table or at the counter, looking at old photo albums, and reminiscing about better days. She couldn't go in through the living room either because her mother would be sure to hear the front door open.

She decided to sneak in through the back door because she didn't want to speak to anybody. If she tried to tell it, she feared she would start weeping again and never stop.

Not even when morning came.

The serene sounds of jazz could be heard from behind the closed door. Before entering the building, Destiny had sat in her car, waiting and watching her friend boo-hoo like a baby pushed from the confines of its mother's comfy womb. Sex. Destiny was certain they fought over that very issue. Apparently, he was ready to do the do. Her intuition told her a vulnerable Miracle Man was simply a threshold away. Yet, she hesitated before knocking.

Destiny's hand shook as she took out her compact and quickly blotted her face with Cornsilk powder to reduce its annoying shine. She pressed her lips together, smoothed down her blouse, then knocked firmly on the door.

Marley opened it a crack and quickly turned away, not even bothering to acknowledge her. Her breath caught in her throat. He had on a pair of red silk pajama bottoms without the top. *What is wrong with Amani?* Already, Marley and his cologne were seducing all five of her senses. Destiny's sixth sense was having enough sense to do whatever he wanted. She would consider allowing herself to be used while getting what she wanted in the process.

Softly, she pushed the door close. Marley lay on the sofa with his eyes shut. With every step she took toward him, her heartbeat accelerated. His right hand was on his chest below the golden cross he was never without, and his left hand tapped on the edge of the black leather sofa, keeping time to the music. Destiny made herself comfortable on the floor beside him and reached for his hand.

It was difficult to ignore the graphic reminder of Amani's hold on him that was staring her in the face. A few months ago he'd proudly explained the significance of the eternal emblem. Before the sun rose, the heart could symbolize that his now belonged to her. The wave, in its center, would represent that hope floats. Hope had kept her believing they would one day be together, one way or another.

Amani unlocked the back door. She kept her fist around the rest of the keys to prevent any jingling. Her plan was to tiptoe from the family room through the living room then up the stairs to her double bed. There she'd struggle to forget until sleep embraced her.

The kitchen and living room lights were on, but she knew the two women were sitting at the kitchen table under a stack of photo albums. Together they were taking their annual trip down those-were-the-days drive. Amani turned and quietly shut the door behind her. She was surprised they couldn't hear her heart breaking with every silent step she took.

Just as she reached the doorway, she heard a familiar cough. Her mother and godmother were in the living room. No matter how much tiptoeing she did, she couldn't sneak up to her room. Amani sighed and shook her head. "I don't believe this."

Amani backed up and lay down on the rust-colored sofa in the family room. Feeling a hundred years old, instead of eighteen, she took off her navy sweater, dropped her purse on the floor, and kicked off her shoes. Then she lay on her stomach and buried her face in her folded arms.

Amani quickly straightened up a few seconds later. She had never been a nosey child, but it sounded like Mama was crying. Her godmother kept repeating the same thing. "Jesus. Jesus. Jesus." Amani crept over to the bookcase adjacent to the doorway and peeked at them. Although her mother was customarily down during the month of June, she didn't usually cry.

Both women's backs faced her as they sat side by side on the loveseat. Her mother's brown curls almost touched her godmother's black micro-braids.

Her godmother was clasping her mother's hands and talking to the lover of her soul. "This is your child, Lord. Help her tonight. Your Word declares we have all sinned and come short of your glory. But when we confess our sins, hallelujah, you are faithful and just to forgive us and cleanse us from all unrighteousness. We're thankful, Lord, that you're not like man. When you forgive, you forget. Heavenly Father, let my sister experience your forgiveness to the depths of her very being. In Jesus' Name, I pray. Amen." She paused. "Olivia, you know I love you and so does God. Years ago, I shared with you how my being so promiscuous when I was younger destroyed my chances of ever giving birth to a child. I carried my secret with me a long time. Bennie was the only person who knew the real reason why I couldn't have children."

Oneita rubbed her sister's back. "Come on, baby. It's time for you to kick every one of those skeletons out of the closet."

Amani held her breath as she listened to her mother's sobs. Many, many moments passed until Olivia was composed enough to speak and, even then, Amani had to strain to hear her mother as she "lay her burdens down."

Olivia focused her eyes on the grandfather clock. "I was pregnant when I married Marcus. Please don't hate me, Oneita. Here you were wanting a baby, and I . . . I . . ." Olivia's shoulders began to heave as Oneita held her in her arms. "*I killed my baby,*" she howled.

What? Amani tried to digest her mother's revelation. If she hadn't heard it with her own ears, she would have called anyone attempting to share this information with her an ugly liar who was going to roast in hell. *Did Mama just say she had an abortion?* No, she must have misunderstood.

Amani stumbled into the living room and faced her mother. Olivia's horrified expression answered her daughter's unasked question. Amani doubled over, grabbing her stomach. She thought she was all cried out. "No, Mama. No! Oh, God. How could you? You lied to me . . . to all of us." She lifted a hand to her forehead. "Why, Mommy?" Amani whimpered.

Olivia jumped up and started toward her daughter, her face flushed with tears sluicing down her face. She extended her arms to her . . . eighth child.

"Don't you touch me!" Amani shrieked and ran up the stairs.

Olivia threw her hands in the air as she turned to Oneita. Oneita's only offering was, "Give her some time to cool off, O."

She usually valued her best friend's words, but this time Olivia ignored her and raced to the top of the stairs.

"Amani, baby," she cried over and over. She had no idea how she could ever make her daughter understand. What she did know was that it was time to begin at the beginning.

Time to accept the truth of her past, acknowledge the lies of her present, and rid her future of all regrets—for her sake and Amani's.

————————

Amani paced her bedroom floor with her arms locked around her. This was worse than Marley changing his mind about sex. Her whole life had been a lie and her mother was the deceiver.

She felt like a thirsty woman lost in the desert. In the distance, she sees a pond full of refreshing water. She takes off running with everything left in her, only to realize it's a mind game. There's nothing to drink, just more sand. All she had believed for eighteen years was nothing more than a mirage.

She crouched on her knees and reached under her bed. Standing, she held the plastic container in which she kept her blow dryer, hair care products, manicure and pedicure kits, her favorite nail polishes, aromatic scented lotions, and a pair of scissors. With one swift movement, she swept everything off the dresser onto the floor and set the container down. Snapping off the lid, she grabbed the scissors she was barely able to see through her tears.

"Amani, baby, let me in." Her mother banged on the door.

She began to slowly inhale and exhale in an attempt to calm herself. Then she looked into the mirror. Had it not been for the little girl in her who still believed the seven years of bad luck story, she would have broken it. Amani did one better. She snatched handfuls of hair and began cutting.

As she opened and closed the scissors, she felt a strange sisterhood with the betrayed wife in the movie *Waiting to Exhale* who ordered her beautician to hack off her lengthy locks to rid herself of the look she associated with her cheating husband. Amani remembered grimacing during that scene because many sisters paid retail for their long hair.

However, tonight she was doing some disassociating of her own. It was time to cut a deceitful mother right out of her hair. The sixth Shephard sister's commentary on the long locks issue was summed up in true Mia fashion. "If ya can't grow it, let me sew it" or "If you can't achieve it, Hair Master Mia will be happy to weave it."

Her crude comments used to make Amani self-conscious. Looking down at the piles of hair on the floor, she felt naked. She picked up the bottle of moisturizing hair gel and quickly molded her impromptu afro. With her high cheekbones and cascades of pearls falling from her neck, she looked like a warring African princess. Amani was on a mission to betray her betrayer.

Continuing to ignore her mother's pleas from behind the locked door, Amani brushed the hair off her neck and shoulders and studied her reflection. *If Mama is not who I thought she was, what does that make me?* She wasn't quite sure who returned her stare, but she was determined to find out. For the last seven years, she had attempted to step in each of her mother's footprints. The time had come for her to carve out a path of her own.

Finally, she opened the door and rushed past her mother, almost knocking her down. Her godmother waited for her at the foot of the stairs. Oneita's mouth dropped and she brought her hand to her cheek. "And what is cutting off all your hair supposed to prove?"

"That I don't want to be anything like Mama. She *lied*."

Oneita took her youngest goddaughter by the shoulders. Her still unlined, dark chocolate face glistened. "God has forgiven all. It's not your place to judge. The good book says children are to honor their father *and* mother. You know better than to be disrespectful."

Amani shrugged off her godmother's hands. "The Bible also says God hates hands that shed innocent blood."

Her godmother winced, a look of compassion with a side of

sternness was on her face. "Just keep going to bed and waking up, Baby Girl. You won't get out of this life without making mistakes."

"Tell me about it." Brushing past her godmother, she stormed back into the family room. Amani snatched up her sweater, grabbed her purse from the floor, and wiggled her feet into her silver sandals. Her eyes met her godmother's who was standing in the half-lit doorway, praying softly under her breath.

Before Oneita could intercede any further on her best friend's behalf, Amani opened the door and stepped briskly into the dark of night.

Oneita felt something brush against her arm and slowly turned from the open door and looked at her friend. Olivia's swollen eyes and face were flooded with tears and pain. She was hugging armfuls of Amani's hair to her chest. Oneita reached out to hold her. Gently, they swayed from side to side while Oneita called on the name above every other, "Jesus. Jesus. Jesus."

NINETEEN

Tonight, patience would be her sole virtue. Destiny listened to Marley's light snores and continued to hold his hand. With her other hand, she opened her brown leather backpack and stuffed the small gift bag into it. It was after midnight. Though the outside air had cooled, she was burning up. Destiny reluctantly let go of his hand, slipped out of her jean jacket, and let it fall to the floor. She was wearing a pair of cuffed jeans and a yellow wrap shirt. Several ponytails had been styled waterfall fashion at the front of her head.

She quickly rummaged through her backpack and took out a small bottle of Purely Pear perfume. Destiny sprayed some behind each earlobe and on her wrist before retrieving his hand. The perfume seemed to revive him because his eyes fluttered then opened. But his brow furrowed deeply as he stared at her.

It was obvious hers was not the face he hoped to see.

Marley rubbed his chest, sat up, and extended his arms over his head. Destiny's nose drank in the scent of him and her 20/20 vision zoomed in for a close-up. His new goatee and regular six-pack made her want to pack her bags and move in.

He squinted. "Hey." His voice was emotionless.

"Hi." She almost swallowed her ears.

"Amani wears Purely Pear perfume sometimes." He yawned. "I was dreaming she came back."

Her smile immediately slid into a frown. "What happened?"

"I'm ready to retire this code of celibacy I've been wearing and—"

"Your girl's not coming to the retirement party, is she?"

He shrugged. "I gave her until prom night to decide, but I think she already has."

My girl deserves a medal. "There are not many sisters who could hold out."

"How about you?"

"What?"

"Could you turn me down?"

Destiny stared into his eyes. *This is your best friend's man. Yeah, but I met him first.* Mesmerized, her eyes never left his face as she shook her head. Marley pulled her onto the sofa beside him.

She wasn't dreaming this time. Marley wanted her. Miracle. Magnificent. Marvelous. All three titles were befitting. *This is crazy*, she thought as she closed her eyes and fell into the sensation of being in his arms. It was better than anything she could have imagined. The muscles in his forearms were taut under her hold. She wanted to kiss his bare torso, but she forced herself to wait on him. Her body would go wherever his led. Waves of exhilaration rolled over her as she received his kisses on her forehead, up one side of her face and down the other. They were a breath away from their lips finally meeting.

His mouth brushed her cheek, "I love you so much, Amani."

She pushed him away. *What was I thinking?* "You better save the playing for the court."

"I'm trippin'." He sat back and rested his head against the sofa. "Destiny, I'm sorry."

So was she. However, the bewildered look on his face touched her and she actually felt bad for him. Destiny stared at him, seeing him for the first time. He wasn't some trophy to be earned but a person with feelings, hopes, and disappointments just like her. There was nothing phony about the pain she saw in his eyes. "You really are into her."

Marley nodded in response.

She knew there wasn't a thing right about what almost happened between them because she also loved Amani and desired to live for the Lord. She surprised both Marley and herself when she offered him a shoulder to lean on. For about fifteen minutes, he rested his head on her shoulder in contemplative silence. In that time, a new alliance was formed as Wayman Tisdale's horn wailed in the background.

Suddenly, Destiny remembered why she had come and moved toward her backpack. Marley fell over.

"Oops!"

"Thanks for warning me." He rested his head on the arm of the sofa.

She unzipped the backpack. "I want to show you what I bought our girl for her birthday."

Seconds later, their eyes were drawn to the door as the knob turned and it opened. Light from the outside illuminated the scarcely lit living room. Marley jumped up as his unexpected guest reached for the light switch.

Amani couldn't tell if they were more shocked at seeing her or her new haircut. Her eyes shot darts of fury at Marley.

She dangled the key. "In case of an emergency, remember?" Amani directed a threatening look toward his visitor. "Did you give him what he wanted?"

Marley walked toward her with his palms facing her. "Amani, it wasn't even like that."

"I thought I had until prom night to decide." She shook her

head in disgust. "You're that hard up, you had to call her?"

Destiny stood. "He didn't call me, and he's telling you the truth. Nothing happened." She reached into her backpack. "Amani, please, let me show you something."

"You already have. Both of you." Amani ignored Marley calling her name and ran as fast as she could to the front of the apartment complex. She was having difficulty sprinting with salt water in her eyes and bumped into a lady who obviously believed in doing her grocery shopping while the masses slept. The bag crashed to the ground and Amani stooped to pick it up.

"Sorry." Amani handed the bag to her. *Was there a full moon?* The lady was wearing a black trench coat buttoned to the top, red high-heeled shoes with no stockings, and a pair of shades. Her long hair spilled from under a red cowboy-style hat.

"No foul. I need to wash the fruit anyway."

Amani grimaced. "Tamera?"

"No. Tamara, like camera."

"Whatever."

"I thought y'all broke up."

He called her, too? "We did. You can have him."

She licked her lips. "I will." Then she took off her shades. "What did you do to your hair?" She laughed and put her sunglasses back on. "Don't worry. He can run his fingers through mine."

"Better hope he doesn't snag his fingers on all that black thread holding it on." Amani forced her head up as she walked to the glass door. She pushed it open, took a deep breath of night air, and continued running.

She slammed the car door; thankful she hadn't broken down in front of Marley and his girls. How could she have been so stupid? Not only had Marley been messing around with that cheerleader, he was also fooling around with her best friend. Guess he pretended to be a virgin long enough to get dummies like her to let down their guards. Destiny had obviously lied about what happened that afternoon with Marley. Maybe Destiny had tried to warn her in her own way. Maybe Perri was right. A lasting love could only be found in the movies. Too bad she hadn't learned this lesson earlier.

During the drive back to his place, she had listened to KJLH's *Rhythms of the Night* radio program. Those romantic songs put her in the mood for Marley. She had practically convinced herself the depth of their feelings justified their making love. Besides, it wasn't realistic for them to continue to deny themselves and not even her mother had been a virgin when she got married.

If she had given in sooner, Marley wouldn't have had to turn to anyone else. She blamed herself—and her mother. "What's going to happen to Mama, Marley, and me?" she inquired of the night. Then she wondered what she could have possibly sown in her first seventeen years of living to be reaping such a disastrous introduction to adulthood.

She turned the key in the ignition. *"Fortunate to ha—"* She quickly turned off the radio, pressed CD and programmed the CD to play the song she needed to hear. Tonight, a sultry serenade from Marley via Maxwell would not do.

The spirit-filled voice of Yolanda Adams filled the car. The lyrics soothed her soul as she listened. Only Jesus could feel her pain and heal her hurt. The song seemed to have been written with this night in mind. Knowing the battle facing her was the Lord's was encouraging, but she was a little confused by the rest of the melodious message. How could God possibly use her in this sad situation?

A sudden succession of raps on the window startled her and another flicker of hope brightened her dark tunnel. He had come and was going to fight for her. She turned her tear-streaked face to the door and opened it.

"I thought that was you."

She jumped back and stared at him through bleary eyes.

He extended his hand. "Clifton Hendrix."

She squinted, trying to place his face and voice.

"I'm on the team with Marley. We live in the same building."

"Oh." She nodded slowly. "You're the Ragu guy."

He chuckled. "Only to you, Tenderoni. I live two doors down from your boyfriend. I was sleeping on the sofa when I heard a brother yelling like he didn't have no kind of sense. I looked out the door and saw Marley standing there in his fire engine-red PJ's. I figured that had to be you booking across the courtyard." He stopped. "Are you all right?"

As she looked away, she was sure her bottom lip was bleeding.

"Come on. You can tell Mr. Ragu anything." His eyes rested on her head. "Not to change the subject, but I'm feelin' your new 'do."

"Really?" She touched her hair self-consciously.

"Really." He watched her chew her bottom lip. "How about this? I'll grab a jacket and we can go for a ride. I'm number ten out of a family of twelve. Seven sisters, four brothers. I can be a great set of ears if you'd like to talk. We can take my car." Clifton pointed to a Honda Prelude parked across the street and she simply stared at it. He did a spin and gave her a goofy grin. "Ro-ni, are ya with me? Oh, yeah. Better than crying and going nowhere. Ro-ni, are ya with me?"

She forced a half-smile. "Okay, Brother Kirk."

"I'll be right back."

After he left, she wondered if this was a good idea. But she wasn't ready to go home and she really didn't want to be alone. She couldn't sit outside Marley's all night either. Besides, Clifton seemed harmless enough. Then again, hadn't she learned tonight that appearances were definitely deceiving?

Before she could change her mind, however, he was opening and closing the passenger door for her. It was an older model, but immaculate. She leaned over and unlocked his door. He put on his seatbelt and watched her do the same.

Clifton stared at her. "What is up with church boy? The last thing I would want is to make you cry." He put the key in the ignition. "Watch out, Hollywood! There's a new cropped-cut cutie in town."

She offered a polite smile. "Where are you from?"

"Lexington, Mississippi. Can't hide that southern pride." He started the car. "Anywhere specific you'd like to go?"

Amani looked at the building where her love no longer lived. She turned to Clifton and nodded. "Yeah."

To not be getting any, he sure had a lot of women. Tamara stepped inside the open door and cleared her throat. Marley dropped Destiny's hand and glanced at her. He looked pitiful. Strong but sensitive. Tamara admired that. She appreciated Marley in a pair of silk pajama bottoms sans the shirt even more.

What was up with his girl and who was this chickenhead?

Tamara reacquainted herself with the contemporary décor of the living room. This, too, suited her taste. She put the grocery bag and pack of wine coolers on the table. After unpacking her version of forbidden fruit, she strolled over to Marley, a peach cooler in hand and her eyes on Destiny.

"I ran into your ex on the way in." Taking off her shades, she pointed them at Destiny. "Was this golden girl her problem?"

Destiny glared at her. "Marley, you better let this midnight cowgirl know Amani is way more saved than me." Her eyes flashed and her waterfall ponytails resembled a charging bull's horns. "I will step to her."

Tamara finally recognized Destiny and returned her stare. "I have a cousin who goes to Tubman. Seems your mouth writes checks your behind can't cash."

"You obviously asked the wrong somebody!" Destiny's eyes narrowed. "It's not a problem for me to deposit my foot in your behind. It'll take you and *your cousin* to withdraw it."

"Ooh, I'm scared." Tamara waved her hand. "You gots to go! Go see a movie, a play, or take a long walk." She removed her hat and carefully raked her hands through her hair. "Maybe you'll catch up to your little friend or bump into Jill Scott. Don't matter. Just get!"

"You bringin' out the ghetto instincts I try *hard* to keep on the down low, Tamera."

"That's Tam-a-ra." She flung her hair over her shoulder. "It rhymes with camera."

Destiny pointed her finger in Tamara's face. "Now you mistakin' me for someone who cares!" She pushed Tamara's forehead with her index finger.

"Destiny!" Marley separated the two young ladies. "It's cool." He raised his hands. "I got this. Go on home."

"Whatever!" Destiny snorted. She stopped committing murder with her eyes and walked over to the sofa. She put on her jacket, picked up her backpack, and dropped the small gift bag into it. She walked slowly to the door, then stopped and looked at the strawberries, grapes, and cherries on the table next to the six-pack of coolers and a large can of Cool Whip. She watched Marley rub his neck, a pained expression on his face. Destiny stared until his eyes met hers. "You're better than this," she said firmly.

Minutes later, Destiny walked through the courtyard and prayed he'd remember who he was before it was too late. Because of his earlier slip-up, she was forced to do the same. It was time to let go of her dream and face reality. She and Marley would never be.

Truthfully, she had gone over to his place with the best of intentions. She had forgotten Amani's birthday present at home and Chazz picked her up right after school. They didn't have time to go by her house before driving sixty miles east to Chino Hills.

Although it was after midnight when she returned from Chazz's uncle and aunt's fish fry, she phoned the Shephard residence anyway. Miss Oneita answered Amani's phone and told her Amani was at Marley's, then she practically begged her to take Amani's gift to her.

Destiny drove up in time to see Amani sobbing behind the wheel of her mother's SUV before finally pulling off. The temptation of being alone with Marley Jamison was too tough to resist, even though her love for her friend was sincere. She was thankful Amani hadn't barged in fifteen minutes sooner.

Destiny thought of that little ditty about friendship. Something about making new friends but holding onto the old ones because new friends are like silver, but old friends are gold. What she surmised from the poem was that friendships able to withstand tests and trials become as strong as pure gold.

Tamara-camera was right. She had been Amani's golden girl for twelve years and hoped their friendship had not been tarnished beyond repair.

TWENTY

Clifton wished he possessed the power to keep Amani's heart and the impending day from breaking. At the same time he felt a brotherly concern, he had an overwhelming desire to take her in his arms and never let go.

Her new haircut was working, and he never knew the scent of flowers could be so sexy. When Amani grabbed his hand, he had to talk himself out of becoming excited. She needed him to be a newfound friend, not some horny toad.

He decided to focus on something else as he waited for her to open her heart and share her hurt.

Clifton's mind tumbled back to where it had landed as they traveled to their deserted destination. On the drive over, he listened silently as Amani told him about Marley and Destiny and Tamara. Clifton thought Marley was closer to God than a mere mortal like himself. Even he had turned down Tamara. Like McDonald's, she had served many.

Clifton continued to mull over the situation and was surprised to discover he was disappointed in his teammate. He was then forced to admit he had been secretly in awe of Marley, not because of his athletic ability, but because of his spiritual prowess. Marley reminded him of the person he used to be.

Since Marley's rookie year, Clifton observed beautiful women off all shapes, sizes, and shades come on to Marley and leave empty-handed.

On several occasions, he watched Taylor defer to Marley instead of leading the team in prayer. An almost tangible presence of God descended when either man prayed, reminding Clifton of his father and brothers. He had more respect for Taylor and Marley than any of the other alleged Christians on the team because their walks were not faulty.

Clifton realized that somewhere deep inside of him was still a high regard for the things of God. That was why he made it a point to apologize to Marley the day after their incident in the locker room.

Marley had looked shocked to find him standing at his door, but was quick to invite him in. Clifton apologized for being out of line. After accepting his apology, Marley extended his own. On his way out the door, he told Marley he could tell Amani was something special. The Miracle Man had smiled and nodded his head. "Man, she is first class all the way."

Clifton believed they developed a new level of mutual respect that afternoon, so he felt a little strange being alone with Marley's girl now, especially since he'd developed a crush on Amani the first time he met her. It was something about the way she carried herself. Marley was right. She was one classy lady.

He glanced at Amani. She was staring into the darkened sky. He finally cleared his throat, breaking the silence.

"Maybe we shouldn't have come here."

"I'll be fine." She sniffed. "It's just so hard to believe my best friend and my boyfriend could do this to me. And that cheerleader . . ."

He proceeded cautiously. "Amani, maybe there's some reason Destiny was there that you're overlooking. Think about it. You two are best friends and if I had a dollar for every time I saw Marley turn Tamara down, I'd be set for life."

She sighed. "I don't know. Destiny said she had something to show me, but I didn't listen. Of course, I want to believe nothing happened but, even if that's true, he had to have called Tamera."

Amani could have called Tamara Tomorrow and he wouldn't have corrected her. He shook his head. "I didn't think the Miracle Man got down like that."

"Guess it's a fact. Men are either on the prowl or under-cover dogs."

"Hold up. You're stereotyping the brothers."

"No, I'm not. Let me hear you bark."

He pulled down the collar of his sweatshirt. "See? No leash. Personally, I'm on a mission to find the right woman." He looked directly at her. "I thought for sure Marley appreciated true beauty." He continued staring until she turned away. "So this is where Marley brought you at the end of your first date?"

Amani nodded.

"Smart man."

She frowned. "What do you mean?"

"Look around. No crowds. No lines. No distractions. Just the two of you and God's creation."

Amani wiggled her hand free and buttoned her sweater. They were sitting on the hood of his car. Per God's instructions, the stars had made themselves scarce tonight. And the light of day was on its way. She quietly recited one of her godmother's often-quoted scriptures.

Clifton repeated her faint words. "'Weeping may endure for a night but joy comes in the morning.' My mother named the toy poodle I bought her Joy because of that scripture. So you believe it, too?"

"I have to but, if it's not true, I'm not going to make it."

"I used to believe the Bible like that."

"What happened to change your mind?"

He turned away from her and squinted into the darkness.

Amani watched him. "God hasn't changed, Clifton, and neither has His word. He loves you." Her voice was gentle.

"Then why did he kill my father the week before my high school graduation?" Leftover anger was in his voice.

She placed her hand on his shoulder. "I'm sorry. I didn't know, but I do know God isn't in the parent murdering business. My daddy was killed by a drunk driver the month before I started kindergarten and—"

"Aw, man. You were a baby." His eyes connected with hers. "At least I had my father for seventeen years."

"You were blessed, but you know what, Clifton? God wants to be your Heavenly Father."

"No!" He shook his head. "I don't need another father."

Amani watched him, opting to remain silent for a few moments. Finally, she reached for his hand.

"You stopped believing when your father died, didn't you?"

Clifton nodded. "Why couldn't it have been someone else's daddy?"

"I don't know." She continued, speaking to both of them. "What I do know is God is the *only* daddy who will never leave you." She squeezed his hand. "I bet He's been missing that drawl of yours."

A slight smile snuck across his face.

She pressed on. "Cliff, it's time for you to come home."

He focused on the dim light of a distant star. "My father was a pastor. All we knew was church. He was killed ministering to a couple of homeless men. One of those fools had a knife. My father died trying to do good."

She winced. "That had to be hard on all of you."

"Yeah, but the rest of my family did what the old song says. They continued to hold on to God's unchanging hand." He shook his head. "Me? I didn't want *nothin'* to do with God. His hand, his church, or his Bible. None of it!"

"But are you satisfied, Clifton?

He looked at her and quickly turned away, but Amani could see his anger subsiding.

"Would you like to rededicate your life to the Lord?" Amani had nothing but time as she waited.

He finally answered, "Yeah."

"Just say what I say." Amani swallowed her own hurt and squeezed his hand. "Lord Jesus, I've been doing things my own way. Forgive me. I stand before you with a broken heart and a restless soul. I don't understand why my daddy had to die and probably never will." Soft sobs escaped as she continued to pray. "But . . . I want to experience your peace and I want to believe again. In you, in your Word, in your plan for my life. Lord Jesus, I humbly admit you are the potter and I am the clay. I'm asking you to mold me into the person you created me to be. Help me to live for you, no matter what. Be my Saviour and be my Heavenly Father. In Jesus' name, I pray. Amen."

Clifton repeated the final word and smiled at Amani. Although he didn't feel different, he knew that he was.

Amani returned his smile then rested her head on his shoulder. Encouraged and restored, they awaited the sun's rising, signaling the start of a new day.

Looking like something the cat had drug in and tossed aside, Marley paced in front of his apartment building. He noticed Mrs. Shephard's Land Cruiser still parked out front when he'd walked a very perturbed Tamara to her car right after Destiny left. Marley was waiting for Amani because he doubted she would respond to the note he placed under her windshield wiper.

She had to be with Destiny. When Destiny showed her the gift she bought for her birthday, Amani had to realize she jumped headfirst into the wrong conclusion. Okay. There was that almost-kiss, but he was grateful he stuffed both feet into his mouth and was certain Destiny would not mention it. After all, she loved Amani, too. What almost happened was a simple case of delicate male ego and fleeting insanity.

He knew Amani would pick up her mother's truck before heading home, so he had been keeping a vigil for her return since Tamara's departure. There was no way he was going to let Amani go home believing he'd spent the night with Tamara.

The only woman he wanted, if only for one night, was her.

———

Several cities away, Amani quickly jumped into the passenger door that Clifton held open. A stack of Denny's buttermilk pancakes and a vegetable omelet usually satisfied her. This morning, her only contentment came from Clifton's rededication to the Lord. He closed his door and faced her.

"I know I'm no Denzel Washington, but you don't even want to be seen with me?"

"Please. I don't want to be seen looking this tore up. I haven't even washed my face or brushed my teeth. Look at me."

"Not a problem." He grinned, staring at her. "Baby, you are blazing! 'Scuse me. We're family now. Sister Amani, not everybody can wear puffy red eyes and still look gorgeous."

She rubbed her eyes. "Thank you, I think. Just so you know, if you did something with your hair, you could give Mr. Washington a few tips."

"Thank you, I think." Clifton blushed, patted his huge Afro and looked into his rear view mirror. His light brown eyes shone more brightly in his mahogany face than the diamond stud in his ear. "So you think it's time for a hair cut?" he asked, smoothing down his thin mustache before turning to her.

She finger-combed her own afro and laughed. "Take it all off, homeboy."

"I don't know about all that, but maybe it is time for a change." He winked and started the car.

Twenty minutes later, Clifton drove up beside the hunter green Toyota Land Cruiser. He took Amani's hand and lightly squeezed it as he helped her out of the car then he shut the door and leaned against it, folding his arms and crossing his feet. "I can't say I've ever spent that kind of night with a beautiful lady before." The smile left his face. "If you need to talk, use the number I gave you. Don't worry about the time, call whenever you need to." He took her hand. "You are something special, Roni. Don't forget it."

"So are you, Mr. Ragu. I can't wait to see your new haircut." She leaned forward and kissed him on the cheek. "Thanks for being a gentlemen and thanks for listen—"

Someone grabbed her from behind, squeezing her forearm.

Clifton straightened and faced off with her assailant. "Step off, man!"

Marley glared at him. "This ain't your business, No Class."

Amani gave him a disgusted look. "Wrong! You're the one who could use some class." She took in his unkempt appearance and wanted to rush heart first into his arms.

Marley looked at her through sorrow-filled eyes, but she coldly returned his stare.

"Let . . . me . . . go!" Though she spoke through clenched teeth, it took every ounce of self-respect she could dig up to get inside the SUV and not look back.

Amani was about to drive off when she noticed the piece of paper. She got out of the car as Clifton stood guard. She could feel Marley watching as she read his message. *Amani, I love you and I'm sorry I hurt you. Please forgive me, baby. I don't want anybody but you. I need you in my life. Please stop by before you leave. We need to talk. Marley.* Amani turned her back to him, tore up the note, and let it fly on the wings of the morning wind.

TWENTY-ONE

It was the third Saturday of the month. Unfortunately. Her sisters were inside reconnecting, sparring or both. Amani closed the car door and stood staring at her family's tree. Instead of looking lush this morning, it seemed sinister. What happened to the familiar tree she'd exuberantly climbed in the past and presently observed from her window while she pondered life and love? She lumbered slowly up the stairs leading to the porch and front door of the Shepherd residence. Never had the three steps seemed so steep. She settled her eyes on *their* porch swing and almost gasped. Where was its warmth? No longer inviting, it appeared rickety and cold. It was as if she was seeing the only home she had ever known through different eyes.

She put her key in the lock. Before she could even turn it, the door swung open. Perri was standing in the doorway with her hands on her hips. "Baby Girl, we were just about to call the police and put out an—" She frowned. "Mama said you cut off all your hair."

Amani looked past Perri. "Where's Mama?" Amani moved past her and saw that four of her sisters were seated at the dining room table.

They looked up when she came in. Nola was the first to jump up and wrap her arms around her, followed by Rosalind, Vanessa, and Krystal.

Perri came and stood beside her. "Mama told us you were at Marley's. We've been calling him since *early* this morning, but his line was busy. We finally realized he must have taken the phone off the hook. Guess y'all didn't want to be disturbed."

Amani snorted.

"I remember those days," Perri continued. Again, she eyed Amani's head but this time she kept her comments to herself. "I'm glad you're okay." She patted her youngest sister's shoulder, then started to clear off the table.

Amani watched her work, then observed the rest of her sisters who had each returned to what they had been doing before her arrival. Rosalind was working on her laptop, Vanessa was sketching in her notepad, and Nola was giving Krystal a manicure. She glanced at the head of the table.

Mama's Bible, reading glasses, and the breakfast that had scarcely been touched were still on her placemat. Amani stood in the doorway that separated the dining room from the kitchen and watched Mia talking on the phone while Perri stacked the dishwasher. Based on the cavalier reception her sisters gave her, Amani knew they all thought the same thing.

The last Shephard sister had pledged to hold on to her virginity in the name of the Father, the Son, and the Holy Ghost, but last night, she had given it up in the single name of love.

Mia finally noticed Amani and spoke hurriedly into the phone. "I love you, too, RJ. See you tonight." She hopped off the stool, hurried over to her sister, and put her hands on her shoulders. Amani bit her bottom lip and looked down, willing herself not to cry. She had done far too much crying lately.

"Hey, you all right?" Mia asked softly, placing her right hand under Amani's chin and raising her head.

Amani's eyes met her sister's. "Mama's in her bedroom?"

Mia nodded. "We finally got her to lie down about an hour ago. She told us *everything*. Baby Girl, she made an awful mistake and she regrets it. She did something she'll have to live with for the rest of her life." Mia looked straight into Amani's eyes. "Mama might have a head start on you, but you'll make plenty of mistakes as you make your way, too."

Talk about déjà vu. Amani sunk her teeth into her lower lip. *Trusting Marley, Destiny, and Mama proved to be the biggest mistakes I've ever made.* She stared at her sister through uncaring, yet enlightened eyes.

Mia easily read her sister's gaze. "Go easy on her, Amani. You didn't hear the whole story. The saddest part is she's blamed herself for Daddy's death all this time." Mia eyed her sister's curly Afro. "Your hair's cute."

"I need you to shape it up for me."

"Sure." She returned to more pertinent matters. "By the way, the mystery of what Perri Shephard, Esquire used to hint at has been solved. Daddy and Mama had a huge argument the morning he left for New York."

Amani's eyebrow rose. "Really?"

"Yep, but I better shut up. She wants to talk to you herself. Are you sure you're okay?" Mia pressed.

"Yeah."

Mia hugged her sister, and then watched her slowly climb the stairs.

As Amani trudged upward, she could hear Krystal.

"Mia, what's wrong with you? You've seen Miracle Marley! She's way better than just okay. Thankyouverymuch."

"Shhh! Be quiet," Mia pleaded. "This isn't funny."

Krystal stared at her, then rolled her eyes. "Chile, don't make me call Roland Jones and get all in your business."

"Don't make me get out the spirit and kick your behind."

"Spare me. Being saved is the last thing on your mind when RJ's rocking your world." Krystal blew puffs of air at her nails.

Mia walked over to her. "We've been together two years and have only been sleeping together for six months. What's your track record?"

Krystal stopped blowing her nails and began waving her hands up and down. "Why should I buy the car when I can lease a new model whenever I want?"

"Because the wear and tear on your engine is gonna catch up to you."

Krystal rolled her eyes. "Don't deceive yourself, honey. The mileage on your motor is adding up, too."

Nola frowned at them then began returning Amani's borrowed supplies to the plastic container.

Rosalind, Vanessa, Perri, Krystal, and Mia began readying themselves to leave. The prodigal daughter had returned.

Amani listened to her sisters fussing and teasing as they left the family home. They either had people expecting their presence or places where they needed to be seen.

A pair of heavy feet and an even heavier heart accompanied her as she made her trek down the hall. She halted outside her mother's door and tapped lightly. "Mama, it's me. May I come in?" She opened the door and peered in. Her mother was standing in front of the window. Amani moved to stand beside her.

Minutes felt like hours as the two Shephard women stood shoulder-to-shoulder in silence. Olivia turned and gingerly touched Amani's short curls. "Your hair."

"It'll grow back."

Without wavering, Olivia looked deeply into eyes that mirrored hers. "Did you have sex with Marley?"

Amani's hesitant response was deliberate. "No."

"Now that you know about me, are you planning to?"

A sudden defiant attitude arose in her. "Why shouldn't I?" She didn't care about hearing her mother's explanations. "You weren't a virgin when you married Daddy *and* you were pregnant."

Olivia didn't want another tear to drop before she had a chance to explain what happened. Maybe it would prevent Amani from doing something she couldn't take back. Olivia was finally ready to confess her sins to her seventh daughter because she needed her baby girl's forgiveness.

However, Amani was out for vengeance. *Somebody needs to hurt like I'm hurtin'.* As this seed began to sprout inside of her, she allowed a spirit of hostility to completely overtake her. "You know, Mama, we're not as alike as I thought. I'm woman enough to tell you the truth and I don't pretend to be something I'm not. You're nothin' but a liar!"

Olivia's hand snaked out and slapped the smug look from her daughter's face. Amani's face registered shock, then anger, and finally, rage. Olivia held her hand in the air, looking at it in disbelief. Her fabricated world was careening out of control. "Oh, my goodness! Amani!" She reached for her redemption, but Amani backed up, out of her arm's way.

Her mother had never slapped her before. Amani's impulsive haircut made her chiseled face look menacing. Her chin jutted out and her eyes narrowed into windows of fury. She glared at her mother through swollen, reddened eyes. "You kill your first child and abuse your last. Some mother you are. *I hate you.*" She stormed out of the room, slamming the door so hard the windows rattled.

Olivia covered her mouth. The muffled sounds of her wailing would, undoubtedly, echo throughout eternity. As she sank to the floor, she cried for herself, her husband, for the baby they never had a chance to call son, and for the daughter she feared she had lost forever.

TWENTY-TWO

For Amani the past twenty-four hours had been an awak-
ening involving individuals she doubted she'd ever forgive. Of the twelve disciples, only one—Judas—had inten-
tionally betrayed Jesus. Her list was three times as long.
Marley, Destiny, and Mama. The only highlight of the past
twenty-four hours was leading Clifton back to the Lord. However, she was on the verge of straying. If you couldn't trust
your mother, your boyfriend, or your best friend, who could
you trust?

Her mother had been drilling abstinence into her although
she had lost her virginity, gotten pregnant, and had an abortion. Then she had the nerve to slap her. Destiny pretended
to be her best friend while all the time she was messing with
her boyfriend behind her back. And Marley. He deserved an
Oscar for his dedicated boyfriend performance. He was a player
on and off the court. She hadn't given him what he wanted,
so he had been handling his business elsewhere.

Her stinging face was turned toward the window as she lay
across her bed. She squeezed her eyes shut as an unrelated

thought popped into her head. The church's annual talent show was tomorrow night. Sister Rachel asked her to sing a solo for the teenage division of the show. Amani told her she'd get back to her, but she never did. Amani was relieved she hadn't committed herself because there wasn't a song in her.

She opened her eyes and rubbed her cheek. *I should have been Mama's eighth child.* If the baby were a girl, she would have been the eighth daughter. A boy, and the place she now held would have remained. But the budding life was ended before her sister or brother could bloom. What made Mama so desperate she decided to abort their baby? Especially after she married Daddy.

In two months, Daddy would have been gone thirteen years. According to Mia, Mama had blamed herself for his death all these years. How could their father being killed in a car accident be Mama's fault? Amani was more confused now than she had been when she first learned of her mother's secret. The mother she thought she knew was a stranger.

Exhausted from unanswered questions and thoughts of betrayal and regret that spun in her head, Amani finally dozed off.

When she awoke, shadows crossed the room and she knew twilight had fallen. Amani sat up, glanced at the clock, and then stared into the mirror, touching her face lightly. Her mother had never slapped her before, and she had never hurled such harmful words at her mother. This afternoon they had each played roles so out of character that Amani felt disoriented. Having already lost Marley and her long hair added to the unbalanced feeling she was experiencing. Losing a mother was more than any child should have to bear.

Her mother's love was the glue that held her together since Marcus Shephard departed for New York and never returned. She needed her mother's guidance. She needed her mother's encouragement. She needed to hear her mother's story, and then share her own.

Amani ran her fingers through her unfamiliar hair and stood to her feet. She needed to piece together this puzzle and make peace with her mother.

Seconds later, she stopped outside of Olivia's closed door. Amani was unsure of the response she would receive, but was certain of one thing. The mother she knew would be standing in a favorite spot. Amani twisted the knob and opened the door. She was relieved to see that she was right. Her mother faced the window.

Olivia waited before her bay window, comforting herself with a hug as she peered at the huge, familiar tree. Through the changing of seasons, it remained a constant fixture in their lives. No more than a sapling when she and Marcus planted it, sometimes it seemed it would not prosper. But it had taken root and proven itself faithful. Despite the testing and challenges of spring, summer, winter, and fall, it stood.

As Olivia stood in the face of nightfall, her silhouette formed a backdrop to the crepuscular sky. Amani continued to watch her mother while easing herself onto her parents' bed. From her vantage point, she had only a side view of her mother. An eternal five minutes passed between them.

Amani was ready to apologize when her mother began to speak. It was a voice Amani didn't recognize, but it reminded her a little of Clifton's.

"Marcus and I attended high school in Bunkie, a small town in Lou'siana. I loved him seemed like my whole life. We became husband and wife a week after we graduated. My father was against the marriage because he wanted me to go to college. My mother . . . she was just against me. I never did anything right in her eyes. To tell the whole truth, she seemed to hate me. I was tired of being the reason for everything wrong with her life. That's why I moved in with Papa and Big Mama when I went to high school."

She fixed her eyes on the tree. "My father came to the wedding, but not my mother. My six sisters were too afraid of Mama Bea to go against her, so they boycotted the ceremony, too. You've heard some of this story many times before. What you didn't know before last night was that I was pregnant when your father and I got married."

Olivia turned away from the window and looked down at Amani. "In April of our senior year, my cousin Claudine and I were sittin' in the backyard under our fig tree. She told me Marcus asked her to have sex with him. Of course, I was crushed. I was ready to break up with him, but she said I could get revenge by going out with Lil' Earl. Earl Wright had liked me from the time we were both in diapers. He was as handsome as Marcus, but was a bit of a roughneck. Claudine was dating his older brother, Juniorman, who was worse than him. Claudine was what the old folks used to call 'fast.'

"I let her talk me into going out on a double date. I should have known better, but I was upset and had no reason to distrust my cousin. *We were blood.*"

Olivia sighed. "The four of us went to a juke joint about forty-five miles outside of town. We danced and I had my first taste of beer. On the ride home, Juniorman pulled off the road and drove across an open field. He said he was too drunk to drive and needed to sleep off some of the alcohol." The four of us traded places in the car. She shook her head. "After a while, it was obvious Juniorman and Claudine weren't doing no sleeping in that back seat."

She turned back to the window. "I guess their noises started getting to Lil' Earl. He pulled me close to him and, for the first time that night, I was scared. His eyes were wild looking. I'll never forget the smell of him—a mixture of cigarettes, liquor, and funk. He put his big, slimy tongue in my mouth and reached under my skirt. I panicked and threw open the door. Lil' Earl caught me by the shoulders and turned me around to face him. When he licked his lips and leered at me, he looked like the devil without a disguise. In that moment, I knew my tomorrow would be different from any that had passed before it."

The silent shedding of tears united the two Shephard women. Amani cried for her mother and her mother mourned for the young lady she'd been.

Olivia's teary eyes were focused on something beyond the tree. "He took what I had been saving . . . for your daddy, out in that open field, under the watchful eyes of the stars."

There was an edge in her mother's voice as she continued. "He hissed in my ear that preacher boy wouldn't be able to satisfy me because he was nothing but a sissy. No real man would ever turn down a piece of Claudine's tail. He hadn't and she was his brother's girlfriend. It took a few minutes before what he said registered. I lay on that ground having to accept that my first cousin was an accomplice to my rape."

Olivia lowered her voice. "When the three of them dropped me off, I got out of the car and tapped on her window. Claudine casually rolled it down. 'You lyin' heifer,' were the last words I ever spoke to her."

Olivia turned to Amani and she could see that her mother was revisiting that night. "If Lil' Earl was the ugly devil himself, then Cous'n Claudine was the devil's wife. She got out that car and looked at me through cold, hard eyes. '*Poor, Baby Sister*. Look at you, with your long, brown hair. Your smooth toffee complexion.' She kicked the car door. 'Y'all ever hear her play the piano? Hmm. This here girl is gorgeous *and* talented.' She turned away from her partners in crime. 'All my life, all I ever heard was 'Olivia this' and 'Olivia that.' 'Why can't *you* be more like Olivia?' I can still see her vicious eyes.

"Claudine leaned in close to me. 'You even have the most beautiful man this side of heaven sniffing around you like some mangy dog. Maybe he'll reconsider my offer now that you're no better than me.' She got back in the car. Lil' Earl had fallen asleep almost as soon as we got back on the main highway. At the slamming of the door, he woke up and yawned, then told me he'd call me. He acted as if we had just spent a normal evening together."

Olivia walked over to her dresser and picked up the last picture she and Marcus had taken together. "The next day, I told your father what happened. He took me in his arms and it was the first time I ever saw him cry. I didn't tell my parents or my grandparents. If I had, Mama Bea would have found a way to make the whole thing my fault. I wouldn't give her nothin' else to hold against me." She returned the photo to the doily on her dresser.

"And I couldn't go to the sheriff. Juniorman, Lil' Earl, and Claudine were killed about two hours after dropping me home. Juniorman tried to beat a freight train across the tracks after he and Lil' Earl robbed a Piggly Wiggly Supermarket. My Aunt Maybelle asked me to play and sing 'I'll Fly Away' at Claudine's funeral. I couldn't. I let everybody think I was too overcome with grief."

Her mother looked through her as she began her visit with young Marcus and Olivia. "By the time May rolled around, I could no longer blame my late period on stress. I felt like Jesus in the Garden of Gethsemane. My God, why have You forsaken me? The hardest thing I ever had to do was to tell the man I loved that I was carrying the child of a rapist."

She twirled a strand of hair and looked off. "We cried together for a second time. When we were all cried out, he kept repeating how sorry he was. Like it was his fault. Then he said something I'll never forget. 'These aren't exactly the set of circumstances facing Joseph, but I love you every bit as much as he loved Mary. Will you marry me, Olivia Ava Dupree?'"

She looked directly at her daughter and smiled faintly. "Baby

Girl, I wanted to spend every second in me with that man. He told my grandparents, and then his parents that I was having his baby and we were getting married in a week." She chuckled. "Reverend Shephard tried to marry us right then, but your father insisted on a church wedding." She blew out a resigned sigh. "Your daddy could be some stubborn."

Olivia sat next to Amani and smoothed the comforter with her hand. "Marcus kept reminding me that the baby was innocent. I wanted to do the right thing, but I couldn't. The thought of having to look into the face of a Lil' Earl or Earline was more than I could bear. When I was four months pregnant, I went to New Orleans to visit my friend, Jacqueline. Her father was a gynecologist." She stared at her hands in her lap. "I had an abortion. Jackie's father covered for me by telling Marcus I had a miscarriage when he came to get me."

"That was August of 1970." She squeezed her eyes closed and continued, tears rolled down her face and into the corner of her mouth. "In August of 1989, I took your father to the airport. On the way there, he started joking about our still being young enough to try for a son. The guilt and the shame of how I chose to solve what Lil' Earl did became an overwhelming weight, but I was too ashamed to tell your father what I did. I was afraid of what exposing the truth would do to him—to us. Instead, I shared another secret I was keeping."

Marcus kept his hands around her waist as they hurried through the terminal. Gate 27A was packed with passengers on their way to New York. Marcus nodded to a few familiar faces before turning his attention to his life partner.

He pulled Olivia to him and nuzzled her neck. "Girl, this is going to be a long weekend. We'll work on our prince when I get back. You're going to be home until my last princess graduates from high school. Might as well have another baby to take care of besides me."

Olivia stiffened. "Marcus, I've been accepted to UCLA's School of Nursing."

His jaw clenched and he released his hold on her.

"I begin the program in September when Amani starts kindergarten."

A sudden closed look clouded his handsome features. "We agreed you'd stay home until she graduated."

"No, Marcus, that's what *you* want. I'll be thirty-seven next month, and I've never worked outside of this house. It's time for me to pursue *my* dream."

A woman's voice interrupted them. "Flight 832 to New York's JFK Airport will begin boarding at this time."

Marcus brushed his hand across his head. "I thought we settled this foolishness this morning when you told me you were thinking about applying to that nursing program. Now, you're telling me you applied and were accepted."

Olivia pulled the band off her ponytail. Lush brown waves cascaded past her shoulders. "Yes. I'm sorry I didn't tell you, but I knew—"

"That your first responsibility is to me and our girls." He kissed her on the forehead. "UCLA will still be there when Amani graduates. If you still want to be a nurse then, I'll support you all the way."

"I need you to support my decision today, not thirteen years from now."

"Olivia, let them know you'll have to decline."

"I won't."

"What do you mean, you won't?"

"I mean if you won't support me, don't bother coming home."

Marcus lips curved into a magnetic smile. Everything he had belonged to her. She owned his heart, his mind, his body. He pulled her into his arms. "Woman, don't you know there's no place I'd rather be than home?" He adjusted his carry-on bag on his shoulder. "I know I'm being selfish, but I'm not ready to share you with the world. I like coming home to you at the end of the day."

Olivia's body relaxed at his words and she melted against her husband. Their heartbeats instantly pulsed as one. There was no way she could live without this man, but what about her dreams?

He lifted her chin with his fingertip. "Mrs. Shephard, every ounce of me loves every ounce of you."

Her eyes filled because she knew he spoke the truth. Marcus loved her though her own mother never did and her father was too much of a coward to show it. Her sisters never accepted her while her first cousin had resented her. Only Papa and Big Mama tried to love her before Marcus made her his own.

"I love you, too, Mr. Shephard."

They embraced so tightly and kissed so passionately that the stragglers at Gate 27A gave them a rousing applause. Marcus and Olivia reluctantly let their fingers slide from each other's grasp.

He grinned seductively, "I'm already looking forward to returning home to you."

"I'll be waiting." With eyes aglow, she watched his rhythmic gait carry him away from her. She didn't leave the airport until she could no longer see his plane.

———

Olivia blinked Amani into her line of vision. "As long as I live, I'll regret having an abortion and telling your father not to come home."

Tears slid down Amani's face. "Was the baby a boy?"

Olivia nodded. Her shoulders shook. "I killed your father and the son he would have loved no less than he loved his girls."

Amani took her mother's hands in hers. "That drunk driver killed Daddy. And Daddy knew you didn't mean what you said." That's why y'all were locking lips like two crazy people in front of a crowd of strangers." She looked directly into her mother's eyes. "I know you repented about the baby, Mama, so God forgives you. And I really believe Daddy would have done the same." Through blurry eyes, she added, "It's time for you to forgive yourself."

Olivia nodded her head mutely, and then buried her face in Amani's shoulder. She released a soul-purifying cry that flowed from her depths and reached the holy ears of God. When she had no tears left, she lay back on the bed.

"Baby Girl, I'm sorry I hit you. Will you forgive me?"

"I already have, Mama." Amani knelt beside her mother. "And I apologize for what I said to you. I didn't mean it."

Olivia reached out and caressed her daughter's wet cheek. "I know, baby." She dropped her hand and closed her eyes.

Amani kissed her mother's temple then reached for her hand. She stared at the profile of the woman who had given her life and love unconditional.

"Mama?"

Olivia sat up and faced the daughter who had saved her life again.

"I have two wishes." Amani attempted to compose herself. "I wish I could give you the peace of God the Bible talks about and I wish . . . I could give you the love of the kind of mother you've been to me." While they embraced, two seventh daughters wept and traded places.

TWENTY-THREE

Their church overflowed with singers, dancers, poets, actors, actresses, mimes, writers, and musicians whose creative gifts glorified God and edified His children, both the faithful and the flaky. The congregation was abuzz with excitement. New Horizons Christian Center's Annual Talent Show grew more spectacular each year.

Destiny was dressed in a long-sleeved golden one-piece leotard covered with a matching wrap skirt. Her feet were bare except for the gold toe ring on her right foot and the dainty gold anklet on her left. Her hair was pulled back in a bun and her bronze complexion glowed with a hint of peach lip gloss, adding an understated yet elegant effect.

Destiny Lafawn Ross had been performing in the talent show since she was ten years old. She loved modern dancing. Her unseen partner was God Himself. But this year she wasn't certain He'd catch her if she happened to fall.

If Marley hadn't slipped and called her Amani, she would have probably lost her virginity to her best friend's man or at least kissed him. What kind of person was she? Better yet, what kind of Christian was she? How could she be saved and still have such a strong desire to do wrong?

Even though Amani was her girl, she had wanted to sleep with Marley. The only reason she introduced the two of them in the first place was to have the chance to resume a friendship with him. She believed her friend's stubborn resistance to having sex would remain firm but had a feeling Marley would begin to weaken. She had been right.

Destiny closed her eyes and took a deep breath. She was on next. Gracefully, she glided onto the stage and prepared for her starting pose. Feet a hip width's apart, she lifted her head, extended her hands to heaven, then placed them together, palm to palm. She lowered them to her mouth, bowed her head and prayed. "Forgive me, Lord."

Fred Hammond sang her heart's cry as the spotlight shone on her. "I'm Running Back to You" searched souls while Destiny danced away her private demons and made her public confession of repentance.

Chazz was accustomed to something stirring inside him whenever he saw her. It didn't matter whether Destiny wore sweats, a dress, or jeans. Her thick brown hair could be pulled into a ponytail or bouncing and behaving. She made him feel deeply without even trying.

Tonight, as he watched her, the stirring in his soul had little to do with her.

Chazz was digging Destiny's dance. The girl who surrendered her limbs to the guidance of some unseen force was a Destiny he didn't know. Her intensity seemed inspired and the emotion on her face matched her strong, fluid movements. He watched and wondered what had gotten a hold of her.

Later that evening, Chazz pulled up in front of the Ross' residence. He shifted the gear into park and his mind started processing. Destiny's parents had gone to get coffee with some of their church friends. The two of them could be alone but, for some reason, he knew not to go there. Chazz faced the divine dancing diva beside him.

"I must have said this two hundred thirty-seven times already, but you were amazing."

Destiny blushed. "Thank you. Actually, it's been more like seven hundred thirty-two times, but who's counting?"

Chazz loosened his tie and ran his hands over his sandy twists. "It's been a while since I've been to church. I wasn't sure what to expect, but it was pretty cool. Y'all have some peeps up in there that belong in Hollywood." He laughed. "And your pastor is a trip."

Destiny smiled. "Pastor Hilton definitely believes in keeping it real. I think he's a little too real for some folks."

Chazz shook his head. "He was straight up trying to pop-lock. I bet he used to get his groove on back in the day." He removed his tie. "Where was your girl? I heard she could sing."

"Somebody told you wrong. Amani can *sang*." She frowned. "At the last minute, she decided not to perform, but I figured she'd still show up."

"She obviously changed her mind about that, too."

"Guess so." Destiny touched his hand. "We need to talk."

"About?"

She looked straight ahead. "I've been a part-time church girl and a full-time wild child." She exhaled slowly. "I don't want to live like that anymore."

She had been so busy fantasizing about Marley she hadn't realized how much she had grown to like Chazz. She was really going to miss him. Her words came out in a rush.

"I'm 'bout to start acting like I'm saved, sanctified, and filled with the Holy Ghost. You need to find somebody else to hang out with."

Chazz grabbed her hand. "Press stop, then rewind. I'm cool with that."

Destiny's eyes widened. "You're trying to tell me if I stop acting like a wild child, you still want to kick it?"

"I thought you knew." Chazz kissed her hand. "You have my heart open, girl."

"Dang, Chazz! I thought you were just hanging around long enough to get in my panties." She was half-kidding.

"We just got out of church so I'm not gonna lie. I wouldn't mind getting with you, but I'm 'bout more than that."

"Then you'll go to church with me next Sunday?"

He laughed and dropped her hand. "A brother's not trying to get all caught up in religion."

She leaned over and kissed him softly on the lips. "How about getting caught up in an awesome spiritual relationship?"

Chazz smiled into her hazel eyes and nodded. "Sounds do-able."

Destiny reached for the handle, but he stopped her and rushed around to the passenger side and gently helped her out.

Seconds later, they stood on her porch. "I'll see you Sunday. Pick me up at nine-thirty." She took his brown sports coat from around her shoulders and handed it to him, then gave him a firmer, but tongue-free, kiss on the lips.

"Thanks for being a friend."

His light brown eyes twinkled. "Is that all I am to you?"

Destiny smiled up at him. It was time to stop playing games. "Goodnight, *boyfriend*."

Chazz's Colgate smile lit up his face and warmed her heart as she turned the key in the lock and opened the door.

A few moments later, Destiny's hand trembled as she dialed a number that was permanently lodged in her memory. She had planned on asking Amani's forgiveness face-to-face, but her friend was a talent show no-show. Destiny did not want the sun to go down on Amani's wrath another day so she forced herself to call.

The phone started to ring, but she slammed it down and

took a deep breath. "Okay, Destiny. You *can* do this. You can do all things through Christ who strengthens you." Destiny slowly put her hand on the phone and lifted it once again.

———

Several blocks away, the ringing phone startled Amani out of her private reverie. Marley had called so many times, she almost felt sorry for him. She never answered the phone, but would immediately call the message center to listen to his voice after every call. All night he had been personalizing verses from Song of Solomon.

Amani, you are my beloved and you are my friend. . . Sunshine, you have ravished my heart, my sister, my future spouse. Nikki, your lips drip as the honeycomb: honey and milk are under your tongue. . .Miss Mani, you are the only one whom my soul loves.

Amani smiled, thinking of Steve Urkel's infamous line to his unrequited love interest, Laura Winslow, on the television show *Family Matters*: "I'm wearing ya down, baby!" That's exactly what Marley was doing to her.

After the ringing stopped, she let a few seconds pass, then picked up the receiver so she could hear what he had to say this time.

"Amani?"

She almost dropped the phone.

"Please don't hang up. We need to talk."

Silence.

"You still there?"

"What's up, Destiny?"

She took a breath and dove in. "I went over to Marley's to take you your birthday present. When I called your house late that night, Miss Oneita told me you were there. I didn't understand why she basically begged me to take you the gift until I saw you. I could see something was up. I just wanted you to know I gave your gift to Mama O tonight."

"All right."

"Amani, you believe me. Don't you?"

"I'm not sure what to believe."

"Listen, I have a confession to make." Destiny gripped the phone so hard her knuckles were white. "I've had a crush on Marley since tenth grade." Tears clouded her vision. "But I want to reiterate that nothing happened. Even if I wanted something to, it wouldn't have. He is *way* into you, Amani. I apologize for not being totally honest with you in the first place. Will you please forgive me?"

As usual, Destiny's candor broke through the wall she had attempted to build between them. "I forgive you, Destiny, but promise me one thing."

"What?" She held her breath.

"You won't ever hook me up with somebody you still have the hots for."

Destiny grinned through misty eyes. "I promise." She stopped smiling. "I love you, Chocolate Mani."

"Back to you, Vanilla Dee." Amani's phone clicked. "That's my other line. I'll call you back, okay?"

"Okay."

Destiny softly replaced the phone in its cradle and knelt beside her bed.

"Lord, I thank you for blessing Amani and me. Help us to continue to practice your love and your forgiveness in our friendship. Guide our footsteps. Put us back on the right path when we go astray. Let us always be here for each other and let our lives glorify you. In Jesus' name, I pray. Amen."

Destiny suddenly felt like dancing, so she did.

TWENTY-FOUR

The Monday morning blues were unable to get their grip on her. Olivia was looking forward to starting the week anew and the talent show had helped her to celebrate her long overdue liberty. She stretched her arms above her head. For the first time in years, the love of Marcus' life was sleeping peacefully through the night. The past no longer held Olivia hostage.

This morning she awoke feeling she could take on the world and then some. Though it was still dark outside her window, she fully trusted the light in her heart to guide her. A simple, yet powerful, verse came to mind. *Trust in the Lord with all thine heart and lean not to thine own understanding. In all thy ways, acknowledge Him and He shall direct thy paths.* She regularly confessed Proverbs, Chapter 3, Verses 5 and 6 over her daughters and herself.

Olivia walked to her bedroom's full-length mirror where she appraised her reflection. She was wearing a silk spaghetti-strapped peach nightie. Not bad for a mother of seven who was banging on the door of fifty. Oval eyes gleamed in a smooth face. High cheekbones and a wide mouth offset her strong nose. Kinky brown waves drifted past her shoulders—the same carefree style she'd worn for more than three decades.

It was past time for a change.

Time to be bold and daring. A chin-length bob would complement her heart-shaped face and add an air of cool sophistication. Only one problem. Hair Master Mia would be too shocked to work the magic that was making her a standout in her field. Olivia grinned. She was crossing over Jordan and would deal with that bridge when the time came. Besides, it was her hair and her choice.

Olivia preened and pranced in the mirror, viewing her body from every angle. She still wore a size twelve comfortably and was quite tone. Her early morning meetings with her treadmill were paying off. Exercise was the one good thing she had given up temporarily, but a few months following Marcus' death, she had gone back to her regular routine.

Though not slim by society's standards, her mirror reflected a fabulous, fit grandmother of twins. She radiated beauty and serenity from the inside out.

Olivia stared wistfully at the last picture she and Marcus had taken together. The month was May and they were celebrating their nineteenth wedding anniversary. Several of their close friends and relatives had come to a backyard barbecue. The exuberant couple was wearing matching khaki shorts and pale yellow shirts. She was sitting on Marcus' lap and kissing him on the cheek. He was smiling into the camera and managed to look elegant even in casual attire.

Olivia lifted the picture and held it in front of her with both hands. Then she attested to her faithful partner and beloved friend. "You were so grateful for God's gift of life. Thank you for being an awesome man of God, husband, father, and role model to all who were blessed to know you."

It was her first time remembering her husband and crying

for a very different reason. Her wet eyes stared into his. "I miss you, Marcus, and will always love you, but I've mourned long enough. 'Those who God sets free are free indeed.' It's time for me to live again." She wiped her cheek. "I believe you would want that."

Due to the sacredness of the moment and the stillness of her soul, she was able to hear the witness in her spirit quietly say, "Go in peace."

————

The rhythm of Monte's English *and* his Spanish flowed naturally. Olivia's English was good, but her Spanish sounded robotic. It made no difference. The two amigos were basking in each other's company as they took turns reading *The Woman Who Outshone the Sun*. It was a Mexican folktale written in two languages. Montana and Olivia looked quite comfy as they turned his hospital room into story time. Surprisingly, they had not tired of the only story they had read over the past several weeks. Olivia wasn't sure how much longer their book club could meet. Each morning, she went to work hoping—for a cure, for a miracle, for one more day.

"Miss Olivia, you remind me of Lucia Zenteno."

"Really? How?"

"You both have glorious hair, except hers is black."

She smiled. "Muchas gracias, mi amigo."

"But that's not all." A wide smile crossed his pale brown face.

Olivia stared down at him. He was a true beauty inside and out. His midnight hair and eyebrows were still thick. The chemotherapy treatments had not yet affected him to the extent that they would. His long, full lashes framed eyes so dark they appeared black, too. He looked up at her.

"My last name is Rios and it means river. In the story, the river fell in love with Lucia." He stopped. "And Montana means mountain. So a river *and* a mountain love you."

"That is a double honor." She leaned over and kissed the top of her 'adopted' son's head. "I love you, too, mijo, and I'm really going to miss you when you go home."

Montana's smile slid from his face. "Can I tell you a secret?" he whispered.

"Yes," she whispered back.

"You know at the end of the story when Lucia Zenteno disappears, and the villagers are sad because they think she's gone?"

Olivia nodded.

"That's going to happen to me. I'll be in heaven, but I'll be here, too. You just won't be able to see me."

Her eyes welled with tears and blocked her words. She pinched her lips together in an attempt to maintain a proper demeanor. Still the water flowed.

"Don't cry, Miss Olivia." Monte patted her arm. "I'm still gonna love you and my papi."

It was very unprofessional, but she cried anyway.

Olivia rushed to the one place in Centerview Memorial Hospital that she purposely stayed away from. The cafeteria. It had nothing to do with the wisecracks about hospital food. After years of serving as a nurse, she could not get over the cavalier attitudes of many of the nurses and doctors with whom she worked.

A profession in the medical field warranted tough skin and even tougher emotions, but she had a difficult time accepting the untimely death of a child. She had never received the across-the-board, high-ranking evaluations she could have because of her one downfall.

Her supervisors felt her too compassionate because, over the years, she did more than pity grieving families, she empathized with them and often cried along with them. What none of them knew was that she cried, too, for the loss of her own child. If not for her keen mind and the meticulous attention she paid to detail, she would have been fired long ago.

Her supervisors appreciated her bedside manner but wished she would not get beside herself when the inevitable occurred. Olivia smiled briefly, remembering her early days. She had made some progress in learning to mask her feelings. However, no patient had ever affected her the way Monte did.

Olivia needed a drink. Something with caffeine. She stood in line to pay for her purchase—a cup of steaming herbal tea and a croissant. There were two cashiers working a double checkout line. A good-looking gentleman across from her smiled. Olivia realized she had been staring at him for some time. She quickly turned her head, paid for her snack, and hurried to an empty table near the back of the cafeteria.

She lifted the plastic bear from the table and added several drops of honey to her tea. Then she squeezed every ounce of juice from the lemon into it and dropped the entire slice onto her saucer. Olivia stirred slowly and attempted to focus on something beside the mountain and river she loved: Amani. Telling her what to do about the Marley situation would be futile. She had six witnesses who could testify to that. Olivia bowed her head. "You speak to her heart, Lord."

TWENTY-FIVE

Amani longed for the times when the biggest obstacle between her and sleep were the snores of one of her sisters. She was tossing, turning, and searching for peace.

She finally gave up trying to sleep and sat up. She turned on her favorite Christian radio station, then grabbed Marley's letter from underneath her pillow. Her ears perked up at the speaker's words.

"When you are planning to marry and you are unequally yoked, you end up marrying someone else's husband or wife. The same principle applies to dating someone whose belief system differs from yours. God does not want believers dating or marrying someone whose beliefs are contrary to His word. The ridiculously high divorce rate in the church can be traced back to the fact that far too many Christians are doing things *their* way instead of His way.

"God is so much smarter than we are. The Bible tells us His ways are higher than ours. Every time. As Christians, we must base our lives on sacred scripture instead of our flaky feel—"

Amani reached out and silenced the message. It was not

the one she desired to hear. And Marley was a believer. He just believed a little differently than she did. Anyway, wasn't love about sacrificing and compromising?

Her thoughts turned to the letter from Marley in her hand. It seemed a lifetime ago since she'd seen him, but it was only a day shy of Toni Braxton's "Seven Whole Days." She refused to take his calls or come out of her bedroom the times he had come to see her. Destiny reluctantly helped her to dodge him when he had been bold enough to show up at Tubman. In his persistence, Marley had finally hand-delivered the letter to her mother.

She yawned and glanced at the clock radio on her nightstand. The red digital read-out displayed 3:09. Oh, what the heck! Grabbing the telephone, she knocked the on-campus housing information she still needed to look at on the floor. She loved Marley. That had to count for something. Hadn't Mia told her that love makes you do what you wouldn't ordinarily do? She wondered if her sister still believed she made the right choice.

Amani dialed the first three digits of Mia's number before she remembered Roland had practically moved into the two-bedroom apartment Mia shared with her girlfriend, Keisha, who was also a hair stylist. Knowing there was a good chance he was spending the night, she hung up and leaned back against the headboard. Amani felt as unsure of herself as she had on her first day of kindergarten. She didn't know whether to put on a brave front or suck her thumb.

She'd been unable to sleep since receiving Marley's ultimatum a week ago, and she refused to read the letter because she was weakening. Amani knew she needed to make a final decision. The prom was being held later that evening. After her mother told her about what happened to her when she was Amani's age, her first decision was never to cry over his trifling behind again. How could she? What she experienced the night of her birthday was puppy chow compared to what Mama had gone through.

When her mother awoke from her nap, Amani had filled her in on everything that happened the night she went back to Marley's. Olivia was ecstatic that Amani's plans to have sex were thwarted, but she firmly reprimanded Amani about going for a drive with Clifton because she didn't know him well enough. She knew from experience that the night could have ended much differently. However, she repeatedly thanked Jesus for "ordering her baby girl's steps and directing her paths," even in that situation.

Tonight, in her moonlit room, Amani gently fingered the envelope. Marley. He was the only man she had given the secret combination to her heart. Until the night of her birthday, he had carefully protected all the love it stored for him.

It was hard having to avoid him because they had become inseparable, yet she was afraid to go back. Without him, her life was at a standstill because she didn't see how she could go forward either. No one or no thing was supposed to come between them. Not ever. *What happened, Marley?*

She looked upward, trying to halt the inevitable. However, the thought of life without Marley was so overwhelming she could barely breathe. Her vision blurred as the dam of tears she had stubbornly refused to shed broke.

Amani felt like a ship adrift at sea.

She needed to let down her anchor and force herself to remember the direction of the sandy shore from which she had come. Only then would she be able to make the decision that would put her back on course.

Like waves at the beach rushing against jagged rocks, thoughts of their last night began pushing against the walls of her mind. She wanted to keep them at bay, fully understanding why the late Minnie Riperton sang about not wanting to go back down memory lane.

But, despite the pain, she needed to make that voyage.

With her back propped against the pillow, Amani surrendered. She carefully opened the envelope and took out the letter. Immediately, his scent filled her nostrils and her temperature rose. He had sprayed the letter with cologne. Amani inhaled deeply. *Mmmm.* She missed his laugh. His smile. His kiss. She missed being in his arms and feeling his heart beat in a rhythm identical to hers.

Amani crawled over to the other nightstand and turned on the lamp. Then she took a deep breath and read the letter. Twice.

Dear Amani,

I see your lovely face everywhere I go. The wind blows and I yearn for your caress. The sun shines but cannot compare to the warmth your smile brings me. Your voice is the first melody I hear when I awake in the morning and the last one I tune into at night. You are so much a part of me that, though misunderstanding, doubt, and confusion have separated us, my heart knows the truth. This is not the end, merely a new beginning.

I'm certain Destiny has told you about the birthday present but, I must admit, I did call Tamara. When you left me that night, I almost lost my mind. But I came to my senses in time to send her home before I did something stupid. Amani, I don't have the words to express how sorry I am. Please forgive me, baby. My love for you is so real and so strong.

I went ahead and reserved that tuxedo you liked, and your chariot awaits. Nikki, I know you want the same thing I do. Once the prom ends, we'll make love until nothing else matters, except the way we feel.

Your love is the only miracle I need.

Marley

Amani wiped her cheek with one hand. Marley's sincere sentiments touched her more deeply than even his telephone messages had. If they reunited, she already knew what their next step would be. The thought of their uniting as one made her pulse race and her heart flutter. Amani couldn't deny that he was right. She wanted what he wanted. However, there was something else she could neither deny nor dispute.

"Knocking boots." "Doing it." "Getting busy." "Making love." They could call it what they wanted, but no matter how they viewed it, God called it sin. True as that was, she was still uncertain of her plans for the evening.

To live her life for the moment or for eternity: it was time to choose. They would either go their separate ways, or tonight was the night.

Amani stood, stretched, and walked over to the bay window. Closing her eyes, she lifted the letter to her nose. *Mmmm.* Then she sat on the bench where she stayed until the morning sun greeted her with a warming smile.

Olivia bounced down the hall to Amani's room. Her smile quickly vanished when she opened the door. Amani was sitting on the cushioned bench. Her head was slumped on the window and her legs were extended in front of her. Olivia glanced at the bed and noticed the envelope. She walked over to her daughter and squeezed herself behind her, gently resting her baby girl's head on her shoulder. She took the letter out of her hand, refolded it and placed it on the windowsill. Amani stirred.

"What time is it?"

"Almost six."

"I finally read it."

"I see." Mama wrapped her arms around Amani's middle and clasped her hands. "You should at least talk to him."

"He said he sent that cheerleader home right after Destiny left." She turned to the tree. "I believe him."

"Then what's the problem?"

"He still wants to bypass the wedding and go straight to the honeymoon."

"Oh." For a brief moment, Olivia's mouth set in a tight line. Experience had taught her to listen more than she spoke at times like these, but she had one thing that needed to be said.

"Amani Nicole, continue to stand on the Word of God and you won't fall or fail." She looked out the window. "Sometimes the fallout from your decisions will make it seem as if you made the wrong choice, but God honors you when you honor His word."

Amani nodded. "I definitely want to do the right thing. Mama, what made Daddy so different? Why didn't he pressure you?"

"I think it was because he was solid in his faith and he knew who he was. Everyone always looked up to him and he looked up to God. Even as a young boy, he had the ability to motivate people to do their best."

Amani chuckled. "I don't think little Vincent would call that punch in the stomach Daddy gave him for teasing you motivation."

"I don't know. It did prevent him from making that same mistake again."

Amani's giggles turned into full-fledged laughter.

"What? Out with it!"

"I wish Daddy were here to slap Marley upside his big head."

Olivia smiled. "Maybe I'll do it for him." She glanced at her watch. "I need to get going and you need to get ready for school. When I come home, we'll start preparing for your big night." She paused. "Are Destiny and Chazz still meeting here?"

"I'm not sure. I'll find out when she calls this morning."

"Either way, your sisters will show up in full force." She kissed Amani on the temple then headed for the door.

"Mama."

Olivia turned.

"Tell Monte and Lucia Zenteno hello for me. I'd like to meet the little fella one day."

285

"That would be nice." The smile that crossed Olivia's face far outshone the sun.

After her mother left the room, Amani turned back to the window and fixed her eyes on the tree. Raindrops or sunshine, the tree remained. Amani hummed the words to "I Shall Not Be Moved," a hymn they used to sing in Sunday School. She wished she could be like the tree in that song, planted by waters that were sometimes calm and other times rushing, still the tree stood steadfast and unmovable.

To be as strong as a well-grounded tree would be awesome. The winds of temptation could whirl as fierce as they chose without her being uprooted. All of Marley's huffing and puffing would be but a breeze blowing through her branches. She'd bend, but not break. Amani was inspired and knew exactly what she had to do.

Today she needed to talk to the gardener of her soul.

––––––––

Monte's bed had become a prison and the cafeteria was the visitor's waiting area.

Monte was too weak for even their morning walks up and down the corridor. When Olivia arrived at 6:45, she attached a catheter to his urethra because getting up to go to the bathroom took more energy than his frail frame could expend.

She read their favorite story to him before her morning break. He lay back on his pillow and tried to get comfortable. It hurt her to see him hurting, but the painkillers took a few minutes before they made a difference. Until then, she almost cried watching him force smiles as she read alone.

Loving him was starting to affect her job performance.

She snapped at a parent griping about how much time she lost from work because of her son's clumsiness, was borderline hostile to the nurse she relieved when she discovered Monte sleeping on urine-soaked sheets, and lost it completely when another nurse casually mentioned that room 111 would be vacant soon.

Finally her supervisor told her to take an extended break.

She stirred her tea and looked around the cafeteria. Her eyes fastened on the clock. 9:52 AM. Time kept ticking, ticking, ticking into the future and life marched on. Olivia understood that death and disease were not a part of God's divine plan, but found it hard to fathom the unfairness of Monte's fate.

A gentle voice above her head startled her. "May I sit with you?" She quickly looked up, and then nodded.

He sat down, smiled, and extended his hand. "Good morning. My name is Gabriel."

His grip was warm and strong. "Hello. I'm Olivia." Her smile was faint in return, but something about him seemed familiar.

"I'm very pleased to meet you . . . Olivia."

"Likewise." She cocked her head. He was wearing a starched denim shirt, a pair of jeans, and a musk-scented cologne. But it was his eyes that stood out.

He picked up his breakfast burrito. "I saw you here Monday afternoon and would have liked to sit with you then, but you seemed preoccupied."

That's it. She snapped her fingers. "I knew I recognized you. You were standing across from me at the register. My mind was elsewhere that afternoon. I apologize for my staring."

He swallowed and shook his head. "Not necessary." A piece of scrambled egg fell on the table. "So, you're a nurse?"

"On a good day."

"And on a bad one?"

"An overprotective mother hen?"

He raised an eyebrow.

This is strange, but I already feel so comfortable with him. She picked up the teacup. "There's a patient I appear to have

crossed the line with. My personal feelings for him are inter-
fering with the professional distance my job requires."

Gabriel raised the Styrofoam cup to his lips. "I'm sure your
patient appreciates the concern you have shown him." He
took a sip of the black coffee. "In fact, he's lucky to have you
taking care of him."

Olivia shook her head. "I'm blessed to know him." She returned the cup to the saucer. "My husband and I lost our first
child. A boy. Seven more pregnancies resulted in seven daughters. I get to cheat and pretend he's my son." *I can't believe
I'm sitting here telling this man all of my business.*

He smiled. "I hope you don't think me too forward, but
your husband is fortunate to have a wife as beautiful and
compassionate as you."

She blushed then stared into his luminous eyes. "I'm not
married. My husband died in a car accident. This August will
make thirteen years he's been gone."

"Forgive me." He touched her hand. "I also know the pain
of loss. My wife was killed in September of 1995. We were
caught in the line of gang crossfire. For months I carried the
blame, thinking if only I'd taken a different route."

She squeezed his hand. "Gabriel, you couldn't have known."

"I tortured myself just the same. We were planning to move
the month before she had the baby."

Olivia gasped. "She was pregnant?"

He nodded.

"And . . . the baby?"

"Was to be born two months later, but they performed an
emergency C-section as soon as we arrived at the hospital." It
was his turn to look away. "Paulina died holding our son in
her arms."

Olivia closed her hand around his. "My God," she whispered.

"Both He and my son got me through." With his free hand,
he took a picture from his shirt pocket and handed it to her.

Her eyes brightened. "This is the mountain I love."
"I know." Gabriel smiled. "Your hair gave you away."

———————

Amani was walking on water.

Instead of going to school to discuss hairstyles and evening attire, she played hookey. When Destiny called to see if she wanted to carpool, Amani confided her plans to go to the beach and think. Her friend wanted to tag along, but Amani declined her offer. The wet sand and the cooling sensation of the rolling tide tickled her toes. The ocean's salty breeze wooed her closer to Him.

She was incognito in a hooded white sweat jacket over a purple tank top with matching sweatpants, the bottoms of which were pulled up to her knees. Her hair was almost completely covered under the purple and gold Lakers cap she wore. The brown frost lipstick adorning her mouth glimmered in the morning sun. Amani had come to wade, listen and obey.

On the ride over to the Redondo Beach Pier, she played only song number seven from *The Mountain High, Valley Low* CD. Yolanda Adam's "Open My Heart" prepared her to hear from her Heavenly Daddy.

She stopped, put her hands in her pocket, and spoke aloud. "Okay, Lord. What should I do? I love Marley and I want to go to the prom with him tonight, but I also want to do your will. It's no longer about trying to be like Mama. It's all about pleasing you." Waves of salt passed by and washed her feet. "Capture my heart again," she prayed, clothing herself in the rays of an ageless sun and savoring the accompanying touch of a comforting breeze.

Amani stared at the houses on the distant hills. The same God created the mountains, Marley, and her with one purpose in mind: to fellowship with Him. God loved her and wanted her to know and love Him in return. Her eyes stayed focused on the highest homes.

"I will lift up mine eyes unto the hills from whence cometh my help," she recited softly. She tried to remember that expression Pastor and Sister Hilton used. The wind from the sea refreshed her memory and she declared out loud. "I feel my help coming on." Amani turned from the hills and continued her faith walk. In the stillness of her spirit, He encouraged her to stand.

Like a tree planted by the waters.

———

When Amani returned home, she read the letter for the third time. Marley's scent combined with the love she felt in her heart for him was difficult to resist. All she needed to do was call and he would be ready. Ready with the tuxedo he already reserved. Ready to play Prince Charming to her Cinderella. Ready to seal their love when the prom ended.

She inhaled the smell of him one last time, then threw the letter on the nightstand and sat on the edge of her bed. Her hands shook as she picked up the telephone and dialed. He answered on the second ring, sounding out of breath.

"Hello."

"Hi . . . It's me."

"I know." He closed his eyes and mouthed the words. "Thank you, *Jesus.*"

"This is late notice, but—"

"Are we on for tonight?"

She hesitated. "Can you be here by six-thirty?"

"Girl, you ain't said nothin' but a word."

TWENTY-SIX

Mia was doing what she did best, working a sister's 'do. First, she washed Amani's curly coif then used the blow dryer to loosen the curls. Next, she used a moisturizing styling gel to slick down her hair and hold the side part in place. Then she pinned a braided bun to the nape of her neck. The final touch was a ring of silk fuchsia lilies circled around it. The effect was jazzy elegance.

Earlier, Perri had created a work of art. Smoky eyes, a berry mouth, lush lashes, arched eyebrows, and even more flawless skin made up a face that belonged on a magazine cover.

Nola's contribution was the manicure and pedicure she had given Amani earlier. Rosalind was going to videotape and Krystal was responsible for refreshments. Olivia and Oneita's jobs seemed simply to smile with pride and remember when.

The pink evening gown was a Vanessa Shephard creation. The halter-top contained a single pink and fuchsia beaded flower in the center. The long pink skirt was form-fitting and flowed to the floor. The dress showcased her slim but shapely size seven frame. When she tried it on two weeks ago, she loved the way she looked and couldn't wait for Marley to see her in it. Together, they had picked out his tuxedo and matching accessories.

Mia finally stopped fussing with Amani's hair and helped her to pull on the dress. Amani slipped into her silver pumps, then stood in front of the mirror. Mia stood beside her.

"Every brother in the house is going to want to switch places with homeboy." Mia laughed. "You look good, girl."

"Thank you." Amani blushed.

The chime of the doorbell serenaded her.

"I hope I'm doing the right thing."

Mia put a hand on her shoulder. "You usually do."

———

Amani was having such a good time she almost forgot what had brought them to this place. He had been the perfect gentleman all evening and was looking suave in a black tailless tuxedo with a white silk shirt and fuchsia vest and bow tie. He was even sporting a new hairstyle himself: tiny chic locs. So far, she had not regretted calling Clifton. The two couples were getting along like four black-eyed peas in a pod.

Destiny and Chazz accepted Clifton as if his escorting Amani to the prom had been the plan all along. The deejay decided to get the party started with a song designed to pull even the most loyal 'flower' off the wall.

Amani grabbed Clifton's hand. "Can you do the electric slide?"

"Can Bishop Jakes milk a metaphor?"

"You've been watching TBN?"

"My mother makes sure I watch it on Sundays."

"A-plus for her."

Chazz and Destiny followed them to the dance floor. It was surrounded by round tables that seated ten. Gold balloons decorated the ceiling and white silk roses with gold petals in black vases adorned every table.

Clifton started dancing as soon as they hit the floor.

Destiny picked up the skirt of her long lavender dress and proceeded to get her slide on. Chazz in a white tux and lavender vest broke it down with her.

Amani made sure her flowers were secure as she scanned the crowd. This was their last high school dance before they each embarked on predestined courses. She cut short the philosophizing. Right now was all she had to work with, so she decided to shake her groove thing and let tomorrow take care of itself.

They danced four records in a row before the deejay slowed it down. Clifton grabbed Amani's hand.

"Let's sit this one out."

She was a little disappointed, but followed him off the floor. Shawna, the nosiest and longest-winded person at Tubman, was still seated at the table. Amani was sure her date had probably gone in search of earplugs. That girl could out-talk a used car salesman. She knew it wasn't nice, but "Shut-up Shawna" was her well-deserved nickname.

Clifton pulled out Amani's chair for her and as he sat beside her, his knee brushed her leg. "Excuse me."

"That's okay." Amani took a sip of water, smiled in Shawna's direction, then leaned forward and whispered in Clifton's ear. "What's up? You don't want to slow dance with me?"

Clifton shook his head. "Girl, that ain't it." He kept his voice low. "My spirit is saved, but my flesh is still waiting to be rescued. If I slow dance with you, I might end up stranded on *Gilligan's Island*."

Amani burst out laughing. "You are crazy!"

"I notice you have that effect on a brother. Marley has to be insane to let you go for any reason."

"I guess I'm not woman enough—"

"Hush. You were too much woman for him."

"Thank you." She kissed his cheek. "You are a nice guy, Mr. Hendrix."

He smiled at her. "No, *thank you*, Miss Shephard." Clifton squeezed her hand. "I'll be right back. I need to make a bath-room run."

"All right."

Shawna turned to Amani before Clifton was barely out of earshot. Her French roll looked more like a French loaf. "So where's Marley? I was expecting him to be your escort. Oh, yeah. Why didn't you come to school today? I asked your girl, but she was her usual South Central self." She adjusted the humongous corsage covering her chest. "So what's the deal, pickle?"

"We broke up." Amani took an extended drink of water.

"That's too bad, but I knew he was flakier than Tony the Tiger the first time I met him. But that's okay because Clifton is definitely a cutie, and I love his sexy little locs. Donald Lawrence, the guy who sings with the Tri-City singers, has some on the front of one of his CDs. What's the name of it? It's sort of unique. Has something to do with the Internet. Anyway, Eddie Murphy wears locs sometimes. He was on Oprah a while back and I believe he was wearing them then. He was promoting one of his movies. I don't remember the name of it, but that guy on that show, *Living Single*. I watched a rerun the other day. Anyway, he wore his hair in locs, too. What was his name on the show? Oh, I can't recall . . . "

Amani looked over her head onto the dance floor. Destiny and Chazz looked comfy. She was jealous for real. As nice as Clifton was and as debonair as he was looking, he wasn't Marley. If they had slow danced, she would have probably tried to pretend that he was. She couldn't get too upset at Shawna. Her question was valid. Where was Marley?

———————

They had a false start last week, but this time she was going for the gold. Tamara's thigh brushed Marley's as they sat on the sofa. She quickly passed him another wine cooler. She couldn't believe this was his first time drinking and hoped what they said about alcohol was true. Her pal Seagram would free Marley of *all* his inhibitions.

Two hours ago, Tamara called and invited herself over. She had heard, through the Bruin 'vine, that Amani would be occupied. Before leaving her apartment, she showered and finger-combed her hair. The time she spent in the salon that afternoon had paid off. In place of the straight look she normally wore were tight chin-length curls her stylist had set using small spiral rods. A quick stop for a six-pack of mood transformers and she was on her way. On the liquor aisle, brothers of all colors tried to get their mack on. She ignored them all. In return, Marley droned on about how Amani had not called him to escort her to the prom.

Tamara knew exactly where she was going to take him before the night ended. She caught the tail end of his comment.

". . . I thought she loved me," he whined.

"Marley, I'm sorry." She bit into the end of an overripe strawberry. "I hate to say this, but looks like your girl has moved on."

"You think so?"

"Think about it. The prom is one of the most important nights of a girl's life. Instead of taking her *boyfriend*, she took some other dude." Tamara took a tiny sip of her cooler and shook her head. "That was foul. You don't deserve that."

He nodded and she opened his fourth cooler. In silence, she watched him down it. There was only one left.

She took the bottle from him in exchange for his hand. "If I were your woman, I couldn't even think about being with another man." She put her hand on his. "I love you, Marley, and I would never hurt you."

"You don't love me." He pouted.

"Boy, I love everything about you. From the way you smile to the way you rub the back of your neck when you're upset.

I even love the passion you bring to the court." She put her hand on his face and kissed him softly on the lips. When he didn't pull away, she moved onto the floor and knelt in front of him.

Tamara leaned toward him and stared him in the eye. "I bet you bring that same level of intensity into everything you do."

She unfastened his bow tie and threw it on top of the jacket on the floor. Next, she unbuttoned his fuchsia vest and added it to the pile. She slowly undid the buttons on his white tuxedo shirt. As she slid it down his shoulders, she kissed his neck and shoulders and licked the birthmark on his chest. Then she stuck her tongue in his mouth and started to unfasten his belt, but he grabbed her hands.

Marley stood and pulled her to her feet and began to clumsily unbutton her trench coat, beginning at the bottom. She stopped him before he could undo the top button. Tamara's eyes never left his face as she unfastened it and let her coat drop to the floor. Though the lights were dimmed, he could clearly see. For a few seconds, he simply stared. The last time, she had worn a red camisole underneath the black coat. Tonight, she had come prepared to bare her heart, soul, and body. His glassy eyes gleamed his approval as he surveyed her nakedness then grabbed her hand.

Tamara let out a weary sigh. She was finally going to have what she had been searching for all her life. Someone to love her. Someone to protect her. Someone to hold her gently through the night. She gave no thought to tomorrow as she kept her eyes on the person she believed to be that someone and followed him down the hall.

TWENTY-SEVEN

Five days to graduation and great expectations. Destiny slammed the car door and looked over at Amani who was on the driver's side. They were heading to what used to be their second home.

Destiny grinned. "This feels weird."

"I bet. You've been doing all the driving. Now, it's my turn."

"Not a problem. I can sit back and chill."

Amani looked into the rearview mirror as she backed out of the Ross family's driveway. "So what's up with you and Chazz? Y'all looked real chummy last night."

She blushed. "I really like him, Amani. He even promised to come to church with me tomorrow."

"Get out of here!"

"But I think it's more Pastor Hilton than me. He had Chazz cracking up at the talent show."

"Mama came home pumped. She said God's anointing was all over you and that the congregation broke out in praise and worship for at least fifteen minutes after you finished dancing. I wanted to come, but I know Sister Rachel would have asked me to sing and I couldn't. All I did was listen to the five hundred messages Marley left on my voice mail."

Destiny stared at her friend's profile. "Amani, please don't take this the wrong way, but that night at Marley's was divinely ordered."

She watched her friend frown but continued. "I met Destiny that night and I didn't like what I saw. I realized how much I needed the Lord. I've wasted so much energy looking to people and things to make me feel good about me when God has been here all the time."

She sighed. "I've hated my father for drinking and my mother for staying. I was angry because I missed out on a normal childhood. Even though your father's not here, his reputation for being a man of integrity lives on. I forgot all about God and tried to ensure a better future on my own."

She shook her head. "'It's not by our might or power but by His spirit.' My father has been trying and I've come to see my mother for who she really is—a strong woman of faith. Pastor Chamberlain and Sister Rachel have been counseling with them."

"A praying woman ain't no joke!"

"You better recognize." Destiny looked out the window. "If I hadn't been at Marley's that night, Amani, you probably would've done something I know you would have regretted. Running into Tamara pushed you into Clifton's arms, so to speak, and he rededicated his life to the Lord. I also got right with the Lord and it even looks like Chazz might hook up a relationship with J.C." She took Amani's hand. "I got love for you, girl."

Amani grinned, squeezing her hand. "I love you, too, Dee." She put her hand back on the steering wheel and turned into the parking lot. They found a space way in the back.

A few minutes later, a humbled Destiny grinned and held the door for Amani as they walked into the air-conditioned entrance of Sears.

Destiny fluffed her hair. "Get ready to lose your minds up in here, fellas. The divine diva duo is here to make your day!"

"I see that ego is still intact." Amani smiled.

"God's not through with me yet, girlfriend. I'm still under construction."

Once again, Olivia was holding secrets. In due time, she would tell it all. For now, she cherished the time they spent together, accepting that it would not last. She remembered Gabe's words and the way his dark eyes glowed. "Your beauty outshines the sun, the moon, and the stars." She turned away from the bay window and got ready for work with a smile on her face. She thanked God it was Monday.

Three days later, Olivia missed spending time with two of her favorite amigos, but she wouldn't have missed Amani's graduation for anything.

The sun was hot, but the tears that stung her eyes were hotter. She framed her hand over them and scanned the lawn area. Where was her baby? Black and white robes with matching caps and gold tassels bobbed up and down. They all looked alike. The only difference was the girls wore white and the boys black. Like the family and friends that sat bumper-to-bumper around her, she had come to celebrate with Harriet Tubman High's Class of 2002.

Olivia glanced down at the top of Ahmad's head. Instead of sitting next to Nola and the boys, her son-in-law was seated on the speaker's platform. She and the rest of her crew were sitting in the front middle section. The Shephard family had been designated reserved seating in 1990. That was to be the first year that one of Marcus' daughters graduated under his principalship.

It was also the first year the Marcus Alexander Shephard III Leadership Award was presented. Since that year, a young man and a young lady each received a plaque and a check for one thousand dollars. The student body, teachers, and administration, as well as the clerical and custodial staff, all voted for the two students showing giftedness in the area of leadership.

Graduation was the Shephards' time to release the bitter and savor the sweet.

Despite the turmoil at the beginning of her senior year, Perri ended it as the class salutatorian. However, during the first several weeks of the 1989-1990 school year, her academics began to slip. The usual A-plus student received mainly B's and a couple of C-plus's on her five-week progress report. A week later, twenty-three-year-old Ahmad Jamal Mills joined New Horizons Christian Center.

The burden-removing, yoke-destroying power of God had transformed a hardcore thug into a warrior for Christ. His impact on the teenagers and young adults in the congregation was nothing short of phenomenal. Ahmad based his life on a single scripture, one to which he easily related: "The kingdom of God suffereth violence and the violent take it by force."

He was on a mission to snatch the lives of young people from the jaws of despair, self-destruction, and death.

What began as a church's youth group had become Growing Boys 2 Men & Girls 2 Women, a community-based program emphasizing spiritual principles. One of the recipients of this year's leadership award was Jalontae Woods, a young man who could have easily been voted the most unlikely to survive had Ahmad not been put into his life. Shamika Brown, on her way to becoming the first African-American *and* first woman President of the United States, was representing for the ladies. Neither of their families were churchgoers, but they had made sure their children were a part of Ahmad's organization. As a result, Jalontae and Shamika had become faithful members of New Horizons.

This morning, Ahmad had the honor of presenting the award in the name of the father-in-law he had never met but to whom he was often compared.

Malachi and Micah started jumping up and down. Olivia started to shush them, and then realized their father had center stage. She cheered with them and reached over and squeezed her daughter's hand. Nola managed to look nervous and proud.

Down on the lawn, Amani nudged Monica Shaw. "That's my brother-in-law."

She elbowed Amani. "Girl, he is *fine*."

Amani smiled. Ahmad was looking very handsome in a brown suit with a tan shirt and a print tie containing brown, tan, and black. His thick black hair was neatly cut and his clean-shaven, golden complexion radiated confidence. His deep dimples accentuated his face. He stood holding a plaque in each outstretched hand.

"Good morning, graduating seniors, faculty, family, and friends. As the name implies, the Marcus Alexander Shephard III Leadership Award signifies outstanding achievement in leadership. It is given to two students who embody the spirit of the late, great Marcus Shephard."

Amani and many of her classmates rose to their feet and clapped. In the stands, she could see her family's standing ovation. She sat down and wiped her eyes and Monica squeezed her hand.

Amani listened intently as Nola's man and Malachi and Micah's superhero continued. "Shamika and Jalontae have cultivated their leadership abilities. They have been using what they already possess to make a difference here at school and also in their neighborhoods and communities. Their gifts will affect society and, ultimately, the world."

He carefully placed the plaques on the podium then pointed toward the sedate and serious seniors. "What's in your hands this morning? What gift have you been given and how are you using it?" He waved his hands. "Don't tell me that your life is too messed up." New Horizon's favorite son shook his head. "When I met Jalontae Woods, he was in his fifth foster home. He mumbled when he spoke and barely raised his head. The boy was so full of rage, he was ready to fight if you blessed him when he sneezed." He looked over at Jalontae who, grinning broadly, returned his stare.

"Don't get me started on Shamika. She lived with her grandmother. The only thing she knew at twelve years old was that a pretty face could get you anything you wanted." Ahmad winked at her and she blushed in response. "Not only have they turned their lives around, but they have made it their duty to help others. They will both be attending USC in the fall, but have already promised me they would be part-time facilitators at Boys 2 Men & Girls 2 Women."

He turned to them. "You all know you can count on me to hold you to that." They looked at each other and nodded vigorously. Ahmad returned his attention to their fellow classmates. "Take the time to find out what your talent is, then develop it until you achieve excellence in that area. Your gift is already in your hands. Whether you use it or lose it is up to you."

He picked up the plaques. "It is with great pleasure and even greater pride that I present the Marcus Alexander Shephard III Leadership Award to Miss Shamika Brown and Mister Jalontae Woods."

To a rowdy standing ovation complete with whistles and "raise 'em ups," they stood and walked over to their mentor with their heads held high, unwavering light in their eyes and smiles on their faces. Ahmad shook Shamika's hand and passed her a plaque, then did the same with Jalontae. He took two envelopes from his jacket pocket and passed one to each of them, accompanied by a hug.

Ahmad leaned into the microphone. "Either of you have a word for your classmates?" He stepped back. Shamika whispered in Jalontae's ear. The young man nodded, then they walked to the podium together.

"Class of 2002, whatever your hands find to do for good, do it mightily!"

Their unified voices echoed across the lawn and into the stands. Their words reverberated in the hearts of two of the women on their feet.

Nola squeezed her mother's hand. Both women knew the deep admiration a wife held for a husband who adored her and willingly invested himself for the betterment of others.

The sky rained black and white caps as the senior class song, "Believe" by Commissioned, gave them their marching orders. They were instructed to believe the unbelievable and dream the unthinkable because they could do all things if they only believed.

The Tubman seniors rushed in different directions, all wanting to be among the first to congratulate their closest friends. Amani and Destiny swayed to the song's lyrics as they held tightly to each other and their tested faith in God.

TWENTY-EIGHT

One month ago, Amani had graduated from Tubman High and fairytale notions of love. She was now able to see things as they were. The white horse was a bleached donkey and the armor had been rented and was dented.

Since graduation her hair had grown some, but she had changed a lot. Amani stretched her legs across the built-in bench and closed her Bible. The Bible was a present from her godparents. *Virtuous Amani Shephard* was engraved in gold across the bottom. In another month, she would be attending college on the other side of the country. She stared at the tree as she began to reflect.

Six weeks had passed since she'd seen or spoken to Marley. Destiny claimed to have seen him at graduation but, if he was there, he left without saying anything to her. Amani missed him for real. As recently as yesterday, she had to talk herself out of calling him.

They were on different levels.

To keep busy, she volunteered at Boys 2 Men & Girls 2 Women. As she watched her brother-in-law in action, she wondered how many of the young ladies had a crush on their mentor. Thirty-five-year-old Ahmad looked pretty good for an old man.

When she returned home in the afternoons, she looked forward to spending time with Olivia, but her mother always seemed to have something to do when her shift ended.

Amani didn't like having too much free time on her hands. She wasn't sure if the saying was in the Bible, but she believed it nonetheless. An idle mind was said to be the devil's workshop. She did her best to keep hers occupied. When she wasn't reading literature specifically targeting her age group, she was listening to teaching tapes on subjects ranging from abstinence to financial prosperity God's way. Jamming with her girl Yolanda Adams was another of her favorite pastimes. She couldn't get enough of Yolanda's rendition of R. Kelly's "I Believe I Can Fly."

Destiny had enrolled in UC Berkeley's Freshman Summer Program. With her best friend gone and her not wanting to lead Clifton on, her social life was nonexistent. Amani pulled the invitation from the back of her Bible. Maybe she would go to Clifton's birthday party.

She quickly opened her King James Version of the Bible, flipped to a passage of scripture she had practically memorized, and read it silently. I Corinthians, Chapter 6, Verses 17-20. Her experience with Marley had shown her the importance of having the Word of God in her spirit *and* on her lips. She was determined not to compromise her Christian values—for any reason or any man—ever again.

Amani watched the postal carrier get back on her truck then walked downstairs to get the mail. Her face brightened when she recognized Destiny's handwriting among the bills and junk mail addressed to Olivia Shephard. She quickly tore open the package. It was a Trin-i-Tee 5:7 CD called *Spiritual Love*.

A yellow post-it note was attached to the front of it. *Mani, I don't think Yo-Yo would mind if you listened to this CD for a while. There are so many fine brothers up in here I have to listen to one song constantly to remind myself "who I be." When you listen to the song, you'll know what I mean. The watch was your birthday/graduation present. Think of song #2 as a gift for your spirit. Love, Dee.*

Amani smiled. She missed her best friend.

She ran up the stairs, two at a time, and hurried over to her CD player. She put her girl back in the case and put the trio of cuties in her place. She set the CD on song number two. Shaking her head with her mouth open, she drank in every lyric. This couldn't be a coincidence. God had her back. She started flowing with the song's beat, letting every line wash over her. Amani grabbed two of the lines and held on tight. She was God's property and her body was the Lord's temple.

When the song ended, she ran back to her Bible. This time, she read the verses aloud. *"But he that is joined unto the Lord is one spirit. Flee fornication. Every sin that a man doeth is without the body; but he that committeth fornication sinneth against his own body. What? Know ye not that your body is the temple of the Holy Ghost which is in you, which ye have of God, and ye are not your own? For ye are bought with a price: therefore glorify God in your body, and in your spirit, which are God's."*

Amani walked back over to the CD player. She needed to hear that song a few more times. Marley wasn't the only man who would give her an invitation she'd have to refuse.

New York was a big place and her name was not Eve. She planned to take a bite out of upstate New York and the Big Apple without breaking fellowship with the Lord.

Amani picked up the telephone. Before her mother made plans for Saturday, she was going to get in her request. After their morning excursion, Olivia could do whatever it was she had been doing. She wondered briefly if her mother had a man, then shook her head and frowned. An idle mind *was* a devil's workshop. The only boyfriend in her mother's life was a little guy named Mountain.

TWENTY-NINE

Olivia thought she had grown accustomed to being alone but recently she had begun to experience acute feelings of loneliness whose only remedy was the cure of Gabriel's company. His smile and touch were just what the doctor ordered. Though hesitant about the afternoon plans she had made, she knew she needed to follow through this time.

The first thing on her agenda, however, was taking her baby girl shopping. Amani's first experience with cold weather would be upstate New York's winter wonderland. She needed long johns, at least two pairs of gloves, a couple of wool scarves, a pair of waterproof boots, and an insulated coat.

For the next four years, Miss Mani would be attending college far away from her, but just a prayer away from God. And, after the way she had had handled herself with Marley, Olivia wouldn't worry about her *too* much. Although she was proud of her daughter's strength, she wished Amani had chosen UCLA, USC, or even gone to UC Berkeley with Destiny. Olivia was proud of both young women and truly appreciated Destiny's most recent gift to her daughter.

When they were out today, she was going to buy six more of the timely CDs—an extra for Amani to carry around with her. She smiled. Well, maybe not in her backpack but to have in case the first one became lost or damaged. The second one was for Mia. The third for Krystal. One for Vanessa and another for Perri. The last one was for her.

She was a vibrant mommy—not an entombed mummy—and had recently been revived in spirit, soul, and body.

Her last bambino was on her way to college. Olivia put her hand over her mouth and pressed her lips together as her eyes began to fill. She quickly removed her hand and spoke aloud to the One who promised in His Word never to forsake her. "She's your child, too, Father. Please take care of our baby."

She walked down the hall to Amani's room and knocked on the door.

"Come in."

Olivia opened the door. "Good morning."

Amani smiled. "Good morning." She was sitting cross-legged on the bench, looking out of the window. Her Bible lay open beside her.

"I'm all yours. We'll do some school shopping first, then find you something to wear for tonight. A few more weeks and you're out of here." She looked over her daughter's head. *When did she stop being five?* Olivia became lost in her own thoughts but quickly caught herself.

"Take a shower and get dressed. I'll make breakfast then we'll head over to Baldwin Hills Plaza. How's that?"

"Sounds like a plan, Miss Ava." Amani stretched her arms above her head and yawned.

Olivia rolled her eyes, smiling. "I'll meet you downstairs in an hour. A true beauty doesn't need much enhancement."

Amani smiled. "You ought to know."

———————

Amani was having an out-of-body experience. She didn't believe in spiritualism in any form, but had no other words to describe what was happening to her. It was as if she was watching her mother, the salespeople, the other shoppers, and the folks just hanging out trying to see and be seen from a distance.

She felt removed from everything going on around her. At the same time, she was in tune with what was taking place within her.

In almost every store they had gone to, she had run into someone she knew from Tubman. She already felt they no longer knew her. Most of them did a double-take before approaching because of the new hairstyle she sported. She exchanged pleasantries and her college address, knowing she had no intention of staying in touch. Amani felt like a fraud, but there was no point in being rude so she played along with the charade.

A couple of the brothers mentioned they weren't into letter writing but would prefer to have her digits. Amani was grateful she really didn't know the telephone number in her dorm room. She politely accepted theirs instead. After the third or fourth such exchange, Olivia looped her arm through her daughter's and kidded as they walked away.

"Seems that girls with short black curls have as much fun as blondes."

Amani playfully pinched her mother. "Let's check out that store on the second floor. I can't remember the name of it, but it has some really nice evening wear. I want the *perfect* dress for tonight."

Olivia dropped her daughter's arm and raised an eyebrow. "Either you're falling for Clifton or you're hoping Marley will be at the party?"

Amani blushed. "Clifton and I are just friends and although I still haven't returned any of his calls, and I won't let him visit, I would like to at least see Marley before I leave."

"In that case, you need to be da bomb!" Olivia posed in a gangster lean. Being loaded down with packages made an already comical stance even more hilarious.

She gave her mother an incredulous look and spoke through clenched teeth, "Olivia Dupree Shephard. Please! You never even lived in South Central."

"That's all right. Your father helped put South Central on the map. I thought you knew, homey."

Amani grabbed her mother's arm. "Okay, gospel gangsta mama. You so down, you make down look up."

Still in character, Olivia snatched her arm away from her daughter. "That's what I'm talking about. Don't make me get ghetto on you." She started walking toward the escalator.

Amani watched her for a moment with a wide grin on her face then called after her, "You don't get out much, do you?"

Olivia turned around. "You say something, little girl?"

"Nope." She stood beside her mother, almost half a foot taller.

Olivia cocked her head to the side and gave her daughter the look. "That's what I thought."

Amani put her head on her mother's shoulder. "I'm really going to miss you."

"Nowhere near as much as I'm going to miss you." She gently rested her head against her daughter's. All joking was shelved and their mood began to somber. Olivia lifted her head and Amani straightened.

"And I'm gonna miss Marley."

Olivia squeezed her daughter's hand. "The next time God sends him a virtuous woman, he'll know how to honor her."

Amani sighed. "Too bad I had to be the guinea pig." She couldn't stand the thought of Marley loving and eventually marrying another woman. "*We* were supposed to be inseparable." Once meaningful words taunted her. *No one or no thing can come between us. Not ever.*

"Look at it this way. You were his first strong Christian sister."

Amani's smile missed her eyes, but she raised her hands, snapped her fingers, and swayed from side to side. "From now on, a brother gets that every time."

"Good." Olivia winked at her daughter's efforts and wished there was something she could do to speed up Amani's healing process. Experience had taught her better. The mending of a broken heart was a delicate procedure best left to time, prayer, and God.

Olivia sat outside the restaurant, debating whether she should stay or go. Glancing into the rearview mirror, she finger-combed her hair then said a silent prayer. Before she could change her mind, she got out of the car and walked briskly to the entrance of TGI Friday's. She stood in the foyer and looked around, but didn't see him anywhere.

"Okay, Lord. I'm going to take this as a sign." She was reaching for the door when he walked in. Instantly, her heartbeat sped up and she felt tingly all over.

"Buenas tardes, Olivia, don't tell me you were about to stand me up *again*." His glowing eyes smiled into hers.

"Uh . . . I was just going to wait for you outside. It's a little stuffy in here."

Gabriel smiled. "I would suggest you trail me to the Long Beach Shoreline, but I'm afraid you'd get lost in traffic."

Olivia's smile was weak. She wanted to say, "If I'm not careful, I'll end up lost in your gaze." What she said instead was, "No. This will be fine. Maybe next time."

His smile widened. "So I'll have another opportunity to see you away from the hospital?"

She hadn't meant to say that. "Maybe."

"Please excuse me, Olivia." He walked over to the hostess.

Olivia was surprised that the restaurant was already crowded. While she usually remained in her house on the weekends except for church on Sundays, people were out and about, living their lives.

Gabriel returned to her. "We have about a ten minute wait." He placed his hand on her arm. "Have a seat and I'll be right back." He strolled up the steps to the bar.

She was glad she had worn her beige sundress with a pair of brown sandals and a brown choker. Gabriel was wearing a tan, short-sleeved polo-style shirt and a pair of khaki shorts with brown sandals.

They already looked like a couple.

Olivia hated to compare. Marcus had him beat in the looks department, but not even Marcus could touch his generous heart and gentle spirit. Gabriel was confident in a different way than Marcus had been. Marcus trusted the Lord and his ability to lead and motivate others. Gabriel's sole confidence was his trust in the God who created him.

After finally accepting he was not to blame for his wife's tragic death, he accepted the hand he had been dealt with great aplomb. For almost seven years, he had raised Montana alone, believing God to provide him with a mother for his son and a companion for himself.

She smiled as he approached her carrying two glasses of water. He extended his hand. "Por una hermosa angel negra."

"Gracias." She took a tiny sip as warm rays beamed on her through the window.

He sat next to her on the red-cushioned bench. "You're even prettier in the sunlight."

"Thank you." Olivia grinned. "I could get accustomed to all this flattery."

"And I would enjoy nothing more than the chance to compliment you every day. You think we could arrange that?"

She smiled and sipped slowly. "Rios, party of two." They were being beckoned over the intercom. As Olivia hurried to her feet, water from the glass sloshed her hand but getting a little wet was the least of her concerns. Olivia was grateful she was saved from having to answer Gabriel and face her growing feelings by a call to lunch.

THIRTY

A mani posed on the staircase so her mother could take one of the last pictures she would include in the photo journal she was creating. Olivia had presented each of her daughters with a scrapbook of joyful memories and love-filled words as a graduation present. Amani would receive hers as a going-away gift. Olivia was having a difficult time feeling happy as she snapped Amani's picture.

Amani made it to the bottom stair and stood before her mother for final inspection. "So what do you think?"

The pastel green skirt of the taffeta dress showed off her firm thighs and shapely legs. The bodice of the dress was halter style and hugged her toned torso. She thought her daughter looked chic and angelic.

Olivia smiled. "Una hermosa angel negra."

"Huh? English pora favoro."

"Your Spanish is worse than mine." Olivia laughed. "You look like a beautiful black angel."

"Oh! Thank you."

Amani was wearing a pair of silver slip-ons. The laces were

tied around her ankles. She had accessorized the mini-dress with a thin silver choker and a pair of silver studs. Her short curly hair shone dark as midnight and showcased her high cheekbones and smooth complexion. The only makeup she wore was a light dusting of bronzing powder and her barely brown lip gloss.

"Baby Girl, Marley is going to forget his name, his birth date, and how to dribble a basketball. All he'll remember is how gorgeous you look."

Amani clasped her hands together. "I'm nervous. I haven't seen him since my birthday. He probably won't be there anyway. It's not as if he and Clifton are road dawgs. Or what if he brings another—"

"Not a chance." Olivia spoke with motherly authority. "Number one. Marley will be as excited to see you as you are to see him. Number two, he and Clifton may not be buddies, but they are teammates and, lastly, trust me. Marley will be flying solo."

Amani breathed a sigh of relief. "Thanks, Mama. You're probably right." She looked over at the grandfather clock. It was ten minutes to seven. "Clifton should be here in a few minutes. I tried to tell him I didn't mind driving, but he wouldn't have it."

Olivia grinned. "I'm really starting to like that boy. I'm not crazy about you driving alone at night." Olivia sat on the sofa and patted the space beside her. "Come here, Amani Nicole Shephard."

"Uh-oh. You used my whole name. What's up?" Amani walked over to the sofa and sat down.

Olivia took Amani's hands in hers. "I want you to have a wonderful time tonight. However, don't get so overwhelmed seeing Marley that you forget who you are." She paused. "I have a feeling you'll be tested."

Amani returned her mother's stare. "This time next month, I'll be in New York and will have to make all of my decisions on my own."

Olivia offered a quick rebuttal. "Oh, no, you won't either. Continue to make your decisions based on the eternal truths found in God's Word like you've always done."

Amani hated to force the issue, but she needed to make a point. She spoke evenly, "The first thing I'll have to decide *on my own* is whether to continue living my life as the Bible says I should." She refused to bite her lip as she waited for her mother's reply.

Silence.

The chimes of the doorbell interrupted them. Amani hurried to the door, but before she opened it she turned to her mother.

"Right?"

Olivia nodded mutely and watched Amani open the door to her freedom to choose.

Several minutes later, Amani was in a reflective mood. She looked at the passing scenery as Clifton headed south on the 405 freeway. A lump formed in her throat as she thought of all the times she had traveled this same freeway with a different escort behind the wheel. Sneaking a peek at Clifton, she had to give him his props.

Knice and Knappy Hair Salon had done an excellent job with his classy afrocentric 'do. She fingered her short curls. A great hairstyle worked wonders for anyone. However, there was something else. Something other than the fact that the black muscle shirt he was wearing over a pair of black slacks highlighted his solid abs and muscular arms. That was enough to give her pause, but there was still something deeper.

Clifton exited on Artesia Boulevard and headed west to Prairie Avenue then south to 190th Street. His family had rented the Portofino Conference Pavilion in Redondo Beach. He told her the room they were partying in overlooked the water. In addition, there would be a soul food buffet, a slide show, and a live deejay. They were celebrating three events in grand style: Clifton's twenty-second birthday; his graduating from

UCLA; and his being a top NBA draft pick.

In two years, Marley will enter the draft, Amani thought. *Maybe the New York Knicks'll draft him.* Amani felt slightly guilty about the Marley situation. The last thing she wanted was to hurt Clifton's feelings. When he called to see if she was coming to his party, she tried to bring up the matter delicately. He assured her he would understand if she and the Miracle Man straightened things out and Marley brought her home after the party.

Amani presented Clifton with his birthday gift after her mother took their picture and exited the living room. He seemed genuinely pleased to receive a personally autographed copy of Pastor Hilton's most recent book *Old Things are Passed Away: Becoming a Real Man of God*. In his birthday card, she had written: "I am thankful for our deepening friendship. You are a class act! Amani."

She wanted to make sure the No Class Cliff nickname no longer fit, but she could tell he'd already outgrown it.

Gone was the tactless, sloppy, ill-mannered basketball player Marley had introduced her to months ago. In his place was a respectful, well-groomed, thoughtful young man she considered a good friend. He had proven himself a loyal ally since the night she'd run half-crazed from Marley's apartment. Over the last several weeks, they had spent a lot of time talking on the phone and she had come to depend on his good-natured humor and his listening ear. They even prayed together a couple of times.

Talking about his renewed faith was one of his favorite topics and one she managed to steer him toward whenever he tried to coax her to go out on a platonic date or to let him come by for a visit. She didn't need another relationship, especially not one on the rebound. Plus, she hadn't completely resolved things with Marley.

Would they make an Al Green "Let's Stay Together" pact or agree to a Manhattan's "Let's Just Kiss and Say Good-bye" ending? In either case, she only liked Clifton as a friend. How-ever, Brother Cliff was looking exquisite and was smelling kind of good. Oh, yeah! He had definitely gone from no class to the top of the class in her book. Amani's smile broadened.

"What's so funny?" Clifton asked.

Oops! "Um . . . I was just thinking about my mother doing her homeboy impersonation in the middle of the mall this morning. I was so embarrassed."

"Your mother is elegant and down? Talk about an oxymo-ron!" he quipped.

"What do you know about an oxymoron?"

He put his hand on his chest. "I'm hurt. Just because I'm from the south doesn't mean I'm country. I have taken a few English classes in my educational career. Check this. Bitter-sweet. Hurt so good. Sweet and sour." He spoke in a singsong manner, moving his head from side to side.

Amani was impressed but teased him anyway. "Are you sure those are all oxymorons?"

He checked his rearview mirror, "Yep. Those words or phrases basically have opposite meanings." He grinned. "Don't tell me you're hating, Miss Shephard."

The birthday boy has the most incredible smile. Amani frowned playfully to mask her thoughts. "Who me? Please! I don't hate. I appreciate."

Clifton started tapping out a beat on the steering wheel then added one of his own anti-player hating messages. "Don't hate. Celebrate."

Amani joined in, tapping out the same beat on the dash-board. Together they chanted over and over, "Don't hate. Con-gratulate. Don't hate. Appreciate. Don't Hate. Celebrate. Then do your best to imitate."

Without realizing it, she had stopped tapping and was mixing in her own soulful, lyrical flavoring in place of the chanting.

Clifton stopped cold, glancing at her with a surprised look on his face. "Well, help yourself, lil' Yolanda Adams. I didn't know you could put it down like that."

Amani blushed then kidded him. "Now, I know you don't know a thing about *my* girl!"

"My mother's been a saint in the temple of the Lord forever. In fact, she knew Moses personally. When—"

"Hold up! Are you saying yo' mama so old, she has an autographed copy of the Bible?" Amani smiled mischievously. "And she swam in the Dead Sea when it was still alive?" She burst out laughing at the wide-eyed, open-mouthed expression on his face. "I'm sorry, Cliff. It just slipped out."

He closed his mouth. "Oh, no, she didn't." He thought for a moment. "Yo' mama so old her birthday expired."

She chuckled. "Yo' mama so *dumb*, she got hit by a parked car."

He grinned. "Yo' mama so *greedy*, she took a spoon to the Super Bowl."

"Okay." Amani laughed. "You got me." *Clifton's real cool. Too bad I'm still in love with the Miracle Man.* She continued smiling. "Now, what were you saying before you started talking about my mama?"

He gently elbowed her. "I was saying when I told my mother I rededicated my life to the Lord, she went out and bought every contemporary Christian CD she could find and express shipped them. Yo Yo's definitely one of my favorite female artists. Do you have her latest?"

"Not yet. I'm still listening to *Mountain High, Valley Low* and *The Experience*. Okay, who's your favorite group?" Amani asked excitedly.

He thought for a moment. "They are so many awesome ones out there. Mary Mary. Kirk Franklin and his crews, Virtue, Natalie Wilson and the SOP Chorale, Winans Phase 2, Brent Jones and the T.P. Mobb, Anointed, Dawkins & Dawkins. Let's see . . . who else?"

Amani gave him a disbelieving look. "Forget I asked, okay? Your mother's not joking."

"No, I'm going to tell you. My favorite group is Fred Hammond and Radical for Christ. Their *Purpose by Design* CD is outrageous."

"Get out of here! I love them, but I'm still jamming to their *Pages of Life* CD. I loaned *Purpose by Design* to my sister Mia before I even listened to it." An undercurrent of anger was in her voice. "She claims her *boyfriend* plays it in his salon. He needs spiritual 9-1-1 so I haven't been after her to return it."

"Spiritual 9-1-1?"

"Why do people dial 9-1-1? Because they have an emergency and need help in a hurry." Her eyes narrowed. "Roland's a jerk. He's self-centered, egotistical, and a player. Homeboy's in desperate need of some divine assistance." The fire in her voice simmered. "Of course Mia's the only one who can't see the obvious." She paused. "Anyway, the CD was a charitable donation. You never know what the right song can do for a person."

"*Amen.*" Clifton nodded in agreement. "You can have my CD because you gotta hear Fred's "My Father Was/Is." I guarantee it'll make you cry."

She shook her head. "No, thank you. I'm all cried out."

"This is another one of those oxymorons. You'll be crying tears of joy instead of pain." He turned off the jazz station they were listening to and pressed CD. Fred Hammond's voice filled the darkness. He sang about his Heavenly Father being there for him although his earthly one was not. He sang about God caring about him in place of his absent father. He sang about an eternal Father's love.

Once again, the message in the music was meant for her. When the song ended, Amani opened her purse and took out a piece of Kleenex and dabbed her eyes. Clifton quickly squeezed her hand, but took his time letting go.

He stopped at the traffic light on the corner of 190th and Harbor Drive. A wooden sign on the southwest corner welcomed them to Redondo Beach's restaurant row. Clifton's hand brushed Amani's. She tried to take a peek on the sly. He was looking directly at her. *No, I'm not feeling all warm and woozy.*

Clifton coughed against his fist, cleared his throat, and softly said, "You let me know if you have a change of heart . . . about the CD."

Amani finally looked away as an overwhelming urge to sneeze overtook her. "Achoo!"

"Bless you."

"Thank you."

The light turned green and he made a left turn. They passed the Cheesecake Factory, Charlie Brown's, and a few other restaurants before entering the parking lot that led to the Portofino Conference Pavilion and Hotel. The trees were strung with white lights, setting the mood for a perfect evening. Clifton put the gear in park and took the key out of the ignition. He was getting out of the car when Amani stopped him.

She shifted in her seat and turned sideways. Putting her hand on his forearm, she ignored the slight stirrings she felt, and made eye contact. "In case we don't see each other much tonight, I want to wish you Happy Birthday again." Amani kissed him lightly on the cheek. "Thanks for being there for me these last couple of weeks. I appreciate you, Classy Cliff."

A wide smile crossed his face. "It's been my pleasure." He swallowed. "If homeboy has any sense left, he'll keep you by his side all night." He stared at her. "I know I would."

Amani removed her hand and shifted again. She pulled down the visor and took a quick look at herself in the mirror before Clifton opened the door and helped her out. They started toward the building. As they walked up the steps, she heard Marley's voice.

Her heart raced wildly though her feet stopped moving.

Clifton felt her sudden hesitation and looked down. "You all right?"

Amani took a deep breath before answering. "Yeah."

Almost to himself, Clifton said, "He must have been inside

already and didn't see you. I guess he wants to get to you before anybody else can." Clifton rubbed his chin. "That would have been my strategy, too." He stopped. "Look, I'm gonna go on in. If you need me, you know where to find me."

"Thank you," Amani whispered.

He trotted up the steps.

She called after him, "Clifton, I—"

Just as Clifton turned back, her real-life dream suddenly appeared at the top of the steps. He gave Clifton the manly man's hug and greeted him warmly, "Happy Birthday, bro, and many more."

Amani was surprised at the warm greeting. Apparently, Marley was growing, too. Maybe tonight would be a new beginning for them.

The two young men tapped fists and Marley eyed Clifton's head. "I'm feeling those locs, man. You got me thinking about changing up."

Clifton faced Amani, but spoke to Marley. "Thanks, Chief. Be sure to give my friend her due. Peace." He turned and disappeared around the side of the building.

Marley stared at her from the top of the steps. He was wearing a gray linen suit over a gray muscle shirt. The jacket had four pockets on it. One on either side of the chest and two more at the bottom. His scent greeted her before he did. In what seemed like slow motion, he caught up with his cologne.

When he was standing beside her, the first thing she did was look down at his wrist. He was still wearing the S.O.S. bracelet she had given him for Christmas. Then it meant Song of Solomon. Tonight, it stood for "Help!"

She may have been standing flat-footed on the outside but on the inside, she was turning cartwheels, back flips, and somersaults.

He took her hands in his and stared into her eyes. "What do you think?"

She was already getting drunk. "About what?" she asked.

"Do you think I'll look as good with locs as No Class does?"

She jerked her hands away. "Don't call him that. He's saved now. That makes him your brother in Christ."

Marley lowered his voice. "Who is he to you?" He paused. "I know he took you to your prom," he added sadly.

"That's because you left me no choice."

"So is he your new man?"

She turned up her nose. "You've been drinking."

"Don't change the subject."

"Marley, Clifton and I are just friends. When did you start drinking?"

"When you broke my heart."

"*Excuse me.*"

"Girl, you had me all messed up. You wouldn't return my calls. Not even when I gave that letter to your mother. Then you took No Cla—Clifton to your prom. I had already rented a tux and everything." He shook his head. "I straight up got cut . . . I thought we were a team." He put his forehead on her shoulder. "And . . . I thought you loved me, Amani."

His voice and nearness were removing every piece of her armor. She felt vulnerable, unarmed, and at his mercy.

"Marley, I did love you." She hesitated, then put her arms around him. "I still do."

He returned her embrace with an urgency that reminded her of everything she had missed for the past six weeks. They held on to each other while the moonlight serenaded them with a night full of glistening notes. The music in their hearts played the same time-honored symphony of love lost and found again.

Voices and footsteps were coming nearer. Amani eased from his embrace and he grabbed her hand. The first pair of eyes she connected with in the group belonged to someone who had already made clear her feelings for each of them.

All the others had the good sense to bid them good evening

and continue on their way. Tamara made it a point to stop and stare Marley squarely in the face. "You haven't returned my calls." Her voice was harsh. Then she turned and acknowledged Amani. "She's back in and I'm out?" She shook her head. "I don't think so." A couple of her girlfriends called to her. "I'm coming," she hollered back. Unsmiling, she turned back to Marley. "We'll talk later."

Amani jerked her hand away from Marley and started up the steps. He ran in front of her and blocked her. Every time she moved, he moved in front of her. They continued this dance for a few minutes before she finally gave up.

He put his hands on her shoulders. "Are you ready to listen?"

She simply stared at him.

"See. You fell right into her trap. This is exactly what she wanted. To get you to thinking we have something going on."

Amani bit her lip. She didn't know what to believe. Her sigh was deep. "It was good to see you again, Marley." She turned and started up the steps.

Marley grabbed her arm.

"Amani, I'm so sorry I hurt you, baby, but you are the only woman I want. Please don't leave me. I meant everything I wrote in that letter. It was straight from the heart." He started singing softly, "It's been six weeks, eight hours, twelve minutes since you went away."

Brian McKnight didn't have a thing to worry about, but she did. She was falling heart first into love again.

Balancing his weight on one leg, he leaned against the railing and drew her inside the circle of his warmth. She put her arm around his neck and rested her hand on his chest. His arms surrounded her waist. He nuzzled her neck then sniffed it like a dog marking his territory.

She giggled. "That tickles."

He sighed. "Yeah. You smell just as good as I remember. By the way . . ." He stared at her. "Your short cut's on point, but

I still prefer it long."

Amani's eyes narrowed as she thought about the two girls in the bathroom and their "homely remark." And she couldn't forget the many nights she had cried herself to sleep because of his ultimatum. She looked at him sharply. "So, how have you been?"

"Baby, I've been walking around like a zombie. A sliver of light slipped in when I found out about the party because I figured you'd be here." He brought her hand to his mouth and gently kissed it. "When I saw you standing at the bottom of these steps, everything in me woke up."

Amani felt like she was right back to where she started as Marley's warm breath caressed her ear.

"Let's get out of here."

For a moment, she couldn't speak, then she steadied herself. "No, Marley."

He turned her body directly in front of his and held her hands to his chest. "I just want to talk to you in private." Their eyes were already making love. "You can trust me, Amani."

Volts of electricity surged inside of her. "Said the spider to the fly."

"The only web I want to wrap you in is my love."

As she allowed herself to get caught up in his rapture, she couldn't understand how she could feel empowered one moment and entangled the next.

Clifton's dance card was full. His new look was a hit with the females. However, they couldn't understand why he was acting so strange. They weren't accustomed to him being a gentleman and treating them like ladies instead of potential sex partners for the night. When he told them he had rededicated his life to the Lord, they laughed. He decided not to force the issue. They would see the truth for themselves.

While he danced, his eyes roamed the tables, the buffet lines, and the patio area. He didn't see her anywhere. Marley had obviously gotten a clue and was attempting to prove himself worthy. Amani Shephard was a gift any intelligent man wouldn't mind waiting to unwrap. But if Marley continued to pressure her, he was beyond stupid and didn't deserve her presence in his life.

———————

Her ears were on fire and she was sick to her stomach.

Tamara wanted to shout after him. Just because you don't see something, Marley, doesn't mean it isn't there. She never made it inside to the party. Upon entering the building with her friends, she complained that something she'd eaten earlier was mad at her and went in search of the bathroom. Of course, they decided to go with her for their last-minute inspections. She had remained behind the stall until they had no choice but to leave her. Her crew liked to get their party on too much to miss out because of a sick friend, especially one with a simple case of diarrhea.

For the last several minutes, Tamara had stood within earshot yet out of sight of the happy couple. Looked like joining the public party wasn't in their private plans. She carefully stepped out of her hiding place and looked toward Marley's parking space. His car was still there. Tamara frowned. "As Cousin Pookie would say, 'What's really goin' on?'" A sudden familiar laugh erased her confusion and helped her to find her target.

Marley and Amani were casually strolling toward the other building. The Portofino Hotel. Looked like Miss Puritan was about to give the Miracle Man something to remember her by.

Well, she would make sure it was a night he and Amani would never forget, no matter how hard they tried.

THIRTY-ONE

Amani walked over to the steps in the middle of the lobby. A small sitting area was on a raised platform. The open room contained two sofas, a love seat, matching floral chairs surrounding a birch wood coffee table, a fireplace, and a mini-bar set off to the side. She went up the steps and stood in front of the fireplace.

Marley turned and watched Amani watching the fire. Grasping the small envelope tightly in his hand, waves of warmth tingled throughout him. Nine months ago, he met the only woman to challenge his commitment to celibacy like no one ever had. Not even Tamara's just-say-when approach enticed him like Amani's I-want-you-too-but-I-can't stance. He licked his lips. His girl wasn't *that* naïve. She had changed her mind or else she wouldn't have agreed to come here.

However, he knew from experience that Amani was sometimes too trusting. She was willing to give him the benefit of the doubt even though he was unable to trust himself. He knew he should just talk to her and try to straighten out the mess he had made of their relationship. Under different circumstances, that's exactly what he would have done. But he was under the influence of the most potent aphrodisiac: love. This one emotion instilled within him a singular focus and inspired him to accomplish what had previously been an impossible mission. This time he would not fail.

He had to keep Mrs. Shephard's Baby Girl from moving to New York. Had to keep Mr. Shephard's Nikki from leaving him. Had to keep his Sunshine from giving her heart to another. The only way he knew to do that was for he and Amani to make love. Tonight. Once she shared her body with him, they would truly be inseparable. No one or no thing could come between them. Not ever.

Being without her for the past month and a half had been a struggle and he made some mistakes, but he was certain that together they could handle anything. A peach-sized lump formed in his throat when Amani turned and caught him staring. She smiled that smile she had to know drove him crazy. He shivered. "I've got to do this."

Marley snapped his fingers. He forgot to get the apple cider from the car. Before he and Amani broke up, he never touched alcohol. Lately, he had been indulging quite a bit. So far he stayed away from the hard stuff but had taken a liking to Seagram's wine coolers.

Hadn't Jesus turned water into wine at that wedding feast? He shrugged. It must be all right then. Yet, he decided against bringing any type of alcohol because he had a feeling a paper bag could hold liquor better than Amani. He wanted her sober and clear-headed.

She would never be able to say she was drunk or even tipsy the first time they made love. The only thing he wanted his lady intoxicated by this evening was Miracle Marley.

In place of wine, he had almost brought his small portable CD player. For a hot second, he even thought about borrowing his parents' T.D. Jakes' *Sacred Love Songs* CD, but he knew that would freak Amani way out. He could just hear her. "Hel-lo. We're not married, Marley. Bishop Jakes would have a fit if he knew we were getting busy to his CD. Uh-uh, Marley. I can't." He shook his head. Those were definitely not the words he was aiming for tonight.

Plan B. He thought about bringing a couple of his mellow fellows along. No woman could resist the crooning of Brian McKnight, Kenny Lattimore, or Will Downing, but he realized the folly in that plan. She would think this whole thing was a set-up. Not good for setting the perfect mood. It didn't take long for him to conclude that tuning into KJLH or The Wave on the radio in their room was the safest route to go.

No fine wine. No sanctified love songs. No personal serenaders. No way was he going to do without the two bottles of sparkling apple cider he had bought especially for tonight. He strolled over to her. She had turned back to the fireplace and was holding out her hands toward the windowed flames. He came up behind her and put his hands around her waist. Then he kissed the back of her neck.

"You're cold?"

She leaned her head back against his chest. "A little."

"Good."

Amani didn't respond and continued to face the fire.

"If you want me to, I can be your blanket . . . while we talk." He nibbled her ear.

Releasing herself from Marley's hold, she made a one hundred-eighty degree turn and locked her hands behind his waist. "Marley," she called his name softly.

"Yeah, baby." His eyes were watching the flames.

She patted his back. "Look at me." *Help me, Lord.* "I want you to know that I *do* love you." Her voice was thick with emotion.

The fire in his eyes warmed her soul. "I love you, too, Amani." The passion in his voice was raw and unrehearsed. "Wid nuff luv an' every ting inna me."

Fervently, they held onto each other and the moment.

She reminded herself that they were just going to talk as their fingers intertwined and they headed toward the elevators. She was surprised when Marley pulled back. Maybe he was afraid of them going too far, too. She waited for him to speak.

He chose his words carefully, "I have a couple of bottles of apple cider in the car. I want to go and get them before we head up. Unless you want to go on and I'll meet you there?"

Amani shook her head. "I'll wait in front of the fireplace." She put her hand on her hip and said half-jokingly, "You had it all planned, huh?"

Marley hid his nervousness with a smile. "Of course not. But I was hoping I'd get a chance to make a toast in your honor at the party. Seriously." He couldn't stop himself. "I'm sure Clifton would have joined in with a special toast of his own."

"Don't go there."

Marley kissed her on the forehead and spoke quickly. "I'll be right back." He stuck out his hand. "Take a key card in case you change your mind. I can let myself in with this other one." He dropped it into one of his top pockets and sprinted out the door.

"Tell me anything. Just don't expect me to believe it," she told the breeze he left in his wake.

Amani returned to the fire and meditated on a scripture she'd committed to memory. *There hath no temptation taken you but such as is common to man; but God is faithful, who will not suffer you to be tempted above that ye are able; but will with the temptation also make a way to escape, that ye may be able to bear it.* The Word was true and her mother was right. She was being tested. Again.

———

"Please, don't let her change her mind. Please don't let her change her mind. Please! Don't let her change her mind." He wouldn't dare call this a prayer, but this was what he repeated all the way to the car. Marley slammed the door shut and started back toward the hotel. A bottle of apple cider was in each hand. In his rush to get back to his girl, he didn't notice someone approaching him until he heard the words.

"Aren't you going the wrong way?"

His grip on the bottles tightened and his heartbeat quickened. Instantly, the muscles on the right side of his jaw began to throb.

Marley stopped and shrugged. "What's up?"

"You tell me."

He started walking away and spoke firmly. "I'll holler at you tomorrow."

"Where's the fire, Double M?"

"Somebody's waiting on me." Marley quickened his pace.

"Tamara?" Taylor asked, trotting beside him.

Marley scowled. "Naw, man." His jaw relaxed. "Amani."

Taylor shook his head, "Better assess your situation before you make a mess of your situation."

Marley was not in the mood. He stopped and squared off with his friend. "Man, you don't know jack."

Taylor attempted to playfully slap his young friend upside the head. Marley stepped back, but Taylor forged on. "Didn't I tell you to get your hormones under control? That's God's property you're messing with."

"Wasn't nobody kidnapped. If she wanted to turn me down, she could have. She's done it before."

Taylor stared hard at Marley for a few seconds. "You know you're my boy, but you're also a man of God." His voice was low, but firm. "You're supposed to set the example." He shook his head sadly. "What are you doing making that kind of suggestion in the first place? Brother, you really need to listen to that CD I gave you a while back." Having had his say,

Taylor turned and continued on his way.

Marley walked back to his car. He sat the bottles on top of the roof and fished around in his pocket for the keys. He was going to drive back to the hotel. He was tripping so hard he hadn't thought of doing that before. If he had, he would have missed Saint Taylor's little sermon. A line from an old song Aundrae Russell often played Sundays on KJLH's *Spread the Word* radio program popped into his head.

Marley unlocked the door and grabbed the bottles. He quickly got in and dropped his head back on the headrest, squeezing his eyes shut. Suddenly, he sat up, put the key in the ignition, and turned the radio on. Usher was crooning "U Got It Bad." Marley snapped his fingers on his right hand and grooved to the music. Nice try, but he couldn't shake that first song. He turned the radio off. Maybe God *was* trying to tell him something.

———

Whenever they embraced or kissed, something on the inside yelled, "More!" Amani tried to tune it out while Marley obviously cranked up the volume.

Tonight, she was listening to a higher station.

Although her flesh would have liked to overturn her decision, the matter had been settled in her heart and spirit. As soon as Marley came back, she would tell him. If he really wanted to talk, they could do that here in the lobby. She didn't plan on retreating, but she finally realized her soul would continue to rage its war.

Amani felt a light tap on her back and turned around, prepared to do what had to be done.

"We need to talk."

Startled, Amani gasped. That was supposed to be her line and *Marley* was supposed to be standing in front of her. "We have nothing to discuss," she replied firmly.

Tamara smeared the tears on her face with the palm of her hand. "I know I haven't been very nice, but don't take it personal. You have something I want." Her lips quivered. "Amani, I really do need to speak with you. *Please.*"

Tamara's humility caught her off guard. Amani pointed to the sofa behind them. "We can sit over there. Marley stepped out for a minute."

"I know. I followed the two of you and I saw him leave." She sighed. "I came to cause a whole lot of commotion, but on the way over I had a change of heart."

"Hmmm. So did I."

A look of confusion mixed with the pain in Tamara's eyes. "I'd like to go up to the room and talk in private."

Amani raised an eyebrow. *Girlfriend's acting kind of strange. How do I know she's not planning on doing something crazy? I'm the only person standing between her and the man she's been hounding for two years.*

Tamara noticed Amani's hesitation. She smiled tiredly. "Believe me, Amani. If I were capable of taking you out, I would have done it long before now."

"I don't know. People do some pretty sick stuff in the name of love."

Amani headed toward the elevator and Tamara followed. Minutes later, they entered room 307. Amani turned on the light then walked to the patio door. Tamara followed her onto the balcony. For a while, they stared into the water in awkward silence. Amani cleared her throat and turned to Tamara who seemed mesmerized by the black sea and sky.

Amani followed her gaze. It was hard to tell where one ended and the other began. Tamara glanced at Amani then turned away. "You have no reason to believe what I'm about to tell you, but I have the proof at home to back it up."

Amani's facial expression hardened and her heart pounded. "What's up, *Tamera*?" she asked pointedly.

The other young woman bypassed the bait. "I'm pregnant."

Tamara looked directly at Amani. "Marley's the daddy."

Right away, Amani noticed two things that surprised her. Tamara was not gloating and she looked terrified. Amani turned away and focused on the seemingly endless horizon as the cheerleader continued.

"I called him the night of your prom. He sounded so out of it. I knew he had it bad when he didn't refuse my offer to come over. I also knew he was imagining I was you when we. . . I stayed at his place the entire weekend. Right after that, he started avoiding me. He wouldn't return my calls and he wouldn't let me in the building when I came over. He always had some excuse."

"Now, he won't be able to pretend that weekend never happened." Tamara rubbed her belly and spoke more to herself than to Amani. "Though I'm starting to regret that it did."

Amani's hands gripped the railing. If Tamara was telling the truth, she was six weeks pregnant by the man Amani loved.

Marley's the daddy.

Those three words ricocheted through her. Swooping out over the water, they returned again and again to torment her delicate heart. Yet, each time, their power to hurt lessened.

She was thankful she had already made the right decision. Tamara's confession was simply confirmation.

Both young women jumped suddenly and turned toward the sound of Marley's whistling. Amani looked at Tamara, shook her head, and covered her mouth with her finger, then signaled for her to move into the far corner.

He stopped whistling and yelled out as the door opened, "Amani, tonight is our night of new beginnings." They listened to him open and close the refrigerator. "Where is the lady I want to spend the rest of my life loving?"

Amani saw Tamara wince. She suddenly felt sorrier for her than she did for herself. Tamara only wanted what most sisters wanted, to be loved by a good brother.

"I'm on the patio, Marley." She forced herself to look at him. "It feels nice out here."

"So do you," he whispered as he took her in his arms and lowered his mouth to hers.

Amani put her hands on his chest and pushed him back. "Wait a minute. I almost forgot. We have a surprise visitor. Close your eyes," she ordered.

A look of confusion then annoyance crossed his face, but he did as she asked because he would need her compliance soon. "That's why it took me so long to get back. I ran into Taylor in the parking lot. Where is he?" he demanded.

"Calm down. It's not Taylor," Amani answered. "That wouldn't be much of a surprise." She beckoned for Tamara to emerge. Seconds later, Tamara stood at his side. Amani didn't know it was possible for her to look worse than she did before her revelation.

Amani's eyes filled. "You can open your eyes now." She took a step back.

Marley opened his eyes, muttered something under his breath, and then reached for Amani.

She slapped his hands away as tears replaced her fake cheerfulness. "It's your baby's mama, Marley." Her voice broke. "Congratulations, Daddy."

Marley's mouth dropped and his eyes looked like two full moons as he looked directly at Tamara.

Although her gaze was steady, her voice trembled. "I'm six weeks pregnant. You were the only person I was with last month, and I haven't been with anyone since."

"You're lying!" He turned to Amani. "Baby, please, let me explain. She got me drunk and it—"

"Was only sex but, tonight, we were going to *make love*?"

Marley grimaced and started toward her. She held up her hand. "You better stay out of my face!" She ran through the open glass door and grabbed her purse from the coffee table. On the way out, she rewrote the ending to their story. It was official. She would have to be another's man's wife.

A few minutes later, Amani was back where she belonged. Taylor grabbed her as soon as she entered the party. He kissed her on the cheek. "I hope you set my boy straight tonight."

She didn't answer.

"Gina had to break up with the bonehead she was dating before me for the same reason. I'll give you her number before I cut out. Maybe she can help."

"All right."

He searched her face. "Are you okay?"

"I will be."

Taylor grabbed her hand. "Look at me, Amani."

She returned his stare.

"Stay encouraged. They are a lot of Christian brothers who appreciate a strong Christian sister."

She smiled thinly. "A brother gets that every time."

Taylor chuckled. "Amen, sister. Are you familiar with that Trin-i-tee 5:7 song?"

Amani softly sang a few lines from "My Body." Then she searched the crowd. "That song was written for me." She spotted Clifton and their eyes met. He finally turned away and glided over to the deejay.

Taylor observed their exchange and gave Amani's shoulder a squeeze. "We'll be praying for you."

"I 'preciate it." She patted Taylor's hand but continued watching Clifton. "Thanks, Tee."

"You're welcome." He excused himself and strolled over to a group of his teammates.

Amani smiled as Clifton started toward her. Bobby Brown's "Tenderoni" blared through the speakers.

"So, where's Marley?"

"Don't ask."

He took her hand. "Care to boogie with the birthday boy?"

Amani nodded, and he began leading her to the dance floor. She was moving to the music as she followed him. Suddenly she stopped and poked him in the back.

He turned around. "What's up?"

"I may be tender, but I'm also tough."

He smiled. "Ain't nothing worse than mushy pasta."

"You're crazy." Her smile almost reached her eyes.

"You have that effect on a brother, Tough n' Tender Roni."

This time, Amani's face smiled in three places, and her heart hurt a little less.

———————

Amani stood in the porch light and faced Clifton. He took her hand in his large ones and stared down at her. *Marley must be mad.* He cleared his throat. "I'm going to miss you, friend."

"I'm going to miss you, too, Classy Cliff. Just cause you're going pro doesn't mean you can't keep in touch. I don't want you to forget about me."

Not a chance. "I've enjoyed our telephone conversations and I want to thank you for letting me down easy."

"What are you talking about?"

"I'm talking about keeping me focused on our building a friendship whenever I tried to see you. You know, I wouldn't have minded letting you use me to get over Marley." He chuckled. "That's what friends are for."

She punched his arm lightly. "Friends don't use friends."

"Girl, you could have used me until you used me up. I'm sure I would have enjoyed every minute of it." He stopped smiling. "Amani, you are a beautiful Christian lady and I'm glad we got the chance to get to know each other." His eyes never left hers.

"So am I." It would have been so easy for her to let him get even closer but she didn't want to take act impulsively. Even though a part of her wondered what kissing him would be like, the bigger part of her would not take advantage of him.

Clifton shifted. "Well, I better get going." *Before I do or say something stupid.* He let go of her hands. "Keep in touch, pretty lady."

"Cliff, I owe you big time for all the nights you prayed with me, listened to me cry and whine, and for listening to me babble on the ride home tonight." *I love his light brown eyes.* "If . . . if there's ever anything I can do for you, please let me know."

Can you forget about Marley and give me a chance? His smile was bittersweet. "You don't owe me a thing." He couldn't say what he was thinking: *One day I'd like everything you have to give.* He gave himself an invisible shake. *Stop buggin', man. She's simply a friend, a sister in the Lord.* "Take care, Roni. God bless you." He turned to go.

"Clifton, wait!" She reached up and kissed him on the cheek, then wrapped her arms around him.

Shock waves rebounded through him at the feel of her body against his. He hugged her back. Hard. Like he wouldn't ever let her go. *This girl just don't know how close I am to making a fool outta myself.* It was easy to ignore the assertiveness of the females at the party because his heart belonged to his teammate's girl. An urge to kiss her became so overwhelming he did the only thing he could. He let her go.

Amani stepped back and stared up at him. The scent of his muted cologne continued to hold her. "God bless you, too, Classy Cliff." Her voice was soft. "I hope everything works out for you."

His smile was wide. "Me, too." He started down the steps, then stopped and turned around. "By the way, I'm really feelin' your new look. It suits you."

"Thank you." She ran her fingers through her short curls. "So does yours." She smiled. "And I'm not referring to your locs."

"I know." He winked. "Our daddies would be proud of us."

"They *are* proud."

"Tell it right." He stepped briskly to his car.

As Amani watched him get into his car and drive away, she already missed her new friend. She said a quick prayer as she opened the door. "Heavenly Father, help Clifton and me to continue to seek you first and to trust you with our lives." She paused. "And please help me to stop loving Marley. In Jesus' name, I pray. Amen." Amani wiped a lone tear from her face and went inside.

THIRTY-TWO

Taylor closed the door of his pre-owned silver Jeep Grand Cherokee, then walked around and leaned against the passenger door. He was trying to gauge his homeboy's mental state before approaching. Marley was standing at the free throw line, his feet apart, his knees bent, and his hands poised to aim the ball into the center of the basket. He held the ball slightly above his head for a few brief seconds before releasing it.

It banked off the backboard and rolled onto the grassy area. Taylor watched this same scenario play out repeatedly before his eyes. Sometimes the ball rolled to the right; other times, it rolled to the left.

Something was definitely up.

Whatever it was, he felt partly responsible. When Marley came to UCLA as a freshman, Taylor, then a junior, had become his surrogate big brother. They prayed together, attended the same on-campus Bible study, and held each other accountable in being doers, and not just hearers, of the Word. For special services, they even visited each other's church.

All that started to change last fall.

Marley hooked up with a PYT, a pretty young thing named Amani Shephard.

Taylor remembered the intense rush of being in love for the first time, the unparalleled thrill of hooking up with someone who was manufactured by God with you in mind. So not wanting to intrude, he gave his boy some space.

For a while this caused a rift in his relationship with Regina. The time he would have normally spent with Marley, he attempted to allot to her. She finally broke it down for him. She still had friends and, as much as she loved him, it was healthy for them to spend time apart.

Taylor did have other associates, but Marley was his road dawg. They had three major things in common: shooting hoops, Jesus Christ, and Jamaican parents.

He and Marley slipped into patois when expressing a deep emotion or when they simply wanted to spice things up some. Their parents regularly spoke this Pidgin English. When family or friends from back home visited, the brethren and sistren in both residences duplicated the atmosphere of the island with the warmth of their laughter and the binding tie of a kindred language.

Taylor ambled toward the court and forced a cough. Marley turned around. Taylor took in his boy's disheveled appearance. His bloodshot eyes had seen no rest and his uncombed hair was in serious need of attention.

Marley didn't speak as he left the free throw line to stand opposite Taylor a few feet away. Taylor took his place and Marley passed him the ball.

Before he checked the ball and passed it back, signaling the start of their game of one-on-one, he nodded his head and spoke casually.

"Wa a gwane?"

"Mi heart brok."

"Da gal de Amani?"

"True dat."

"Some say young luv a puppy luv. So wa yu tink?"

"Mi no know wa mek dem call it puppy luv. Dis feel lek a big dawg luv."

Taylor returned the ball to Marley and quickly got in position to defend. The ball was in Marley's court and Taylor was prepared to be there however his friend needed him to be.

While he guarded Marley and worked to block the shot, Taylor gave his only sermon for the day. "Only one luv a pure luv. Com'on bak home."

Marley drove past him and did a perfect lay-up. Taylor went back to the free throw line and dittoed their previous ball exchange. Marley had on his game face and again drove forward for another point. On the third attempt, Taylor became more aggressive in his blocking. He wanted his homeboy to win, but he still needed to put up a fight. Taylor appeared to have manifested eight arms as he blocked the third shot.

Marley had been on simmer since leaving the hotel last night. Everywhere he turned, someone or something was out to stop him. He wasn't having it this morning. He ran right into Taylor with everything he had, elbowing him in the ribs as he drove to the basket and slam-dunked the ball.

Then he picked up the ball and flung it against the backboard. The basket reverberated as the ball rolled across the blacktop. Marley turned to look at Taylor who was sitting on his butt holding his knees. The look on his face said, "I know you're upset, my brother, but I wouldn't advise you to do that again." Marley extended his hand.

Taylor jumped up and put his hand on Marley's shoulder. "What's up?" he asked quietly, letting his hand drop.

Marley avoided his friend's eyes as he answered. "Tamara's pregnant." He put his head down and began massaging his neck as he continued. "She said I'm the only one she was kicking it with. It was the weekend of Amani's prom. Tamara brought over some coolers and I . . ." A few moments passed before Marley lifted his wet face and looked Taylor in the eye. "What am I supposed to do, man? One lady might be having my baby, but another one already has my heart." He bent over, put his hands on his knees, and shook his head. "I want to do right, but my life keeps getting in the way."

"That's because you've been leaving it in the wrong hands." Taylor walked over to Marley and patted his back. "Brother, it's time to pray." Taylor strolled over to an empty bench and waited for his friend.

At their last meeting, Marley had gone in the opposite direction. Only a few seconds passed before Marley straightened up and followed him.

THIRTY-THREE

Staring at the Queen Mary was quickly becoming one of Olivia's most anticipated pastimes. They sat on a grassy area facing the blue sea of the Long Beach Shoreline. Gabriel's arm was around her shoulders and her hand rested on his leg. They were both wearing jeans: he wore Levi's and she wore Khalil Love's. He had on a long-sleeved red button-down shirt. She was wearing a magenta tank top and a rare pony-tail with a necklace made of golden leaves adorning her neck and golden sandals on her recently pedicured feet. They had been sitting in silence for almost an hour.

Olivia was reluctant to disturb their private reflections, but there was something she meant to ask him. She turned to face him.

"Gabe, when your wife was killed, did you ever turn your back on God?"

He squinted his eyes, never taking them off the water. "There was a baby born a few days before my son. He had several serious conditions. Every day I would look at Montana and I would look at him. Even though Monte was premature, he was perfectly healthy. The other boy lived nine days. How could I not thank God, Olivia?"

"But Paulina was killed and now Monte is sick." Her eyes began to fill. "How can you not hate God?" She stared at his strong profile.

He thoughtfully studied the sea.

Olivia needed to understand his steady faith, so she pressed him for a response. "Do you say like Job did, 'Though He slay me yet will I trust Him?'"

"God doesn't kill His children."

She flinched and looked away.

"Satan took the lives of your husband and my wife." Gabriel placed his hand on hers. "And God received them both because they served Him."

Her eyes were on the brink of overflowing. "My heart believes that, but sometimes my head . . ." She wiped her face. "Gabe . . . soon . . . Montana . . . will be gone."

"I know." He took her face in his hands. "But can't you see, Olivia? The light in Gabriel's dark eyes pricked her soul. "*God* sent me you."

She rested her head against his shoulder and released a river of tears for their mountain.

———

Olivia needed to speak to the one person who knew her better than anyone else, the one person who could stop her from making an avoidable mistake.

They each carried an Ultrasonic Dog Repeller as they walked through the Armstrong neighborhood in sweat suits. Oneita's thin braids were pulled into a high ponytail at the top of her head.

Olivia laughed, tugging at her own. "We've been friends so long we can feel what the other one's doing?"

Oneita's smile was mischievous. "Did you feel what I was

doing early this morning?"

"Sister Armstrong, you better watch out. You keep Bennie in too good of shape, some of those single sisters are going to start eyeing him."

Oneita quickly covered her giggle.

Olivia stopped walking and stared at her friend. "What?" she asked with a gleam in her eye.

Oneita laughed harder.

"Tell it."

She took a deep breath. "You remember Sister Bridgette?"

Pursing her lips, Olivia tilted her head to the side. Her name sounded familiar. She was trying to picture her face. She snapped her fingers. "She was cute as a button. Everybody thought so, especially her. Had a short blonde Afro."

"And a great big behind. Wore her skirts so tight we all had to repent before the end of service. The sisters for envying her and the brothers for worshipping her."

"You're a mess. What about her? She left New Horizons a long time ago."

"Been about fifteen years now."

Olivia raised an eyebrow.

"You bet your sweet patootie I remember. That heifer wanted my man."

"As your youngest goddaughter would say, 'Get out of here!'"

Oneita smiled. "I'm serious. After her husband left her, she started stopping by the school under the pretense of volunteering. Before I knew it, she was calling our house, day and night. Wanting Bennie to help her with this or give her advice about that. I tried to explain to him what was going on, but he accused me of being selfish." She placed her hand on her hip. "I told him if my not wanting to hand my husband over to another woman was selfish, then he was right."

Olivia chuckled. "Even smart men can be naïve."

"Who you telling? We had just come home from dinner one evening. Bridgette called almost as soon as we stepped in the door. I could hear Bennie on the phone in the bedroom. Her sink was backed up and she needed him to unplug it."

She noticed the goofy look on Olivia's face. "Don't go there, Sister Shephard! When Bennie came out of the bedroom, he was wearing overalls. I asked him to wait because I wanted to get ready for bed before he left. I could tell he was irritated, but he sat down and started messing with that remote. A few minutes later, I came back and stood in the doorway. I was freshly showered, wearing his favorite perfume, and *butt naked*."

Olivia gasped and put her hand on her cheek.

"I posed in the doorway. 'Honey, are you going somewhere?' Bennie looked over at me and scratched his head. 'Uh, uh . . . I guess not.'"

Olivia was laughing so hard tears were running down her face.

"That was the end of our Bridgette situation. She stopped calling and soon after that she left the church."

"You don't have any sense." Olivia wiped her eyes with the back of her hands.

"I have enough sense to protect what's mine."

Olivia looked off.

"You might as well tell it."

"Not only is Gabriel Hispanic, but he's five years younger than me."

Oneita grabbed her friend's hand and pulled her along. "I hope *you* have sense enough to recognize God's hand in action."

Later that evening, Olivia knelt beside her bed and prayed as she never had before.

"Dear Heavenly Father, forgive me. I've been so wrong for so long. Forgive me for blaming myself for Marcus' death and for harboring resentment against you all these years." She squeezed her eyes shut. "I thank you for being merciful, gracious, and protective. In spite of my grudge and in spite of . . . the abortion, you've kept my girls and me." Her eyes filled and tears spilled along her cheeks. "Help me to believe, without wavering, that you've already forgiven me and that you *still* love me. In Jesus' name, I pray. Amen." She remained on her knees. "And thank you for placing Gabe and Monte in my life."

Refreshed and renewed, she lifted herself from the floor and climbed into bed, fully expecting to receive sweet slumber.

THIRTY-FOUR

Quite some time had passed since Marley last fell on his knees, but he had recently dropped his moral standards even lower. After Taylor prayed with him in the park, he promised he'd try to pray for himself. He didn't know where to begin and wasn't sure God would even hear him.

Marley surveyed the mess surrounding him. Empty bottles cluttered his bedroom. Drinking was his futile attempt to drown out visions of that weekend. He reached for his bag on the floor and dumped all of its contents on the bed. The CD Taylor gave him months ago was still there. Marley walked into the living room and removed Brian McKnight's *Back at One*. He replaced it with Men of Standard's *Feels Like Rain* CD and forwarded to "In Your Will," setting the repeat option on number three.

As the music played, he humbly knelt before the Lord. The song expressed his sincere sentiments. Men of Standard sang about being consistent in pursuing the perfect will of God. His only goal was to get back in and stay in the Father's will.

After leaving Taylor that morning, he drove over to his parents' restaurant and told them there was a possibility they had another grandchild on the way. His mother cried, and his father just looked numb. When Marley informed them that the alleged mother was not Amani, his mother almost fainted, and his father finally stirred. "It's that cheerleader," his father said quietly.

Though he hated to hurt his parents any further, marrying Tamara was not an option, even *if* the baby proved to be his. He didn't love her and she had a reputation for being scandalous. That weekend he had sex with her more than once, so what did that make him?

With tears streaming down his face, he raised his hands and lifted his heart to the Lord. He didn't have any elaborate words or Bible verses but spoke meekly. "I messed up, Lord. Please forgive me and give me another chance to do Your will. Another chance to make it right with You *and* Amani." He sowed the rest of his prayer in tears.

Then he crawled over and scanned his stack of CDs through blurry eyes. There was another song he needed to hear. Finally, he retrieved Hezekiah Walker's *By Any Means* CD and set the repeat option for the third song.

The song's lyrics were the same as those his spirit sang. He was tired of doing things his way and needed the Lord's forgiveness. It was time for him to totally surrender to God's will for his life.

He took it as a sacred sign because both songs were number three. Suddenly Marley rose, feeling certain God was listening and that everything would be all right. "Second Chance" was the name of his new favorite song and he was certain he would get his.

Amani stepped into the house of God in the company of her favorite women. Praise and Worship had already begun and the glory of the Lord filled the temple. A tangible feeling of peace enveloped her.

Spirit-filled music continued to play softly as Pastor Chamberlain Hilton took his place behind the clear podium that bore the emblem of New Horizons Christian Center. The atmosphere was one of expectancy and anticipation. Their pastor believed in letting the Spirit dictate the order of service. Their seventy-five-hundred-seat sanctuary removed any burden of time constraints. Their only morning service started at ten AM and ended by one o'clock. Usually.

Pastor Hilton began with a prayer of thanksgiving before asking the church to be seated. Then he went on to talk about the importance of letting God be God in our lives and yielding ourselves fully to His sovereignty. He then left them with his customary closing. "The church is not full of super men and wonder women but ordinary people who love Jesus and are striving to imitate Him. Amen?"

"Amen!" The members heartily agreed.

He smiled at his wife on the front row. "Now, I'd like to ask my queen to come to the podium."

When Sister Rachel stood beside him, he put his hand around her waist and addressed the church. "One of the best things about being married to a minister is the Lord has somebody else He can wake up before dawn." Pastor Hilton lifted his right arm, made a fist, and then pulled it toward him. "Yes!" He looked down at his wife. "Dis morning be her turn."

He switched places with his wife so she could stand in front of the mike. Sister Rachel took the microphone out of the stand and smiled at her brothers and sisters in the Lord. "Y'all have to excuse your pastor. You can take the man out of the country, but it takes some time to get the country out of the man."

He interjected. "Just like when we come out of the world. It takes time to get the world out of us. Much longer for some of us than others. Apostle Paul—"

"Dis morning be my turn, remember?" She kissed him on the cheek then stepped from behind the podium. Pastor Hilton forced a stern look, then jogged down the steps, and strolled back to his seat. Sister Hilton was casual chic in a black pantsuit and white silk shirt. Her silver Afro accentuated her glistening, golden skin and a pair of gold-rimmed designer glasses framed her eyes.

She gazed over the crowd before she began. "At about three o' clock this morning, the Lord began ministering to me about His daughters. Some of our young ladies will be leaving for out-of-state or out-of-town colleges and universities soon. Too many of our single women are raising children alone as a result of divorce or plain misguided decision-making. And even more of our young girls and ladies are being lured by the media, through songs, movies, and television, into making costly and, with the rise of HIV and AIDS in our communities, sometimes deadly mistakes."

She paused. "The Lord spoke to me in my spirit early this morning. He said, 'Daughter, I want you to invite every female in the church from eleven on up to gather around the altar. Instead of making a confession of chastity, I want them to make a POP covenant with me.' 'Lord, what in the world is a POP covenant?' I asked Him. He explained that P-O-P stood for Preserving our Purity and that a covenant is more powerful than the confession we've made in the past."

She wiped her face with the black handkerchief in her hand. "I'll refresh your memories and break it down for those of you who are visiting with us today. A covenant is a contract or binding agreement made between at least two individuals. In this case, we will be making a sacred agreement between ourselves and God."

Sister Rachel walked down to the second to last step on the platform. "For those of you who are still virgins, you are agreeing to practice abstinence until marriage. However, for those of you who are single and are getting your sex on anyhow, you are agreeing to stop having sex until you get married. The married women are agreeing to remain faithful to their mates. Those of you who are married, but getting a little somethin'-somethin' on the side, you're agreeing to break off any improper relationship and to have sex solely with *your* husband."

She adjusted her glasses, peering around at the congregation. "You can get those shocked looks off your faces. I'm not talking to you unless'n it's you. But I know I'm talking to a *whole lotta* somebodies. Don't worry. Y'all are coming down at the same time so no one will know who is who."

Sister Hilton held up her hand and spoke gravely. "I'm telling you now. Don't come down here unless you mean business. If you think coming to this altar is going to instantly—" She snapped her finger "—take away *all* temptation or physically prevent you from going to bed with someone who is not your husband, you go on and remain seated, baby.

"The Word of God warns us, in St. John, Chapter 10, Verse 10, that, 'Satan comes to steal, kill and destroy.'" She walked off the platform and stood next to her husband, placing a hand on his shoulder for support. "That verse goes on to say, 'But Jesus has come that we might have life and have it more abundantly.' Pay close attention to the word might. God's abundant life is a possibility not a guarantee. How *might* we enjoy God's abundant life? We've got to fight the temptation to sin when it comes. Don't fool yourself. It's gonna come, more often for some of you than others."

She slipped off her jacket and passed it to her husband. "If you've forgotten, let me remind you. We're in a war. Our spirit and our flesh fight daily for control of our lives. We decide who wins by what we choose to *do, say,* and *think.* All sin begins in the mind. Why do you think Romans 12:2 encourages us to be transformed by the renewing of our minds?"

Pastor Rachel wiped beads of sweat from her face. "When you and I follow the leading of our spirits, we win. God's abundant life is ours. When we allow ourselves to be led by the lusts of our flesh, we lose and ultimately receive the devil's reward of an empty, unfulfilling, self-destructive life."

She smiled. "Please don't mistake me for some old fuddy duddy. I know sex feels good. It's supposed to. Our Heavenly Father made it that way *on purpose*. And I'll be the first in line to thank Him for doing so." She laughed and patted her husband's shoulder.

"God had two purposes in mind when He designed the act of sexual intercourse. It is His ordained method of procreation so that a husband and a wife can make babies and continue to populate the earth. It is also a pleasurable source of recreation for *a man* and *a woman* to enjoy together."

Sister Rachel leaned over as her husband whispered something to her and then quickly straightened. "Don't misunderstand. I'm still talking within the confines of marriage, whether it is for the purpose of procreation or recreation." She looked down at Pastor Hilton. "Thank you, honey. We have to make sure we are *very* specific when it comes to this subject."

She grinned and moved further down the aisle and scanned the faces of her brothers and sisters in Christ. "When we make love with our mates, we recreate the sense of oneness Adam and Eve shared in the Garden of Eden where Adam declared Eve flesh of his flesh and bone of his bone. Through sexual intercourse, we become one." She paused. "Each of us has the awesome responsibility of cherishing and protecting this gift of physical intimacy God has given us."

Her words dripped with compassion. "Ladies, too many of you have been trying to fill the wrong hole and others been thinkin' about it. Let's settle this once and for all. Only God can *fill* the void you *feel* in your spirits." She walked briskly to the top of the platform then turned and said somberly, "I'm asking those of you who would like to participate in this POP covenant to stand to your feet."

Sister Rachel turned her glistening face to the congregation. "Begin marching toward this altar with your fighting clothes on and a renewed determination to be a part of the Lord's army. Jesus is the general and the Word of God is our ammunition. It won't be easy to give up wrongful sexual relations. A couple of battles may be lost along the way but, with God on your side, you can win. Romans, Chapter 8, Verse 37, reminds us we are more than conquerors because God loves us. Get that down in your spirits. The Creator of heaven and earth loves *you*! And He wants us to have the victory. Not by and by when the morning comes, but right here and right now."

Amani stood along with her mother and all of her sisters. She turned around and was surprised to see Destiny standing beside her mother. The two covenant friends smiled at each other through moistened eyes. Harmoni held tightly to Destiny's hand as they stood together.

Streams of God-fearing females took to the aisles and began flooding the altar.

Sister Rachel looked over the multitude. "Is Sister Olivia and Sister Amani in the house?" She cupped her hands over her eyes and searched the crowd. Olivia raised her and Amani's locked hands high above their heads.

Sister Rachel acknowledged them with a warm smile. "We sure are going to miss Amani's anointed voice in the young adult choir. Come on up here and sing us a song, baby. Sister Olivia, please accompany her on the piano." Amani whispered in her mother's ear as they made their way up the platform. Sister Rachel gave them each a hug before handing a microphone to Amani.

Under Olivia's nimble fingers, the piano's melody washed over the souls of those who had come to the altar out of a desire to live holy and an abiding love for their Saviour, the only true lifeline.

Amani lifted her head and her right hand then opened her mouth. "All to Jesus, I Surrender" floated out in perfect pitch. Her heart's harmony reached heaven as a rivulet of tears washed her whole. It was her battle cry and, as she sang, she re-suited in her armor. Though she'd worn it in a previous war, it was still strong enough to carry her through all future fights.

The Holy Spirit showered her soul as she yielded herself to God in song and submitted her life to His divine plan.

When the last note had been sung, she and Olivia joined the others gathered around the altar. Many of them were weeping. Amani's tears joined theirs as she held fast to her mother's hand.

Moments later, she felt a tapping on her shoulder. She let go of her mother's hand and embraced Destiny tightly. This past year had tested their friendship and their faith. As long as they sought the Father's will above all else, both would remain intact.

There were still many rivers to cross, but their trust in God would not leave them shipwrecked. His Word would be a compass as they traveled and an anchor in seasons of rough winds and turbulent waters.

He was the captain of their souls.

THIRTY-FIVE

Amani was in a state of regression. Today, she was feeling ugly, insecure, and five. Again. So she went in search of someone she hadn't seen in a while. Someone who had the ability to make any five-year-old believe in herself. Someone who knew her before she knew herself. Someone who was a second mother to her.

Amani hadn't visited New Horizons Christian School since elementary. Wearing a princess t-shirt and a pair of cut-off jean shorts, she walked through the halls, observing the work displayed on the walls. She knew that every story, every drawing, and every painting had been done to the best of the students' abilities. Mister Bennie and Miss Oneita never settled for less than anyone's highest potential. Before a student left New Horizons, excellence would have become habit-forming.

Amani walked into the main office and worship music greeted her as she entered. A student helper glanced at her, and then resumed filing papers. An older lady spoke into the phone and nodded at her. After she hung up, she hurried over to her. "May I help you?"

Amani grinned. "I see my godparents still believe in manual labor for rule offenders."

The woman returned Amani's smile. "Good thing, too. It helps me out tremendously. You called earlier, right?"

"Yes."

"Miss Oneita is expecting you." She walked over to the intercom and paged her.

A few moments later, the school's first teacher and current director strolled into the office. Oneita was wearing a short-sleeved lavender linen dress with a pair of low-heeled white sandals. Her micro braids were pulled into a low ponytail. A pair of pearl earrings and a thin gold chain with a cross were her only accessories. Although she was sixty years old, her dark complexion was flawless.

Oneita wrapped Amani in a solid hug, giving her a whiff of her signature fragrance. A sweet blanket of Estee Lauder's Beautiful encircled Amani. "Baby Girl, when Miss Jean told me you called, I 'bout had myself a party. Too bad your godfather's out of town. He's going to be sorry he missed you." She released Amani and looked her over from head to toe. Her smile was genuine and bright.

Amani wasn't quite as enthusiastic. "Hi, Godmommy." She pecked her cheek. When she saw her godmother the night of her birthday, she was trying to be someone else. Today, she needed help remembering who she was supposed to be. "That's okay. Not that I wouldn't love to see him, but I really came to see you."

"Good. I was beginning to think you done put me down." Oneita's eyes twinkled. "Wait for me in my office. I'll go get us two cold drinks from the teacher's lounge."

Amani pushed open her godmother's office door and made herself comfortable on the sofa on the wall adjacent to the door. She looked around at the hundreds of books lining the bookcases, the oak desk in the center of the room, and the computer and table on the far wall. Photographs of her godparents, her father and mother, and her and her sisters, at various stages of their lives, lined the walls and decorated the huge desk.

She picked up the last picture she had taken with her father. They were both grinning, but neither looked into the camera. Although their eyes were closed, the expression of pure joy on their faces was apparent. Amani remembered that day.

She had walked Daddy out to the car so that her mother could take him to the airport. He started teasing her. "Here I'm thinkin' my baby girl's crying 'cause she's gon' miss me. And what you say? You're crying over Barbie." He tickled her, she laughed hysterically, and Olivia snapped the picture.

Amani heard the door shut and turned around. Her godmother smiled and went over to her sitting area. She sat the bottles of water on the coffee table and sat on the sofa.

Amani continued holding the picture and plopped down next to her godmother. "I haven't seen this picture in years."

Oneita looked at it. "It's one of my favorites. I call it Royal Love."

"Daddy was the king, Mama was his queen, and we were his princesses." She raked her hands through her loose curls. "But things change."

Oneita's eyes followed her gesture. "Your new haircut becomes you."

"Thank you."

"You're welcome." Oneita twisted the top off her water and swallowed a sip of water. "There's nothing we can do about things changing. Only God never changes." She kicked off her sandals, rested her feet on the coffee table, and looked over at Amani. "Well, Baby Girl, no more sweet potatoes. The frost done spoiled the vine."

"Huh?" Amani lifted her eyes from the picture in her hands. "What does that mean?"

"It's just an old southern expression." Oneita chuckled

lightly. "Your mother told me you and Marley broke up. Is that what you wanted to talk to me about?" she asked softly.

Amani placed the picture on the table and picked up her water. "I thought he was the one I was supposed to marry. I wanted us to be like Daddy and Mama and you and Goddaddy, but he got this cheerleader at UCLA pregnant." She took a long drink of water. "I tried to show him how much I loved him, so he wouldn't mind waiting for us to get married before we had sex. I obviously didn't do a good enough—"

"That boy knows you love him and so do I. Wanna know how I know?"

Amani bobbed her head.

"Because you put your whole heart into whatever you do. That's always been your way. It's not your fault he couldn't care for it properly."

"Maybe if I loved him better, it would have stopped him from doing something I think he regrets."

"None of us has the power to save anybody else. Each of us has to trust God to save us from ourselves. Marley included." She turned eyes that had seen much on her goddaughter. "We all have choices to make. You, my dear, have chosen wisely."

Amani tugged at one of her gold hoop earrings and stared at the picture on the coffee table. "A couple of weeks before Daddy died, I overheard two girls in the bathroom talking about my sisters and me. They were basically saying the only reason people thought we were pretty was because of our hair." She combed her curly fro with her fingers. "They said we'd be ugly without it, especially me because I'm the darkest."

"Those poor babies. They had no idea who they were so they built themselves up by tearing others down." Oneita shook her head. "Listen to me good, Amani. Real beauty begins on the inside." She put her water bottle down and took her goddaughter's hands in hers. "Before you heard Clueless

One and Clueless Two in the bathroom, you believed you were beautiful because your daddy told you so. Then Marley came along and confirmed what your daddy used to say. Now, it's time for you to believe what your Heavenly Father says about you." Oneita walked over to her desk and flipped through her Bible, then she returned and plopped down next to Amani. "I want you to memorize I Peter 2:9. Hold your head up high, Amani. You're a part of a chosen generation and a member of a royal priesthood." She leaned forward and kissed Amani on the forehead. "You carry yourself on to Cornell and make sure you set the record straight. Everything that comes out of L.A. ain't make-believe. Some of us are bonafide queens. Royal as we wanna be."

Amani's eyes glistened. "I love you, Godmommy O. Thank you."

"You're welcome, Baby Girl, and I love you, too."

Oneita prayed Psalm 91 over her goddaughter, declaring that angels were protecting her and would continue to do so as she traveled to New York. Then she held Amani tightly, wishing she could pass down years of experience through an embrace.

Amani left her old stomping grounds with a bounce in her step and renewed confidence in her spirit. She was feeling beautiful again. That evening, an epiphany stirred within her. Her godmother was the first person with whom she wanted to share her new affirmation. Oneita answered the telephone on the first ring.

"Hey, Godmommy. I want you to hear a poem I wrote."

"Sure thing." Oneita closed her eyes and listened to see what God had done.

Amani cleared her throat and read with a newfound, hard-earned emotion.

The Queen That I Am

Once upon a time,
long, long ago
I believed in fairy tales
and I wished for a magic wand.

With a wave of my hand,
all of my insecurities,
my shortcomings would
instantly disappear.
But I've recently been
enlightened.
I don't need magic to become
who I already am.

So starting right here and
right now,
I give myself permission:

To stand regal with my backbone straight.
To glide with a confident and purposeful gait.

To hold my head way high.
To stretch these earth-toned wings and finally fly.

To humbly acknowledge the truth, I am divine.
To let this great big light of mine shine.

To speak not only when spoken to, but when I have some-
thing to say.
To embrace every twenty-four hours as another chance to
do things His way.

To make mistakes, repent, and not wallow in guilt.
To accept that I'm a valuable piece of God's hand-woven
quilt.

To do what I was designed to do without fear.
To adorn Amani in royal gear.

Today, I crown myself with courage, grace, strength, and
love
and I make a decree, too.

Hear ye, Hear ye,
Be it known throughout the land,
This Queen is ready to reign!

"Watch out now!" Oneita opened her eyes. "Amani Nicole, your beauty's starting to overflow."

Amani smiled in return, but said nothing. In her silence she realized she was evolving into the woman God created her to be, step by step. Moment by moment.

———

They were having an informal picnic that consisted of chasing butterflies around the park, monkeying around on the jungle gym, and eating peanut butter and jelly sandwiches. Amani was wearing a pair of white stretch jeans with an orange and yellow blouse. Her now medium-sized Afro was pulled back with an orange and yellow scarf that she had tied in the back, allowing the ends to dangle freely. Golden hoop earrings decorated her ears and white leather canvas shoes covered her feet. She smiled serenely into the sovereign sky and prayed silently. *Thank you, Jesus.* Surprising to her was something that was apparent to those around her. She was falling in love again, but this time was different.

All traces of heaviness were gone and she felt weightless as she pushed one-half of the Z-team on a swing. She looked over at Jade. "Girl, I see why you stay so slim!"

Jade smiled. "I don't have to work out. *This* is my exercise."

"I believe you." A sudden frown marred Amani's face as she squinted in the direction of the parking lot. Jade followed her eyes.

"I'm sorry, Amani. He's been hanging around our house a lot lately. Zack told him we were meeting you at the park today. I didn't think he'd show up."

The uninvited guest was looking good in a pair of Khalil Love jean shorts with an orange tank top that showed off the perfection of his muscled arms and gave her a visual reminder of what they once shared.

In his hand was a plain white gift bag.

Zachary's eyes lit up. "Uncle Marley!" He jumped out of the swing and ran to meet him.

Marley stooped down and Zack hopped on his uncle's back. When he reached them, he got down and unloaded his precious cargo. Kneeling in front of Zoie, he kissed her, then stood and kissed Jade's cheek. Lastly, he turned his attention to Amani.

"For you." He extended the bag to her.

"Thank you."

"So you're out of here tomorrow?"

"Yes."

Silence.

"Uncle Marley, can you push me?" Zack asked excitedly.

"You'll have to play with your Uncle Marley later. We need to get home and make dinner for Daddy." Jade reached out and hugged Amani. "Take care of yourself, my friend. You have our address and our number. Please don't forget to use them."

Amani kissed Jade's cheek. "I won't." Then she knelt down and put her arms around Zoie and Zachary's waists. "You all be good. I'll see you when I come home for Christmas."

"Where are you going?" Zoie stuck out her bottom lip.

"To a school in New York called Cornell University."

"Is that far away?" Zachary piped in.

She nodded. "It's pretty far. But you know what?" Amani pointed to her heart. "I have both of you in here. So although I'll be far away, I can't forget either of you."

Zoie hugged her neck. "Are you going to be a cheerleader at your new school?"

Amani smiled and shook her head. "I don't think so."

"What about when we go to Jamaica?" Zachary tugged his uncle's hand. "Is she coming with us?"

"No." Amani's voice was soft.

"Come on, you two." Jade waved good-bye and took their hands.

They broke away from their mother and clung to Amani. After a few moments, Jade plied them away. "Amani will come to see us when she comes home."

"Cross my heart." Amani smiled through moistened eyes. "And I'll bring presents for both of you, okay?"

"Okay," they said in unison. Usually so animated, they looked like two deflated balloons as they followed their mother to their burgundy Ford Expedition.

Amani sat in the swing Zachary vacated and carefully placed the bag on the sand. Marley squeezed his bulk into the one beside her. A sudden breeze blew his cologne purposely in the path of her nose. Her temperature almost remained steady and her heart skipped a mere two or three beats.

They both remained silent.

Finally, he turned to her. "I messed up, baby. I hurt you, let my parents down, and failed God. I'm sorry." He looked straight ahead. "What happened with Tamara was a mistake." Marley faced her and gently took her hand. "I'm in love with *you* and I need you in my life."

"You *need* to accept the facts facing you." She eased her hand out of his. "You have a baby on the way, and I'm on my way to New York."

His words tumbled out in a rush. "We won't know until the baby is born whether it's mine or not. It's not too late for us. We can get married. You could move in with me and enroll in UCLA for the winter or spring quarter."

She stared into the sand, but wasn't about to stick her head in it.

"Amani, did you hear me?"

"Yes."

"Well?"

She looked into his eyes and gripped the chains of the swing. The warm steel in her hands reminded her to stay strong.

"The fat lady has sung and gone home, Marley. It's over."

He knelt in front of her. "Amani, how can it be? We're each other's first loves."

"That's where we both messed up, Marley." She swallowed the lump in her throat. "God should be our *first* love." She picked up her gift. "The only thing left is for us to wish each other well."

He quickly stood and grabbed her hand. His misty eyes stared into hers. "I'm not ready to say good-bye."

"Then I'll say it for you." She reached up and kissed him on the cheek. "Good-bye, Miracle Man. Please take care of yourself." She turned and hurried away.

"Amani!"

She pivoted around and met his gaze.

"At least open your gift before you leave."

She waited for him to catch up.

He drew her close and her breath caught in her throat. Her heart pounded the same tempo as his. Being in his arms felt good. It felt right. Familiar thoughts and feelings played havoc with her emotions and she almost forgot that she had to let go.

Marley's tears on her forehead reminded her of the tattoo's truth. *Many waters cannot quench love; neither can the floods drown it.* But apart from God, it could not remain afloat. She took in a deep breath, filling herself with the smell of him before moving out of his embrace. Then she pulled a shoebox out of the bag. She tipped her head to the side, her confused gaze resting on his chiseled handsomeness.

"Open it, baby." His soft voice invited her to make other plans.

Amani took the lid off and placed it underneath the bottom of the box. She lifted one red satiny pump. It contained tiny sparkles that reflected the light of the sun. She turned the shoe over. Size nine. She stepped back and looked into his eyes. "They're beautiful, but I don't under—"

"You already have a big heart, lots of courage, and a good brain." Marley's smile waned. "But there's something missing." He tilted her chin upward with the tip of his forefinger. "I need you to *believe* we can get through this." He waited a beat. "I still want to make a home with you, Sunshine. Someday, somewhere, over our very own rainbow."

Her stomach fluttered and her heart banged in her chest. "Marley, I'm sorry, but—"

"There's another gift in there for you."

She reached into the box and pulled out a Yolanda Adams CD. It was the only one she didn't have. If her heart weren't beating so crazily, she would have laughed. The title of the CD was *Believe*. Amani's throat tightened as she dropped the CD into the box and shoved the box in the bag. Her salty tears washed away the beginnings of a bittersweet smile.

Marley wiped away a few of her tears with the pad of his thumb, and then brushed her forehead with his lips. Amani shut her eyes and allowed him to pull her close one last time. They hugged tightly, each knowing the hold they had on each other would not be easily broken.

Marley breathed a final plea into her hair.

"Don't leave me, Sunshine."

She struggled for air against the pounding of his chest, the strength in his arms, and the love that radiated from his heart to hers. It would be so easy to stay and give them another chance. Love was the last thing that should have come between them. She reached up and stroked his cheek. "Goodbye, Marley."

"Amani." He took her hand, this time allowing his eyes to speak for him. She saw his sorrow and it was making her weak. Before she faltered, she slipped her hand out of his and walked away. Amani didn't stop until she had reached her destination. She opened the car door, slammed it shut, threw the bag on the passenger's seat, and started the engine. Immediately, music filled the empty space. When she turned for a last look at Marley, he was still standing where she had left him.

She wept for them both as the soothing sounds of "Open My Heart" played in the background. When the song ended, she prayed aloud, her wet face shining. "Father God, I thank you for ordering my steps and directing my paths because my faith is in you and my broken heart is in your hands. In the name of Jesus, I pray. Amen."

Amani tracked the *Mountain High, Valley Low* CD to "In the Midst of it All" because God had her back and He kept her from falling, even when she was tripping. That was something she would always believe.

THIRTY-SIX

Tamara was on her way to living the fairytale life she had dreamed of since she was a little girl. In her quest, she was forced to kiss a lot of frogs. This was the worst possible time for a nightmare to catch up with her. The drumming of her heart roared in her ears. Her hands were shaking so hard she could barely reread the results of her most recent blood test.

There had to be a mistake because this was the first baby she decided to keep. No way would she end up like her mother. Five kids by four different donors. None staying around long enough to be a real man, let alone a daddy.

Tamara's eyes welled with tears and she dropped to her knees, holding her stomach with one hand and the test results in the other. The first results had told her she and Marley were going to have a baby. But these second results informed her that her chance to have a normal family life was over.

Finally, the backed-up tears burst forth. Her body trembled while she wailed and rocked. It was several minutes before her moans subsided. Tears clouded her vision, but she lifted her head and held up the hand gripping the soggy piece of paper.

Tamara couldn't ever remember being a member of a church and grew up doubting God even existed. But now she knew He was the only one who could help her. She struggled to talk to the God of Taylor, Regina, . . . and Marley.

Her crying eased and she lifted both hands toward heaven. "Lord, if you're real, don't let this be happening to me. *Please* don't let me be HIV positive." She clutched her middle and tried to hold back the moans that tumbled from within the depths of her troubled spirit, her distressed soul, and her battered heart.

EPILOGUE

Last night, Amani dreamt of butterflies and Marley.

She awoke with a poem in her heart as sunlight flittered through her open window. For the last hour and a half, she had been fine-tuning it and was finally ready to share it. Amani walked down the hall to her mother's room and knocked softly.

"Come in." She took her seat at the foot of her mother's bed.

Her mother turned from the window and the tree. "I'm surprised you're already up. I didn't think your sisters and godparents were ever going to leave."

"It's good to be loved."

Olivia smiled. "Yes, it is." She noticed the sheet of paper in Amani's hand. "Another letter?"

"Nope. It's a poem I wrote. Wanna hear it?"

"Of course."

Amani's hands shook a little as she began reciting, her voice wavered, and her words wobbled at the onset. But, as she poetically expressed the ending to their love story, her hands stilled and her voice steadied.

Metamorphosis

So hard it was, the letting go,
the turning away,
passing into the land of never never,
the only if I'd tried harder, been sweeter,
and idle thoughts of love remembered.
Surrendered.

So hard it is, the fading into dreams
to be forgotten
and purposely misplaced,
the changing into a new being
not colder, but wiser.
More cautious.

This metamorphosis,
this forming of wings of faith
for flying the flight for freedom
toward new happenings
is not easy.

But the future awaits
and the Spirit bids
this beauty-full
butterfly,
"Come."

Amani finished the last word and sighed. Olivia clapped like someone who was crazed.

"That was awesome, Baby Girl! I want an autographed copy."

"Thank you. As soon as I get a chance, I'll type it up and mail it to you."

"You'd better." It was Olivia's turn to sigh. "Well, we need to take off our favorite peach nighties and get dressed. If you miss your flight, you'll have to stay in L.A. and go to UCLA or USC."

"I'm going to miss you, too, Mama." She grinned, and then glanced down at the poem in her hand.

"Amani!"

She quickly lifted her head and looked at her mother peering out of the bay window.

"Hurry, come here!"

Amani rushed to join her mother. Both women smiled as they watched the graceful butterfly glide high into a seemingly limitless sky.

Olivia put her arm around her daughter's waist and pointed. "There goes my baby."

Emerging from a cocoon filled with the sun's illumination, her mother's pride, and her fathers' love, Amani believed she could fly—no, *soar*. For real.